A STEP
THROUGH
THE EMPTY

H. E. SALIAN

A STEP THROUGH THE EMPTY by H. E. SALIAN

ISBN: 978-1-7348004-0-1 (paperback)
ISBN: 978-1-7348004-1-8 (ePub)

To the dear Lord and my family for giving me the stubbornness to keep working.

CHAPTER 1

Princess Istoria watched as her home disappeared and the Empty closed behind her. She squeezed her eyes closed to block out the nightmare, to awaken. She breathed in, out, and waited. The carriage jostled and her father's voice carried on with the same conversation as before. Stori opened her eyes and forced a small smile as she pretended to listen.

King Tristram's frown was unconvinced when he glanced at her.

"I know this is hard, darling," he said as he wrapped his arm around her shoulder and gave her a reassuring squeeze.

Stori nodded but glanced away from the pinched expression on his face. She might give up and cry again if she had to witness how much this was hurting her father too.

"I would have wished for any other solution, any that didn't require this sacrifice from you, if I believed one existed," the king continued.

"Father, I know." Stori turned to him and grabbed his free hand. "You wouldn't wish this." She relaxed her grip as she ducked her head again. "There are limited ways for us to resolve this conflict before it reaches all-out war."

"I just wish there was a better solution than marrying you off to that bastard of a king." King Tristram clenched his fists as his rage began to surface again. "Whatever kind of king that bastard Vlasis's son turns out to be."

Stori nodded again, but it didn't stop a few built up tears from escaping down her face.

"I'm sorry, Stori darling, I didn't mean for this…" He stroked her hair. "I didn't mean for any of this responsibility to fall to you."

"Father, it is my duty now." She mumbled again, pulling out her handkerchief to clean her face of the tears. She stared at the piece of cloth with its embroidered *N* written in fanciful calligraphy.

Mother wouldn't have cried for this. The thought made her stomach turn as another tear escaped. *She would have been strong.*

Silence filled the carriage again and settled across the caravan. Stori returned to staring out at the void space, lost in her own thoughts.

A scream echoed through the blackness from the front of the line. Glancing at her father, Stori saw he was already opening the door and calling to the driver for information. More screams rang out, louder and closer than the first.

Stori heard the king shouting orders but she couldn't make out the words he was saying. His white-knuckled hand gripped the carriage door. Finally, one word reached her ears—*Shades.* That was enough to make her blood freeze as she moved closer to her father.

The carriage lurched with force enough to knock Stori against the seat. The king sat back down with the same ungraceful effect. He grabbed an AaD from its place under the seat and began smashing at the screen of the tablet, inputting commands.

A sharp turn threw Stori back again as the carriage adjusted course without slowing down. Stori pressed her face against the window and could barely make out the other carriages following behind.

"Father?" She pulled away from the glass and turned around.

King Tristram was still typing furiously and cursing in a quiet voice. Stori turned back to the window. A ball of fire lit up the distance from where they had come. Clapping a hand over her mouth, Stori tried counting the number of carriages behind them.

Six? I must have miscounted.

She hoped desperately and started counting again. The fire faded in the distance and darkness returned all around. She counted seven this time. Still less than half of their caravan.

She sat back in her seat and prayed more of the carriages made it. She prayed Leha's carriage had made it. She couldn't go through whatever misery awaited her in her new life without her faithful maidservant and friend.

A light spread in front of the carriage as Tristram used the AaD to open a doorway. The carriage raced through before the driver could even pull them into a slower pace. Stori had barely blinked and they'd already put distance between them and the doorway. She turned around and quickly counted again. Seven carriages followed them through before the doorway shut. Stori's stomach knotted at the low number, but she breathed a sigh of relief that Leha's carriage was one of the few which made it.

"Darling?" Stori jerked toward her father when she realized he was talking to her. The king rested a hand on her shoulder and gave it a gentle squeeze as his eyes continued searching her face. She supposed he had asked her a question and was waiting for an answer.

"I'm fine." She lied, hoping her stomach wouldn't betray her. "What happened?"

The king took in a deep breath and released it with slow deliberation. "It was a Shade." He paused and waited for her to nod before continuing. "It attacked the front scout and carriages first, which is the only reason we got away. If it had attacked anywhere else in our caravan, its damned powers would have affected us too."

Stori nodded again with a frown that didn't soften. "I thought…" She waited for her father's attention to return to her. "I thought Shades didn't travel often, especially not through the Empty." She made a conscious effort not to bite her lip even as she was trembling. "What in all the seven sphaeres would it go in there?"

The king's jaw tightened hard enough to crack a tooth. He stared out at the space in Medius they now found themselves sitting in. His expression darkened.

"You don't think the Median king…" Stori trailed off as her throat tightened against the thought of the man she was to marry.

"Silence, Istoria." Her father's tone was enough to silence her. It was also enough to assume he agreed with her.

Stori nodded and cursed her fiancé in her head. There would be no proof the Shade was his doing, but it was something the former king of

Medius, Vlasis, used to do. Stori cursed her poor luck to be marrying the Median.

King Tristram pulled up the tablet again and glared at the screen for a long moment. "We are still about 35 met-reaches from the capital. We should be there by midday."

Closing her eyes, Stori attempted to steady her breath and, if possible, her mind and stomach as the uneven ground made for an uncomfortable ride.

"Darling." King Tristram waited for Stori to open her eyes and look at him before continuing. "If you'd prefer, when we get to the castle, I will have you brought up to your private suite immediately. That way you won't have to meet him right away."

Stori sniffled in relief at not having to face the man she would marry just yet. "I would not want to cause you any trouble in explaining my absence," she mumbled, hoping her father would disagree.

Tristram shook his head with a smile. "It has been a trying day. I will make the Median king understand you need your rest and that he should not even consider disturbing you."

Stori nodded with her best excuse for a smile before closing her eyes again.

CHAPTER 2

L ate morning in Sentre saw an unusual bustle as the whole city
prepared for the royal wedding. There was a tangible stirring of
extra life in the mountain side city.

An added tension had been building throughout the latter half
of the morning—a low mumbling between passersby when no guards or
castle folk were present. In the castle, however, the rumors were more
pronounced and more hushed.

The Sylvan Princess was late. After her expected arrival time had come
and long gone, doubt began to grow—doubt and fear of war—a fear which
had only grown since then and now had a vice grip on the city.

On one of the top floors of the castle, last moment preparations were
being made yet again. The rooms fitted for the guests were immaculate, but
every moment they remained empty, the servants added just a few more
ornaments, cleaned one spot just a bit more, and re-polished everything
that could be polished. It seemed there was a mutual effort to make up for
the lack of occupants by making the rooms even more magnificent in and
of themselves.

On the floor above, in a large study attached to the king's bedchamber,
King Brynte pushed his advisors out the door and closed it, trapping the
peace and quiet inside. He let out an unsteady sigh. With his fiancée so late
to arrive and no signs of the Sylvan caravan in the Empty or on the roads
yet, all his advisors seemed to think he was responsible for it. A ploy his
father might have used, they had said. Bry could have kicked them for that
comment.

Stomping back to his desk, Bry ignored the amusement in the glowing blue eyes that followed his every move. Sitting down with a thud in the chair, he grabbed a handful of papers that were threatening to spill over the edges of the desk and tried to focus on reading. Several moments dragged by as he reread the same line over again without comprehension.

After another half moment passed, Bry gave up and threw the papers back onto the pile. Blue eyes continued to stare and Bry could sense the cheshire grin behind them without looking up.

"Shad, if you have something funny to say about all this, now is a perfect time to shut up."

A half-shadow, half-human shrug of innocence followed from Shad's position in the dark corner of the attached bedroom where the wraith had been hiding from the judgment of the royal advisors.

"I was just going to say, if you glare at those papers any longer they might burst into flame." The disembodied blue eyes moved forward into the light where the wraith's form materialized into a more solid state.

Shad's gray and bluish skin tone showed his wraith side. Black wisps of his Shade blood moved underneath his skin, alive, betraying that he was not all wraith even when he wasn't dematerializing in shadows.

"I don't know what happened. The guards searched for dozens of met-reaches around where the closest doorway should have opened," Bry said, tapping the edge of a discarded AaD resting in the mess on his desk. "If they missed the door…"

"Then there would be nothing you or them could do until the next doorway. And they couldn't call you either." Shad leaned against the desk with a heavy groan. "I thought you being king was gonna make our lives easier. Now *your* people might just string us both up."

Bry scoffed, "This is Sentre. They don't hang people." Pinching the bridge of his nose, he continued frowning. "They might behead us though."

"I know." Shad cracked a grin, "I just like that Terranian expression. It's so fun, isn't it?" Shad wagged his head side to side and smiled at whatever fun he found in it. "And beheadings seem more brutal." He remained thoughtful for a moment before turning back to Bry with a grin in place.

"Yeah, well. Let's try not to get there just yet." Bry stood and began pacing an already worn path on the rug. "Assuming they didn't reach the exit point in time—"

"Then there is still nothing you could do," Shad added, earning a scowl from the king. "Just sayin'."

"If they didn't, we could send a patrol to the next doorway opening." Bry walked back to his desk and began searching on the AaD for more information.

"And what's that going to do?" Shad watched his friend without moving from his spot. "The best a patrol could do is call us, which is what the caravan would do."

Bry growled and paused his search. "But I'm supposed to do something! That's what kings do, isn't it?"

Shad shrugged. "If you can't do anything, then don't do anything."

"And what of the stringing up and beheading part? Remember?" Bry growled a heavy sigh and dropped his head. "Everybody here already thinks I'm the same as my father. Just 'cause we look alike." Bry muttered the last part, pulling calloused fingers through the tangles in his flaming red hair.

Shad looked thoughtful again. "Nah. You look younger than he did in pictures."

Bry kicked his friend's leg and ignored the yelp, growling, "I'm being serious."

Shad hopped a few steps away. "I'm not." He rubbed his shin before moving with care out of striking range, back to the desk. "Bry, there is nothing you can do."

"I hate this!" Bry yelled as he went back to pacing. "Maybe I should have sent an escort to bring them back." He paused at the idea before frowning again. "If we go to war with Sylva because of some stupid… I'm going to be a dead king. And I've only been here a few weeks."

Running footsteps and a heavy knock on the door interrupted the conversation.

"Wow, the executioner's here already," Shad teased, though he frowned as Bry called for the person to enter.

A guard came in panting. "Your Majesty. We have spotted a caravan about eight met-reaches out." The man gestured to Bry's patio with the sightglasses in his hand.

"Thank the Vis," Bry exhaled as he followed the guard to the open space and looked with the glasses in the direction pointed. "For all the blessings of the seven sphaere, thank the Vis again. But I thought they'd have more carriages."

"They should have, sir," the guard offered, taking the glasses as Bry handed them back. "The stable master had space reserved for twenty."

Bry frowned at that before thanking and dismissing the guard. Shad sauntered to the railing and leaned his back against it, eyeing Bry.

"How many were there?"

"Eight," Bry answered. "They must have run into trouble somewhere. But..."

"But why didn't they call?" Shad finished, glancing over the railing into the distance. "Maybe they lost all their AaDs."

Bry shifted his jaw, grinding his teeth as he thought about it. "Not likely. If whatever happened came after they arrived in Medius it's possible, but that might be worse."

Shad hummed. "Yes, your sphaere, your responsibility. And if something happened in the Empty, they would have had at least one working AaD to get out. Either way, I think it's going to be a ton of fun, your beheading."

Bry glowered.

"I meant wedding."

Bry rolled his eyes and moved back inside. He sat down at his desk with less huffing this time. "I'm not sure this is gonna work out, Shad. I mean, she's just a kid."

"Seventeen isn't that much of a kid," Shad muttered, poking at the odds and ends he found on the bookshelves as he passed. He paused at the glare Bry was giving him and shrugged. "I'm just saying, you're only, what? Six, maybe seven years older than her?"

"Eight," Bry grumbled into the hand he was resting his head on. "Practically half her life."

"And a third of yours. Err... Wait." Shad starting counting on his fingers. "Where was this math going?"

"Over your head?"

Shad shrugged. "Anyway, my point was... It's not that much of a difference." He slouched into a chair on the other side of the desk. "'Sides, she's willin' to marry you. With your reputation—or your father's anyway—it shows fortitude at least."

A growl emitted from behind the pile of papers.

"I know, I know, don't mention Vlasis." Shad leaned over the back of the chair to gaze at the ceiling. "But you know she has to have heard of him and all the comparisons people make between you two."

"We're not at all similar." Bry spat shifting some papers to see across better. He propped his head up on his hands so he could see Shad's tilted head over the pile of documents. "But I know the rep I get from him."

"You never know." Shad stretched as he threw Bry a grin. "You give her a chance, and you might end up liking her."

"She's still just a kid," Bry repeated with a sigh.

"Two chances, then." Shad scoffed before continuing, "Do you remember us when we were that age? I don't think anybody called us 'kids' when we were... What was that Terranian expression?" Shad paused and scrunched up his face as he tried to remember.

"'Kickin' ass and takin' names," Bry offered with a sigh.

"Yes! That was it. 'Kickin' ass and takin' names'." Shad snapped his fingers with a rare, true grin flooding across his features.

"And how does this relate to me marrying the princess?"

"Well, I'm just sayin' you shouldn't go about dislikin' her when you've never met her." Shad nodded almost as if to himself and said in a quieter voice, "That'd be the same as her judgin' you by your father's reputation."

Bry grumbled at that and dropped his head against the desk and papers. "Did you have to put it like that?" He groaned.

"Yes. Yes, I did." Shad stood and leaned against the desk, staring at his friend. "Come on, we've got some time before they get here. What do you wanna do?"

Bry lifted his head and glanced around. A scowl settled on his face. "Not that it's gonna be fun, but hell, I need to clean this room."

Now Shad groaned. "Really? Your last bit of freedom and you wanna clean? That's kinda pathetic."

Bry threw a handful of papers at the wraith. "I'm not getting married 'til tomorrow, so it's not my 'last bit of freedom'. And, I want to make a good impression with King Tristram." He glanced around the messy room and rubbed his head. "I at least need to appear to have shit under control."

Shad tried to scoff and chuckle at the same time, only to choke for a moment. "Good luck with that."

"You're helping," Bry ordered as he started sorting the heap of documents.

"Why?" Shad crossed his arms.

"'Cause your king ordered it and you've got nothin' better to do."

"That's not true. I've got plenty of nothing better to do, and I've never listened to a king's orders before."

"Your friend is also asking and you listen to me all the time," Bry said as he gathered some papers off the floor.

"Only in battle," Shad said with an arched eyebrow, but relented and began gathering a handful of books to stuff onto the nearest bookcase.

Bry grunted in satisfaction at that and went about his own organizing and hiding of messes. By the time a guard appeared to relay that the caravan had arrived the study was as close to presentable as possible. As long as Bry steered the guests away from the drawers or behind one particular sofa in the corner where all the unknown and odd-sized objects had amassed, everything should be fine. At least, that's what he hoped.

CHAPTER 3

Kingly, he repeated to himself, trying not to grit his teeth at the reminders his advisors always gave him. He tried and failed to keep his gait casual as he strode down to the courtyard to greet the carriages.

Shad kept perfect pace next to him, grinning his sun-bright smile at everyone who passed and ignoring the nervous-bordering-on-disgusted glances everyone gave in return. Bry noticed his friend had grabbed an extra cloak before leaving the study to hide the skin on his arms and hands; though it didn't do any good to hide the bits of Shade smoke that moved across his face.

Bry made sure to send an extra glare to anyone who looked at his friend with anything close to hatred. Sometimes he wished Shad didn't hate his Shade powers as much as he did. Otherwise he might be able to use them to make people like him—at least for long enough for them to see him as a person, not a monster in disguise.

Damn these people, Bry thought despite himself.

He did love his people, he reminded himself as another group of servants turned away without trying to hide their disgust at his friend.

"Is it just me or is everyone a bit out of sorts for a wedding?" Shad chirped with an overly bright smile.

Bry just scoffed. He was still too irked at his people for a follow-up comment.

"Hey, just a thought, but..." Shad stopped walking just as they reached the doors to the courtyard.

Bry motioned the guard not to open the door yet as he turned to Shad.

Shad stumbled over his words for a moment before finding a good way to say what he was thinking. "Maybe I should wait in my room, or with Klaas and Eleanora." He failed to hide his fidgeting.

"Why? I'll need your good opinion of my fiancée, won't I?"

Bry was only partially joking. Mostly, he wanted to see how she would react to Shad. Bry hadn't considered earlier what he would do if the princess insisted on hating Shad the way everyone else did. He supposed he'd just have to find a nice courtesan.

"Bry, maybe it wouldn't be a good idea to give the King and Princess of a sphaere we're nearly at war with another reason to mistrust you. By, let's say, meeting them for the first time with a half-blood Shade present," Shad suggested, trying and mostly failing to keep up a smile.

"Nonsense," Bry growled and added a few choice words in the Glasic tongue.

"Bry…" Shad paused again as the sound of carriage wheels on cobblestone caught both of their attention. "I'm just suggesting you don't do something that could be questioned by all the people who are going to be hearing of this."

"I'm not." Bry put extra effort into smiling as he walked back to Shad. "I'm also thinking that it might be worse if they think I'm hiding you for some reason."

Shad thought about that for a moment before yielding. "Fine, but if they flip out, I get to say I told you so, and you know I will." Shad leveled a finger at Bry before stepping past him and waving for the guard to open the door.

Bry walked passed Shad who made a sweeping gesture toward the great outside. In the bright courtyard now filled with silver crested carriages, Bry watched the Sylvan king exit the largest one with a sweeping grace he wouldn't have imagined. The king stood in regal silence, seemingly taking in the entire courtyard, including Bry, before settling his facial features into a look of elegant distain.

All fears that the marriage was somehow off and the threat of war came crashing back down on Bry's shoulders.

"Not a princess in sight." Even Shad's whispered voice was strained.

Bry swallowed hard and moved down the flight of steps to the cobblestone as fast as possible without looking, even if it was—as his advisors would call it—un-kingly. He hated the constant reminder that he was sorely out of practice in acting like a king.

"Your Ma—King Tristram," Bry caught himself, remembering that he now held the same title as the foreign diplomat. Such an odd thing that was. He shook his head at the idea. "It is a pleasure to welcome you to Sentre," Bry spoke as properly as he could, then remembered to smile.

The Sylvan king glared at him, his frown settling even deeper into his lined face. He took a step to greet Brynte but stopped short as his gaze focused on something behind him. Tristram gripped his sword as he shifted immediately into a fighting position.

Shad, Bry thought at once, glancing back to see his friend reach the same conclusion. "Shadric here is a personal friend, so I'd suggest you damper any hostilities before this becomes a problem." Bry shifted to stand between Shad and King Tristram.

A tap on his shoulder drew Bry's attention back to his friend.

"I told you so," Shad grumbled with a sigh as his smile fell away slightly.

Bry grimaced at the reminder and his friend's poor sense of comedic timing. A small movement in front of him brought his gaze back to King Tristram.

The Sylvan king had straightened out of a fighting stance, though he still gripped his undrawn sword with a white-knuckled hand.

"Why does the King keep company with a Shade?" He growled without taking his steely eyes away from Shad.

"I don't." Bry struggled to keep his own voice above a growl. "I keep company with friends. And if it's escaped your notice, Shad ain't a full-blooded Shade." Bry bit back a few choice words he would have liked to add.

King Tristram shifted his intense gaze between the two of them, searching for an answer to a question Bry couldn't guess. After a moment more, Tristram seemed to reach a decision and released his grip on the sword.

"I apologize, King Brynte." King Tristram stepped forward to greet his host, keeping a cautious eye fixed on Shadric. "I meant no insult."

Bry glanced at Shad, surprised at the sudden change in mannerism from the foreign king. Shad just shrugged and mouthed the word 'kingly' while making a small gesture to remind Bry to straighten out of the fighting stance he hadn't notice he'd slipped into.

Bry paused for a moment, remembering not to call the other king "Your Majesty" before continuing his greeting. "Apology accepted, King Tristram. I too must offer my apology if my speech was or is… crass."

"Your apology is accepted but unnecessary. I understand you are just coming to castle life from a long journey away, some mild differences in thought should be expected," Tristram said with a light, tense smile that didn't reach his voice or eyes.

Bry tightened his jaw and made a conscious effort not to frown. This king was mocking him. Still, Bry carried through the motions of a formal greeting with Tristram before asking after his fiancée.

"I fear she was rather exhausted from our unexpectedly exciting journey. She went up to her rooms as soon as we reached the first entrance of the castle." Tristram smiled again, the same rather mocking smile. "You can meet her tomorrow."

Bry did grimace at the other king this time. "Yes, there's no rush. I suppose I can meet her anytime."

Tristram narrowed his eyes and focused his already intense gaze. Bry surmised he had found something he didn't like in that statement, though Bry couldn't imagine what.

Shad cleared his throat and took a careful step forward, still acting with caution not to startle Tristram. "May I ask about your 'unexpectedly exciting' trip… Your Majesty?" He added the salute with an uneasy glance to Bry.

At the very least, Bry was secretly glad he wasn't the only one who couldn't remember the proper mannerisms for dealing with a king when they weren't being paid for it.

Tristram shifted his steady gaze between the two of them as a new frown formed. The silence lasted a moment longer before he decided on the wording to use. "A Shade attacked our caravan. In the Empty. We lost 12 carriages."

"What!" Bry and Shad shouted in unison. A frown passed between them as Bry shifted his weight and started pacing in tight circles around the spot Shad stood thinking.

"Shades so rarely travel in the Empty and I haven't heard of any in Medius," Shad thought aloud, rubbing his chin.

"Yes, there haven't been any reports of Shades in this sphaere, so it must have come from another." Bry carried on the thought. "Sentre is closer to Eidola this season, but that is still too far a distance for a Shade to travel on its own."

"If they were attacked closer to an edge of Medius, it may not have been that great a distance," Shad pointed out as they both turned back to Tristram for an answer.

Tristram glanced between the pair with some level of surprise and confusion written across his face. He blinked a few times before remembering to answer. "We come out about 35 met-reaches East of Sentre."

Bry growled, "Wrong direction."

"That would have been much longer for the Shade to be traveling. And very convenient for it to appear at just the right place to attack the caravan." Shad went back to frowning.

"If you're suggesting—" The obvious rage in Tristram's voice was interrupted as Bry continued his thought.

"It is possible someone was trying to ruin this truce by stopping the wedding, but..." Bry trailed off as Shad picked up the thought trail, both ignoring Tristram's anger as he sputtered in confusion.

"Moving a Shade is no easy task and there would have been much easier ways." Shad finished. He turned slightly as Bry stopped his pacing and they ended up facing each other. "Using a Shade though..."

"Something people keep telling me my father used to do." Bry grimaced at the thought.

"And since you keep company with me, that would be a great way to throw doubt onto what kind of king you'll be." Shad shifted to look at Tristram. "If it wouldn't be too much trouble, sir, if we could prevent these events from becoming wide spread knowledge it may be best for the success of the truce."

Tristram nodded, still glancing between them with an odd look on his face. "Yes, that is what I thought for the time. I have ordered my men and servants not to say anything on the matter."

"Very good, sir." Bry nodded with respect to Tristram and shifted his attention back to Shad. "We need to hunt it, I could take a—"

"You're king," Shad interrupted. "Kings don't go hunting Shades in the Empty, especially not the day before their wedding. I can go."

Bry cursed in the Glasic tongue. "The hell I'm going to send you to hunt Shades. The men you hunt with would be just as likely to mistake you for the Shade and kill you."

"Well, you. Can't. Go," Shad sneered at Bry. "And you just called him 'sir'. You're not supposed to do that now," Shad added, pointing to Tristram.

"I did not." Bry stepped into Shad's space with a glare.

"Actually, Brynte." Tristram motioned for the two to settle down. "You did."

Bry swallowed his inclination to swear.

I was doing so well.

Bry glanced between Tristram and Shad, hoping they'd drop the subject. The sneer on his friend's face told him he wasn't going to get away that easy.

"You 'bout called him 'Your Majesty' before too." Shad continued smirking, seeming to enjoy Bry's discomfort.

"I caught myself on that one," Bry defended, glancing at his feet.

"Barely."

Bry cleared his throat and determined to steer the conversation way from himself. "Weren't we discussing something more important?"

"We already decided," Shad said, giving Bry a pitying pat on the shoulder. "You and I will fight no monsters. You'll have to send out a hunting party to settle it."

"I also think that would be wise," Tristram stepped in, though he looked amused at having witnessed the last conversation. "It might also be prudent to continue keeping these occurrences to ourselves for now. Of course, I will let my people know that you are handling the situation. They should feel more secure that way."

"We'll have this matter settled before the events tomorrow." Bry gave a nod and glare to Shad, whose smile was ever-lingering.

Shad continued smirking to himself and jumped the steps up to the front, waving for the door to be opened as he did. Bry turned and tried to smile in what he hoped was a kingly way, clearing his throat again to beckon the greeting party inside.

CHAPTER 4

Staying in her room through dinner and even through the next morning, Stori observed the final preparations for the wedding. She ignored the fussing of her maidservants and ladies-in-waiting as she stared out a window and watched the bustling city move. The early morning sun caught the pale stones of the city walls and buildings in its rays and set them glowing. *It is rather pretty*, she admitted to herself with bitter contempt, rather pretty indeed.

The sound of swords clashing pulled her attention to the inner castle grounds, to a large lower terrace that was partly obscured from her view. Stori watched as a wraith and a redhead seemed to be having a friendly match. At least, she hoped it was friendly, since they were in the castle. The two were striking with such speed though she wondered if they might injure each other.

Stori leaned out the window for a better view of the two soldiers. She could only guess they were soldiers from their common dress. She squinted to see better and couldn't help but notice that the redhead was quite handsome, though quite scarred too. Even from this distance, she could make out a nasty scar on his cheek. She supposed he had to be a soldier to have received that kind of injury. She reached this conclusion just as the wraith punched the redhead in the face.

"Not the face, Shad! Not the face, remember!" The redhead's shout turned into a laugh as he spat blood and wiped his mouth with a gloved hand. The wraith shrugged and responded with something Stori couldn't hear but which received a retaliatory slap to the back of the head from the redheaded soldier.

Stori clapped a hand over her mouth to keep from laughing. Though the punch was not a legal move in proper sword fighting, the laid-back manner in which both soldiers responded was more than a little entertaining.

"Miss Stori?" Leha called from inside the room. The words pulled Stori back to her unfortunate reality; marrying the damned Median king.

She straightened up, sparing one last glance at the soldiers just beginning another match.

"Miss Stori, we must have you try the dress one last time, there are still some modifications to make and..." Leha trailed off for a moment as sorrow caught up to her voice. She paused for less than an instant before she tried again with a small, teasing smile. "Listen here, you're halfway through the morning of your wedding already, and afterward, you never have to wear the thing again."

Stori returned a small smile at that as she moved to the center of the room where her maids helped her out of her robe and into the dress again.

As the time passed and brought her closer to the dreaded event, Stori wished she could have spoken to her father one last time. She hadn't been able to the night before and since she also skipped breakfast, avoiding her fiancé, she had unfortunately avoided seeing her father too.

Stori chastised herself for that decision. She would have to meet her fiancé eventually. Wouldn't it be better to meet him before the wedding? She shrugged off the idea, no point in thinking of it now that the time had already passed.

The rest of the morning slipped away until the moments just before the procession down the aisle. It seemed to her that the time between watching the soldiers fight, and this moment now, straining against the stiffness of her dress, outside the doors with her father by her side had passed with impossible quickness. She knew her father was speaking to her, but she was too focused on the doors of the church to hear what he said.

The melodies started before she was ready and then the doors began to open, moving with infernal slowness. She would have run in surprise at the motion if her father hadn't taken her arm, leading. He paused and gave her a slight frown as he tried to step forward and she remained still.

Stori remembered what she was to do and started forward, taking a moment to correct her steps in time with the music and her father's gait. She kept her head ducked as she walked. She chided herself for the childish behavior, but she still couldn't bring herself to look at the bastard she had to marry.

Also, she couldn't bear to look at the guests who she knew were staring at her as though she was their only hope at peace with a rival sphaere. That thought of the promised peace was almost enough to make her look up, just as the shoes of the guests pulled away and a scarred hand reached out and waited for her to take it. Almost. She took the hand and moved to her position without even a glance at her betrothed.

As the ceremony continued for a short eternity, Stori stared at the hands holding hers' and traced the scars in her mind. What business did a king have with that many scars? The question kept coming back to her and when it did, she considered looking up to see if she could find the answer in her groom's face. She always banished that thought as soon as it floated into her mind, however. Hands were more honest anyway, faces lie. And from his hands, she guessed he was a fighter... or else an idiot who always stood too close to moving blades. Probably the latter.

So, she continued watching his hands and dreading every moment of the future. He must have been uncomfortable too, the way his hands were sweating. Though what he had to be uncomfortable about, Stori couldn't imagine. He had nothing to lose, at least not the same way she did, on their wedding night. She blanched at the idea and clenched her fists, unintentionally giving his hands a sharp squeeze and digging her nails into his palms; with all the callouses, he didn't even flinch. She hated him a little more for that.

Stori almost ripped her hands away when he tapped hers' with a finger, a question. She turned her head a little more toward the archbishop and hoped he'd take the hint that she was ignoring him. He seemed to understand as he returned a gentle squeeze and didn't move again until the end of the ceremony.

As the archbishop said the dreaded phrase 'you may kiss the bride', Stori clenched her jaw and, if possible, tucked her head even more. She squeezed her eyes closed as her betrothed—*no husband, what a dreadful thought*—pulled back her veil.

She felt a light peck on her lips and breath a sight of relief that the wedding was over. Still without looking up, they both turned to the guests and listened to the cheers for a moment before walking down the aisle, out the door, and toward the banquet hall.

"You know," the voice next to her startled Stori almost enough to make her jump. "You'll have to look at me eventually."

Stori grimaced but didn't lift her gaze from the floor as she followed his lead down the hallway. "I imagine so," she murmured in as cold and uncaring tone as she could muster.

Her husband hummed an answer next to her but didn't say anything more as they reached the banquet hall and took their seated positions next to each other. Stori grimaced again as her father sat on the other side of her new husband—out of talking range.

Stori sat straight and still throughout the lunch feast, only picking at her food when she had to for appearances. Scarred hands occasionally entered her peripheral vision. She became extra engaged in any conversation that faced her in the opposite direction when they did.

As round after round of toasts and cheers were extended to the new king and queen, a familiar twinge of guilt grew in Stori. The relief on the faces of both her people and his was almost blinding as she ventured a look out at the crowd. War was prevented. The relief of the people in the room, every person in the room, from the nobility to the servers and guards, added a tangible weight to the Vis in the air.

Stori clenched her teeth, chiding her selfish feelings for their existence. As the feast drew to an end and the festivities of the wedding day started, Stori eased herself into the notion that all the people in this room were now her own—the Medians had become hers; she had married their king.

She repeated that idea to herself as she walked around the room on her own and accepted with grace wishes of prosperity and congratulations from the guests. Working up the courage, she glanced around the faces in the crowd, hoping to overcome her hesitation when she found her husband's face.

A small frown formed tugged at her own face. She realized she didn't know what he looked like and couldn't remember what he was wearing. If everyone could put their hands up, she'd be sure to recognize him. Stori almost laughed at the thought. She couldn't find her own husband in a crowded room.

"Are you alright, dear?" A smooth female voice asked from behind.

Stori jumped and the hairs on the back of her neck stood on end. She turned to the speaker and stared for a moment in awe at the woman she knew was her husband's mother. She thought her name was Lora, or something that started with an *L*, from her father's brief overview of the Godric family tree.

"I am the King's mother, Loreda Iano-Godric," the woman stated with a graceful little nod.

Stori blinked for a second at every graceful feature of the older woman before returning to her senses and recalling her manners. "Queen Loreda, it is a pleasure to meet you."

Loreda waved the greeting away with a graceful hand and lazy indifference. "Istoria, dear—may I call you Istoria?" She paused long enough for Stori to nod before continuing, moving to the young woman's side and gently steering their walk to the balcony doors. "I think it would be helpful if we were friends. We do have a great deal in common, you know, and I've been in most every situation you will be."

"Oh?" Stori heard herself respond automatically, then regretted her lack of manners as the older woman guided her to the balcony railing and a breathtaking view of the kingdom—*her* kingdom. Stori remained silent for a moment, looking out at the lovely view and hoping she could act naturally amazed at the gorgeous city long enough to come up with a better response than 'oh'.

Loreda was looking at her with one eyebrow raised in a teasing manner. Stori forced a smile and tried to think faster.

"I was married in a similar manner, you see," Loreda continued after the silence lasted a moment too long. "I only meant I might be able to assist you in… becoming accustomed to life here." She paused and gave Stori a meaningful glance. "And if you should decide you would be happiest living away from Sentre, I have a few estates you might enjoy staying at. After you've completed your duty to the crown." Loreda placed her hand over

Stori's and gave it a light squeeze.

Stori gritted her teeth at the thought, though the woman was right, of course. She wouldn't be free to leave or do as she wished until she'd born the kingdom an heir. But still, hiding in some remote estate didn't sound like something a queen should do. At least, it was something she hoped her mother wouldn't have considered, if she had lived long enough.

"It sounds like a horrid idea, I'm sure," Loreda continued quickly when Stori didn't speak.

"No, I…" Stori tried to protest as she realized this was probably something Loreda, herself, had done. And after all, the former king, Vlasis Godric, had to have been a much worse person than her father, if even half the rumors about him were true. "I did not mean to insult, I was just thinking about it. I only just arrived in Sentre, you see." Stori failed to explain without tripping over her words.

Loreda purred a response but didn't say anything more for several moments. "If you wish to stay here with Brynte, I'll admit I don't know him well, he has been away so long… But no matter what kind of… no matter what he turns out to be, I won't be able to assist you much here. When Vlasis was king, I only stayed in Sentre when I couldn't avoid it." She turned to Stori with cold eyes that remained so until a small smile softened them. "After you've stayed here for a time, at least long enough to bear the king an heir, I think you might come to see things as I did. My offer will remain open."

"I— Thank you," Stori stammered, unsure if she should even try to suggest that she might not need to live somewhere else. Loreda sounded sure that she would, and after all, the woman had been through this before.

Another squeeze of her hand brought Stori's attention back to her conversation partner. Loreda moved away from the railing toward the festivities but paused before she'd taken more than a few steps. "I don't know him well. When he was a boy I didn't know him at all. But he was raised by his father, and I knew his father. Vlasis was a cruel, cowardly man. I don't mean to frighten you, dear. Only to warn you. I was constantly in fear for my life after I gave the king the heir he wanted. Living away was not a choice, it was a necessity." Loreda gave Stori one last sad smile before returning indoors.

The weight of the woman's words hovered over Stori's head as she repeated them to herself, trying to find every bit of meaning in them that she could.

When she had turned inside out the idea that her new husband might have her killed in the future, she gave up on figuring out what plan he might have. Stori decided she'd have to find Brynte and ask. She always hated the games played in her father's court. She wasn't ready to play those games here, especially not today.

With that determined, Stori marched back inside and was faced with the same problem as before. She still didn't know what her husband looked like. Stori sighed and started looking around then for either Loreda or her father; one of them could surely point him out.

Stori couldn't find her father, but Loreda was making rounds speaking with all the guests. One guest in particular she spent a great deal of time greeting; a rather short military officer, a general, Stori might have guessed though she wasn't sure what all the medals and stripes meant in Medius. The general had dark hair with more of it pooled to his eyebrows and beard than on his head. Stori couldn't help but stare at the pair from across the room. The time they spent greeting each other was filled with enough phantom touches and whispers in ears, Stori averted her gaze. The notion that she was spying on an intimate moment between lovers filled her head as she avoided looking toward either of them for the rest of the event.

CHAPTER 5

fter what seemed an infinite amount of time, Stori gave up on finding out who or where her husband was before they had some formal engagement together. She focused instead on finishing her rounds as a new queen, smiling and nodding with demure at her new subjects. She managed to speak to her father but only in passing before he had to speak with someone else.

In a moment of inspiration when no one was looking, Stori came to the decision to give up for a time and slip away. She maneuvered through the crowd to one of the small side rooms and snuck in, closing the curtains behind her without checking inside the room first. She let out a small sigh, relieved to be cut off from the crowd, even if just by a few layers of fabric.

"Uh?" A voice queried from the back of the small room.

Stori's nerves were too shot even to jump. Instead she sighed again.

Just my luck.

"I apologize for intruding." She turned around slowly in case she'd interrupted anything private. Her father's advice was to always be cautious when entering private, dark nooks.

Stori blinked at the scene in front of her; at the two soldiers she had seen sparring that morning. They sat on the only couch, hunched over an unfamiliar board game. The handsome redhead was sporting a bruise across his jaw on the opposite side of the scar. A scar that, up close, looked less roguishly handsome and more like someone had tried to split his face in two and almost succeeded. It was hideous, but his smile was warm and Stori smiled back before she could stop herself.

She distracted herself by turning to the wraith. The wraith... Stori stopped breathing for a moment as she caught sight of the Shade presence in the wraith's face.

"He's not a Shade. He's my friend and he ain't gonna be any danger to you." The redhead jumped up between Stori and the wraith with his palms out as though to calm a frightened animal. "Please don't scream or anything, that'd just be the worst for this wedding party."

The request not to scream broke Stori out of her initial panic. She swallowed back a scoff at the insult that she would scream over this, even if she almost had.

"I'm not going to scream," she snapped.

It must have sounded harsher and more unladylike than she'd meant it because the redhead blinked at her with surprise written over his discolored face. He shared a glance and a half-smile with the wraith half-blood.

Stori marched the short distance to the wraith, gave a small curtsy that may not have been entirely appropriate for a soldier, and looked back to the redhead with an expression that might almost, *almost* be considered a smirk. Stori remembered her manners enough to swallow the grin and the comment she had planned. Though maybe she shouldn't have; the big grin spreading over the redhead's face could have used a sarcastic comment.

A sudden grab at her hand brought Stori's attention back to the wraith, who was also wearing an ear-to-ear smile. He kissed the back of her fingers, grin never faltering. He gave her a wink as he let go of her hand.

A silence settled over the three. The quiet remained long enough for the sounds of the outside world to pass through the curtain and remind Stori where she was and what she was doing. "I apologize for interrupting. I didn't mean to disturb your—" Stori frowned at the funny looking board game with so many different pieces. "Game." She took a step toward the curtain, toward the redhead who was standing between her and the way out.

The redhead remained still as he glanced between her and the wraith. Stori guessed from his facial expression that he was having another silent yet animated conversation with his friend.

Stori straightened her neck and held her head firmly facing forward. She wasn't going to try to guess their conversation. Besides, the responsible thing to do would be to return to the tedious, drawn-out party celebrating the end of her free life.

The queenly thing, she reminded herself.

Her shoulders gave up a bit of good posture at the thought.

"You don't have to leave," the redhead said in a hurry, returning all his attention to Stori. He took half a step forward, running a hand through his flaming hair and resting it there for a moment.

Something about that hand was familiar. Stori frowned at it as he moved his hands to make his words come alive.

"You could join our chess game. I mean, it's a two-person game, but we could teach you if you want...?" His attention shifted behind her again and she caught a wild hand motion from the wraith out of the corner of her eye. The redhead rolled his eyes at his friend.

Stori spared a quick glance at the board before returning her focus to the scarred hands. Images of those same hands holding her own flashed to mind. Stori's stomach dropped for a long moment as she tried to remember how to breathe.

"You're not gonna start doing that again, are ya?"

The redhead... King Brynte!

How did she not realize it already? He had such a distinctive look.

He raised his hands slowly up to his face, watching her track them with a pinched and confused frown. He cleared his throat and snapped his hands behind his back, trapping her attention on his pitiful and confused smile.

"Other than the scar and bruise," the wraith piped up, finally standing.

Stori flinched—she had forgotten he was there as he moved to lean against the wall next to Brynte.

"And that hair, of course." He made a point of frowning and shook his head. "He's not that bad to have to look at. Though I'll admit, there is a lot to ignore." He snuck her another wink before returning his full attention to frowning at Brynte's hair.

"My hair's fine," Brynte snapped. "And the bruise is your fault."

"Oh, come on. You're the one who didn't dodge or parry. Your fault," the wraith returned with a crooked grin.

Brynte almost succeeded in not sneering back at his friend but couldn't quite keep the twisted look off his face. "I told you not to hit my face, Shad. Since I had a *wedding* to go to!" He enunciated each word of the last sentence as he threw a wild gesture in Stori's direction.

Stori startled herself by snorting with laughter at the absurdity of the encounter.

Shad shrugged. "Figured it couldn't make you look any worse."

"How 'bout a rematch?" Brynte said, slinging the first words together and drawing out the last one for an odd rhythm—almost like the rhythm of a sword fight.

"How about the bride gets a-a word in?" Stori interjected, trying to match the rhythm, but missing terribly as she tripped over the last few words.

Both men turned to her as though they'd forgotten she was there. Surprised blinks were exchanged.

"Sorry."

"You're King Brynte!" Stori barely remembered not to shout as the outside world loomed close. "I thought you were a solider."

More blinks were exchanged.

"Well, I used to be, sorta. We both were," Brynte said, shifting his weight. "Bodyguards, actually."

Stori blinked at him, her husband. He looked serious. She supposed being a bodyguard for a time could lend one such scars.

Still, why in all the worlds was a king ever a bodyguard?

"I had to make a living," Brynte answered her thought, as though a king having to make a living was a normal occurrence.

"It was either that or work as a male courtesan," Shad added. "And he just doesn't have the body for that—or the face. Ya know?" His mocking frown grew deeper. "Good manners are missing too."

Stori's jaw dropped as Brynte slapped the back of Shad's head.

"Don't say shit like that in front of her. She might get the wrong idea." Brynte waved off his friend.

"Don't cuss in front of her. She might get the right one," Shad returned with a cool smile.

"A courtesan? Why ever would you... I mean. How would..." Stori sputtered to a stop as she wasn't sure what question to ask or if she should even be trying to ask any.

Brynte rubbed his head as he shot one last glare at Shad. "He was joking. I never considered making a living like that. I wasn't that desperate."

"But…" Stori stopped, hoping he would continue.

She didn't know anything about him. No one in Sylva did. Even her father hadn't been able to tell her much before they arrived. Stori was suddenly aware of the glaring hole in all her thoughts and the assumptions she'd made about her fiancé. They were all based on his father, Vlasis, who was a terrible man. She knew nothing about Brynte.

A short hum brought her attention back to the two in front of her.

"Okay, fine," Shad surrendered. "But it would have been a funny thing to explain if you had."

"I doubt it would have been funny."

"Woulda been for me." Shad grinned.

Brynte crossed his arms and shot an annoyed glance up at his friend. Stori hadn't noticed until now, but he was nearly a head shorter than the tall wraith.

Average height or just under, her brain filled in the comparison. The wraith was just that tall.

"Could you explain to me?" Stori spoke, gaining their attention. "About being bodyguards."

"Oh, sure." Brynte turned in her direction as he spoke. "It's not that complicated. I spend, what, 13 years in exile?" He glanced at Shad to check the number. Shad shrugged. "'Bout 13 years. I needed to work. Me, my tutor and his wife—Klaas and Eleanora—have you met them yet?"

Stori shook her head. She hadn't known he'd been exiled either. Most of the people in Sylva who knew anything about the politics in Medius only knew he'd been away for several years—presumably doing Vlasis's bidding abroad in places where he wouldn't get in trouble.

"Well, you'll meet them. They're great, practically raised me. Both of us, actually," Brynte said as both he and Shad nodded emphatically. "Anyway, with Shad joining our group within a year of my exiling, we needed jobs. Klaas and Eleanora did what they could especially when we were younger, but Shad and I had to start working pretty quick to survive.

29

Being bodyguards was just a reasonable thing to do since it let us travel freely. We were already okay swordsmen, and we improved from there."

Stori stared as she consciously made sure her mouth hadn't fallen open again. She glanced between them. It was that simple for them. Stori searched for something to say but found nothing. For a king, or a crown prince at the time, to be working as a bodyguard for other royalty or powerful people? She almost smiled at the thought. It was a funny notion. Her attention went back to Brynte's hands as he unfolded them. The scars made sense. She noticed for the first time that Shad had many similar scars, they were just harder to see against the wisps of Shade in his skin.

"So…" Brynte drew out the word until Stori's attention returned to his face. "I'm a few years out of practice with all this." He waved his hand generally toward the party going on behind the curtain. "If I get a few things wrong, well, you may have to forgive me a couple mistakes. I'm still not used to interacting with the royalty and nobles as equals again."

"Alright." Stori paused and glanced around. She wasn't sure what she should ask about or say. She had already learned so much more about her husband than she'd known before she entered the little nook. Though she did wonder what they were doing away from the party.

Stori frowned and glanced at the game then back to them.

Even if he isn't used to this, she thought. *That doesn't necessarily mean he was in here avoiding the party—like I am*, a petty part of her reminded.

"So, what are you doing in here?" she asked, hoping to silence that petty part.

"Hiding," the men replied at once.

Stori blinked at their honesty.

"I had planned to 'hide in plain sight', as it were," Brynte said, rolling his eyes toward Shad. "But Shad said we shouldn't pretend to be guards here."

"We wouldn't be getting payed for it," Shad pointed out, as though not being payed to guard one's own wedding was the most important deciding factor. "And *you'd* stand out too much, for once," he added with a sly grin.

Brynte snorted but said nothing.

"Oh. Is that so?" Stori managed to ask, glancing between the two of them to make sure this issue too was that simple for them. They nodded in unison.

"Sorry to just leave you out there by yourself," Brynte said, giving her a sort of pinched half-smile. "But you didn't seem to want anything to do with me, so I figured you wouldn't mind."

Stori opened her mouth to deny that. She had been looking for him, but... not for any good reason. She closed her mouth and shifted in the awkward silence.

"Okay, okay. Mistakes of the past—let's not dwell," Shad said, stepping between the two of them. "Though it might not be a good idea for you both to be away from the party for a long period of time. People'll start talkin'."

Stori sighed and Brynte growled at the reminder. Silence returned to the trio as the sounds from the party now seemed louder and more foreboding.

"Okay, how 'bout this." Brynte started waving them into a huddle. "Since we both want to spend as little time out there as possible, we need a good plan of attack."

Stori listened with a bit of awe at the way her husband planned out their casual reintegration to the party, and ways to periodically slip away— with Shad adding a few points of help and sarcasm. They came away with a strong plan to avoid as much of the party as possible—and Stori felt something she hadn't before regarding her impending future—hope.

CHAPTER 6

From the Empty opened a doorway and the albino stepped through pitch darkness into the nighttime shadows of a Terranian city. Sverre glanced both ways down the dirty alley, noting a couple of shadows moving at one end before checking his AaD tablet for the location of the next doorway. He exhaled with a mutter somewhere between annoyance and relief that the hacker he needed to find lived in a natural gaet; an area where another doorway would open in the vicinity within the hour. The hacker seemed to have a propensity for odd things.

He must have been attracted to the gaet for all the oddities that would arise around it, Sverre mused, shaking his head.

The shadows moved close enough that Sverre could recognize them as two young men. He wanted to groan in exasperation at their predatory behavior, blocking the direction he needed to move in.

"Hey pal," one of them started in a Boston twang, looking at the AaD in Sverre's hand with an appraising eye. "That's a nice tablet you got."

"The hell's up with your hair?" The second stepped closer. "You tryn'a look like an old geezer?"

The first one laughed. "Hey, what brand's that tablet?" He turned to the other. "Looks pretty new. You could afford another, right?"

Sverre tried not to sigh as he glanced at the AaD in his hand. Giving up the device would be the quickest way out, but he didn't have a spare. He tucked the AaD into its proper pocket in his cloak.

"You're not thinkin' of pulling somethin' funny, are ya?" The first of the two pulled out a knife and waved it at Sverre. "Hand it over."

Sverre bit back the twinge of annoyance that these men couldn't think of something more entertaining to do.

At least act less predictably, he chided in his head.

Sverre stepped forward and caught the careless knife-hand. A quick squeeze of the sensitive nerve in the wrist and Sverre caught the knife as the man dropped it.

He tossed the knife to his other hand and held it to the second man's throat when he stepped within range. Both men stared wide-eyed and Sverre waited a moment for their brains to catch up to what had happened in the last two seconds.

When the proper amount of fear flooded the eyes of the man he had a knife on, Sverre withdrew the weapon.

"It's unbalanced." Sverre tipped the knife to one side then the other in his hand. "Won't throw straight." He demonstrated this with a quick flick of his wrist, sending the weapon some distance away into the side of a cardboard box with *Walmart*com* scrawled across it. The knife stuck out two letters away from the star symbol he'd been aiming at.

Sverre stepped between the men, in the opposite direction he'd sent the knife flying, and moved to put as much distance between himself and them as possible before they overcame their shock.

He pulled his dark hood over his head to prevent any moonlight from reflecting off his snowy hair as he stepped out of the alleyway and moved down a side street. He glanced at his surroundings and was glad no one was following.

Sverre made his way up to the roof of a short skyscraper where the doorway would open. He walked the rooftop perimeter and paused for a moment to notice that one side offered a view through an open window to the target of this escapade.

Sverre crouched for a moment to observe the middle-aged man. Lawrence Dara seemed oblivious to the fact that he was being watched. The cybersecurity expert continued shifting his attention between his computer and a mass of books open on his desk.

Another small sigh escaped from Sverre; he hoped he'd picked the right person for this. Not that he would ever know. Sverre presumed his eventual, bloody death would occur long before his plan worked. He shook his head, such wonderful things he had to look forward to.

Moving away from the edge of the rooftop and out of the older man's sight, Sverre pulled his own laptop out of his shoulder bag. He waited for the machine to boot up and checked the position of the doorway again. Another 15 minutes, at 2237, the same as the last time he'd checked. He logged in and waited again for the applications to set up. Another minute passed as he waited for his secure connection and link to the dark web to open. Sverre prodded one of his fingers that didn't have a nail on it with a careful touch, testing its sensitivity. It still hurt.

Damn that clown and his obsession with fingers, Sverre thought.

Finally, the laptop was ready for use. Sverre scowled at his watch, a full two minutes and 38 seconds. *Slow machine.* He could kill a dozen people faster than it could wake up. *Or maybe it's up to 13 now?* Sverre puzzled over the thought. He hadn't tested it yet, but the clown's latest modifications certainly increased his reaction time.

Sverre shook the thought out of his head and turned his attention back to the task at hand: Completing the encryption for the files and uploading them to the chatroom his target frequented.

He paused again in his work to glance over the new threads that had been started. It ever amused and surprised him how close to the truth some of the ideas hidden on this backroom chat were. He'd even seen references to some of his own work in this sphaere. Not by name, of course, but several people in the chat had linked some of the disappearances and deaths with the shadow organization they were chasing. They had reached the most accurate conclusion for those "mishaps"—assassination; his specialty. Not that Sverre wasn't great at the rest of his job, but death was, after all, his forte.

He scowled. He was starting to sound like Atanas. The man had said things similar when he was Sverre's master. He wasn't sure he could even consider Atanas any less his master now. He still took orders from the damned man.

A flash on the screen notified Sverre that the files were successfully uploaded. He was thankful for the excuse to drop his last line of thought to finish what he was working on.

Moments passed in silence except for the uneven sound of typing. The few of Sverre's fingers that still had nails clicked across the keyboard while the rest padded the keys in silence.

Moments passed as Sverre continued in his singular focus on completing the best level of encryption he could. He was sure that a hacker could break it within an hour, but he was still going to make it as much of a challenge as he could. Computers were definitely *not* his forte.

Finally he paused before entering the last command. He glanced toward the opposite building even though Dara's apartment was out of his view.

"I'm trusting you here," Sverre muttered to himself. "Please make this right." He finished the command and closed his computer, tightening his jaw at the click of the lid.

Sverre stood and packed away his things with greater haste than he had taken them out. He checked his AaD and entered commands to open a doorway as soon as one was available. Another minute and 43 seconds. He walked toward the building's edge to check on the hacker one last time.

Dara remained as he had been before. He closed one of the large books and moved to set it on the edge of the desk. In his focus on the computer he missed the desk and the book toppled to the floor, taking a stack of papers and smaller books with it.

The ghost of a smile touched Sverre's lips as he watched the security expert growl and drop his head against his desk before moving off his chair to collect the papers.

Sverre almost turned away when a young lady entered the hacker's room with a flourish and threw herself onto the couch. Sverre paused to watch the girl with a quizzical eye.

She's pretty. The thought was surprising and took away from his observations. She was very pretty, in fact, with an easy laugh and soft features. Though she seemed to be in a bit of a bad mood.

"*Atanas calling,*" the AaD in Sverre's hands started singing. Sverre stared wide-eyed at the device.

How did Atanas know? The thought screamed through his head. He had expected his bloody end sooner than later, but not this soon.

Sverre steadied his breath and answered with a curt greeting.

"You have a new mission," Atanas spoke without preamble.

Sverre almost let out a sigh of relief. He snapped his jaws together before he could give himself away and waited for Atanas to continue.

"You're going to Sentre. You have a king to kill and don't let your feelings get in the way, Alvidar. I'll send a message to you with the details. And with this one, make Oracaede proud of your work." Atanas hung up as Sverre scowled.

Make it messy, huh? He finally let the sigh escape.

The doorway opened behind Sverre, startling him out of his concentration. He moved away from the edge of the building after one last glance at the hacker and the pretty girl. He wished them both luck in surviving the mess that he was about to start.

Sverre turned back to the darkness of the Empty and stepped through the doorway. He didn't look back at the moonlit world as the doorway closed around him.

CHAPTER 7

Lawrence frowned as he moved the thick book of unhelpful cybersecurity guidelines out of his way. The hairs rose on the back of his neck as the sensation of being watched returned.

He scowled as he searched for movement in his environment and out the window while trying to not seem obvious. Nothing had changed since the last time, but the sense of an intrusion on his privacy didn't dissipate.

He dropped the useless book he'd been holding as far away as possible. A swish and thud brought his attention to the edge of his desk where piles of papers were slipping in a steady stream to the floor. He groaned at the world's continual vendetta against him as he dropped his head onto his desk with a satisfying, painful *smack*.

Lawr crawled from his chair to the floor, imagining how enjoyable it would be to worm his way over to the couch and take an unending nap.

Excessive sleeping is a sign of depression. He groaned at the internal reminder. *Wouldn't want Ali to notice.*

On cue, the sound of a lock turning and the front door opening pulled Lawr out of his thoughts. Alisha waltzed into the living room, tossed her backpack onto his lovely couch, and flopped down after it. She glanced over the paper and book mess he was picking up and laughed.

"At least your day is going well," she said with an empathetic smile as she kicked at one of the pillows on the sofa.

"You know what they say, attitude is everything." Lawr sighed at his hypocritical statement and dropped the papers he had collected into a stack on his desk before returning to the floor to gather the rest.

Ali scoffed and kicked the pillow again. "Well, I am officially done with university." She paused a second to wait for his reaction. "And good riddance, too."

Lawr hummed a response as he set the last of the papers and smaller books back on the desk and lined them up so they were square with the laptop and other books. "Congratulations," he added, seeing his niece was waiting for an actual response.

Ali groaned. "I'm just happy to be done."

"Yeah, now you can spend all your days standing in the burning sun, staring at rocks and picking up trash."

A growl emanated from the couch, followed by a pillow that bounced off Lawr's head. Lawr smiled as he caught the pillow before it fell to the floor and threw it back.

"You make the last five years of my life seem so worthwhile," Ali grumbled.

"That's what I'm here for." Lawr paused. "That, a place to live, a tutor, and a lot of moral, if not emotional, support."

"Yes, Uncle Lawr." Ali rolled her eyes and smiled as she sat up. "You're the greatest."

Lawr waved off the adoring fanfare with mock seriousness. "I know, I know." He shifted one stack of papers that was just the barest bit out of line. "You gonna call your parents." He said the question as a statement of suggestion, though he already knew the answer.

"No," Ali started, pinching the bridge of her nose as though she had just reached a decision of great importance. "The cost of international calls is expensive. Besides, they were worried about monitoring on their cell phone last time I called." Grumbling the last bit, Ali glanced at Lawr's one raised eyebrow at her excuses. "I just don't want to bug them. If I get a job at the company, then I could go to Ghana and surprise them."

Lawr caught the dull look in her eyes at the thought. He wanted to tell her she didn't have to leave if she didn't want to, but he stopped himself. He didn't know what his niece wanted for her life anymore then she did. He still thought she should have continued studying to be a veterinarian, but...

Lawr's shoulders sagged. He was biased in that thought. He glanced at the photo on his desk. His wife's smile made it worse.

A sigh brought his attention back to the couch. The dullness was gone and Ali seemed to be wrestling with an idea of great importance.

Lawr chuckled. *She's probably thinking about dinner already.*

"Sure." Lawr was content to drop the subject as he sat down. *But wait...* "Weren't they in Nigeria?"

"Industrial waste is everywhere. They moved last week," Ali said with a scowl as she stood and headed for the kitchen.

"Oh." He must not have been listening when she told him her parents were moving somewhere else. He frowned after his niece. *Poor communication skills must be hereditary.*

Ali called from the kitchen to let him know she was making dinner. She started listing off all the possibilities as she went through the fridge and cabinets. Lawr ignored her since she wasn't really asking for his opinion anyway and would make whatever she alone decided on.

He turned his attention back to the laptop and logged back in. Lawr sifted through his email, checked his favorite sites, ignored the angry messages his boss had sent him, and finally ended up on the deep web for a quick check of his favorite sites and chatrooms.

Two new threads had started in his favorite chat group, though not the sanest one he frequented. Lawr frowned at his screen for a moment as he opened the most recent thread. This one was altogether dedicated to complaining about how awful the second thread was. Lawr gathered this was because it couldn't be opened.

Moving to the second thread, Lawr found it was indeed, difficult to access. The encryption alone could have been used for government security. Lawr cracked his knuckles. Good thing his years of designing security systems wouldn't be completely wasted.

Less than an hour later, and long passed a forgotten dinner, Lawr had access. With the thread finally open, Lawr took a moment to revel in his triumph and scarf down a few bites of... whatever it was Ali put on a plate. He wasn't sure it contained any of the basic food groups, but it tasted good.

Lawr opened the file and stopped at the first document. It was addressed to him by name. Lawr froze.

Hacked? How could I *have been hacked?*

This had to be a script that addressed itself to the person logged in. But there was still no way it could have reached his computer through all the precautions he had set up.

After thinking through it again and checking the software and logs, he reached the same conclusion, his system wasn't compromised; whoever uploaded the file just knew his name. That was worst. Lawr leaned forward again and opened the document. It contained a short message that requested his assistance in a matter he'd soon learn much about. Listed was a name. A name for the ghost organization his chat group had been theorizing about.

Oracaede.

Lawr frowned again. He didn't recognize the name and Wikipedia could only come up with a weak reference to a Greek python goddess. Lawr ignored the name for a moment to click through some of the other files. They mostly documented plans for places Lawr knew nothing about. Though some of the files were about past events Lawr recognized and listed more details than had ever been made public.

"Well," Lawr whispered to himself. "This is going to be fun."

CHAPTER 8

ry woke up with a start and searched the room with frantic eyes for... something. His father maybe. The nightmare faded from his mind with a few blinks into the still dark world. The nightmares had started again ever since returning to the castle. Bry rubbed a hand across his face.

I wish I could leave again...

He groaned and collapsed back into the too-comfortable bed. He'd been sleeping on it for weeks now, but he still worried the fluff might swallow him up and never let him out. Bry asked if the servants could put a board or something hard under the first layer of fluff, but they'd stared at him like he was crazy, and he swore the bed was even softer afterward.

He stood up in one quick motion and began moving around the room. Exhaustion from the previous day hung over him as thick and tangible as the duvet he'd just escaped from. The party had been endless and suffocating, without a suitable amount of drinks for an event of that size. The only thing he had focused on was avoiding politicians.

"Oh, well," he said aloud, just to hear something.

The room was too quiet. Bry hated the quiet. Life was only ever quiet before an attack. He scanned the room again, just to make sure.

Ah. Still alone.

He sighed at that too.

At least his wife wasn't some politician with an agenda—and she seemed rather nice. He could almost see himself liking her.

After she's grown a bit, maybe.

He was still so near Terrae and abiding by Terranian laws that even the thought of sleeping with the princess, a minor, made him squirm—even if the notion was normal in Medius—and in Sylva too, apparently. Istoria had been less than forceful about the "duty to the crown" or whatever she called it, but made it clear she was willing to do her part as both their people expected. The idea made Bry frown.

"Silly girl, if you don't want to do something you just have to say so. I'll listen," he grumbled to himself, moving from the dark bedroom to the attached study.

This room was also dark, but not, as Shad always put it, obsessively so. Light wasn't blocked out of every crack near a window, or gap by the door. Bry wasn't sure why his servants thought he needed a pitch-black room, or even when they'd had time to add all the extra curtaining. He wished they'd stop doing things behind his back, no matter how much they thought it might help.

Bry stood in the middle of the study for a moment, staring around into the nooks and corners before moving to open the curtains of the giant window. Bry stared out for a moment to take in the quiet city, where all the decent people were still asleep. The sun had yet to rise, but was giving the world its first taste of pale light.

Bry moved away from the curtain and found one of his shirts on a chair. He shrugged it on, followed by his boots after a short search for them. Shad, at least, would be up. Klaas and Eleanora too. He could get breakfast.

A soft knock sounded on the study door just before Bry grabbed the door handle.

"Damn." He'd been beaten again.

He opened the door, careful to avoid the one spot that squeaked as he slipped out. Glowing blue eyes in a nearly disintegrated shadow greeted him. Bry could sense the smug grin radiating from his friend even if he couldn't see it. Bry replied to it with a glower and a nod and said nothing.

They moved in silence through the castle halls, down several flights of stairs, and through many back passages, avoiding notice by any of the guards. They reached the door at the bottom of one last flight of stairs and paused to catch their breath from the little bit of exercise traversing the castle always was. The smell of breakfast wafted through the door.

Good old Eleanora, Bry thought, smiling to himself.

He could sense a quiet smile about Shad too as the shadow gave a couple light taps on the door before entering.

"Morning!" Shad called as he entered the room and Bry closed the door behind them.

They walked into the brightly lit living room that was, as usual, buried in a sea of books, plant clippings and roots, small glass containers, and loose papers stuffed into every nook. The pair carefully picked their way through the mess toward the kitchen.

"You boys came at the perfect time." Eleanora's voice floated from a back divide that hid the kitchen. "I'm almost done," she added as they entered the even messier kitchen.

Eleanora stood over the wood burning stove, staring into an oversized pot with a look of tangible disappointment. She half-heartedly attended to another pan of breakfast-looking food.

"The medicine… experiment… whatever that is… not coming along well?" Shad asked, moving to take over the breakfast pan.

Bry smirked as he sat next to Klaas and watched Shad carefully save the meal by inching it away from the older woman.

"It should be working." Eleanora frowned, jerking the wooden spoon in a semi-circle around the pot's edge. "This should be translucent by now." She lifted a scoop of dark green sludge from the pot.

The older woman shook her head and gave the pot one last stir before taking pot holders and moving the mess to one of the thick stone side counters that was already burned black. Eleanora looked back at the stove and Shad with a smile working its way onto her face. "How's breakfast? Saved?"

"Well, it is hard to mess up one of your meals, unless you do it yourself," Shad started, eyeing the contents of his pan with feigned interest. "But it doesn't seem too bad. Maybe just a little dried out."

Eleanora shooed the wraith away as she came to examine the meal. "It'll be fine," she announced to scattered applause from the three men. "Let me just spiff it up a bit." She moved quickly through the kitchen gathering random ingredients.

43

Shad moved to join the seated crowd with a short nod of "you're welcome" to the other two. Nods were returned in full.

"So," Klaas started, turning toward Bry with a bushy eyebrow raised. "How's the new wife?"

Bry was not so obtuse as to not notice the other question in his tone. After all, Klaas had just come from Terrae too. "She seems a nice girl, but we only talked a little at the party and I didn't see her after."

Klaas nodded with solemn approval and Eleanora hummed a similar thought.

"And she seemed not to mind Shad," Bry added, since that had been one of the more important discoveries about his wife.

"Yeah, I don't think she minded me at all," Shad chipped in with a happy voice and relaxed smile.

"Well, that is wonderful." Eleanora pitched in as she worked, "Though you know she would have had to warm up to Shad at some point regardless. You two are practically attached at the hip."

"Are not," Bry and Shad protested in unison.

Klaas laughed uproariously at this and earned a pair of scowls in return before Eleanora could turn their attention back to the usual morning proceedings, complete with rounds of bickering and lighthearted jabs. These were the moments Bry longed for.

CHAPTER 9

Brynte concentrated hard on remembering the good times from earlier that morning with his little family. He tried remembering why it was so nice to live in Sentre and be king.

As he half-listened to his Castle Manager drone on with a report he never asked for, remembering became harder. Bry blinked as he realized he'd been focusing too much on his inner thoughts and had completely tuned out from the matter at hand. He focused hard on listening again— hard enough that he still wasn't listening, only focusing on doing so.

Bry almost gave up and let his head drop to the desk for a healthy smack, but an ever so slight change in the speaker's voice brought his active focus back to the Castle Manager, Chesler or something. Bry had forgotten the man's name immediately after being introduced and now he could only go off what the other guards called him. Bry had the distinct impression that the man despised him, or at least wouldn't be willing to give him half a chance at anything.

"This new movement from the Nomads is a disturbing change from where they have been operating for the past several months. Their move into Medius has already displaced many villages and towns who are flocking to their neighbors and the capital for safety," Chesler droned on—though now he wasn't reading the report as much as speaking what he knew from memory and watching Brynte. His beady eyes seemed to analyze Bry's every motion.

Bry tried not to bristle under the scrutiny. He couldn't guess what the man was looking for or expected to find, but he hated being examined for weakness.

"This new activity may bring up civil unrest about your rule. The people will remember that Queen Loreda worked hard to fight the Nomads out of Medius." Chesler paused at the last sentence to watch Bry's reaction.

And there it is, Bry thought.

This was a problem Loreda solved in her short rule, but it had returned shortly after he'd taken the throne.

Great.

Bry almost rolled his eyes at the tone and the carefully placed accusation.

"Do you have any suggestions for handling the people's mistrust?" Bry asked after a moment, since he certainly didn't.

He'd only ever had to deal with the aftermath of letting this kind of problem fester—when one of his clients grew so unpopular, people attacked. An attack he could handle. How for the fate of all the worlds was he supposed to mitigate one from an entire sphaere?

Chesler raised an eyebrow and stared for a moment as though he must have misheard and was waiting for Bry to say something smarter.

"Any suggestions?" Bry repeated after too long of a moment passed in silence.

He disliked the man for more than just the boring reports and hidden accusations. Now Chesler was staring at him like he was an idiot. Bry crossed his arms, leaned back in his chair, and waited. He could play this staring game too.

Chesler held his frowning gaze a moment longer before he turned his attention back to the tablet he'd been reading from. He looked over the information on the tablet for a moment before answering.

"I might recommend a show of force, sir," Chesler said, speaking in a slow and careful tone. "To demonstrate that you won't tolerate the Nomads brazen moves into Medius."

Bry nodded. He guessed mitigating wasn't that much different than a simple counterattack. "Who is the general in charge of the region under attack? He can lead this counteraction."

Chesler was frowning again and bristled at the question. Bry almost sighed.

This man never stays happy, does he?

He waited with some impatience, watching the other man's body language.

Chesler didn't seem to like Bry's idea and his voice as he spoke reflected as much. "The general is Jeshua Harailt, one of the former King's trusted generals."

Bry could hear the hatred Chesler had for the general as he spoke. *Good.* Bry didn't so much care for Chesler. Maybe Harailt would be an improvement.

"He can take over the offensive in a shorter time than any other generals. Have him informed of the new plan." Bry stood to stretch as Chesler made a few notes on his tablet.

"Yes, sir."

A frown crossed Bry's face as Chesler left the room with only a slight, grudging nod in respect. Bry slumped back into his chair.

"I thought he'd never leave," Bry sighed, turning toward his adjoining bedroom. A quick scan of the room revealed it was empty. "Shad!" Bry called and waited. No movement in the vicinity as the silence returned. Bry wished he could have skipped out on that meeting too.

He crossed his arms on his desk and dropped his head on them. He groaned into the nook of his elbow, a small compromise against screaming.

An AaD broke the silence with an unwelcome *ding*, signaling a new message. Bry groaned again with hope of ignoring the intrusion. A second ding. He gave up.

Bry took a moment to rifle through piles of important and useless kingly documents on his desk, checking each AaD he found until the one with the messages. He unlocked the device and checked the name of the sender. Aarkdal… the Lucian.

Great. Bry rolled his eyes.

He stretched in his chair and popped his neck and knuckles before opening the first message. Bry frowned at the contents for several moments. It didn't make sense. Someone had found files of recent activity regarding Oracaede.

Oracaede is gone, Bry assured himself.

He had seen to that—so had Shad and Aarkdal. That damned monstrosity had been destroyed before Vlasis had even died. There was no way… He reread the message.

But Oracaede wasn't gone somehow. That's what this meant.

Bry held his head between his hands and squeezed until the pressure started making him nauseous. He released his head and opened the second message, hoping it would say the last message was all a prank, a lie, another sign that Aarkdal merely hated his guts, anything. The second message contained specifics of where the information was found.

Terrae.

Bry stood and paced the room for several moments, trying to pull his thoughts together. He marched back to his desk and messaged Aarkdal, asking if he knew anything else. The reply came in moments with as much scathing as could fit into so few words that Aarkdal had already sent everything he knew. Bry growled at the response and dropped the AaD back onto his desk.

What to do with this information.

Bry scowled and pinched the bridge of his nose. He didn't even know where to start. He called a servant to go and fetch Shad, wherever he had wandered off to.

If nothing else, Bry thought. *It'll help to talk out some potential plans and see if they're workable.*

The moments of waiting dragged by and began unnerving Bry as he waited for his friend. He reread the messages again, trying to analyze the words to see if he had missed anything. The information remained the same no matter how he looked at it.

The door swung open and hit the wall just short of slamming. "You *summoned*," Shad said as he entered, putting noticeable effort into not frowning. "How kingly of you," he added with a smile that was all bitterness and no mirth.

"Sorry, Shad. I didn't have time to try and find you myself." Bry grabbed the AaD and moved to where Shad stood, waiting. "Aarkdal sent this. Read it." Bry shoved the AaD into Shad's hands and moved to reread the first message again over his shoulder.

Shad read in silence. He stared at the screen for an inordinate amount of time by Bry's standards. Bry fidgeted and shifted as he waited for any form of response. Finally, he reached around his friend and scrolled to the next message.

Shad didn't move and his gaze remained focused, so focused that Bry could sense his Shade powers trying to claw their way out. Bry sensed the force touching his mind, pulling at it. He tried not to flinch as the pain increased.

"Shad."

The powers snapped back. Shad blinked as he focused on Bry and the world around them again. "Well, this is bad."

"No shit." Bry grabbed the tablet back and glanced at the message again without reading the words as he started pacing.

Shad stood still except for one hand which pulled anxiously through his hair. "What...?" Shad broke off and waited until Bry stopped pacing and faced him. "What are we gonna do 'bout this?"

Bry threw his hands up. He wanted to scream. He had no idea what they should...

He dropped his hands and rubbed his head. That wasn't true, he did have some ideas. Bry paced back to his desk and set the AaD down. He leaned against the desk.

"We need more info," he said finally, voice quiet as he turned to Shad.

His friend nodded and stepped forward, already awaiting orders.

"We can't start another war based solely on this—" He waved toward the AaD. "The people won't jump at the idea of attacking an enemy that's supposed to be destroyed already."

Shad nodded and moved to the desk to look at the messages again. "I could find whoever discovered this leak. See if there's any more info."

"Right. And we need to get to them quickly. Oracaede will try to find them too," Bry said, starting to fill with energy now that a plan was forming.

"I can leave now for Terrae to get whoever it is," Shad said, already writing the information in the message that could track the person who found the leak.

"I..." Bry grimaced. "Can't come. There is still too much I have to take care of here, being king."

"Finally, ya got that one without me having to tell you." Shad smirked at his friend before becoming serious again. "If nothing else, it would be a horrible idea for you to leave your mother around with the throne empty."

49

Bry nodded in agreement. "True. Maybe if Istoria wasn't still so new and her father and the other ambassadors from Sylva weren't leaving tomorrow."

Shad nodded along with that. "I'll be fine taking care of this myself. Don't worry." He straightened up and headed for the door. "I'll grab some supplies in case this takes a while," he said over his shoulder as he left the room.

"Hurry," Bry said, mostly to himself. He grabbed the AaD from the desk and started searching for the nearest doorway with the fastest travel time. He frowned as he found the closest one would still be a stretch to reach on time, even on horseback. Bry called a servant to prepare two horses and get one of the stable hands ready to make the trip.

Ducking out of the room, Bry nearly ran—slowing to a fast walk whenever he passed someone—down to the stables. Shad was only a few moments behind him and ready to go as soon as he reached the horses. Bry gave him a quick rundown on the doorway location and time limit before Shad took the AaD and rode out.

Bry sighed in relief as soon as Shad was on his way. He made his way back into the castle but stopped as he noticed an odd person watching him from between a buttress and the side of a bridge near the lower castle. The man, whose appearance would have looked young if not for a shock of white hair, was dressed in all black. The clothes were odd in a city that either wore bright colors if one was rich or shades of browns if one was a peasant.

Bry turned to call to the man and entice him to come down from his high position off the path. The man turned and disappeared into the castle before Bry could speak. He frowned and waited for the man to reappear. There was nowhere to go from the buttresses, except maybe into the castle through a window. Bry growled at the idea and snapped an order to his guards to look for the stranger.

This day is going to be a bad one. Bry resigned himself to the thought as he trudged the long way back up to this study.

CHAPTER 10

B ry sat alone in his study, failing to focus on the piles of paperwork
he needed to do. He glanced again at the AaD open to the doorway
patterns indicating where Shad should be in Terrae. Even if the
hacker cooperated, the trip back would still take another few days in
Medius time.

That and the twisting in his gut which came with the knowledge he
was being watched kept Bry anxious and his sword close. It was a sensation
he knew well and always preceded an attack. He scanned his study again,
but there were still no signs of threat.

The hairs on the back of Bry's neck rose as he did. There was
something dangerous there that shouldn't be. He walked to the center of
his study with his sword and waited. Moments dragged by in silence except
the ticking of a few clocks.

"I know you're there," Bry called to the silent, empty space. "Come
out and stop wasting my time."

Silence returned. Another tense moment passed. A shadow moved by
one of the floor-length windows.

The wanderer in black from the day before stepped out and closed the
window.

"Most astute, King Brynte Godric." The speaker's voice was low as the
white-haired man moved between shadows along the edges of the room,
making a large circle around Bry.

Bry couldn't ignore the sense in his gut that this man was dangerous as he studied the stranger, careful not to turn his back to him. The man looked about thirty and albino. His shock white hair and skin combined with blood-red eyes and overall demeanor gave him the focused presence of a demon. Bry could make out various weapon outlines under the man's dark clothes.

An assassin, Bry's gut told him. *This man is an assassin.*

Bry knew danger when he met it. The only ghost assassin Bry knew of was from rumors of one that had worked for Oracaede. Bry made a conscious effort not to gulp at that realization.

"What are you here for?" Bry snapped the question. "And who sent you?"

The albino continued his slow pacing circle and gave no sign he'd heard the questions. A moment of silence passed before he stopped walking and faced Bry.

"I'm only here to extend congratulations on your coronation—and wedding," the low, flat voice responded. "Oracaede wishes you best in this... escapade of yours."

Bry's breath caught as he waited for the assassin to continue. Had Oracaede merely sent this man because they knew they'd been found out, or because of his war-preventing marriage?

He breathed out, remembering he'd seen the albino right after learning of Oracaede's continued existence. Even Oracaede wasn't fast enough to have someone in Sentre in that short of a time—especially not someone as high-caliber as the Ghost.

"Tell Oracaede to keep their congrats. I'll keep my sovereignty as king." Bry tightened his grip on the sword and cocked it out of its sheath.

The albino didn't seem surprised. Maybe a little relieved, but the expression disappeared before Bry could fully recognize it. The man continued his circular pacing with no reply. When he reached the window again, he paused and looked out it at the city below.

"Your people are suffering. The shortages of food, threats of war, taxes." He caught Bry's eye for a moment on the last one. Bry thought he too must realize the idiocy of mentioning taxes when their inflated rates were Oracaede's direct bidding, a leftover of Vlasis's reign.

The assassin turned back to the window. "The suspicion and mistrust of the united sphaeres is against Sentre." He paused again to look through Bry. "An ally would not be the worst thing for the people of Medius."

"Medius has already tried allying with Oracaede, hence all of our problems," Bry growled.

He knew Oracaede wouldn't take no for an answer; he could only presume the albino had orders to kill him if he declined the "help" they offer. He just wished the man would get on with an attack already.

Instead, the albino continued pacing. "Your father, King Vlasis, was not a great leader and it reflected poorly on the stance and attitude of Oracaede. They hoped your rule would make a better show of Oracaede's true nature."

"Oracaede's *true* nature was shown honestly in Vlasis's rule," Bry spat back.

The albino gave a short hum which might have been amusement.

"You will expect Oracaede to be displeased at this response," the albino said as a matter of fact, ceasing to pace with his back to the outer door.

"Naturally," Bry said behind gritted teeth, slipping instinctively into a fighting stance, waiting for the damned assassin to act.

The albino remained stubbornly stationary. Then, in a sudden movement, the albino turned and walked out the door.

Bry blinked, mouth opening and closing. The albino didn't reappear. Bry crossed the short distance to the door and jerked it open with his free hand. The albino was gone.

Looking down both sides of the hallway, Bry didn't see anyone except the guard that should have been stationed outside his door meandering back to his post. The guard caught sight of Bry and stared in surprise for a moment before snapping to attention.

"You're supposed to guard this doorway, are you not?" Bry tried to keep the anxiety out of his voice as he continued checking the hallways for any signs of the assassin.

"Yes, Your Majesty. I took a short break to relieve myself," the guard explained stiffly. "I apologize. It won't happen again, sir."

"Humph," Bry huffed as he stepped carefully back into his study and closed the door after one last scan both outside and inside.

The albino was gone. But now Bry was more uncomfortable than when he'd been facing him.

He paced the same circle the albino had as he tried making sense of the odd meeting. Bry opened the door once more and ordered the guard to check on Istoria, Klaas, and Eleanora. Several finger-biting moments passed before the guard returned to report they were all fine.

That was strange. That the albino had left with no bloodshed was the most surprising thing about the encounter. Oracaede always did things bloody, no matter what.

Bry paced a long-since worn path in the rugs on the floor until the evening lights were already burning hot.

This is a nightmare.

CHAPTER 11

Lawr held his head in his hands as he tried to keep his focus fixed on the article on the computer in front of him. Not that reading about various disappearances, deaths, and massacres was boring, but after three days, he was numb.

That and he still couldn't figure out how the author of the thread knew his name. It was that question that was driving him particularly crazy.

With a sigh, Lawr decided a break could be beneficial as he stood up, grabbed his coffee mug, and trudged to the kitchen. The data still puzzled him. Most of it was regarding things and places he had never heard of. Places neither Google nor any deep web search had heard of. Lawr would have thought this was just some hacker's joke, except for the events in places he knew—the deaths of people he'd heard of. The files gave more information about the planning of those events than had ever been public. Those files scared him.

Lawr reached the kitchen and glared at the empty coffee pot, then at his mug. He could have sworn he made a full pot sometime recently. He sighed again as he made another. A note on the fridge from Ali caught his attention. She was out celebrating and would be back late. Lawr tried remembering if he'd even noticed her leave.

Nope.

Lawr's stiffened, spilling coffee grounds onto the tile. The pins-and-needles feeling of being watched was back. He turned slowly and caught sight of a huge black shadow standing in the divide between kitchen and living room. Lawr froze mid-breath.

The shadow held out its arms in a nonthreatening manner. "I'm not a Shade. I promise," it said in an airy male voice, as though that would mean something to Lawr.

Hearing a human voice come from the shadow was enough to pull Lawr out of his stupor.

"That's nice," Lawr snapped back.

He was still deciding whether to run or wait and see what this shadow was. His curiosity won out. The longer he waited, the less threatening the giant shadow seemed.

For one, whatever it was, it wouldn't stop fidgeting. Its electric, glowing blue eyes darted around as it continued trying to appear unthreatening, arms still raised with palms facing out. The longer Lawr watched it, the more the shadow looked like a person with layers of black sheets hung over them. Lawr would have thought it was some kind of elaborate prank except the shadow was hovering several inches from the floor and the shadowy cloth was fluctuating in size, disappearing and reappearing as it floated.

"You're... not afraid of me?" The shadow asked again in the same light—but now surprised—voice.

"Should I be?"

"No! No, you need not fear me," the shadow said quickly, floating forward a few steps and waving his hands in a weak motion as though to dispel the idea. "I'm not a Shade, not a full one at least."

"Uh-huh." Lawr sidled toward the edge of the kitchen and a view of the front door. Still locked. "And how did you get into my apartment?"

"Through the door."

Lawr frowned. "It's still locked, Shadows."

"My name's Shad, actually. And I did come through it. Or rather, the shadow under it." The shadow held out its hand to cast a shadow on the wall. The hand dispersed into the shadow for a moment before reforming with a wave. "See?"

"Huh." Lawr stared. He resisted the urge to poke the shadow, as if that would prove whether it was solid or not.

"So, what do you want?" Lawr remembered to ask.

"Information." The shadow shifted with a sudden look of extreme discomfort. "You found some information about Oracaede and I'd like to see what the rest of the data you have looks like." The shadow spoke fast now, fast enough to almost trip over his words. "If that would be alright."

"You want that info?" Lawr chewed on his thoughts, resolving to speak slowly to give himself more time to think. "I assume that means you know a bit about the places and people it references."

"Which places?" The shadow almost jumped at the topic.

Lawr considered if he shouldn't have said anything.

Well, there's nothing to do about that now.

"The files mention somewhere called Sentre in Medius a few times."

"*Sentre?*" The shadow jerked at the name. "Does it say anything about Bry? I-I mean, Brynte Godric, the King of Medius?"

Lawr blinked. A few files referred to someone by that name, but he couldn't remember what exactly they said. Now he knew the shadow knew something about the information in the files, other than just the few bits he had shared in the chatroom online. "It may have mentioned something about that person," Lawr said, moving deliberately back to the coffee machine and setting his mug down.

He glanced through the doorway, past the shadow, and could just see part of his computer screen. It had timed out and locked. Lawr almost sighed in relief. At least he'd have leverage to reach the information if he needed it.

"I think I need you to explain a few things," Lawr said slowly.

The shadow let out a huff, though not an uncooperative one. "Yes, I suppose." He turned halfway around to the living room. "I was in a bit of a hurry, but nothing for it, I guess. Could we sit?"

Lawr nodded and followed the large flowing thing to the couch in the other room.

The shadow sat, shifted, and shifted again. "So, do you know much about the other sphaeres? I know some people in Terrae know about the sphaere system, but most don't. Do you?"

Lawr stared at him with eyebrows raised before shaking his head.

"Oh, okay. Well, uh…" The shadow trailed off, glancing around the room. He spotted what he was looking for and lurched over to grab a notepad and pen. His sudden movement and the odd way he jumped made Lawr flinch. The shadow was too fast for how big he was. It reminded Lawr that most of the cloth-draped shadow was probably empty space.

Shad started drawing before glancing up with an expression Lawr would call chagrin, as if asking permission to use the paper. Lawr gave a slow nod.

This shadow is gonna be amusing.

"So, this is the Caelepta," the shadow said as he handed the notepad to Lawr. The drawing was a simple diagram of seven circles arranged with five surrounding one, and the seventh—being more than twice the size of the others—on the outside of the circle.

"Okay, and what is the Caelepta?" Lawr asked, glancing back at the shadow.

The shadow stared at him as though he had asked what two plus two was. Shad blinked. "Uh, the universe. The Caelepta is the universe."

"Uh-hum," Lawr nodded and pretended that was normal, and that the universe had a fancy name now.

"If you know nothing about the other sphaeres," Shad started, rubbing his hooded head. "How did you get the information about Oracaede?"

"The power of the internet," Lawr deflected, then pointed back at the doodle of a map. "So, these circles are…"

"Oh, those are the sphaeres—the worlds," Shad said. He pointed to the big one on the outside of the other circles. "This one is Terrae, or Earth. Where we are now."

Lawr hummed but added nothing as he waited for Shad to continue.

"These other ones," Shad pointed to the five circles that sat around the sixth one. "These are Lucianca, Sylva, Lux Aequor, Glacius Tesca, and Eidola. This center one is Medius."

"Of course they are," Lawr said absently. He'd already forgotten the names of the five sphaeres other than Medius and Terrae. The files had mentioned the others, but not nearly as much as Medius. "And you're from Medius, right? Is this—" He waved at the oversized shadow's appearance, "Is that what all Medius people look like?"

"No, no. I'm half-wraith. Medians are humans like you. Medius is the most similar sphaere to your world."

Lawr remained quiet. There was something Shad had said when he'd first seen him he was curious about. If only he could remember what his question was.

"... so that's where I'm originally from, Eidola. But I've been traveling with Bry—before he was king, that is—for years," Shad was saying. Lawr had missed the first bit of what he said, but now he remembered what he wanted to ask.

"And what are Shades? I assume they look like you?"

Shad's eyes widened and his body stiffened. Lawr guessed the question was a surprise—and that it made him uncomfortable.

"That's... How did you know that?" The shadow blinked.

Lawr just shrugged. He didn't care to take the time to explain when he still had other questions to ask.

"I—I mean, you're right, this is what a Shade would appear as," Shad answered the question while he wrung his hands and fidgeted. "I'm half-Shade, so I appear as a Shade in some sphaeres."

"And I'm assuming a Shade is... bad." Lawr waited for Shad to continue or correct him.

"Yeah, Shades are monsters," Shad said with guilt in his soft voice. "They wreak havoc and have mental powers."

"Mental powers." Lawr didn't like the possibility that this giant shadow in his living room had ways of messing with his thoughts.

"Yeah, just mental stuff. They make a mess," Shad mumbled, shrinking in on himself.

Lawr stared at the shadow. He seemed so disturbed by the powers he had, Lawr didn't think he'd be likely to use them. That thought was a bit of a relief to consider.

"So," Lawr started, tapping the sketch. "You said Medius is most like Earth, or Terrae. What are these other sphaeres?"

Shad visibly brightened at the topic change. He jumped at the chance to talk about anything else. Lawr's interest in the other worlds grew as he listened. Especially his interest in Lucianca. He couldn't imagine a world that, as Shad described it, was all light and information with no physical form. The shadow's information was going to change his life.

CHAPTER 12

More than an hour passed discussing the different worlds and their physical traits—long enough to exhaust Shad's limited knowledge of physics and to convince Lawr that he needed to travel more.

In a show of equivalent exchange, Lawr pulled up the files on his laptop to show and explain what information he'd found. He showed the documents that referenced a Brynte and Medius. Though what they talked about was more focused on someone named Vlasis and his death by heart failure.

Shad stared at the passage with as close to wide-eyed shock as two orbs in a shadow could look.

"Something wrong?" Lawr asked, ignoring the sudden headache he was getting as he shifted the text to show the continued account of a queen taking command of Medius for a short time followed by the coronation of the Brynte person.

The shadow continued reading until the end of the section before leaning back and rubbing his head with a shaking hand. He gave a half laugh that sounded closer to a cry. "I was hoping I could come here and find old news about them, something that stopped when we destroyed their infrastructure. But this…"

Lawr followed the shadow's attention to the computer screen. "Isn't something they should've been around for?"

At least his headache was subsiding. He rubbed his own head as he waited for Shad's response.

Shad stared at the screen a moment longer before shaking his head. "Bry's coronation was a few weeks ago. Last we heard about them was over a year ago. We thought we'd destroyed the organization—or at least forced them to disband. Everyone thinks they're gone." He turned his attention to Lawr for the first time since starting to read. "How'd you find this?"

Lawr watched the bright blue orbs for any sign of unstable panic, but the shadow had calmed, returning to a state of determined problem-solving. Lawr almost grinned despite the situation; that was a personality trait he loved seeing in anyone. Instead, he grumbled an explanation of how the information came to him.

"Someone addressed this stuff to you?" Shad questioned, leaning back against the couch as he thought.

Lawr grunted an affirmative. He tapped his fingers together as he thought. "How did you and that Bry fellow find out I had discovered something?"

"A Lucian, Aarkdal. He's someone Bry and I worked with when he was fighting against Oracaede a few years ago."

"How'd he find it?"

Shad shrugged. "Magic? I don't know."

Lawr held Shad's gaze as a question.

"No, there isn't 'magic' in the other sphaeres." Shad rolled his eyes. "There's Vis, but that's not magic, and you can't use it to find computer files."

Lawr grunted again. "I'll have to have someone explain this 'Vis' stuff."

"Not me. I don't know enough of the science about it. Few people do, that's why it's Vis."

Lawr grumbled at the odd explanation, "Yes, clearly not you." Lawr rubbed his messy hair as he thought again about how the Lucian could have gotten access to the info. "Would the Lucians have internet?"

"Sort of. They have access to all kinds of information. And I know Aarkdal connected to Bry's AaD before when we were in Terrae last. Why?"

"Because I posted clips of the files in that chatroom. If he was one of the members, he'd have seen those pieces." Lawr watched the shadow as he thought about it.

"It's possible," Shad finally agreed. "I don't know Aarkdal well enough to say he would have been in a chatroom like that, but he would have the technology needed to be there."

"That's one problem solved." Lawr stood up and stretched, remembering the pot of coffee he'd started before the shadow's arrival. He offered some to Shad as he moved off and poured them both a cup.

When they both settled back in the living room, the looming issue of who had sent Lawr the data settled over them both. They couldn't decide if the person might be an ally or not. Their discussion on the matter fizzled to silence without being resolved.

"Look, Lawr, I think it might be a good idea for you to come back to Medius with me," Shad started on a different topic, setting his coffee cup down. "All information of the worlds flows through Lucianca, so we'll probably be needing to go there. If they secured the data the way it was here, I know I wouldn't be able to open it—but you could."

Lawr blinked a second at the proposition. It was ridiculous. He had to be at work tomorrow. His stomach twisted at the thought as his gaze drifted to the stack of books on his desk—tomes really.

Tombs, more like. He'd need one if he had to open those books too many more times.

Shad said something, probably meant to be a convincing argument, but Lawr wasn't listening. He couldn't leave. Ali would have... No, Ali was finished with school now. She would be working, and her name was on the lease for the apartment. She could keep it with no issues.

Lawr felt a twinge of guilt at trapping his niece with the apartment, but he also couldn't see her wanting to go to Nigeria or Ghana or wherever his brother had flown off to.

Besides, there really couldn't be a better way of getting to the world of light, now could there?

The shadow was still talking. "... asking you to pack up and go to another world is a bit sudden, but we could really use your help." Shad seemed to be taking Lawr's silence negatively.

"Yes, a bit sudden." Lawr stood and glanced around for what he'd need. "Give me twenty minutes to get some stuff together."

Shad watched blankly for a moment as Lawr moved to gather his things.

"Well, that was easy."

Lawr wrote a quick note to Ali, trying to leave out as much of the insanity of this decision as possible. He tried ignoring his internal cries of warning at what he was doing. He'd rather hide behind the insanity than the idea that he was running away. He shook his head at the thought.

You can't run away from self-loathing, he reminded himself. *But a change of scenery will be nice.*

He left the note on the fridge and walked out the door with the shadow in fifteen minutes flat.

Shad pulled out a tablet and started messing around with some settings on it.

"What's that?" Lawr asked, trying to read what was on the screen without being obvious about it.

"It's an Aequorian device for figuring out when pathways to the Empty will be thin enough that we can open a doorway. It's also a phone. It's called an AaD," Shad explained, following Lawr into the elevator.

"Odd?"

"AaD. A-A-D. It's short for an Aava Device."

"Okay, you can call your odd little device whatever you want. What's the Empty?" Lawr asked, still watching what Shad was doing on the device.

"Oh, I didn't explain that already?" Shad looked up at the question.

"That and a million other things, no." Lawr stepped back as the doors opened on the ground floor.

One of Lawr's neighbors moved to step in. She stopped as she caught sight of Shad and screamed. Lawr immediately tried to hush her, but she abruptly stopped and wished them a good day as she moved into the elevator as they stepped out.

Lawr looked back at Shad. "How'd that just happen?" He narrowed his eyes at the shadow's glowing blue orbs.

"Um, mind powers. Remember? Shades." Shad fidgeted during this short explanation.

"Oh, yeah." Lawr remembered. He remembered he thought it wouldn't be a problem if Shad wouldn't use them.

Maybe this trip won't be such a good change of scenery after all.

"I haven't used it on you. I never use that power, except in emergencies." Shad gestured toward the elevator. "Please don't be afraid of me."

Lawr stared hard as the large, veiled shadow looked more like a kicked puppy than he should have been able to. Lawr sighed. He wasn't sure how seriously he should take this guy. One thing was for sure, no matter what kind of terrifying power he had, he wasn't the scary sort.

"Sorry pal. You've already lost all your scare points for the day. Try again tomorrow," Lawr said with a smirk as he headed out of the building.

Even though he couldn't see it, he sensed Shad's jaw drop as the shadow followed him. Once the surprise wore off, Shad remained a beaming ray of happy-go-lucky sunshine the whole walk to the doorway—at least, as much as a six-foot-tall shadow without a defined face could. Lawr almost considered saying something mean just to tone the shadow down.

CHAPTER 13

Istoria sighed as she walked up one hallway and down another. She really should have thought to take a map with her that morning when she decided to explore the castle. The idea to explore the halls beyond the passages from her rooms to the main hall had seemed a good one just after breakfast. She had even convinced Leha she wouldn't need company to guide her back. The condition was that Leha could come only if she would divulge everything she knew about a sudden request Bry had made to talk with the servant girl the day prior. Now here Stori walked alone, regretting the inclusion of that condition and both her and her friend's stubbornness.

Lunchtime had come and gone and Stori still had no idea what part of the castle she was even in. The area must have been short on guard staff, as she hadn't run into any for quite a stretch of time now. From the windows she passed, she knew she was on a lower floor than her own, but all the stairs she came across only seemed to lead further down.

This trend continued as she came to yet another staircase leading downward. Stori let out a very unladylike groan and stomped her foot. She marched down the stairwell after only a quick glance back at the maze of hallways behind her.

The bottom of the stairs was extraordinarily similar to dozens of others she'd already reached. The hallway split in two directions with a few doors spaced at large distances. One of these two hallways ended in a door, which was different from the others.

Stori's first thought was that it might be best to go the other way, but a faint smell of food changed her mind as she started toward the dead end. The door was cracked open, she noticed upon approaching.

She paused outside to consider if she should intrude on someone's meal. She wouldn't want to impose herself too much, especially since she still didn't know much about what cultural differences the Medians might have from her own. Moments of hesitation dragged on as Stori began to convince herself more and more that wandering a bit longer might be better than rudely barging in on someone.

"Are you gonna come in or not?" A creaky voice asked from behind her.

Stori yelped and jumped, almost hitting her face on the door. She spun around to the speaker, an older man who was chuckling unabashedly to himself.

"Sorry, missy. Didn't mean to startle you," the man said with a warm smile that made his eyes crinkle at the edges.

Stori doubted that, if the way he was still coughing back his chuckling was any indication. She nodded as she gathered her composure to greet him properly. She took the time to notice the man was old enough to be her grandfather and looked it too, except for his eyes, which were as bright and mischievous as a child's.

"What was that? Who's there?" A shrill feminine voice called from the room beyond the door. "Klaas, are you scaring cats again?"

The man, Klaas, chuckled again before returning with a shout, "Nope! Just Bry's new wife."

"What?!" The shout was even more shrill as the owner appeared at the door in an instant. The door flew open and a stocky woman of the man's same age appeared. Her eyes lit up as she caught sight of Stori.

"Ah, darling! Welcome!" The woman pulled Stori into a tight hug, ignoring the startled noises she made.

"Ma'am, if you please—" Stori tried to start after she'd been freed.

"Oh, 'ma'am'. Did you hear that?" the woman interrupted and asked over Stori's shoulder to Klaas.

Stori heard him chuckle again as she was pulled inside the room.

"Now, now, my darling," the woman was already speaking again in a fast voice. "You have such manners—and very pretty—but you'll have to call me Eleanora, I insist. You're Bry's wife now—practically my daughter-in-law. Anything else would just be rude."

The woman had walked Stori into the kitchen and sat her down at a thick, wooden dining table with many burn spots on it. Stori remained dumbfounded at the casual manner both these people treated her and referred to Bry in. Their names, however, were familiar.

Maybe Bry mentioned them, she thought. *They must know him very well.*

A plate of cookies and a cup of tea appeared in front of Stori, forcing her attention back up to the smiling woman.

"You know King Brynte well, then?" Stori asked, taking a timid sip of tea. She paused to savor the shockingly lovely taste.

"Oh, good heavens of Vis. He didn't tell you to call him that, did he?" The woman rested a horrified hand over her heart.

"Um, no." Stori blinked.

"Good." The woman straightened up again. "I'd have had to have a few words with him otherwise. Young people can be foolish sometimes, you know."

Stori remained again, speechless. Though somehow she didn't doubt this woman would scold a king.

Klaas hummed in agreement with Eleanora's sentiment as he entered the room, unburdened of the coat and hat he'd been wearing earlier. The man sat at the table a chair space away from Stori and watched her for a moment.

"Younger than I thought you'd be," he mused absently. "Maybe you just looked older in the wedding dress." He turned to Eleanora, who was nodding agreement.

Stori wasn't sure if she should blush or be angered by the comment. Anger seemed a most inappropriate response though, so she just ducked her head.

"My wife, Eleanora Lodem," Klaas was speaking again, as a way of introduction. "Is the Court Healer. And my name is Klaas. I've been Bry's tutor and guardian for nearly his whole life." Klaas paused to pat down his beard and chase a few crumbs out of it before reaching for a cookie. "When Bry was exiled, we left with him to look out for him and continue his education."

"Oh, now dear. No need for such formalities." Eleanora patted her husband's hand as she set down a cup of tea.

Klaas held Stori's gaze. Stori did appreciate the explanation; it helped explain their closeness to the new king. Klaas nodded, as though he could tell his "formalities" were indeed appreciated.

Stori broke from his gaze and focused on her tea and cookie before she thought of something embarrassing, just in case he could read her mind. It wasn't hard—the tea and cookies were some of the best she'd ever had. She wondered briefly why Eleanora was the Court Healer instead of the Head Cook.

The more she thought about the couple, the odder they seemed. To have raised the king, and yet they seemed content to live on a lower level of the castle with only simple conveniences.

She glanced back at Klaas as she tried to think of a polite way to ask. Klaas held her gaze but didn't offer any answer.

"Would you mind if I ask," Stori started, because it was the politest way she could think of. "You live on this level of the castle, but surely a higher floor would have a better view." She cringed internally at the rudeness in her latter words.

"This apartment has a good root-cellar to store herbs," Eleanora said in a matter-of-fact voice without even turning around, as though the matter was that simple.

"Eleanora and I prefer to live simply," Klaas added with a nod. "Bry too, I believe. He'd live closer to the ground too, if he wasn't required to stay up with all those fancy-dressed people."

Stori nodded, suddenly aware of her own expensive wardrobe. She didn't doubt that Klaas was right. Other than at the wedding, Stori had never seen Bry dressed in anything that could not have passed as a simple soldier's clothing.

"Besides, Bry is down here enough that he might as well live here." Eleanora chuckled.

Stori snapped her attention to the older woman. "Bry comes down…" She trailed off, realizing her mistake.

In Sylva, the royalty and nobles never went to levels of the Giant Trees lower than their own station.

Medius is a different world, she reminded herself. *Different rules.* She breathed easier about being down on this lower level of the castle, now that she knew it was alright for even Bry to come down here.

Klaas chuckled at something, and this time Stori did blush. She didn't know if he'd somehow realized her mistake in judgment or not, but she would count it as a most embarrassing one.

"My, my, you've turned all red. Are you alright, darling?" Eleanora had finally turned and sat at the table, setting down a large pot of stew and a stack of small bowls.

Stori flushed more and tried to hide behind her teacup. "I'm fine," she mumbled.

Eleanora narrowed her eyes at her husband, who shrugged with innocent indifference. The older woman scoffed before turning back to Stori.

"Have some lunch, darling. You looked quite pale when you came in."

Stori thanked the woman as she served herself as fast as she could without seeming too impolite. The stew smelled delicious, like strong herbs and broth.

Klaas stood up momentarily to collect a loaf of bread and a knife. He returned to sitting and cut a slice for everyone.

Stori was again forced to pause her thoughts to admire the hearty taste of the food. It wasn't the most elegant meal she'd eaten by any means, but it had a wholesome and full flavor she'd hardly tasted before and found she very much enjoyed.

The rest of the afternoon lazed on as Stori listened to stories of the group's time in exile. From the stories they told, Stori was surprised Bry and Shad had lived as long as they had. They seemed to have been troublemakers—even more than now.

CHAPTER 14

The sun was sinking low on the horizon when Stori departed from the older couple and, with the assistance of a map Eleanora had drawn, made her way back to more familiar passages.

She found herself looking forward to her next run in with Bry. Eleanora had shared many stories she could use to tease Bry with—and Shad too, when he returned from wherever he'd gone off to.

Stori was practically skipping with new optimism when a familiar voice called to her from an open terrace. Halting, Stori peered out to the open area and recognized the figure of Loreda standing next to the railing.

"Stori, dear. Are you well?" Loreda asked with a cool smile, holding her hand out to Stori.

"Loreda, it is good to see you again." Stori returned the smile and clasped the woman's hand warmly as she moved to the railing to take in the view. She tried remembering everything she could about her original meeting with Loreda almost a week earlier at the wedding. "I am doing quite well."

"Oh." Loreda seemed almost taken aback by Stori's demeanor. "I would have expected that becoming accustomed to living here would be more strenuous."

Stori shook her head, "Not at all. In fact, it seems our fears about Bry may have been a bit premature."

Loreda scoffed in a manner quite contrary to her elegance. Stori couldn't help but stare.

"He is just playing tricks dear. You should not be so easily swayed," she snapped, eyes flashing with something venomous.

Stori blinked at the unexpected outburst. She swallowed and moved her hand the slightest bit away from Loreda. "Your son appears to act quite differently than what I've heard of his father. I think—"

"You didn't know Vlasis." Loreda cut her off as she stepped back from the railing. "Do not lecture me on matters you know nothing of."

Stori's jaw dropped as Loreda marched off with a last scornful sniff. Stori took a moment to reel back her indignation and confusion over the odd conversation before returning inside herself.

Stori walked back down the familiar hall to her rooms in a markedly more dejected mood than before. As she entered her front room, she expected Leha to be worrying about her all-day excursion. However, though the girl did bounce to greet her and gave her mistress a hug, she was much more excited than worried.

"Stori, you have to see! His Majesty sent a post-wedding gift," Leha said, almost bursting with poorly contained enthusiasm. Leha almost dragged Stori into the bedroom where a knee-high wooden crate sat with a white ribbon and envelop tied on top.

Leha knelt on one side of it and beamed up at Stori, waiting for her to sit on the floor too.

"Leha, what...?" Stori puzzled over her friend's excitement as she knelt. A soft scratching met her ears as she came closer.

Undoing the intricate knots securing the lid, Stori finally removed the top. A ball of fur jumped into her lap and began licking her face.

"Oh!" Stori nearly jumped back at the animal's sudden appearance. Leha clapped and laughed, utterly delighted.

The small creature bounced off Stori's lap and ran to greet Leha before returning to Stori again. The animal was about the size of a fox, with marbled black, white, and gray fur and a bushy tail. Leathery wings were folded against its back and as it rolled happily on the floor it exposed a shockingly scaly underbelly. Stori observed how the scales continued down its legs, and the way its feet were more reptilian than canine.

Stori laughed as she pulled the little beast onto her lap again. It licked her face frequently in between trying to spin in circles on her lap.

"What is it?" Leha asked, reaching to pat the animal.

Stori shook her head as she released it, letting the animal run around the room, barking and yipping as it scurried about, smelling every corner.

Leha pulled the envelope from its secured position and read the address before handing it over to Stori. "From His Majesty."

Stori tore it open while trying to keep an eye on the creature as it explored underneath her bed. The letter was written informally and gave a short description of the creature—a Pyxis, it called the creature. They were native to Glacius Tesca and eventually grew to the size of the dire wolves that inhabited Sylva. This one was just a pup.

Stori and Leha giggled as they watched the small Pyxis hop around, flapping clumsy wings in an attempt to fly. They debated names for a time, until Stori decided on Fenrir; a name from one of her favorite stories her father used to tell about the other worlds and their histories.

Stori marveled for a moment that Bry had already realized her love of animals. Then another thought hit her. She swatted Leha's arm.

"That's what Bry wanted to talk with you about yesterday, isn't it?"

Leha beamed unabashedly. "I couldn't tell you. I didn't know when he'd get you something, and he wanted it to be a surprise!"

Stori laughed as Fenrir ran and jumped back into her arms. "It is a lovely surprise. I'll have to thank him for this little darling." She held on tightly to the exuberant animal as she stood up. "I'll do that now."

Leha nodded and pet the animal again as Stori walked past. Stori carried the animal up the narrow passage of stairs connecting Bry's bed chambers and her own. This was the first time she had used the passage. Only halfway through the passage did she consider that it might not be a good idea to interrupt whatever Bry was doing. He was busy after all. Her steps slowed as she reached the door at the top.

Maybe I should wait...

Fenrir licked her face and barked, effectively announcing their presence.

Too late to turn around now, Stori thought with a sigh.

She kissed the small creature on the head before knocking on the door, hesitating, and letting herself in. The king's bedchamber was a dark, empty mess. The only thing neat was the bed, clearly unslept in. The rest of the room's contents were in piles on the floor or overflowing from the top of the dresser. There was a single chair in the room, almost invisible beneath piles of clothes whose level of cleanliness was anyone's guess.

Stori wrinkled her nose, sighed, and carefully picked her way toward the attached study. She couldn't help noticing how similar this room was to Eleanora's and Klaas's apartment.

Through the open door to the study, Stori could see that the mess continued, though only in the study, and was mainly confined to the top of the desk and just a bit of overflow on the floor below.

This room was empty too. Stori paused, uncertain.

I'll have to thank him later.

Stori was surprised by the disappointment resting heavily in her chest now.

Fenrir squirmed and nearly jumped to the floor before Stori bent low to let the animal down before it could escape her grip. Fenrir took the opportunity to jump again and this time succeeded.

"Fenrir!" Stori yelped, failing to grab the little creature as it ran to the desk, creating a flurry of papers. Fenrir barked and yipped from the other side of the desk as Stori picked her way through the mess on the floor.

"Oh, hello, pup. Did she not like you?" Bry's familiar, but sleepy voice startled Stori as she moved close enough to see Bry shift from his position, previously sleeping with his head on the desk, entirely hidden behind the pile of paper. He picked the small animal up as he rubbed his eyes and yawned. Fenrir licked his face and open mouth, to which Bry coughed and shook his head, wiping his mouth against the back of his hand.

Stori tried to hide her laugh behind her hands, but Bry had already snapped his gaze to meet hers.

"Sorry," he apologized at nothing. "I thought you might like this little Pyxis. If you don't..." He trailed off, hugging the little creature closer to his body.

"Oh, no—I love him!" Stori jumped forward, almost close enough to snatch the animal back.

Bry looked surprised at her sudden movement, but the expression quickly faded into a relieved smile. "That's good." He handed Fenrir back and rested his head on his hands, propped up by the desk. He smiled sleepily at them both.

"I didn't mean to disturb you," Stori returned the smile. "I just wanted to thank you for Fenrir."

Bry waved off her concern. "Don't worry about it; I must have dozed off, but I still have a lot of work to do. I'm glad you like him. Fenrir, eh?"

"You should get some sleep." Stori's suggestion was met with a frown, but Bry nodded.

"Suppose I should," he replied without moving to do so.

Stori smiled and nodded as she moved back toward his bedroom and the passage back to hers. "Have a good night," she said as turned and walked to the stairs.

"Night," she heard him call behind her.

She descended the passage with a more relaxed attitude than when she had ascended. Stori hugged the little creature tight to her chest as it started licking her neck and face again.

CHAPTER 15

Alisha stumbled into the elevator of her apartment building and leaned against the wall as the lights on the elevator button crawled slowly upward to her floor. She teetered down the hallway, trying to hum the beat of the last song the club had been playing.

After a failed try at a door that wasn't hers, Ali made it into her shared apartment. She threw her purse at the entrance table and didn't notice if it landed on the table or flopped to the floor as she fumbled to get the lights on. She was surprised in a dull way that Lawr wasn't still awake. He always kept odd hours and was generally awake when she returned from parties.

"Lawr!" Ali shouted to wake him. "Uncle!" She tried again, wandering into his bedroom. She pawed the lights on only for an empty room to greet her. "Where are you?" She mumbled to herself as she stumbled back to the living room.

He's fine, she told herself. *He'll be back.*

She slumped down on the couch. Now it was her turn to wait for Lawr to get home. Her drunken mind laughed at the thought. She was asleep within seconds.

Ali slept undisturbed until rays of late morning sun light found their way through the open blinds and onto her couch. Waking up was a groggy, miserable experience that she would have preferred to forego.

Downing a few aspirins, Ali padded around the apartment again, careful to hold her aching head. Lawr still wasn't there. A note on the fridge caught her attention as her heart leaped to hide in her throat.

It's not that kind of note, she told herself as she unfolded it and squinted to read what it said.

Hey Ali,

A talking shadow has invited me to go and help destroy an evil empire. Can't say no to that, can I? Take care of the apartment until I get back. Don't know how long it'll be. Stay out of trouble. I mean it. - Lawr

Ali sighed as relief flooded her system. The relief was short lived though and followed immediately by annoyance.

She growled and crumpled the note, dropping it in the trash. "Lawr, why can't you write something useful?" she muttered to herself, making her way back to the couch. She wasn't sure what her uncle was trying to say, other than that he decided to take a spontaneous trip.

That wasn't particularly like him, but he did surprising things every once in a while. She'd have to think about it when she was more sober. She laid back down and fell straight to sleep again.

The sun had disappeared from the window side of the apartment when Ali woke up again to clamoring sounds near her. She grumbled for Lawr to be quiet and tried to ignore the noise, to fall asleep again.

Ali became aware of a man's voice saying something to her as a large hand grabbed her arm and pulled her up.

"Lawr!" she growled, trying to jerk away.

She turned to face a young man with dark hair and bright, dark eyes. He was talking in a language Ali didn't understand to someone behind her.

"Let go of me!" Ali screamed, jerking away from the man before someone grabbed her other arm. Ali whipped her head toward the new person. Another man she didn't recognize with sandy hair and eyes and a goofy grin spread across his face.

"Allo there, missy," the second man chirped. "My name's Aike. Bother it is, but we need ya to come on a lil trip wi'd us."

Ali screamed and thrashed as the man behind her shoved a gag into her mouth and pulled a bag over her head. She continued to thrash as the smiling one's voice continued talking.

"I don't tink she appreciates my asking."

76

"Course not, *hermano*," the other one said in a different accent, voice soft. Then he continued in another language.

Suddenly, one of the men clamped a rag over Ali's mouth and nose, and whatever was on the rag was so strong it immediately permeated the bag. She thrashed harder as the sweet smell from the rag turned rotten. Her head bobbed lower and fighting became harder as her consciousness faded. Her awareness of one of the men picking her up and carrying her dulled until she was lost in blackness.

When Ali woke again, the experience was even worse than before. Her head was still throbbing, and this time a wave of nausea washed over her. Her vision was dark, and it didn't improve as she continued to awaken. As consciousness settled on her, she realized she still had the bag over her head.

The horror of the most recent events in her memory flooded her mind and she almost puked. The adrenaline that began flooding her system, however, settled her stomach as she tried moving, attempting to free herself of whatever was blocking her vision.

Ali felt a strong cord pulling her hands together, tied to something wooden behind her. The gag pulled against her cheeks as she tried rolling into a different position.

The initial shock of waking up to her situation settled enough for Ali to notice the loud noises around her—the shouts of rushed people, objects, and animals colliding, and the grind of whatever she was on as it rolled over gravel. The sounds were deafening and added to her splitting headache.

Not just the sounds, but the smells too. The smell of feces, sweat, and bile mixed with dirt was strong enough for Ali to notice even with the bag over her head. She slowed her breath in hope she wouldn't lose her battle with nausea.

Ali curled in around herself and cried softly as she prayed this nightmare would end.

The cart she was in jerked to a stop and a pair of large hands grabbed at the cords binding her to the cart. Ali waited, tense, until her hands were freed, then tried to jump away. She only made it a step before a rough hand grabbed her wrist and jerked her back. Ali fell. She met the gravel on the ground with a thud that left her head lolling as she tried to stay conscious.

Someone yanked her up by her arms and tied her hands together, in front of her this time. She was too tired to care or struggle. Her headache was reaching migraine levels after the fall. The same hands kept her standing as she began slumping again. The man spoke a few commands in another language and pulled her along behind him, dragging her if she didn't run to keep up.

The short distance they traveled ended as the man dragged her up a short flight of stairs after she tripped on the first step. Ali could hear the yelling more clearly as she jogged after the man. The shouts seemed directed at her.

A sudden stop made Ali run into the man's back. She would have fallen over if he hadn't still been holding her. Laughter replaced several shouts for a short moment.

The man held her up as he pulled the bag off her head. Blinding sunlight flooded her view. She tried pulling away and hiding her eyes as the gag was pulled out of her mouth. Squinting, Ali could just begin to make out her surroundings. She was standing on a crude wooden platform in front of a crowd. The people in front of her were a mix of every possible culture, but a distinct layer of dirt coated everyone equally.

The man holding her up was a deep shade of tan and more than three times her size. He started yelling to the crowd in the same rough language while gesturing toward her. After a short round of shouting, the crowd started taking turns yelling short phrases.

It sounds like an auction house. The thought casually made its way through Ali's head.

It is *an auction*, she realized.

She was being sold. Ali thrashed against the man again, kicking his legs now that she could see one of them was wooden. A sudden pain in her head stopped Ali's struggles. She slumped forward, only held up by the large man. She tried to fight off the dizziness as she watched red splotches appear on the platform beneath her.

Blood.

It took her a moment to put the notion together. It was blood dripping from her head. The man had hit her with something.

What a jerk, the thought floated lazily about her mind.

With no energy to start thrashing again, Ali stared out at the crowd and watched who was shouting the most. A middle-aged man with a crooked nose was particularly loud and clearly intent on winning. The twisted grin on his face whenever he looked at her turned Ali's stomach.

Another person, an older woman, was also bidding consistently, much to the annoyance of the crooked-nosed man. The woman sneered up at Ali with an ugly look, showing the black rot of her teeth every time she opened her mouth.

The bidding was over before Ali's mind could catch up. By the angry looks on the faces of the two leading bidders, neither of them had won. The man holding her started moving again, half-carrying, half-dragging her this time as she let her feet drag, not even trying to walk after him. The man moved to the back of the crowd and into a large tent. The tent was hot, compared to the chilly temperature outside. The enclosed space was humid from so many people trapped in the small space.

The big man dragged Ali to a table where coins were being exchanged with papers. A white-haired old man clad in all black stood handing the coins to an ugly fat man who meticulously counted and bit every piece of gold and silver coin.

The process was long—long enough for the big man holding Ali to get bored. He handed the cord tied around her wrists to the white-haired man. Ali blinked at the man. He wasn't actually old, just albino.

He can't be more than a few years older than me, she thought. He met her eyes just briefly as he took the cord before turning back to the merchant in front of him.

The exchange concluded a short time later as the albino took the papers and led Ali out of the tent. He moved at an easy pace that seemed more for her benefit than his. She was just happy not to be dragged around at that point. They moved through the maze-like market place, past the platform where the crowd still milled as Ali saw a young man being dragged up, kicking and thrashing.

Past the crowd, the array of tents and stands looked like a third world marketplace. That was where Ali convinced herself she was until they reached a stable area. The man stopped in front of an oddity of an animal. It stood taller than a horse but looked reptilian and had a long scaly tail.

"Down," the albino gave the creature an order. The beast knelt to its stomach.

"You speak English?" Ali hoped as the man lifted her onto the animal's back.

"Yes," was the only reply as he climbed on behind her and pulled the animal up with the reins.

Ali remained silent and the man didn't speak again. They rode out of the dusty market and into an expansive desert without a word. The desert spread out as far as Ali could see in every direction ahead of her. Ali's relief at being out of the cramped marketplace was short lived as the only sign of civilization and the one connection to her way home disappeared into the desert. Ali curled into herself as much as she could as the weight that she'd never go home sunk into her heart.

CHAPTER 16

Take reptilian creature could run at amazing speeds. Ali was mesmerized by how fast they were moving. They had been riding for what seemed to be hours and had covered an expansive distance. Without any distinctive landmarks to reference though, Ali couldn't tell how far they'd really traveled.

Tall-and-silent behind her wasn't much help either. The albino hadn't said a single word since they'd left the marketplace. The only thing he'd done during the ride was pull out a tablet device and check something quickly before tucking the device away and continuing on. Ali had been spending the journey trying to figure out what exactly this mess was she was in. Her first thought was that she'd been sold as a slave in some market in either the Sahara or the Arabian desert. However, this desert wasn't like any she remembered from college. It should have been the middle of summer and it was cold. Even though the sun was still high, the ground was covered in frost and her breath was fog. She shivered.

Her second thought on her situation was far simpler and possibly worse. The men who kidnapped her had probably drugged her. She might have been in some hallucinatory drug coma while whatever was happening in the outside world just… happened. The thought sent chills down her spine. Ali tried pinching herself every so often to wake herself up, but the nightmare continued.

A change in the animal's speed brought Ali's attention back to reality. The albino slowed the creature to a stop and jumped the distance to the ground. Ali watched the man with cautious curiosity as he glanced around the empty desert landscape before pulling the odd tablet-looking device out of the folds of his jacket. Ali tried to watch what the man was doing.

A large black hole sprang up in front of them. Ali jerked back and tried to pull the creature with her, but it remained motionless.

"Wha—?! What the hell is that?" Ali managed to question as the albino grabbed the reins and started leading the creature to the giant, empty void. Ali shrank back as they stepped into it. She tried asking again but could only stammer sounds as she gaped into the black hole.

"It is the Empty," the albino said after they were completely inside.

"What? Empty what?" Ali managed to ask as she turned in her seat and watched the desert disappear as the blackness closed behind them.

The albino remained silent, but now Ali was fascinated by him—and the creature—and her hands. Despite the complete darkness all around her, Ali could still clearly see everything that had come into this Empty. They almost seemed to be glowing in the darkness.

The minutes spent walking began to draw out as the much slower process, even in such an odd space, was less of a mesmerizing lull than the speed of riding had been. The walking, however, ended soon enough. The albino, who still had the tablet out, paused his walking as another hole opened. This one opened into the desert.

Ali marveled at this phenomenon again as they passed through the opening and back into the cold desert. This desert was different, however. The sun was now lower, and the landscape wasn't completely empty. Mountainous rocky outcrops spread to the horizon. The albino climbed on the creature again and off they went. This ride was shorter and the man pulled the animal to a slower pace as they rounded a rock bluff. A house appeared in the middle of this nowhere and the albino guided the animal toward it.

The building was a small, but comfortably-sized wooden house with a large awning attached to the side. Another of the strange creatures stood in the stable and growled a greeting. The creature Ali was riding growled back.

The albino led the creature to the stable and ordered it down again before helping Ali off. She stood and looked about nervously as the man put the creature away before leading Ali into the house.

Once inside, Ali continued watching the albino's movements carefully as her anxiety ramped up again. The man motioned for her to wait before he moved down a hallway and ducked into a room. Ali heard him mumbling, talking to someone for a short moment before stepping out and moving into another room across the hall.

Ali glanced around at the layout of the house, at the living room and off to the other side away from the hallway, a kitchen and dining room. The living room had a cozy, lived-in look to it. The few pieces of furniture were worn and the whole house smelled of cleaning oils, old books, and desert sand, with a hint of coffee somewhere. Ali was surprised how homey the place was. It didn't seem to fit with the cold, silent albino.

Ali turned from the kitchen area and bumped into the albino now standing right next to her. Ali jumped back and clapped her hands over her mouth to catch her scream.

The albino stood stock still, watching her. He tracked her hands as she lowered them again and stepped forward without making a sound, catching them.

Ali flinched in surprise as he held her still-tied hands and reached into his jacket, pulling out a small curved blade. Ali flinched back, but the albino held her still as he cut the cords binding her hands.

He tucked the blade away then but didn't release her hands. Instead, he pulled her gently toward the couch. After she was seated, he turned to a large toolbox Ali didn't remember seeing when she first scanned the room. She carefully touched the rope-burns on her wrist where some of the skin had started to pull away. She trembled at the look of it and flinched at the pain where she touched it.

Returning her attention to the albino, her fear of him spiked again. He was laying out several items from the toolbox. The box itself seemed to serve as either a med-kit or a torture box, depending on what he planned to do with it. Now the coffee table, covered in a layer of pale cloth, had an assortment of scissors, threaded curved needles, vials, and needles of drugs. Other items were scattered about that Ali didn't even recognize.

The albino held her arm and swabbed a small wet cloth that stank of alcohol over the inside of her elbow.

Ali tried to shrink further into the couch as the albino set the cloth down and picked up one of the needles, squirted out a little of its contents and moved it to the arm he was still clutching.

A whimper escaped from Ali as she tried to pull away.

"Please don't," she begged.

The albino paused to look up at her before sticking the needle in her arm and emptying the contents.

"It will not hurt you," he said in the same cool, low voice as he put the needle down and picked up a piece of gauze, holding it against the small puncture.

Ali tried to keep her vision straight as she slumped against the couch; everything began to blur into blackness. He was saying something else, but she could neither hear nor see him as her consciousness faded.

CHAPTER 17

L awr pestered his unhelpful, shadowy guide about the Empty as much as any human could. Unfortunately, Shad didn't know much about the physics of the void. He still tried answering the questions but didn't have much success making sense.

All too soon, Shad opened another doorway, this time into a completely strange world. Although Lawr knew it was another world, Medius looked like some more rural places on Earth. Lawr ignored the lackluster world and straddled the opening of the Empty. He tried touching the very edge of it—only the absolute edge seemed not to exist. He could reach at the air of Medius or into the Empty, but not both at once.

"Come on." Lawr felt Shad tug at his sleeve. "You can study it another time. Maybe with someone who knows a single thing about it."

"I don't think you know just how marvelous and contrary to Earth's modern physics this is," Lawr said, stepping out of the Empty. A sudden weight surrounded him. The air itself seemed heavier. Lawr blinked and stared at the still same world. He shook his head.

One crazy abnormality at a time. When he had someone useful to ask, he would get to the bottom of all these new things.

Behind him, Shad had laughed and was finishing a thought Lawr hadn't heard the start of. "…you guys aren't even the most advanced sphaere."

"What?" Lawr almost jumped at the thought. A new pool of beings able to answer his infinitely growing list of questions sounded important to know. He spun to Shad. "What sphaeres...?" Lawr's thought sputtered out as he stared at Shad.

Shad's appearance had changed from shadows and draped cloth to almost human. His clothes consisted of the same dark grays, blues, and blacks, but many black ties and bands of cloth wrapped around his limbs and torso to keep the otherwise loose cloth in place. Shad's electric, blue eyes still glowed between the changes in worlds.

Lawr blinked. Shad's skin was an ashen blue gray, but unless Lawr was losing his mind, there were shadows in his skin that moved like ever-changing tattoos, covering him head to toe.

Pointing a questioning finger, "Wraith?" Lawr asked.

Shad, who seemed to still be waiting for the end of Lawr's previous question, glanced down at himself. "Oh, yeah. Yep, this is mostly what a wraith'd look like." He smiled and waved his arms in a *ta-da* motion.

Lawr continued squinting at him. "You know your skin is moving, right?" Lawr knew he'd have to ask sooner or later, but... maybe he should have asked later. He didn't miss the way Shad tensed and his smile fell flat to his feet.

"Yeah. That would be a bit of the Shade in me," Shad mumbled, wrapping his hands around each other and twisting them further out of sight. He ducked his head, keeping his eyes on Lawr as he seemed to be waiting for a response.

A negative response, Lawr guessed, was what he was waiting for—given how much the kid had tucked into himself. Lawr regarded him in silence for a moment. He still wasn't sure what a Shade was, only that Shad seemed prepared for him to hate him because of it. Lawr wondered how often that happened.

"You know, I still have no idea what a Shade even is," Lawr said, taking a few steps closer to Shad to get a better look.

More like wisps of smoke than shadows, he decided.

Shad opened his mouth, then shut it again, remaining silent.

"Only thing I know about Shades is that you're half one. And you're really not that bad."

Shad dropped his gaze to the ground. "That's just because you haven't met a Shade yet. Shades are bad. They're monsters."

"That's nice," the words slipped out of Lawr's mouth before he thought about it. "So, if you ever get all scary Shade-like, cue me in," Lawr finished with a roll of his eyes, stepping past Shad and starting up the short hill they'd come out behind.

Lawr could hear Shad sputter a weak retort, but the attempt died before it was fully formed.

Soon enough, Shad came bouncing up behind him. His look of sad dejection had morphed to honest joy as he started talking fervently about nothing again.

Lawr furrowed his brow and shook his head at the young man. "I knew you'd been grinning like an idiot the whole time you were in your other form."

"Hey, now." Shad looked mockingly hurt, though the look didn't come off well since he was still grinning. "Come on, Sentre is only a couple of miles." He gestured wide as they reached the top of the bluff.

Lawr paused at the top of the hill to stare at the castle city. It was beautiful. The stones of the city were almost translucent, like quartz or fractured crystal. They reflected the midday light and the blue sky and green fields through broken cracks that shifted softly to gray.

"Pretty awesome, isn't it?" Shad said, tipping from his heels to his toes as he too stared at the city.

Lawr hummed an agreement as he started walking again and tried to ignore the twisting of his stomach. The idea he was in another world hadn't seemed real before, but now... Lawr glanced between the castle city and the wraith next to him. Even the air around him was still too heavy to be normal. He shook his head as he tried thinking of something normal in this moment, anything he could cling to.

Normal is a question, Lawr reminded himself vaguely, though he wasn't even sure what he meant by it. He needed a question, though. That was his normal. He tried remembering what they'd been talking about before he'd been sidetracked by Shad's appearance. *Oh, yeah.*

"So which sphaeres are the most advanced?" he asked.

The question was met with a moment of silence as Shad scrunched up his face, staring at Lawr. "Oh, right." Shad snapped his fingers. "The sphaeres. Well, Lucianca, the light sphaere, obviously. Since they aren't 'hindered' by physical bodies." Shad air-quoted as he rolled his eyes. "They can do and understand things far beyond us, so they say. But they can't really travel anywhere outside of Lucianca. Which seems like a big downside to me."

"What happens if they do?" Lawr questioned as he thought about the answer, "They're consciousness would disperse or get absorbed into the other worlds, wouldn't it?"

Shad blinked at him for a second before rubbing his head. "Um, I guess so. Lucians never travel, because of that, so I'm not sure."

Lawr hummed again. "And what about these 'Odd' devices?" Lawr pointed to the tablet Shad could barely fit into one of his pockets. "And shouldn't it be pronounced 'Add', based on how you spell it?"

Shad frowned. "Tomato, tom•to. Some people pronounce it 'add'— the Sylvans do. The Aquarians who made it just call it an Aava. Take your pick."

Lawr shrugged. "So, the Aquarians made them. Who are they?"

Shad grumbled something Lawr didn't catch before answering with a sigh. "They're the most technologically advanced sphaere. And since they mostly live underwater, all their stuff is waterproof, which is nice."

"Right." Lawr tried remembering what Shad had said about the Merii earlier. "Lux Aequor was the ocean world, right? You didn't mention the mermaid people were smart."

Shad stared at him with his mouth agape for a moment before bursting out laughing. "Ah, mermaid people." He wiped his eyes as he straightened back up and tried coughing out the last laugh. "As a word of advice, you don't want to call any of the Merii, even the women, 'mermaids'. They might kill you for the insult."

Lawr raised an eyebrow.

"I'm serious, they would. The Merii are particular about manners and using the proper names for things."

"Huh." Maybe he should avoid Lux Aequor after all. His sense of sarcasm would probably get him killed.

That sucks.

"Of course, after the Merii, there's you." Shad pointed at Lawr's chest. "Terrae is next in the line of pretentious smart-people sphaeres."

"Oh, someone's jealous." He was a bit disappointed there weren't more worlds he could visit and learn from. Including this new world he was in. He sighed at that idea.

"I'm not jealous of your annoying, smarty sphaeres. I can't even stay in most of them." Shad crossed his arms as they kept walking.

"Can't stay in…" Lawr was getting a bit bored of this conversation, but sphaeres Shad couldn't remain within seemed important. He waited for Shad to continue.

"Well, Lucianca, I can only be in for short periods of time at once. I'd get absorbed into that sphaere. The Merii generally hate me—though that could be more the manners thing than anything else. And there are only a few places in Terrae where I can stay in my wraith form, since you guys don't have enough Vis. Besides, most of you Terrains don't take kindly to peculiar things."

Lawr remained silent. That last part was true, but he still didn't know anything about Vis.

"What's Vis have to do with if you can stay or not?"

Shad blinked at him with the same how-do-you-not-know-this-stuff look he often had when explaining things. He paused and rubbed his already messy hair before answering.

"Well, Vis makes the worlds go round, ya know? Without it, everything would die."

"Then if Terrae doesn't have any Vis, why is there so much life?"

Shad had taken up a look that he was trying to explain a simple concept to a child. "I didn't say Terrae didn't have any Vis, I said not enough. Not enough for things that need a lot of Vis to live, like wraiths, the Merii, and dragons. And Shades. They need lots of Vis too." He was frowning again.

Lawr's jaw dropped at the mention of dragons, but he let it go for the time. He had other questions. "I still don't understand why there would be less Vis. I mean, couldn't—"

Shad let out an annoyed groan. "It's because you ask so many questions, that's why there's no Vis. Vis is what can't be explained. And you guys just can't just let anything be." Shad managed to frown and smirk at the same time, daring Lawr to ask another question.

"Fine." Lawr shrugged but kept a careful eye on the wraith. The outburst was unexpected. He couldn't think of anything he'd said that was that insulting. Though Shad had mentioned not being able to travel around much in Terrae.

Maybe that's it. Lawr was doubtful, but he wondered if Shad was resentful. He slid his gaze over to Shad. The wraith had found a beetle crawling on the sleeve of his cloak. He had named it Beets and was holding a conversation with it. Lawr rolled his eyes as Beets flew away.

Probably not a resentful sort of person.

The conversation changed topics to Shad's time in Terrae and continued as the pair grew closer to the castle city.

The sun was setting as they approached the city and the stones reflected it by glowing fire red. Shad pointed out specific parts of the city; a food court he liked, an honest-to-goodness armory, a small shop that always got the newest Aquarian tech first.

Lawr kept one eyebrow raised in awe and amusement the entire time as they walked generally upward toward the castle. While the culture of the city was, in many ways, reminiscent of the Middle Ages, it also seemed more akin to present day Earth. But the bits of technology that were so futuristic compared to Earth made Lawr marvel at the complete clash of time periods in the city.

Lawr started making notes in the travel-sized notepad of what-he'd-need-to-learn-about-before-he'd-be-content-with-leaving. By the time they made it to the top of the castle where Bry's study was, Lawr had filled several pages of the little book.

"Lawr, will you keep up?" Shad asked for the third time as Lawr fell behind again, this time to examine one of the Aquarian torches. "At this rate, we won't reach Bry until tomorrow."

"Impatience, you know, is an unattractive quality," Lawr said straightening up and wiping dust off his hands. "I know because people are always telling me."

"Unattractive or not." Shad motioned tersely for Lawr to continue moving.

"Fine, fine." Lawr padded after the shadows of the wraith. "But I'm coming back to look at that." He motioned to the torch he had his eyes on.

"Whatever," Shad's voice emanated from his dispersing figure that seemed to melt into shadows and reform when he passed by torches.

Lawr had considered asking about that but decided against it. He could guess enough that it was because of his companion's Shade blood.

No need to bring that up again.

"*Shade,*" a harsh voice snapped behind them.

Lawr froze, half-thinking he might have muttered that aloud as he thought about it.

Shad turned toward a guard who stepped out of the shadows down the hall from them. "Yes? It's Cleeves, right?"

The guard, Cleeves, growled, "His Majesty requested that you be informed upon return, he is with the Court Healer."

"Right, thanks," Shad said to the guard as he began down the way they'd just come. Shad hummed to fill the silence as they walked down all the flights of stairs they'd come up.

Lawr watched the back of Shad's head as they walked. The wraith was still tense and Lawr noticed he had mostly stopped dispersing into the shadows. He seemed to be putting extra effort into looking as human as possible.

Lawr hummed to himself over that. He reminded himself not to make any mention of his companion's Shade side anymore unless he couldn't help it.

They reached the bottom of one more staircase and Shad turned toward a dead end with a door. He knocked once and let himself into the warm, brightly lit room, with a loud greeting to the empty living room.

"In here," someone called from another room in the back.

Lawr followed Shad, tentatively picking his way through the piles of mess on the floor. They rounded the corner to a kitchen area where an older couple and a young man with fiery hair sat around a charred wooden table.

Shad was greeted as one of the family by the room's occupants before he turned to introduce Lawr as the hacker who'd found the data they were discussing.

"Lawrence, then, is it?" the young king questioned with a firm smile and handshake. "Or may I call you Lawr, as well?"

"Well, that depends. What do I have to call you?" Lawr asked with too much sarcasm. He bit his tongue. He should really work on not being overly sarcastic when he was nervous. It was becoming a bad habit.

Brynte blinked in surprise for a moment as Shad and the old man—Klaas—snickered in the background.

Bry laughed. "Just 'Bry' is fine. I haven't been king for too long, but already, all this 'your majesty' and 'sir' bit is getting tiring."

"Oh, yes, I'm sure all the polite formality is exhausting," Lawr said, before he could stop his sarcasm.

"It is." Bry protested with a grin. "You have no idea how much that kind of thing slows down a conversation."

"Really." Lawr thought about it seriously for a moment. "Yes, I guess it could take a while to get anywhere in a conversation if people always have to slow down to salute you."

"Exactly."

"I knew you two would get along." Shad sighed, shaking his head as he shared a grin with Klaas and Eleanora. "Just knew it."

CHAPTER 18

The conversation in the Healers chambers eventually turned somber as the information about Oracaede was brought up. Lawr explained what he'd found and how. The others agreed about not necessarily trusting whoever had addressed the files to Lawr. They also agreed that going to Lucianca would be a good next move.

"I can go to Lucianca to find more information on this," Lawr offered after a pause in the conversation.

Bry stared in silence for a moment. "Are you sure you want to? This isn't your fight."

Lawr nodded before disagreeing. "If what you've said about Oracaede is true, there isn't a world whose fight this isn't. Sooner or later, this will come to Terrae. More than their policies that already have. Besides, if the info is hidden even half as well as the first bit was, you'll need a hacker."

"Yeah, Bry," Shad jumped in. "Lawr here is very excited about seeing a world of light. Physics and all. I really wouldn't try to stop him."

Lawr nodded as Bry gave up his position. "Fine, but you shouldn't be traveling alone, especially with what we're after. Nobody should."

"I can go with him." Shad volunteered.

"No, you can't," the other four occupants of the room spoke at once.

Shad blinked and stared around in surprise for a moment. "Okay, now that was just too fast."

"And too true," Bry said bluntly. "Shad, you can't stay in Lucianca."

"I didn't say 'stay', I said 'go'," he corrected. "I can bring him to

Lucianca and hang around between that world and the Empty until he's done." He raised his hand as Bry started to argue. "There is no one else who we could send. You can't leave. Klaas and Eleanora have to stay with the court, and there is no one else we know to trust here."

Bry growled and clenched his fists at the argument.

"He's right, Bry," Klaas agreed, stroking his beard into a pointed goatee. "It's not a great situation, but Shad will need to go with Lawr to Lucianca."

"There's something else too. Two things actually," Bry growled. "One, the Nomads are becoming active again in Medius, I could easily be getting blamed for it."

"What?" Eleanora looked as though she was ready to stomp on someone one over the last part. "Now who would..."

Bry held up his hand before her anger could manifest in more than words. "Secondly, Oracaede knows we're not going to be cooperating with them, and they've promised repercussions."

"*What?*" This time Shad and Klaas were the loudest in expressing their surprise.

"So," Bry continued after the uneasy silence returned. "We're about to have a lot of problems at the same time."

The silence spread out a moment longer before Lawr broke it. "How does Oracaede know that exactly? Do you think they know about this data?" A sudden fear for Ali's safety gripped him.

"No." Bry shook his head.

Lawr sighed in relief.

Ali will be fine, he reassured himself.

Bry continued speaking and Lawr mentally hurried to focus on the spoken words again.

"... an albino from Oracaede was here within an hour of Aarkdal sending that info. They don't have that kind of reaction time."

"Yeah, that's more likely their reaction time to you becoming king," Klaas added, only half-joking. "The speed of bureaucracy is always impressive."

Shad snorted a laugh of agreement before frowning at something. "Wait, you said an albino, right?"

Bry sighed and nodded. "I was thinking the same. Oracaede's Ghost. Only thing I don't know is, why didn't he try to kill me."

"That phantom was here?" Eleanora covered her mouth and moved a little closer to Klaas, who wrapped an arm around her shoulders.

Lawr blinked and shifted his gaze between the four. "So, who's this albino again?"

Shad offered a weak smile along with an explanation. "Oracaede's albino is their best assassin. Medians don't really have a word for albino, so most people refer to him as a ghost. He usually does Oracaede's bidding when they want people to know they're responsible. Everyone in the six united sphaeres knows the Ghost."

Lawr nodded. This Ghost sounded more like a comic book character than a person, but he guessed that was what happened when so many people feared the same idea of a person. Fact got lost in myth.

"We can be expecting a displeased response," Bry was saying with a frown and a heavy exhale.

"You're not regretting the answer you gave them are you?" Klaas placed the question in an ever-calm tone.

"Of course not," Bry snapped too hastily. He rubbed his temple with a heavy hand. "Just... I probably could have been more cunning in my reply. Bought us some time."

Klaas hummed in a tone heavy enough it could have been a growl. "That wouldn't have worked. He probably would have killed you."

Shad and Eleanora nodded agreement.

Bry sighed. "Fine, but that's still only one of two problems."

"Two of one," Lawr mumbled a correction to himself. The others in the room didn't hear and continued.

"Right, the Nomads." Shad rolled his blue eyes. "Can't those barbarians just keep their filth to themselves?"

Lawr raised an eyebrow at Shad's extreme dislike of anything, much less a whole group of people.

Bry caught Lawr's look. "The Nomads are slave traders and pillagers. They wander and don't call any world home, but they've been keeping mostly to themselves in Glacius Tesca until just recently."

Lawr nodded. He didn't know if he'd hate the whole group for that, but it seemed reasonable enough to avoid them.

"People are going to start making connections between you taking the throne and the Nomads becoming more active," Klaas stated, continuing to fiddle with the shape of his beard.

Eleanora hmphed. "They'll just have to get over it. It's not your fault those people want to start making a mess."

"Why are your people so quick to blame you?" Lawr asked slowly.

"Well," Shad started slowly. "It's something about Bry only having been king for a few weeks. This starting up after Loreda, his mother, put an end to the problem when she was the temporary ruler. That and Bry's father, Vlasis, was a royal ass who worked with Oracaede and sometimes the Nomads too." Shad paused, tapping his fingers rhythmically against the table. "Somewhere between all that, Bry's people are low on trust for their new and untried king."

Bry glowered at his friend.

"What?" Shad shrugged. "It's true."

"I know," Bry growled. He turned to Lawr. "My people don't have a reason to trust me yet. With the Nomads moving, and if Oracaede makes good on its threat, they'll have good reason not to."

Lawr hummed again at the explanation. "So Oracaede is using the Nomads to further your people's distrust of you, potentially starting a civil uprising." He hummed again and paused, noticing the surprised and confused stares directed at him.

"No," Bry started. "I learned about the Nomads before the Ghost ever came to visit."

"Yeah, the timing..." Shad trailed off.

"The timing is too perfect," Lawr finished, meeting each of their gazes. "If your ghost fellow wasn't here because of the data I found, something else must have been important enough for Oracaede to send him, if he's as high in value as you say and didn't kill you. If they knew you were going to say no to their offer, why would they wait to position their pieces? And why should they kill you if they can get your own people to do it for them?"

"Huh," Bry grunted.

Shad blinked for a moment before coming back to his senses and finding his speech again. "Yeah, he kind of scares me too."

"In which case," Lawr continued, now that they were on the same page. "We should get to Lucianca as soon as possible. Having some proof against Oracaede should help your case with your people," he finished with a nod to Bry.

Silence returned. This time, the quiet was much more content than before. Plans were made and a better understanding of what was going on made Lawr more at ease, even if what was going on was a mess. Plans were important. Like Bry, he could take on the world, if he had a plan for it.

CHAPTER 19

Ali woke up to a headache and fuzzy thinking as she tried remembering where she was. She stared up at the off-white ceiling and walls that seemed familiar as she propped herself up on her elbows. The old couch she found herself laying on was familiar too.

A sense of dread knotted in her stomach. Memories of recent events flooded her mind. Ali held her breath as her gaze darted around the room for any sign of the albino. Her 'master'—she winced at the thought. She didn't see him anywhere, and she let a sigh escape for that small joy.

Ali sat up slowly, giving herself a quick once over, and sighing again as she found herself in no worse shape than before the albino had drugged her. In some ways, she was better. Her wrists were both bandaged and the gash on her head was hidden from touch under a layer of gauze.

After a moment of observation, Ali realized the house wasn't silent. The sound of voices made their way to her through the closed French doors that, if she remembered correctly, led to the dining room and kitchen.

Ali swallowed her fear after a moment and stood. Careful to remain quiet, she tip-toed forward to the glass doors. As she moved closer, she recognized the albino's voice and froze. After a few words, the albino's voice ceased and a questioning, chipper voice picked up. Ali clapped a hand over her mouth. The second voice sounded like a child.

Ali moved closer to the doorway until she was standing almost against the glass but still out of view. She could see into the kitchen, but the dining room where the voices were coming from was behind the wall, out of her view.

"So, right here," the childlike voice started. "The remainder would be five, right?"

The albino answered something Ali couldn't hear, but his tone sounded positive.

"Okay! I get it," the little voice chirped.

Ali bit her lip as she breathed in sharply. The second voice did belong to a child. A young boy. Ali tried thinking of what reason the albino would possibly have for keeping a child. She couldn't think of any good ones.

"Eavesdropping is not polite, you know," the albino's cold voice spoke loudly enough for Ali to hear. She jumped back, screwing her eyes shut and drawing a short shaking breath through clenched teeth before opening her eyes again.

She waited a moment, but the voice didn't speak again. She hesitated a moment longer, hoping for courage that didn't come before pushing the glass doors open. The albino sat at a table and had twisted around in his chair to face her. Next to him, Ali bit her lip at the sight of a young child, a boy no older than seven.

A huge grin lit the boy's face as he saw Ali.

"Ah, you're awake!" he jumped up from his chair and ran the short distance to Ali. "Hi! I'm Leon," the boy said, grinning from ear to ear.

Ali's jaw dropped at the child's cheerful demeanor as she glanced between him and the expressionless albino.

"What's your name?" the boy asked, looking confused at Ali's silence.

"A-Ali," she stammered, returning her attention to the boy. She tried to return his smile, but she could tell she was failing miserably.

"Alley?" the boy cocked his head to the side in question.

Ali nodded. "It's short for Alisha." Ali dropped the failed smile as she looked back at the albino. She almost jumped to see he was standing next to her, and she hadn't even seen him move.

"Sverre." He motioned briefly to himself before gesturing toward a chair at the opposite side of the table from where he'd been seated. "Sit."

Ali ducked her head in a nod and moved quickly to comply, to get away from him as fast as possible. A small hand grabbed hers as she moved. She jumped again before she looked down to see Leon holding her hand and walking with her to her chair. The boy moved back to sit in his seat as soon as Ali had taken hers.

"It's okay," Leon followed Ali's gaze into the kitchen, where the albino, Sverre, was moving about in silence. "Sverre looks scary, but he's really great."

Ali gulped and cut her gaze quickly between Leon and Sverre. Luckily, the albino either didn't hear or more likely didn't mind the comment.

"So, um," Leon started talking but paused to shovel some sort of food into his mouth. Ali returned her attention to him. Watching him eat suddenly reminded her how hungry she was. "So, Sverre bought you at the Aynur's slave market, right?"

All thoughts of food vanished from Ali's mind.

"Yes," she mumbled. *I guess.*

"Yeah, he bought me too," Leon chirped.

Ali snapped her head up and stared at the boy.

How can he say something like that so easily?

He was tugging one of his sleeves up. A nasty looking brand on the inside of his upper forearm stared back at Ali. "Different tribe though. The Tromix always brand everyone. It was a long time ago."

Ali's eyes watered suddenly as she wondered what could count as a long time for someone so young.

"An' I'm free now," Leon said around a mouthful of food as though finishing a thought as he pulled his sleeve back down.

Ali blinked at his easygoing nature about all of this.

He can't possibly understand the meaning of this, she thought warily.

A pale hand appeared from nowhere in front of her and lowered a tray to the table. Ali tried to jump sideways, away from the albino, but only succeeded in scuffing the chair over a few inches and banging her knees against the underside of the table. Ali twisted sharply to look up at the albino's face. He stared with a ghost of a frown at her reaction and pulled back to a standing position, several feet away from her.

Ali swallowed. She hated how quiet he was, how silent he was when he moved. She hadn't even seen him leave the kitchen, much less sneak around behind her.

Damn it.

She hated him. She hated how afraid of him she was. She'd always thought of herself as tough, but he was making her realize just how helpless she really was here, the knowledge of how helpless she'd be if he tried to hurt her. Her stomach twisted. She clenched her teeth and her fists under the table.

"Eat," Sverre said, taking his seat across from her again. "You must be hungry."

Ali stared back at the food; an oatmeal-looking goulash in a bowl, with smaller bowls next to it filled with nuts and chunks of fruit. A handle-less mug on the side held a dark sludgy liquid that smelled of coffee.

Ali glanced from her meal back at the albino. He was speaking to Leon in a low voice while pointing at something in one of the many books strewn across the table. Leon nodded, sparing a confused look and smile for Ali. He mouthed "eat" and pointed to the food before returning his attention to his lesson.

A shaky breath escaped Ali as she gave in to the hunger that twisted her gut as much as the hatred. She took a tentative half-bite. It was good. She gulped down as much as she could. The food was *really* good.

She managed to glance up after she'd inhaled the entire bowl. The albino was looking at her with a small smile.

"Would you like more?" he asked in the same steady voice.

Ali nodded despite herself.

Sverre reached across the table to take the tray. He kept his movements slow and nonthreatening as he pulled the tray back and stood up to return to the kitchen.

Ali watched the albino carefully as he moved around the kitchen and returned to the table. This time he moved slower and made sure to catch her eye before coming near her and setting the tray down.

He returned again to his seat and watched with his head cocked slightly to the side. Ali started eating again, not worrying about eating as fast now that she knew she could have more.

Sverre nodded contentedly to himself after watching her eat a few bites before turning his attention again back to Leon.

Ali finished the second helping and downed the last of the coffee sludge before attempting to ask a question.

"So, you, um…" She stuttered, too uncomfortable to force the words out. "You bought me." It wasn't a question. Her question was 'why', but she hoped she wouldn't have to ask that.

Sverre leaned back in his chair and regarded her quietly for a moment.

"Leon." He turned his gaze to the boy. "You can play outside now."

Leon glanced nervously between Sverre and Ali before getting up and moving carefully through the glass doors. He gave Ali one last smile and a short wave before closing the doors.

Sverre waited in silence until the front door clicked shut behind the boy. Then he waited a moment longer and seemed to be thinking on something before he spoke.

"You are, I know, familiar with Lawrence Dara. He located some significant information about Oracaede a short time ago." Sverre spoke slowly and paused, waiting for Ali to nod along like she knew what he was talking about. "The information Dara found is valuable to Oracaede. They had the Aynur's Wolves kidnap you for the purpose of leverage against Dara."

Ali breathed in and huffed an exhale as Sverre's words started to make sense. Lawr had been excited and a bit disturbed by what he'd found. He hadn't told her everything, but she did remember him saying something about an "Oracaede" doing bad things. A fear for Lawr hit her.

"Is Lawr safe?" She half-stood from her seat, searching the albino's face for an answer.

Sverre raised an eyebrow and nodded. "Mr. Dara was taken to Sentre in Medius, another world, by the king's wraith friend. He will be safe there."

Ali sighed in relief as she sank back down to her chair.

"Unfortunately," Sverre continued. "The half-breed forgot that anyone with a…" He paused, seemingly trying to think of a word to use. "A *familiar* relationship with Mr. Dara would also be a target." Sverre nodded toward Ali.

Ali almost gagged. "He's my uncle," she snapped, then immediately regretted it.

Maybe if he thought she was in a relationship, he wouldn't try anything with her. She could have kicked herself for not thinking of that a half a second sooner.

"I see," Sverre said with a nod and no recognition of Ali's internal struggle.

Sverre shifted and Ali caught the barest notion that he might be uncomfortable. Just maybe.

"Miss Ali," he began, catching her eyes again with his bloody ones. "I must tell you that it was my actions that directly brought about your current situation. I made the data available for Dara to find. I must offer my apology that these actions have caused you trouble." Sverre shifted again and gave Ali a sympathetic nod. "I will, of course, do everything I can to make sure you make it back to your world when it is safe." Sverre stood as he finished speaking and moved a step toward the door. "I understand this might be a lot of information to take in, so I will leave you to think on it as you will." He opened the glass doors and paused. "As another note, I can appreciate how terrifying this must be for you. However, I give you my word, I mean you no harm. I would not hurt you. Please rest assured of that." He nodded again as he moved silently through the door and closed it behind him.

Ali breathed again only when she heard the front door open and close again too. Sverre was unnerving to be around. She was glad he had left her alone. She pushed the tray away and folded her arms on the table. She rested her head on her arms and stared at nothing, thinking over the mess she was in.

She sniffled and wiped her eye to remove the moisture gathering there.

What a mess, her thoughts whispered.

Ali wiped her cheek. She wanted to go home. She just wanted to be home. Ali didn't know when she'd started sobbing, but now that the tears had started, they wouldn't stop.

CHAPTER 20

Inside the Empty, Shad assured Lawr the remaining journey would be short. Relatively speaking, Shad had corrected himself.

Lawr grimaced as Shad used the words 'literally' and 'relatively' right next to each other, as though they didn't mean completely different things.

Though, he had to correct himself mentally. *In the physics of the Empty, that was accurate.*

Lawr bit back a manic chuckle before it could vocalize. He loved the wonky physics of the Empty. It was going to be so much fun to try and figure out on paper with math. Maybe a new type of mathematics would be needed to describe it.

"Are you listening?" Glowing, disembodied blue orbs tilted sideways as Shad waited for a response.

"No." Lawr sighed at the distraction to his train of thought. He returned to trying to come up with a math that would work to describe the physics of this space.

Time passed unmarked as Lawr went from trying to think of the math of the Empty to actively trying to ignore Shad.

Shad was bored, Lawr intuited. Mostly from the beginnings and random snippets of conversation he was having with his shadows. Maybe he wasn't bored, so much as oddly entertained by his conversations, but it was equally distracting.

"Would you stop that?" Lawr finally gave up after having been distracted by a question asked to a shadow in the empty black space if it could see itself in the dark.

Shad's blue orbs of eyes blinked in the dark. "It's a valid question."

"You're asking yourself. Not even yourself, a shadow of your shadow," Lawr tried to explain the absurdity.

"So, not directly myself then."

Lawr opened his mouth but didn't know how to reply. He hadn't explained that last bit well.

Shad's eyes shifted in size and tilted again to the side. Lawr could tell he was grinning at the joke. He'd probably laced his hands behind his head at the idea, but Lawr couldn't quite see that in the shadows of the darkness.

"Whatever," Lawr grumbled as he started walking again.

Shad hummed beside him. The humming had started as a hum of victory but had now morphed into some sort of song.

Lawr exhaled heavily. This kid was going to drive him nuts before he got any of his questions answered.

"You okay?" The shadow asked, blue eyes again leaning out in front of his vision.

"No."

"Oh, okay." The blue orbs leaned back.

Blissful silence returned for a time. Shad had become preoccupied with the AaD and Lawr was left to think in peace.

The thinking was put on hold all too quickly as Shad stopped walking and Lawr stopped to wait for him. Lawr frowned and counted the seconds before Shad either started moving or talking.

A sudden, blinding bright light filled the blackness in front of Lawr. He staggered back, squeezing his eyes shut and clapping a hand over them.

"Welcome to Lucianca!" Shad's over chipper voice spoke beside him. "We're here."

"Next time," Lawr began, squinting through the cracks of his fingers for a few seconds at a time. "Maybe open the door just a crack, you know. Ease me into it. Or a warning? A warning would have been nice."

Shad grunted, uncommitted.

Lawr slowly removed his hands as he stepped out of the Empty into Lucianca. The world was bright. He'd expected it to be since it was made entirely out of light, but still. It was blinding.

Lawr glanced around. There was nothing. Nothing could be seen. But there was an entire rich world here, he could sense it. The air, he noticed immediately, was heavy, more so than it had been in Medius.

"Why's the air so much heavier?" Lawr asked back at Shad who was moving somewhere behind him.

"It's Vis," Shad's voice wavered and distorted the space. "You probably could sense it a little in Medius, but it's much stronger here."

"Vis," Lawr muttered to himself as he stepped forward again. Less than stepping, he shifted relative to the world around him.

Vis, he thought again, the weight of it gave the empty, bright world an infrastructure and form. The power and energy wrapped around and moved through him as it moved through the world. He could see the history of the place, sense the emotions and thoughts of hundreds of presences nearby. *Lucians*, he could tell.

The most prevalent emotion from the Lucians was annoyance at the Empty opening near them—and a small bit of anger and disgust directed behind Lawr. He turned. Shad stood in his Shade form, his bright eyes searching the empty white space.

Lawr snapped his eyes closed and jerked his head back around, reaching at nothing to steady himself as a wave of dizziness and nausea made him sway. The sickness passed as Shad's chipper voice broke the silence with endless chatter. The pain of looking at Shad was a relief, though. Maybe all the Lucians he could sense didn't hate Shad for his blood, but rather for his form. Lawr faced forward. He still couldn't bear to look at the shadow. He would puke.

"Are you alright? You look a bit sick." Shad's voice moved toward Lawr.

Lawr turned his head away. "I'm fine."

"Oh." Shad breathed next to him. "I know I'm kind of hard to look at in here. Bry almost vomited the first time."

"Yep," Lawr said.

"Oops, I forgot about that. Maybe I shouldn't have come," Shad's voice shifted away.

"It's fine," Lawr said quickly, though he still didn't try to turn around. He couldn't read Shad's emotions nearly as well with the Vis as he could the Lucians, but he'd learned to read him well enough to know he was upset—genuinely upset. Maybe Lawr *could* read him easier with the stronger Vis.

"Sorry," Lawr mumbled.

"Okay, then." Shad's voice moved around behind Lawr.

Lawr almost turned back at the sound of his voice. It was strained.

"Are you alright?" Lawr asked. "Being here in Lucianca? You don't sound good."

"It's just a little tiring. I can handle it, don't worry. I'm not at my limit yet." Shad's voice wasn't convincing.

Lawr grunted. He didn't agree, but he also had no way of finding Aarkdal without Shad's help. "So, we should find Aarkdal quickly then. How do we go about doing that?"

A laugh sounded behind him. "Use your head, duh."

"You're not helpful."

"Yeah, yeah." Shad's voice moved closer. "You can sense all the Lucians here, can't you?"

Lawr nodded after checking all the Lucians he could feel again. None of them 'felt' like Aarkdal.

"Okay, search for him."

"I just did. I didn't find him."

Shad hummed a moment. "Did you search the Lucians in the area, or search the sphaere for someone named Aarkdal?"

"The area," Lawr grumbled. He tried focusing on the name of the Lucian and searched an increasing area. Several moments passed and several breaks were taken as the mental search was exhausting. Finally, Lawr could sense a connection with the name.

"He's this way, maybe." Lawr started shifting in that direction. He stopped after a moment of shifting. "Will you be okay? We're moving away from where the last doorway was."

Shad grunted. "I'm keeping an eye on where the doorways are going to be in this area." Shad moved and Lawr saw the end of his black hole of an arm waving the AaD.

"Alright." Lawr turned away from the movement and started moving again.

They moved for a period of time over some amount of distance. Lawr was fascinated by the complete lack of visual references for the passage of time and distance. He wasn't even the slightest bit tired from the traveling. The only sense of reference was if they were near Aarkdal or not. Finally, they were getting nearer to him.

Lawr stopped as he felt the Lucian he was looking for somewhere close in front of him. "Um… Aarkdal?"

"You summoned me," the airy voice dripped with distain.

"Oh, summoned? Sorry, I just meant to find you is all. I'm a bit new to this," Lawr said, ignoring the angry tone.

"I know exactly what you are, Terranian," Aarkdal spat, enunciating every word as though it was its own sentence.

"Great, then you should know why we're here," Lawr said as soon as the Lucian finished his sentence, before he could say anything else.

Shad had been standing back, but he tried pitching in. "We're interested in any references to more of the information you sent Bry. Possibly some—"

"Silence, Shade," Aarkdal growled. "When I need assistance or information from a mongrel monster, the worlds will truly stand at a dismal place."

Lawr raised an eyebrow and focused hard on keeping his twitching lip from forming a scowl and possibly a rebuke. He braved the dizziness to glance back at Shad. The big shadow didn't seem disturbed by the comment. But he'd likely grown accustomed to Aarkdal whenever they met last.

"Well, for the record," Lawr started, turning back to Aarkdal and pausing for the lightheadedness to pass. "He's helping me out with the whole 'save the sphaeres' spiel. So, I guess it is that dismal of a time."

Aarkdal's hostility refocused on Lawr. "You can speak easily to this Shade because you know nothing of what they are. You don't know what they can do and have done. Foolish Terranian, you could never—"

"You know, Shad," Lawr cut Aarkdal off, and tilted his head back toward the wraith without looking at him. "I could find this guy just from feeling his name. Do you think he just can't find mine, or does he just think he sounds all superior calling me 'Terranian', like a sphaere is an insult?" Lawr turned his attention back to a seething Aarkdal. "I'm leaning toward the latter, personally. Unseemly as that would be."

"Don't interrupt me!" Aarkdal barked.

"Then don't waste my time." Lawr kept his eye's from rolling as he sensed the being seething. He could tell Aarkdal was smart, but he was becoming tedious.

Aarkdal growled something caustic.

"So," Lawr started again slowly. "Do you know where we might find more records that would continue from the files I found on Earth, Terrae?"

"Of course." Aarkdal ground the words out.

"Great, so why didn't you give the full files to Bry before now?" Lawr asked politely, tipping to his toes and back to his heels once.

Aarkdal snarled. "If you're implying—"

"He's not." Shad jumped in. "We assumed the information would be locked away somehow." Shad jabbed Lawr's side hard enough that Lawr flinched. "That's why no one else has found anything. That's why Lawr is here."

"And to be someone a Lucian would talk to, apparently," Lawr grumbled.

Play nice. Shad's voice spoke in Lawr's mind. *We still need his help.*

Lawr glanced back for a second, trying not to let his surprise at the sudden intrusion into his head show on his face. He grunted his agreement after a moment.

Shad started talking again to Aarkdal, "But someone had to have access to it to leave those files on a chatroom on Terrae."

Aarkdal growled reluctant agreement. "Fine." He moved away and made a motion for them to follow.

"I did find where the information is." This time, when Aarkdal spoke his anger finally seemed to be directed at something other than Shad and Lawr. "Unfortunately, I couldn't access it." He stopped next to something Lawr could sense more than see was a computer terminal.

"Yeah, well." Lawr moved in front of the familiar device after Aarkdal turned it on. "You didn't get into the original files either. I did."

A growl emanated from Aarkdal's direction and Lawr could sense Shad facepalm himself.

I said "play nice." Shad sighed in his head.

Lawr shrugged and smiled. "I tried. I failed."

CHAPTER 21

O verlooking the royal garden from an outdoor terrace, Bry
contented himself with watching Stori and her maidservant
enjoy teatime on the lawn. The idea seemed odd to him, but
apparently tea breaks were important to Sylvans. Stori always scheduled
time for them in the midmorning and mid-afternoon.

The Pyxis, *Fenrir* as Stori called him, also seemed to enjoy the garden
breaks. Bry tried not to laugh as it made bounding laps around the lawn,
only occasionally tumbling and rolling as it tried to catch a bird, only to
return to the girls to beg for some of their pastry treats.

Bry relaxed and leaned against the railing. He was also starting to enjoy
these little breaks. Even if he wasn't invited, per se, it was still a chance to
pause and remember how much he loved his city. He had started to forget
how gorgeous it was. Bry continued staring off into space. He missed this.

A familiar scent brought Bry's attention snapping back to reality. His
mother's perfume announced her presence before she even reached the
terrace.

"Loreda, are you well?" Bry asked politely, turning toward her as he
did.

Loreda paused in her approach. Surprise and annoyance clouded her
features for a short second before they were replaced with an easy,
nonchalant smile. "Yes, Your Majesty, quite well. Thank you."

Bry nodded as he straightened his posture and rolled the slouch out of
his shoulders. He stood stiffly as Loreda approached the railing and

breathed in the view. Bry tapped his fingers against the railing. He wondered if he should have greeted her more formally, like she had. He knew she must still dislike him; she'd been careful to avoid speaking with him since his coronation.

"How does your bride please you?" Loreda asked in her graceful, light voice.

The sudden question startled Bry out of his thoughts. "Oh, uh, she seems nice." Bry mentally kicked himself. "Nice" meant nothing.

"Nice?" Loreda questioned.

"I mean..." Bry paused and watched Stori for a moment. She was laughing at a story her maidservant was telling with great animation. A smile played over his lips. "She has the makings of an excellent queen."

Loreda stared at him. He almost missed the confused look that floated over her face before quickly disappearing. "Surely after an heir is born there will be no need to keep her around as queen."

Bry frowned at the implication, "So she should leave? Hide out in some castle and ignore the troubles of the sphaere and her kid?" He had spoken more harshly than he'd meant to. He would have apologized, but the ugly snarl on Loreda's face made him pause.

Loreda took a moment longer to smooth her features. "I only state what is obvious. You won't need a queen around when the heir is born."

"Well, she's not pregnant. So, I guess she'll be staying for a while." Bry frowned and held in a sigh. He'd spoken before thinking again.

That may be something Loreda didn't need to know.

"You couldn't know that for sure..." Loreda started.

Bry turned back to the view and watched his wife.

Loreda gaped at the sudden realization. "You haven't been with her!"

Bry grunted, but otherwise remained silent. Loreda was getting on his nerves. It wasn't any of her business, but after all he'd been stupid enough to answer.

Loreda remained blissfully silent for too short a time. When she spoke again, her tone had turn nasty. "Medius needs a successor to the throne. The people need to know that the future of the Godric line is secure." She paused and grabbed Bry's arm, pulling his attention back to her. "You're letting your personal feelings get in the way of your rule." She finished her sentence as she tightened her grip, digging her nails deep into Bry's skin.

Bry yanked his arm away. "Don't tell me what the people need, or how to rule." He snapped. "I can figure that out for myself."

Loreda seethed but grit her teeth and pulled her lips back into an ugly smile. She didn't say another word but turned and stormed off the terrace. He heard her mutter something about being his father's son as she left.

Bry glared after her a moment before turning back to the overlook and leaning his arms against the railing and his head on his arms with an angry huff.

He noticed Stori staring up at him with confusion and concern written over her face. She cocked her head to the side—a question. Bry smiled and waved back, hoping she hadn't seen too much of his interaction with Loreda. Stori returned the smile after a moment and turned her attention back to her maidservant and the Pyxis.

A heavy sigh escaped Bry as he turned and headed back inside to his study.

That's enough of a break for one day, he thought.

The mess of papers, maps, and drawn-out battle plans remained on his desk, just as he had left it. Bry sat down heavily and picked up one of the battle plans he'd sent to General Harailt to use against the Nomads. It hadn't worked.

"I don't get it," he grumbled to himself. The plan should have been effective. The many before it should have as well, but the Nomads kept countering and his ideas kept failing. "You used to be good at this." He reviewed the most recent information sent to him and pulled out a fresh piece of paper.

The rest of the day muddled together as Bry finally had a new plan laid out just as the sun was eaten by the horizon.

Bry finished sending the plans to General Harailt when he noticed Stori standing patiently by the door. Bry blinked and stared; he hadn't heard her come in. He motioned her to sit, chagrined that he didn't know how long she'd been standing there.

"I hope I'm not disturbing you." Stori started moving toward the desk but stopped suddenly and caught her breath. "Are you alright?" she rushed forward and examined Bry's arm.

"What?" Bry stumbled over the single word. Her concern dumbfounded him as she moved to lightly hold his arm and examine where Loreda had grabbed him.

Her nail—claw—marks were still visible. Most were just bruised but two had drawn a few beads of blood. The blood had long dried, but Bry hadn't noticed it until now.

"Oh, it's nothing." Bry brushed the dried blood away. "Just a scratch." He smiled.

Stori pouted at him. "From Loreda."

Bry grimaced. She had seen.

Damn.

"It's not important." Her concern surprised him; he wasn't sure what to do with it.

"She shouldn't have done that," Stori said softly, gently stroking the bruised skin.

Bry froze. Stori's concern was surprising. No one except Eleanora would make such a fuss over a little scratch. Well, maybe Shad, but he was an overprotective softy.

I guess Stori is too. The thought made him smile.

"It's just a scratch," he mumbled again.

His soft tone seemed to catch Stori's attention. Her big eyes found their way to Bry's and held them hostage for a moment.

Stori dropped her gaze and moved back, blushing as she did. "Sorry, I didn't mean to intrude," she said in her gentle voice.

"It's fine." Bry rubbed his arm where she had held it. "Not intruding."

"I wondered, if it isn't private, what Loreda was upset about," Stori asked in her kind but determined way.

Bry liked that about her. She wasn't pushy, but he had the sense she could tease answers out of anyone.

"It was... n't." Bry rethought the matter of a private discussion. His talk with Loreda certainly involved Stori. He sighed.

We're going to have to talk about it sometime.

Bry moved to the couch and motioned for Stori to sit, too. "She wanted to know how we were... getting on, as a couple, I guess," Bry winced at his lame attempt to explain.

Stori cocked her head to the side and frowned. "Getting on what? Do we have to climb something?"

Bry coughed out a laugh, "No, that's—um." This was going to be an awkward conversation. Stori's face remained a pleasant vision of patient confusion. "She... wanted to know if I had an heir coming." Bry barely managed to get the full sentence out. He peeked over at Stori, hoping she would take the discussion better than he did.

Stori had paled several shades and Bry was close enough that he could hear her breath catch. He blinked and waited nervously for her to start breathing again.

"Oh," she finally said, her figure pulling in on itself to take up as little room as possible.

Or maybe she was simply moving away from him. Bry couldn't tell.

"Sorry," he said with a cringe, then sighed at his own apology. "It's sudden, but..." He trailed off. He didn't have an end to that sentence and they both knew it.

"I apologize," Stori said, startling Bry out of his own thoughts. "I realize I have been thinking selfishly, not considering the needs of Medius."

"Don't apologize. It's my decision too." Bry rubbed his face and noticed Stori's features relaxed a little out of the corner of his eye.

They sat in silence for a time—not uncomfortable silence, but maybe a little uneasy.

Stori's posture straightened suddenly as she prepared to speak. "My birthday will be in a few months. Can... Would it be fine to wait until then? For an heir? I'd like some time to think and... prepare, if it would be alright?"

Bry stared for a moment. He swallowed and remembered that he still needed to thank the Heavens and all the Vis that this woman was his queen. "Yep, that'd be great."

CHAPTER 22

"So, it's gonna be a special birthday then?" Shad's sing-song voice asked through the AaD.

Bry sighed and let his head fall heavily to the desk. He should have asked for a status update first. Or maybe he just shouldn't have mentioned anything to Shad. That would have been better.

No, Bry reminded himself. *It would have been worse if they'd had this conversation in person. So. Much. Worse.*

"Shad…" Bry growled his friend's name.

"What?" Shad asked with singing innocence.

"Ignoring my personal life for a second," Bry started, in response to which Shad *'uh-huh'*ed. "Have you guys made any progress?"

A moment of silence followed. "Well, the weirdo genius and the annoying one haven't killed each other yet, so that's something."

Bry exhaled in frustration. "That's all?"

"Hey, that's a big thing here. They've come pretty close. But the only real update here is that things are worse than we thought."

"How so?"

"Do you know what a 'digital self-destruct mechanism' is?" Shad asked.

"No."

"Neither do I, but Lawr does, and it's bad news. Something about how it'll destroy all the data if anyone meddles with it wrong." Shad sighed. "Unfortunately, Lawr's gone into a don't-talk-to-me-I'm-thinking mode so he's not really talking. And Aarkdal, of course, still hates my guts, so he's not telling me anything either. There's another Lucian here now, a kid named Biirkon. You know him?"

Bry thought a moment, but the name wasn't familiar. "No. Who is he?"

"A friend, or apprentice or something of Aarkdal. He's friendlier than Aarkdal, at least," Shad muttered. Bry guessed something was bothering Shad, but he let it go for now.

"So, I shouldn't count on being able to use the information you guys find any time soon. That the gist of it?"

Shad hummed negatively. "Yeah, Lawr says what he found in Terrae was meant to be found. This stuff is meant to stay buried."

Bry held back a groan. "Do you think it was a Lucian that hid it, working with Oracaede?"

Shad paused a moment before answering. "Maybe, but it's not like this terminal access is restricted here. Anyone could have added information and secured it, really."

"Great."

Shad hummed agreement. "Any other news from your side?"

Bry glanced over the battle plans spread over his desk. "The fight with the Nomads isn't progressing well."

"Ah, all your charming plans aren't working out." Shad's voice almost made it sound like a joke, but Bry caught the strain in it.

"No," he said then growled. "Nothing I've sent has worked. I asked for Harailt's input, but it's still not enough to affect the Nomads. I don't understand how they keep slipping around the traps I set up. There should be no way for…" Bry trailed off as the only other possibility started to make more and more sense.

The other end of the line remained silent. Bry couldn't even hear Shad breathing until he spoke again.

"No way unless someone's giving them a preview of your attack plans before a battle." Shad said it as a statement, not a question.

Bry bit his lip until he tasted blood. Hearing someone else come to the same conclusion only made the likelihood that they were right even stronger.

"Bry?"

"Yeah. I'm still here, Shad." Bry pulled his focus back to the conversation and swallowed the blood he'd drawn.

"If there is a traitor leaking intel to the Nomads," Shad paused at the thought. "Any idea who it could be?"

Bry shook his head as he thought. "Soldiers wouldn't have direct access to the whole plans before the battle and I couldn't imagine an officer would be able to repeatedly slip out and contact the Nomads without anyone noticing."

"An aide of one of the officers?" Shad offered.

"That's more likely," Bry muttered. "But I still don't know. It could be anyone. Or no one, if I'm wrong."

Silence filled the line again before Shad spoke.

"What are you going to do?"

Bry sighed. "I'll have to go there myself sooner or later."

"Really, you can't send someone?" Shad questioned.

Bry grunted as a response.

"I'm just thinking," Shad started, speaking with unusual care on his word choice, "If that would be the best idea, leaving the capital. Istoria is still new and with your mother being strange and sticking around..." Shad trailed off for a moment as Bry sighed at the thought he knew Shad was getting to.

"You think Loreda will make a play for the throne while I'm gone?" Bry said finishing Shad's unstated thought.

"Ya think she won't?" Shad asked in return.

"No, she'd try."

"Then giving her such an open opportunity might—"

"Be a terrible idea," Bry interrupted. "I get it. But there is no one I trust at the battlefront, and no, I'm not going to send you to investigate."

"I'd go. I could stop by on our way back, if that's soon, anyhow."

Bry sighed again, "You could, I guess. But I can't keep sending you to do my work, Shad." Bry paused to think. "Loreda's going to make a play for the throne sooner than later. I might as well give her the rope to hang herself when I know she'll do it. As for Stori, I'll have to learn whether she can be trusted to rule in my stead sooner or later, and again, it might as well be sooner."

Shad hummed. "It's still risky. Your people might not help you take the throne back from Loreda."

"My people aren't going to trust me no matter what if I don't start proving that I can be trusted. Dealing with the Nomads myself might help that. Even more than being able to show them proof that Oracaede is behind the Nomad attacks. People respond with trust to action, not finger pointing."

"Wow, when did you get all wise?" Shad quipped.

"About thirty seconds ago. This power burst only lasts about a minute," Bry returned sarcastically.

"Oh, you won't get a chance to wax poetry," Shad scoffed. "Pity."

"Yeah, pity." Bry's chuckle faded as the weight of the problem settled back on his shoulders. Silence returned for a moment as Bry could hear Shad shift uncomfortably.

"Well," Shad finally broke the quiet. "I'd better get back to the two geniuses, make sure they're both still alive. Or that Lawr is at least."

"We'll probably need Aarkdal, too," Bry reminded his friend.

Shad grunted in disagreement. "Whatever, I'll talk with ya later. If and when you decide to make a move, let me know, I'll be there."

"Thanks, Shad." Bry sighed. Shad disconnected from his side.

Bry sank down to rest his head on top of his desk. He yawned. This was going to be a problem. He glanced out the windows. It was pitched black already. He yawned again and crossed his arms under his head. Maybe a quick nap before he started work again.

CHAPTER 23

More than a week, for sure. Maybe even two, Ali thought.
The days all blurred together, but she was certain she'd been in this new world at least that long. She sat cross-legged on the folded sofa hide-a-bed in the little library that had become her room. Bookcases lined every wall except the one with a small window facing the front of the house.

As much as Leon had tried explaining how the sphaeres of this universe worked, he hadn't been very helpful. The boy kept telling her she should just ask Sverre, that he'd give a better answer. Ali didn't doubt that, but she was still hesitant to talk to the assassin. That's what he was. She'd learned that when he'd casually mentioned it in a conversation with Leon.

An assassin, she repeated the word to herself. *Why on Earth—or Terrae, or Glacius Tesca—whatever planet I'm on, am I trapped with some assassin? A killer.*

Ali sighed and flipped through pages of a book she wasn't reading.

A killer, but not a scary one. At least, not after she became used to the quiet way he moved and that he didn't talk that much. Behind all that, he didn't seem like a bad person.

And it was becoming increasingly difficult to think of someone as a terrifying killer when they spent hours a day teaching Leon reading, writing, and arithmetic with more patience than most people could, including herself. Hard to be afraid of someone who would carefully prepare every meal and clean the house, even in between polishing and practicing with a truly astounding number of weapons he stored in the attached stable.

The clash between what Sverre was and how he acted was too confusing for Ali to wrap her head around. She was going to have to ask him about it sometime—why he did the job he did.

"Ali," Leon's whispered voice interrupted Ali's thoughts and raised her concerns. Leon was rarely quiet, and never whispered.

"What's wrong, Leon?" Ali whispered back as Leon crept into her room on his hands and knees. He closed the door behind him and waved for her to get down in his normal, animated manner.

Ali scrambled off the couch and sat on the floor with her nerves rising. "What's wrong?" she whispered again.

Leon didn't answer but crawled over to her and pulled her to a corner near the window.

"Listen," he whispered after a moment.

Ali bit her tongue as she tried listening for whatever it was that had scared the boy. Leon continued gripping her hand tightly as he too strained to hear something.

Minutes passed in silence. Ali focused on hearing something, anything out of the ordinary. A faint voice or two was all that reached her ears.

Ali's heart skipped a beat. Two voices. There was someone else around. A stranger. The one rule Sverre had imposed on her after she'd come to this house: If he ever had a visitor, no matter what, she and Leon were not to be seen. Not seen, not heard—their presence in the house had to be nonexistent.

Ali hadn't been in a mind to ask questions when Sverre told her that rule, but now she wondered. What Leon had told her was that if Sverre's boss found out he had other people around him that didn't work for Oracaede, they'd be killed.

Ali gulped and held her hand over her mouth.

Absolute silence, she thought, trying to focus on the idea.

Leon was frowning. His grip on her hand loosened and he crawled over to the window before Ali could stop him.

"Leon," she whispered after him.

She crawled after him as he pulled himself to his knees and peeked through the window. Ali barely stopped from pulling him back down when she saw the look of complete relief that washed over his face.

"It's Dain," he half-whispered, glancing down at her before running out of the room, not bothering to try and be quiet anymore.

"Leon!" Ali called after the boy in a whisper.

She pushed herself to her knees to see out the window and caught sight of Sverre immediately. He was standing a distance from the front door, talking with a dark-skinned man leading a horse. The dark man looked a bit older than Sverre by, Ali would guess, no more than 10 years. He was lithe, like Sverre, though taller and well-built.

He'd have to be, Ali thought. The high-powered sniper rifle slung over his back must have weighed a good 50 pounds, but he moved around and shrugged the weapon as though it were nothing.

Ali's gut reaction would have been to run and hide from someone swinging such a weapon around, but the memory of the relief on Leon's face made her pause. On cue, Leon shot out the front door and ran to the dark stranger. He gave the man a flying hug which the stranger returned by swinging the boy around. A sloppy grin stretched over the man's face as he set Leon down again and ruffled his already messy hair. The gunman took on an energetic manner that rivaled Leon's own as the two started an animated conversation.

Sverre interrupted their conversation a moment later. He spoke a few words to the darker man and clasped his arm in a solemn gesture the stranger returned. The gunman said something to Leon and waved goodbye as he mounted his horse and promptly rode away.

Sverre pulled Leon around toward the house as the boy glanced with confusion between the disappearing figure and Sverre.

Ali stood and hurried to the front door. She reached the living room as Sverre opened the door and walked in, followed by a string of questions and then Leon.

"But when will he be back? He was only here for a quick second. I don't understand why he left so quick," Leon came close to whining as Sverre closed the door behind them.

Only when it seemed Leon was done did Sverre speak. "You know Dain would have stayed if he could. He loves spending time with you." Sverre paused and patted Leon's ruffled hair down. His tone was gentle and cautious when he spoke again. "He had a job."

Ali wrinkled her nose. She could guess this 'Dain' had the same kind of job Sverre did.

Killing people.

Two weeks ago, Ali would have thought of that with nothing but disgust—maybe she still did—but somehow, knowing Sverre even the little she did, her next thought was pity. She didn't understand any of their situation, but somehow, it seemed forced. She doubted Sverre would choose this kind of work.

"How long?" Leon asked, bringing Ali's attention back to the scene in front of her.

Sverre didn't answer immediately. Ali could almost see the wheels turn in his head as he worked out some problem in the answer. "A week, maybe two."

Leon nodded and seemed content. Ali saw the lack of confidence in Sverre; he didn't know when Dain would be back.

If, Ali thought. *If* Dain would be back.

Leon turned to walk away but Sverre rested a hand on his shoulder, holding him there. When the boy's face turned up curiously, Sverre sighed and knelt, keeping a firm hand on Leon's shoulder.

"Leon, I have to leave for a while. Dain was here to relay a message. It's not a job—I just have to meet with my boss," Sverre added the last sentence in what was a rush for him when he saw the look of panic spread across Leon's face.

The panic didn't dissipate at all with the extra information. If anything, Leon looked more upset.

"Those people always hurt you! Don't go!" Leon lunged to swing his arms around Sverre's neck in a hug. Leon seemed to be trying to hold Sverre in place so he couldn't leave.

Ali tip-toed forward. She didn't feel like an impartial observer, but she wasn't sure if she'd prefer Sverre to leave or not.

He's an assassin, she reminded herself. Of course, she shouldn't want him there. *And yet...*

His presence in the house made it a home. She doubted it would be the same if he wasn't there.

Or if he never came back, a small part of her complained.

Sverre exhaled. Ali saw his shoulders slump as he hugged Leon back. "It'll be alright. I'll be back if I can."

Ali paused in her movement.

When.

When was the right word. *When* he could, not *if.*

Ali saw the cold, sad look that had slipped onto Sverre's face. It seemed "if" was exactly the word he meant.

"If I don't, Dain will look after you. You know that," Sverre continued. The words he added were worse than the silence. Sverre caught Ali's eye and nodded to indicate that meant her too. Dain would look after them both.

"No!" Leon jerked away. "I don't want Dain. I want you to stay." He sniffled as he spoke but continued staring into Sverre's eyes defiantly.

"I'm sorry, Leon," Sverre apologized, smoothing out the boy's shirt where it had crinkled up. He squeezed Leon's shoulders after his shirt was straight as if to provide any extra comfort he could by showing he was there. "I have to leave now. The sooner I get there the better."

Leon sniffled and nodded. He waited where he stood as Sverre stood and moved quietly past Ali without a word, directly into his bedroom with Leon still trying to wipe away tears; he failed every few seconds as more streamed down his face.

Ali stared vacantly at the living room.

You should want him gone, she told herself. The idea made her frown. She glanced at Leon. *I could take him back to my world. He'd be safe.*

She watched Leon still trying to wipe away his tears.

Couldn't protect him from this. Ali's stomach twisted on itself in pain for the boy.

She didn't understand why Sverre had this job. It didn't make sense. She turned on her heels and walked to Sverre's room. She entered without knocking and immediately regretted it. Sverre was half-changed into the same all-black outfit Ali had first seen him in. He paused in pulling his shirt on to glance at her as she came in. He didn't blink as he pulled his shirt down, hiding the myriad of scars and discolored skin that wrapped around his torso. Ali stopped in her tracks and stared. Even after the marred flesh was covered, she stared at his shirt where they hid.

Ali slowly brought her eyes up to Sverre's, but he hadn't seemed to notice. He was moving with unusual speed, still graceful, to pack the few things he might need into a small canvas bag.

Biting her lip, Ali moved forward into the room just enough to disrupt the paths he moved in. Sverre stopped to look at her.

"Why…" Ali started, but her voice and mind failed to find the right question for a moment.

Sverre blinked and frowned as though he didn't understand.

"You and him—D-Dain. Why do you do this kind of work?" Ali finally managed. She watched Sverre's face darken.

"Because we don't have the right to choose differently," he said simply.

It was Ali's turn to blink and stare.

That doesn't make any sense.

"Do you think I enjoy this work?" he asked when Ali didn't make a move to speak. "Enjoy putting Leon in danger? Because I don't. I *really* don't." Sverre paused and waited to see if Ali was going to say something.

Ali swallowed, but stayed silent, hoping he would say something that made sense to her.

"You think Dain is a monster because he carries a gun and works a job nobody else wants to do." Sverre's words were a statement, not a question.

Ali dropped her gaze.

"He has a wife and two kids, you know," Sverre's voice was a whisper.

Ali's stomach dropped at the thought.

"He hasn't seen them in two years, because if he goes near them, they'll be killed," Sverre continued.

Ali flinched as Sverre stepped closer so he could whisper in her ear. "Do you have any idea what they'd do to Leon, if they found him? If I didn't complete my missions?"

Ali's stomach twisted further. Her mind flashed with images of Leon with the same scars Sverre sported. She wanted to gag at the idea, but she managed to swallow her horror before it visually manifested.

Sverre's shoulders sagged again as his gaze moved in the direction of the living room. "I was younger than him when they started training me to become this kind of monster," he said absently before his sharp gaze snapped back to her. "I'd do anything to make sure that doesn't happen to him."

Sverre paused again and hesitated before touching Ali's chin just gently enough for her to lift her gaze to his. "I hate this. I really do." He looked so sad and... broken. Ali almost had to look away, back away, get away. But he spoke again. "I don't get a choice. People in my position are never allowed that. It is a privilege of the free."

Sverre stepped back and watched her. Ali wrapped her arms around herself and remained quiet. She took several half-steps back toward the door but couldn't find it in her to leave.

An unusually heavy sigh brought her attention back to Sverre. His gaze was flitting around the room before finally landing back with her. He held her gaze for a moment and she could see him thinking hard.

"I'm sorry, for bothering you with this," he said finally.

That wasn't what Ali wanted to hear, but he spoke again before she could interrupt.

"I know this isn't your problem, by any means. I'm the one who forced you here. I apologize for... ranting." He tipped his voice up at the end of the word, as if it were a question.

"Don't apologize, please," Ali tried to snap, though the "please" sounded much closer to begging in her own ears.

Sverre stared at her with what Ali assumed to be a stunned look on his face. None of Sverre's expressions were expressive enough that she'd ever noticed them when she first arrived, but now she could tell the slight differences. And right now, Sverre was surprised—shocked even—at her response.

His face darkened ever so slightly to a confused frown. "Why would—"

Ali's heart leaped into her throat and she heard herself shout, "Just don't!"

She immediately put her hand over her mouth and turned, waiting for Leon to bust into the room. She dropped her hand when she didn't hear anything unusual and forced herself to turn back to Sverre. He remained standing as before with his head cocked to the side as though he were trying to figure out a particularly difficult puzzle. She knew the feeling.

"I'm sorry," Ali muttered, her emotions seeming as out of place to her as ever.

They both stood, shifting their weight as the silence quickly became awkward.

Sverre glanced at her with a questioning look, waiting for her to say something—or not—she couldn't tell what he was thinking.

He shifted and started packing again in silence.

Ali watched, trying to think of something to say—anything.

Nothing came to her. The moments passed in confusion as Sverre finished packing. He stepped past her with a nod and moved back to the living room.

Ali breathed as he left.

What's wrong with me? Am I upset about what he said or am I actually afraid he might not come back? Why on earth do I care?

Low words spoken softly pulled Ali back to the living room. Sverre released Leon from a hug and kissed the boy on the forehead before standing. His gaze fell back on Ali with an unsure look. He approached her with caution, maintaining a comfortable distance.

Ali bit her lip. The awkward silence was back and she didn't know how to fix it.

"I do apologize for forcing you into this," Sverre repeated with forceful determination. "I know it can't be easy for you, being here away from your home and your world. But… thank you, for staying here with Leon." He looked at her questioningly.

Ali nodded stiffly and moved until she could rest a comforting hand on the boy's shoulder. She could feel him shaking with yet unshed tears. Ali swallowed and willed herself not to cry. Whether it would be with or for the boy, she wasn't sure.

Sverre nodded to himself and moved to open the door. Ali and Leon followed him to the porch as he went to get one of the creatures ready.

Moments later, Sverre was gone.

Leon and Ali watched as his silhouette disappeared into the distance. They continued watching as the cold of night set in.

CHAPTER 24

"That isn't going to work," Aarkdal chided with a sneer in his voice.

"Well, maybe if you'd shut up and give me a chance to try this in peace…" Lawr snapped back. He changed a few lines in the source code. The changes didn't work. Lawr growled and kicked at nothing since there was nothing to kick at. He was pretty sure Aarkdal said, "I told you so," but he didn't listen as he fumed over the idea that didn't work.

It should have gotten through the security system, ODPAA. Aarkdal hadn't found his name for the system amusing, One Damned Problem After Another, so he guessed it was as good a name as any. He now threw "odd-paw"—his pronunciation—into a sentence every so often just to annoy Aarkdal. Not that it was hard; everything annoyed Aarkdal.

Lawr pinched the bridge of his nose with a sigh as he glared at the light that made up the computer system ODPAA was on. He couldn't tell if it had been days he'd been working on it or weeks. Sleep and food weren't required in Lucianca. Although this had been a dream of his, to be able to live without having to take care of the necessities, the company now was greatly lacking.

He had made a good deal of progress working around Aarkdal's useless nagging, but it wasn't enough to open the files. And he was so close, he could feel it.

Abrupt laughter nearby shifted Lawr's attention briefly in the direction of Shad. He'd gotten used to looking at the shadow now, for a few seconds anyway, without getting nauseous. The big shadow against the light was laughing at something the friendlier Lucian, Biirkon, had said.

Lawr shifted his gaze away from Shad to the presence, Biirkon. The kid—as he sounded a bit younger than Shad—was an apprentice of Aarkdal's or something. He had come to watch the annoying presence at work. Not that Lawr had been listening or paying much attention to what was going on around him. Rather, he had paused what he was doing for a moment and suddenly noticed another presence hanging around.

That wasn't anything surprising, the only thing different was that Biirkon knew Aarkdal, and liked him, for whatever reason. After all, Shad had been trying to be friendly and talk to all the Lucians that moved passed. From what Lawr could tell, most of them seemed to ignore him.

Lawr paused in his thoughts, noticing Biirkon and Shad sauntering toward him.

Great, he thought, rolling his eyes. *Now they're going to pester me.*

"How's it coming?" Biirkon asked with a deeper voice than his lighthearted nature would suggest. "Anything I could do to help?"

"Yeah, shut up," Lawr growled. He didn't find the kid as irritating as Aarkdal, but Lawr also didn't want anyone else to be messing with ODPAA. Not when it could be so easily destroyed if someone didn't know what they were doing.

Aarkdal snarled at Lawr's response. "If you gave him a chance, he probably could have gotten this done by now, you stubborn ass."

Lawr snorted but didn't say anything. He didn't see any reason to trust someone he'd just met.

"Hey," Shad said softly, moving next to Lawr. "How's it coming?"

"It's going just peachy, Shad." He hadn't really meant to growl at Shad, but Aarkdal was still irritating him.

"Okay, okay." Shad held his shadow hands up in surrender. "Uh, listen. I'm gonna pop into the Empty again for a bit, okay?"

Lawr glanced at the shadow quickly. For a large black hole, he looked terrible. He'd faded noticeably since they'd first come to the light world. Lawr grimaced; another reminder of how much he needed to solve this problem quickly.

Lawr gave a sharp nod. "Take your time."

A sudden headache accompanied Shad's voice echoing in his head. *Lawr, don't let that Biirkon fellow mess with ODPAA.*

He frowned; he thought Shad liked the kid.

Shad noticed the frown and the headache came back. *There's nothing wrong, per se, just sort of a gut feeling. I don't trust him.*

Lawr gave a slight nod, pretending he was talking to himself for the Lucians' benefit. Gut feelings and intuition he could work with; Shad's he might even trust.

Shad gave a quick nod too and stepped back, raising his voice for the Lucians, "Alright then. I'll be back from the Empty in a bit. Have fun kids."

Aarkdal growled and Biirkon waved after the departing shadow.

Lawr glanced back at the Lucians. Aarkdal was still growling about something. Biirkon was standing next to him, making light of the situation with his cheerful deep voice; Lawr could tell he was smiling.

Lawr turned back to his work, but he was still thinking about Shad's words. It surprised him that Shad had noticed something awry about Biirkon before him. Lawr was the distrusting one by nature, not Shad. It only concerned him more that Shad might be right.

This is going to be a hassle, Lawr thought, rubbing his head.

"If you try—" Biirkon's voice right behind him startled Lawr out of his thoughts.

"What?" he asked, snappier than he'd meant to be.

"Oh, sorry. I didn't mean to startle you." Biirkon's voice shifted up slightly. He was grinning again, probably looking very friendly. "I was just saying, if you increase that offset range—" He pointed. "Then you—"

"Thanks, but if you don't mind," Lawr paused as Biirkon stepped back, giving him time to think of an actual reason. "I prefer to stick with the idea I was working on, before muddling it up with something else."

Aarkdal scoffed and started to say something about Lawr's useless ideas.

"If it doesn't work, then I'll try what you were saying," Lawr acquiesced to shut Aarkdal up. He'd been saying roughly the same thing for a while now, whenever Aarkdal mentioned it, but it always seemed to work to get the light presence to back off.

He leveled his glower at Biirkon, willing him to back off too.

"Alright," the younger presence agreed. He moved back to where Aarkdal was standing.

Lawr almost sighed out loud. He hoped Shad could get back quickly to keep distracting Biirkon.

He continued glaring at ODPAA. He didn't really have any new ideas. He'd almost been willing to let Biirkon make some suggestions before Shad's warning. He grimaced again at that.

Lawr sighed and crossed his arms, staring at the system. He hadn't spent much time recently analyzing the problem. Since he was out of ideas, that seemed to be the best option. Even the Lucians stayed uncharacteristically quiet while Lawr ran through the problem in his head.

Time passed without recognition before Lawr touched ODPAA again. He was pretty sure he had the issue sorted straight in his head, now he just had to get ODPAA to agree with him.

He made small modifications here and there, undid the few problems his last attempt had created, and then waited. Lawr was sure now that he had the configurations correct. Now he would just mess around enough to look busy as he waited for Shad to get back.

Lawr ignored a familiar twinge of guilt for his lack of trust. He did think Aarkdal, irritating as he was, was generally on their side. But Lawr didn't want to be outnumbered when he opened the file system.

An idea struck Lawr. He'd make a copy of all the files after he opened it, then lock the system again and hand it over to Biirkon to see if he'd break it. *Brilliant...* Also, potentially impossible.

Lawr chewed his lip. He assumed the AaD Shad had could connect to ODPAA to copy the files, so that was one problem down. That and distracting the Lucians were the only real problems. And he assumed Shad could do that. Being distracting was his shtick, after all. Lawr grinned to himself over that. The kid had really grown on him. He shook his head. Lawr waited, checking and double-checking his work to make sure it was correct. It seemed so. The moments crawled as he waited for Shad's return.

"Hey, hey, hey!" Shad's sing-song voice called, pulling Lawr back to reality.

"Hey Shad." Biirkon waved as the shadow moved closer. "Doing any better?"

"Doing awesome," Shad chirped. His wavering form said otherwise, but he did look a touch better than before. That would have to do.

"Making progress?" Shad asked, ever cheerful, as he approached Lawr.

Lawr grunted as he turned to the wraith and away from the Lucians. He wasn't sure what Shad's mental abilities could really do, but he assumed if Shad could talk to his mind, he could read it too. Lawr made a quick snapping motion with his fingers when he saw Shad's attention shift away from him. He ducked his gaze from the shadow and steadied himself before glancing back. When Shad's focus was back, he tapped his temple and raised an eyebrow.

Shad stiffened but nodded.

Lawr quickly thought through his plan, stressing that he'd need the AaD and the Lucians distracted for it to work. He thought through his idea as a loop, unsure of how much Shad could actually pick up.

After the second time thinking it through, Shad moved closer to Lawr then stumbled a little and almost dropped the AaD.

"Well, damn. Maybe I'm not doing as well as I thought," Shad laughed it off. "You'd better hold this though." He nonchalantly handed the device to Lawr. "If I drop it, we'd be in serious trouble." Shad smiled his innocent smile; Lawr could sense it as he grinned back.

Shad moved past him without missing a beat and parked his shadowy form between Lawr and the Lucians. "Biirkon, I think you mentioned a project Aarkdal was helping you with, I'd been meaning to ask…"

Lawr tuned out their conversation with a grin at Shad's acting as he executed the last commands to open ODPAA. It didn't work the first time and Lawr frowned.

Oh right, one more line of code.

The second time opened the holy grail.

Lawr clenched his fist close to his chest in victory. A glance toward the Lucians proved they were still distracted as he attached the AaD and started copying the files over. A small, progress bar popped up and snail crawled toward completion.

How's it coming, Lawr? Shad's stressed voice in Lawr's head almost made him jump. *Aarkdal's getting impatient. You know he really doesn't like me.*

Almost there, Lawr thought back, not sure if Shad was listening or not. *Just hurry.*

The progress bar was still less than halfway. Lawr swallowed and glanced back at the Lucians. Sneaking like this always made him twitchy, even just watching it in movies. He turned back to ODPAA. Just over halfway. He sighed.

Lawr moved around in the system, preparing to put all the security features back in place as soon as the files were copied.

A short eternity later and they finally were. Lawr disconnected the AaD and locked the system back up. He clenched his fists again to stop them from shaking with something between nervousness and excitement. Hacking was an adrenaline rush he sorely missed.

Lawr breathed out to steady himself. "Damn it," he snapped, taking a step back.

Shad spun around in surprise. *Everything okay?* His voice was thick with concern, even in his head.

Yep, Lawr thought back, trying not to let his joy at the triumph show on his face.

"Stupid, piece of shit ODPAA," Lawr continued the charade, stalking a few paces away so he wouldn't have to look at the Lucians. Lawr knew his acting skills were not great, even as he felt a smile tug at the corner of his mouth.

"Now are you going to let Biirkon try?" Aarkdal sneered with something close to triumph in his voice too.

"Go ahead." Lawr waved a hand. He was glad Aarkdal had said it first, it would have sounded much more unnatural if he had to. "Just don't break it," Lawr added, crossing his arms and hugging the AaD to his chest.

"All right, let's give this a try." Biirkon cheered as he moved toward ODPAA.

Shad came up behind Lawr, but the headache and his cheerful voice gave away his approach long before the shadow stood next to him.

Did you get everything? That's awesome. I never had a doubt! Shad cheered.

Lawr motioned for him to pipe down, even though he too couldn't help but grin. He schooled his features before turning back to the Lucians.

He moved a little closer to see what the young Lucian was doing. A moment of watching confirmed his suspicions.

What d'ya think? Shad's voice returned *Is he going to get it open?*

Lawr glanced at the shadow briefly before giving his head a small shake. He tapped his temple again to make sure Shad was listening.

No way in hell. I left it pretty near to open. What he's doing now is putting more of the security back in place. I'd guess he'll make it self-destruct in an hour—two if he's really trying to throw off suspicion.

Shad hummed. *Yeah, he seemed like a nice kid, but something's just off about him.* A moment of silence and decreased headaches followed before Shad spoke again. *Now we just wait for him to destroy it, right? Then we leave? That's a pretty good plan you came up with.*

Pretty good? Lawr raised an eyebrow as he struggled to keep his cockiness hidden from the Lucians. *I'd say it was a bloody brilliant plan. We get the info and they don't even know.*

Shad chuckled softly before his blue eyes shifted back to the Lucians. *What are we gonna do with Biirkon, though? Aarkdal's gonna be really upset. He lost his family in the last war, you know.*

Lawr looked at Shad sharply. No, he hadn't known that.

Shad nodded, more to himself than as a communication to Lawr. *He wasn't as difficult to deal with back then. Biirkon I guess... Well, Aarkdal sort of treats him like a son. This is gonna break his heart. Again.*

Lawr sighed as guilt for his dislike of Aarkdal set in. He could understand that. He thought of Ali. She was family to him, now that he didn't have his own. He swallowed and pushed those thoughts down into the dark corner where they belonged. He didn't have time to be distracted like that. Especially not when Shad was still in his head.

What are we gonna do with Biirkon? Shad asked again.

Lawr thought about it. The only real thing he could think of was that they shouldn't do anything until they got the AaD safely back to Sentre.

I agree, Shad thought. Lawr flinched. He'd forgotten Shad had been waiting for a response.

Sorry.

Shad shrugged. *I think it would be a good idea not to cause a fuss when our only copy is vulnerable.*

Lawr nodded and they returned to watching Biirkon in silence.

CHAPTER 25

Sverre strode down the lengthy and brightly lit, unadorned white halls of the complex. He replayed the explanation he'd prepared for Atanas in his head. It still didn't sound believable, even if it was true. Mostly. He clenched his jaw a little tighter. He'd still disobeyed an order. That would not go over lightly even if Atanas didn't have him killed.

The only reprieve as he reached his supervisor's door was that Leon and Alisha would still be safe. Dain would take care of them; he'd make it back from his mission to do that. A moment of weakness escaped in a sigh at the thought before he clamped his jaw together. Now was not a time he could afford to look weak.

He knocked on the heavy steel door that stood out against the rest of the over-white hallway. A faint "enter" called from the other side of the wall.

Sverre obeyed but remained wary. He scanned the room for any surprises or traps placed to test his reaction—and for Duqa. That clown was the worst kind of surprise.

The rectangle of light from the doorway illuminated the room clearly as Sverre walked in. He closed the door and the office was again thrown into shadows created by the one desk lamp that was lit. A shadow moved away from where Atanas was sitting before Sverre could recognize it. Not that he needed to. Echo was the only man Sverre knew who could move like that and be allowed in the boss's office. Atanas's silent messenger disappeared through a side exit without a sound.

Sverre stepped forward and stood stock still before the oversized desk that made the short man seated behind it look even smaller. Atanas didn't look up as Sverre entered and he continued to ignore him as he finished the paperwork he was doing. His only acknowledgment of Sverre's presence was an absent wave toward a tea tray on the corner of his desk.

Sverre snapped to obey. He poured a steaming cup of tea, added a little cream and three scoops of sugar, before carefully setting it down in front of Atanas. He hoped his former master hadn't taken to liking his tea even sweeter since his time as the man's slave.

Atanas didn't pause his work as he took the cup and sipped. He set the cup back down without a word.

At least some things don't change, Sverre noted with relief. He scanned the room again to make sure Duqa hadn't entered from the side door when he'd been preoccupied. The silence hadn't been disturbed which was the most telling sign that the clown wasn't there, but he did try and fail to sneak around sometimes. The room remained empty of other occupants.

A rustle of paper snapped Sverre's attention back to Atanas as the man straightened the papers he was working on with a compulsive hand. He set his pen down and shifted it until it was parallel with the papers before lacing his fingers together and resting them on his desk.

Atanas looked up at Sverre for the first time to acknowledge his presence. "Do you have any objections to my having you executed for your crimes right now?" he asked, waiting for the inevitable answer.

"I will accept any punishment you decide, but I have not acted in any way that would warrant death," Sverre lied through his teeth. He was convincing though. Years of practicing against Atanas payed off.

"Nothing to warrant death?" Atanas repeated. He raised an eyebrow in distaste at the notion, but Sverre could tell how much he enjoyed this. "You disobeyed a direct order. 'Kill the Median King should he refuse to assist us'. That king is still breathing, is he not? Torture is too light a punishment for such a blatant disregard for order. I told you not to let your feelings get in the way, didn't I?"

Sverre remained silent a moment after Atanas stopped speaking to make sure he was finished. "My actions were only made to better serve Oracaede."

Atanas almost scoffed at the notion. He tapped the paperwork under his hands with his pinkie fingers as he asked, "Why didn't you complete your mission, then?"

Sverre gave a long, polite nod for being allowed to state his reasons. "I observed that the shift in power of that sphaere wouldn't bring Oracaede any further benefit. However, the increasing tension between the king, the queens, and the people of Medius may be manipulated for a better result."

"Well, doesn't that just sound like a ton of bullshit?" a chipper voice spoke from the side entrance.

Sverre almost sighed. He had dared to hope he could go through this entire trial and evaluation without the clown's presence. Such naiveté. Sverre continued to stand stiff and still. He didn't glance over at Duqa.

"Sverry, didn't ya miss me?" the half-cyborg asked, skipping his words together in a sing-song way. He meandered to stand between Sverre and the desk. Way, way too close for Sverre's comfort.

"Codrin." Sverre worked to keep his voice above a growl and his face blank. If the stupid clown realized his proximity was uncomfortable, he'd probably try standing on Sverre's shoes. Sverre cursed silently at the oblivious mental case.

"And still in one piece?" Duqa turned his torso an unnatural distance around to face Atanas without moving his feet. "Ata, ya want me to see about that? I think he'd look much better without a head."

"So would you, Cod," Sverre replied quietly. "Maybe just leave that metal exoskeleton of yours in place and make a lamp out of it."

Duqa twisted back around; his one mechanical eye twisted as it refocused on Sverre. A sloppy grin spread across his face. "Sverry, you warm my metal heart." He twisted back to Atanas. "Isn't he sweet?"

"Now, now, boys. Play nice." Atanas mocked warmly, a smile tugging at his lips. His gaze latched onto Sverre and the smile disappeared. "Alvidar, the analysis from our spy in Sentre concluded that removing the new king would be the most efficient way to gain control. How was this incorrect?"

Sverre nodded and ignored Duqa who was trying to check Sverre's fingernails to see if there were any he hadn't ripped out already. Sverre curled his hand into a fist and batted Duqa away before speaking. "That was my first conclusion when I arrived there, however, upon observing the dynamics of the ruling parties, and the underlying feelings of the people." He paused as Duqa straightened up and scoffed at the word 'feelings'. The clown turned to say something to Atanas but was silenced with a glare.

Sverre continued, "The people don't believe in the king because they think he might be working with us. Killing him could raise suspicions against us. Having me, a recognizable figure of Oracaede, kill him would have made him a martyr to his people and united the queens against us."

Atanas remained silent as he considered Sverre's argument. He moved his hand to read the top of the paperwork in front of him. A moment of silence, except for Duqa's constant nosiness, passed before Atanas spoke. "If your assessment is correct, then your decision was adequate." He nodded to himself, picking up a pen and pulling out a fresh form. He began writing again. "I'll have the situation reevaluated."

Sverre nodded but made no further move.

"Can I have him now?" Duqa whined, leaning on Atanas's desk.

"Duqa, get off my desk." Atanas didn't even look up. "Sverre Alvidar, as for your punishment." He looked up as the corner of the smile returned. "Your disregard for a direct order cannot be overlooked. As such, Duqa will be in charge of your punishment. Duqa—" he turned his gaze now to the idiot clown who was hopping up and down like a giddy five-year-old. "A day should be sufficient."

"A day?" Duqa's jaw dropped, showing off his sharpened metal teeth. "Only a day?" Duqa repeated, dropping to his knees and resting his chin and hands on the edge of the desk like a begging dog.

Atanas sighed as though he was tired of Duqa's behavior. Sverre could have scoffed at the show. Duqa was the one person Atanas liked and could stand to be around for any period of time. Why that was, he'd never understand.

Duqa held up two fingers. "Two days?" he asked in an almost sweet-sounding voice.

Atanas groaned.

"You know he's been disobeying more orders, right? He always does." Duqa twisted his head to look at Sverre, as though he thought Sverre would incriminate himself with a blatant agreement. The clown was right, and they all knew it, but Sverre wasn't about to add to his own misery. He wasn't sure why Atanas continued to use torture as a means of punishing him. Other than to make Duqa happy, it didn't have any affect other than to slow him down on his next mission. And he'd still disobey orders.

Atanas grunted again but gave Duqa a nod.

"Yay!" Duqa jumped up and cheered with pure, childlike joy. "What d'ya think, what d'ya think?" he asked, bouncing back into Sverre's personal space again. "Ooh, I know. I just got this new toy. It stabs in just under your sternum and spreads it 'til we break a few ribs. What d'ya think?"

"Sure. Hand it over," Sverre said without blinking. "You'd want to christen it with your own blood first, right?"

Duqa hummed with excitement as they turned and moved toward the main door. "You still have some fingernails, I noticed. We'll get rid of those for sure. Only a few though…" Duqa said, half to himself as he tried to think of more creative ideas. He thought for a moment more before jumping at an idea. "*Oooh*, I could drill holes in the tip of all your fingers and put some claws on." Duqa wiggled his own mangled fingers with metal claws surgically attached.

Sverre held back a gag at the idea. He'd never be able to comfort Leon again—or anyone. He swallowed and spoke, addressing no one. "That would get in the way of my ability to wield a knife, possibly even fire a gun quickly."

"Duqa," Atanas called, waiting until the clown turned to him before continuing. "You know the rules. He's a valuable asset. Nothing that decreases his ability to function. No permanent damage that affects his skills."

"Ah," Duqa complained. "Sverry, when're you gonna do something worth an execution? Then I could play with you for ages." He grinned fondly at the idea.

Sverre nodded to Atanas with genuine gratitude for reminding the clown of the rules. He exited the office with Duqa bouncing around his heels as they walked to the clown's workroom.

CHAPTER 26

"Tall, dark hair, warm blue eyes—quite a catch," Stori teased, bumping Leha's arm as they walked down the busy main road through Sentre.

"We were just talking," Leha said, trying to hide her blush with a scowl.

Her attempt at discretion is sweet, Stori thought as they turned another corner.

"Oh, yes. Just talking. I'm sorry I interrupted. I'm sure that conversation could have covered many more topics," Stori continued teasing, though her slight annoyance somehow found its way into her voice. She hadn't really cared that she'd interrupted Leha entangled in a kiss with a Median soldier, just that Leha seemed intent upon denying it now.

Leha blushed a little redder. "It was just a kiss. Chess and I aren't really…" She trailed off, staring at the ground beneath her feet.

Stori dropped the topic as they reached their destination: the city's marketplace. The girls stopped as they entered the market. It was… *empty?* The few stalls that remained open only had a few items and even fewer people looking at buying.

"Wow, I expected…" Leha didn't finish the thought they both shared. *More.*

They'd expected more.

Stori had been spending all her time trying to reverse the useless and inane laws Vlasis had set in place to stomp out free trade. The empty marketplace was a sad reminder of how much she'd still have to do to make even essential trading business legal again.

The city somehow seemed darker with that realization, and not from the rain clouds that were returning from that morning. Stori remembered the few things Bry said about the economic state of Sentre when she'd first arrived. The one thing he'd stressed was that legal trade had become so difficult that the black market had become the most common way to trade goods. It had simply become a necessity for the average household to survive.

Bry had spoken in such specifics of what parts of town to avoid, and where she might find certain items, that Stori assumed he'd spent at least a few weeks sneaking out and exploring the illegal markets.

Stori suddenly wondered where the little Pyxis at her feet had come from. A few laws she remembered working to null out were about the tight trade of exotic animals between sphaeres; these were almost impossible to get around and stay within the law.

Stori swallowed.

Damn Oracaede.

She hadn't seen the results of their meddling in Sylva, but the damage their political influence had caused Medius was almost overwhelming. Their laws had completely destroyed any incentive for the ambitious to accomplish anything—at least to accomplish it legally. Average citizens had become outlaws in the mere attempt to live their lives.

Stori had worked herself into an angry fit just by thinking about it. She had long since begun regarding the Median people as her own, and she despised any harm coming to them.

"Sorry, Leha," Stori said through gritted teeth. "I think I'm going to need to get back to the castle for work." Stori turned on her heels and started marching back the direction they'd come.

"Stori, do you mind…?" Leha began speaking timidly but halted.

Stori turned, frustrated that Leha wasn't following. Didn't she notice the suffering of the people as a result of too many political leaders trying to further their own ends? Leha pulled out Stori's leather money purse and counted its contents for a short moment. "I'd like to buy a few things." She smiled almost nervously at the idea.

Stori straightened as she blinked at her friend. Leha was right, of course. They might as well support the few merchants who'd been able to keep their wares for sale in a legal way.

Stori marched back to her friend with a much gentler step. "You're right."

Stori clasped Leha's free hand tightly and started around the circular marketplace, buying some item or other at every stall.

The sun reached its highest point in the sky and started its decent before Stori and Leha finished their shopping. They even had one of the castle guards who'd accompanied them help carry some of their purchased items. When they reached the castle, Stori apologized again to Leha for cutting their trip short, though she was mostly apologizing for her own thought that Leha hadn't cared. She could kick herself for thinking so little of her friend's sense of compassion.

"It's fine, really," Leha said with a puzzled frown, as if she didn't fully understand the reason for the apology. A quick smile flashed across her face as they parted ways. "I'd have rather continued talking with Czesiek anyway."

Stori nodded, not fully listening, but paused to frown. She couldn't think of anyone they knew by that name. "Czesiek?"

"Oh, you know." Leha grinned as she walked backward down the split hallway, away from Stori. "Tall, dark hair, gorgeous blue eyes. He actually goes by Chess."

"Ah, yes." Stori laughed. "Yes, you go have another good conversation with him."

Leha beamed as she turned around and walked off to take their wares somewhere useful.

Stori shook her head. She was a little jealous of her friend, though she couldn't figure out why. Bry was a very sweet husband.

But we've never kissed.

Stori flushed at the thought and shook her head. She didn't know where that idea had come from. She shook her head and tried to block it out as quickly as possible.

Stori was so engrossed in her own thoughts that she missed the first few calls of a servant boy to her. Stori paused to glance around for the voice.

"Your Majesty, Queen Loreda… wishes for you to join her for tea in… in the Lavender Sitting Room," the boy tried to speak formally between huffing for breath.

"Thank you for the message," Stori said, pulling out a coin and placing it in the boy's hand.

He blinked at the tip. It was admittedly a bit much for the task, but she didn't have any smaller change after her shopping. The boy glanced up at her and paused.

Stori glanced down the four hallway choices at the junction where she stood. She hadn't even noticed that some of the rooms in the castle had names, much less where they were.

"If Your Majesty would like," the boy started slowly, chewing his lip as he paused to find the rest of his sentence. "I am going back to the west section of the castle. I could walk with Your Majesty to the Lavender room."

Stori smiled warmly at the boy and nodded. She could see he was lying about having to go in that direction. She would appreciate any guide she could get. She could swear the architect of this castle had been working from a maze design and she told the boy as much, though his responding laugh was more nervous and confused than entertained.

The two walked the short distance down a few hallways and up a flight of stairs before reaching the room that was, as its name indicated, pale purple and filled with fragrance from freshly cut lavender.

Stori thanked the servant boy and sent him on his way. As she thought, he went back in the direction they'd come. She took a deep breath and entered the open little room with no joy at seeing Loreda again. The older lady hadn't spoken to her, even in passing, since their short talk on the terrace. And Stori was still peeved at her for digging her nails into Bry's arm.

A mother shouldn't hurt her own son, she thought. Though most of her anger at the time had been that Bry didn't seem to think it was unusual.

"Queen Loreda, how are you?" Stori spoke formally to the woman. She wanted to escape as fast as possible and return to working on the laws.

"Oh, it's 'Queen Loreda' now?" Loreda smiled easily. "So formal. Have you been talking with Bry?"

"Yes," Stori answered the rhetorical question, her impatience finding its way into her voice.

"Yes, well. I suppose." Loreda's smile dropped a little as the comment seemed to annoy her. "I hear that is all you've been doing with the king."

Stori recoiled at the comment. "I don't think it is any of your business how I spend my time with my husband." Loreda laughed at the response. Stori gritted her teeth. Loreda's easy laugh at any topic was impossibly irritating.

"None of my business?" Loreda looked amused at the statement. "I am a queen—and he is my son." Her serene face sported an ugly expression for a moment at the word 'son', but her beauty returned as she continued. "More importantly, the lineage of the throne needs to be fulfilled. You have a duty to your people and you're cowering before it."

Loreda paused and gracefully crossed the distance to Stori to rest her hand on her shoulder. "The people will rest easy when the king has an heir. The king will rest easy with you—" She smirked and tightened her grip on Stori's shoulder. "—when you give him an heir."

Stori tried not to flinch away as the grip was starting to hurt. "Loreda," she started with a near-snap as she reached up and forcefully pulled the older woman's hand from her shoulder. "I know my duties to the Median people, and I will complete them as I see fit for the sphaere. Your meddling in this matter is not required."

Loreda's face contorted again as she listened. She didn't waste a moment after Stori finished speaking to loose her venomous tongue again.

"Child," she pronounced every sound of the word as though it was the greatest insult ever devised—and from her lips, it might as well have been. "You know nothing of your duties or how they should be completed. You're a worthless game piece for the king to discard after you've served your purpose."

Loreda grabbed both of Stori's shoulders and shook her. "Your only job is to go to the king and lift your skirts for him, you useless girl."

Stori remembered how to breathe and tried to keep her angry tears back as the lump in her throat prevented her from making a quick retort. She hated how being angry make her tearful.

Loreda's features softened after a moment of seeing Stori's tears.

"Don't... You don't understand, child," she said softly. "I'm trying to help you. Once you bare the king an heir, you won't have to stay with him. You can leave and live your life away from anyone in the Godric line."

Stori steadied herself in her anger. "Like you did. Abandoning your son and running away from your responsibilities. Bry was your child. You abandoned him."

Loreda pulled back as though she'd been struck. "Don't patronize me, Istoria. I didn't abandon my children, and I certainly didn't have any remaining duties to perform for the crown."

Stori was about to respond in anger, when she noted Loreda's words more carefully. "You didn't abandon your *children*..." The last statement became more of a question as she stared at Loreda.

Loreda's face dissolved in a second from anger to ashen. Stori thought she was going to faint.

"It's none of your business. You'd do well to forget about it and do as you're told," Loreda said, almost stumbling over the last words, as though she'd forgotten what she'd been telling Stori to do. She stepped around Stori and left the room in a manner close to fleeing.

Stori stood still for a moment before sinking to a nearby couch. She breathed out heavily as she tried to make sense of what Loreda had revealed.

Does Loreda have more children?

Stori sighed and sniffled. Tears of anger were still trying to slip down her cheeks no matter how quickly she tried to wipe them away. She breathed for a moment and thought. Stori wasn't sure she'd find any useful ideas hidden in her memory, but she also couldn't leave the room yet. Her face was always red and puffy after crying, and she was determined to get more work done with Bry today. She would just have to wait for her face to settle.

"Ah, Stori."

Stori's stomach dropped as Bry spoke from the entrance of the room. She spun away, hiding her face and trying to wipe away any tears before Bry could see.

Bry continued talking as he entered the room. "There you are, I was looking for ya. So listen, I was looking over some of the documents for those laws you were asking about today and I wondered if you could help with…" He trailed off as he approached the couch and looked up from the AaD he'd been reading from. "Stori, are you alright?" He knelt in front of her.

"I'm fine. I'm fine." Stori tried to brush away his concern. "I can help. Which laws?" She reached for the AaD, but Bry pulled it back and set it down on the floor behind him.

Stori sniffed quietly and shifted her gaze up to Bry's face. His knitted brow and attentive, concerned eyes twisted her gut with guilt. He was worried for her.

"I'm fine. It's nothing." Stori tried to make him believe it, but his features remained unconvinced.

Bry shifted his weight as he regarded her. "What happened?" he asked gently, reaching up and brushing a few upset strands of hair out of her face. Stori could see the focus in his eyes as he was trying to figure out what could have upset her.

"It's nothing, Bry, really. I just…" Stori trailed off, lost in her repetition. She didn't really want to push her problem with Loreda off on Bry. She could see from his paling skin over the weeks and the dark circles under his eyes that he had enough problems to deal with. She could only help with a few of his; he shouldn't have to take care of all of hers. Plus, a petty part of her wanted to prove Loreda wrong on her own—just to show the spiteful woman that she could.

Stori fidgeted as she tried to think of an excuse for her tears that didn't involve Loreda.

Bry sat back on his heels. "If you don't want to tell me, that's fine. You don't have to." He dropped his gaze to the floor with a look Stori might call hurt. Her gut twisted with more guilt. "I understand if it's private. But you don't have to lie to me. If it's something you don't want me to know, that's fine."

"No, it's not. It's—" Stori grabbed his hand before he could pull away further. "It's just… an issue I'd like to deal with myself. Just so I know I can. It's nothing that…" She paused as she caught his eyes again. He looked so relieved that Stori almost laughed. He was easier to read than she was.

Bry raised an eyebrow as he regarded her. "If you're sure it's fine?"

Stori nodded

"And it won't be causing you harm?"

She shook her head.

"Then I won't try to interfere," he promised.

Stori smiled. "Thank you. It really isn't an issue—I was just caught off guard." Stori wiped her face with her hand.

At least the tears have stopped.

Bry grunted and nodded before offering her a small smile. "By the way, not that I mind of course, but…" He held up his hand that she was still tightly gripping. "Am I gonna get my hand back?"

Stori blushed. She released his hand and pulled her own back to her chest as quickly as she could, mumbling an apology as she did.

Bry just cocked his head and smiled his bright smile. Stori couldn't help but grin back.

"So," Bry drew out the word as he shifted his weight onto his other leg and picked the AaD up in one fluid motion. "Do ya have to go off fightin' dragons now, or could you help me out with these damned laws first?" He winked and grinned as he spoke.

Stori nodded and smiled, sighing internally with relief. "Of course. I was just on my way to help with that, but I may need to stop by my room and clean up first. I know I must look a mess."

"Not at all, but I shan't get in your way, milady," he said grandly with another wink, opening his arm wide before shifting to a standing position and offering her a hand.

Stori laughed as she took it. Bry took her arm after he took her hand and walked with her back to her chambers. He made jokes of everything on the way until Stori realized he was trying to cheer her up. And he was succeeding.

CHAPTER 27

A few Median coins changed hands as Lawr and Shad left Lucianca. The bet on how long it would take Biirkon to cause the self-destruct ended in just an hour, according to Lawr's watch.

The pessimist always wins, Lawr told Shad.

Aarkdal and Biirkon wandered off almost as soon as the system was destroyed. Aarkdal seemed too busy nursing his ego to notice how unsurprised or upset either of the two outsiders were at the destruction.

Lawr pocketed his winnings without counting it—not that he knew how to anyway. He hadn't had the chance to sit down and work out the Median money system yet, but he figured he would whenever he had a few spare moments and maybe Shad's input.

"By the way," Shad started as they stepped into the Empty. Lawr paused and blinked against the darkness. "There won't be any doorways close to Sentre from here until tomorrow."

The Empty closed behind them.

"What?" Lawr blinked and walked in the direction Shad's voice was moving within the Empty. The wraith must have been facing the other direction, as he couldn't see the glowing eyes. He tried following where the voice had been. "So, where're we going?"

Shad made a sound somewhere between humming and groaning. "Uh, well, this is the only one I could find..." He stumbled over his words as he glanced back. Lawr could see from his widened eyes and the tilt of his head that he was trying to smile, it just wasn't working.

"Shad, you're not really eliciting any feelings of warmth or trust in your words right now."

"Oroitz. The closest doorway comes out right next to Oroitz," Shad admitted and quickly followed up with how that wouldn't be an issue. "We'll leave as quickly as possible. No issues—just a quick in-between stop."

Lawr blinked at Shad for a moment before rolling his eyes. "Would you be so kind as to remind me of my geography, since I never learned it for a different world? What's Oroitz? And where?"

Shad continued to hum-groan, and paused for a moment to answer. "You remember the fighting Bry talked about before we left? With the Nomads?"

Lawr sighed. "The battle is in Oroitz?"

"Well, not 'in', per se," Shad quickly tried to correct. "Last I checked the battlefront is a ways from the little village, but it is where all the officers have taken up residence." Shad shifted as he walked and watched Lawr for a response.

Lawr bit the inside of his lip not to sigh again. He stared at Shad's waiting eyes for a moment. He was looking like a kicked puppy again, Lawr noticed. "Alright."

Shad blinked in confusion. "Alright?"

Lawr shrugged and stepped past Shad, whose pace had slackened. "If that's where we have to go, then that's where we'll go. Just keep that AaD safe. That's the only copy of the data now."

"Oh, right." Shad caught back up again and tucked the AaD safely into the folds of his shadowy form.

The two walked in silence for a time in peace. Lawr busied himself thinking about the Empty—and the sounds in the Empty. They always seemed hushed, as though any whisper or rustle of cloth was eaten up by the blackness.

It must be the air, Lawr decided. The air seemed light. Compared to Lucianca especially, with all the "Vis" or whatever Shad called it. Lawr needed to investigate that too, he recalled.

His thoughts on the darkness around him turned inevitably inward. His role was finished. Neither Bry nor Shad would need his help anymore and he'd be sent back. Back home. The idea caught in his mind and twisted until it became morbid. He hated his home. He loved and missed Ali, the sweet-hearted girl she was, but he hated everything else. His work, his life, everything drained away his soul.

Could I even live in that world anymore? Lawr frowned at the thought of being stuck in one place; his chest felt tight. He shook his head and tried focusing on the Empty around him to escape the panic. But the beautiful Empty, void of feeling, wasn't enough to drown out the emptiness in Lawr's mind.

The long, eventless journey through the Empty neared an end as Shad slowed and brought out the AaD again. He continued walking without a word as he tried to find the exact point of exit.

The change in pace brought Lawr's attention back to the real world. It was a welcome relief to escape his thoughts.

"Based on the coordinates, we shouldn't be too close to the battle. Hopefully it hasn't moved since I last checked," Shad finished the last bit under his breath.

"Hopefully." Lawr shook his head. He'd never been that close to a battle before. He wasn't sure he wanted to be—definitely not with that valuable AaD.

Light poured into the blackness as Shad opened a doorway out. They watched the forest of the outside world with caution. The bright morning sunlight painted the trees a muddy gold. Low clouds nearly to the point of fog tainted the light, dispersing the rays filtering through the trees.

Shad poked his head out tentatively. The appearance of his head shifted to that of a wraith. He stepped out entirely as his form shifted to catch up. He grinned back at Lawr as he too stepped through to the outside world.

Lawr glanced around. The world was still and quiet. "Well?" He turned to Shad.

"Well, we don't appear to be in any immediate danger," Shad said nodding to himself as he started typing furiously on the AaD.

"Thanks, Sherlock. I couldn't see that for myself." Lawr rolled his eyes as Shad did the same.

"I'm checking, okay," Shad said as he spent a few more moments moving around on the device. "We're about ten met-reaches from the battle on our side. Lucky." Shad breathed in and looked quite triumphant.

"Uh-huh," Lawr grunted. "And do you have any conversion table for miles?"

Shad groaned and started counting on his fingers. "Err, five-ish miles, I think."

Lawr nodded. "When's the next doorway open up?"

Shad was already checking and didn't answer for a moment. He groaned again when he did. "A day."

"What?" Lawr blinked at the wraith. "Aren't there usually more?"

"Well, not really," Shad said as he started walking away from the closing Empty. "There are doorways before that, but they all lead much further away, and doorway hopping is too unpredictable to try. Beyond what we're already doing, of course."

Lawr hummed at that as he watched the forest, wary of any signs of danger. Shad messed around with the AaD settings as he walked and Lawr guided him around a few trees he wasn't paying attention to. The distance to the village wasn't far and they reached it without problems. The sounds of life were refreshing after the unsettling, natural silence of the forest. Sounds of children's laughter were especially soothing—a sign that the battle had yet to touch this place. They moved cautiously into the town. Relief met them as Shad pointed out the soldiers milling around were all Sentrian.

The officers had made themselves at home in the town. Taking up residencies in the houses where they could and tents on the side roads where they couldn't. The sight of the tents made Lawr sigh. He guessed they weren't going to have any luck finding lodgings for the night.

Not indoors at least.

The idea of sleeping outside was dismal, but options could be worse, he reminded himself.

CHAPTER 28

Ali sat again at the dining room table, spacing out as she stared out the window. Leon continued his schoolwork, unencumbered by the lack of attention or help. Not that she was that helpful anyway, as he constantly reminded her.

The boy had tried to keep his spirits up the first few days Sverre was gone. After a few days though, he'd started continually reminding Ali that time passed differently in the different sphaeres; it might only have been a day or less for Sverre. After a week had passed though, Leon grew quiet.

Ali caught him staring at the thirteen-digit number Sverre had left on the fridge for getting a hold of Dain. Both Leon and Ali convinced each other on a daily basis that they didn't need to call him yet.

Another day without their favorite albino was already half over and Ali was losing hope that Sverre would return. His absence was a hole in their existence that she couldn't ignore. Without his safe presence around, Ali started to remember that the Nomads and their Wolves operated in this sphaere.

Ali tried not to squirm at the thought.

"All done," Leon said in a tired, too cold, voice. He slid his papers across the table and slumped onto his elbows as he waited for Ali to grade the problems.

Ali finished grading and the two moved on to the next habit they'd formed over the week. Sitting out on the front porch with books they each struggled to keep their attention on while watching the sandy landscape for any signs of Sverre's return.

After some time, Ali's attention turned to the boy.

I could still take him back... She couldn't call her old apartment home now though. *This place could...* She shook her head and sighed. She wasn't sure where she'd be going back to.

Leon shifted, straining for a moment to see something on the horizon. After a moment he sunk back in disappointment and went back to staring at the book in front of him.

Ali shook her head again. *It was a stupid idea anyway.* There was no way he'd go. Even if he could give up on Sverre returning, he'd want to live with Dain, not her.

The hours passed without any disturbance across the landscape. Ali finally beckoned Leon inside as the sun set to help prepare dinner. They ate in silence. The dinner mess was cleaned up before Leon wandered off to his room while Ali cleaned up some of the mess in the house.

She heard Leon crying when she passed his room but continued on. What could she say to comfort the boy anyway? Ali never felt more like an outsider than on these nights. She'd miss Sverre but knew her loss was nothing to compare with Leon's. Her heart ached for the boy. She wished the albino would return and soon, even if only to make Leon happy again.

Night settled around the house before Ali went into Leon's room to tuck him into bed and read him the book Sverre had started before he left. The boy had since dried his tears, but his eyes were still red.

Ali said goodnight and quietly closed the door behind herself after a short struggle to do the book justice. Apparently she didn't do the voices nearly as well as Sverre, and Leon was quick and snappy to remind her. In the hallway, Ali's eyes automatically glanced toward the empty room across the hall. Sverre had left the door half open, but neither Ali nor Leon even glanced inside; just to provide a little privacy for if—*when*—the assassin returned.

Ali sighed again as she moved back to the kitchen and sat heavily at the table. She pulled out all of Leon's books and started reading over each lesson for the next day. She'd seen Sverre do this task every night and hadn't thought anything about it. Now, every time Leon scolded her for getting something wrong she remembered how much she'd forgotten. Or in the case of the history and geography of the sphaeres, had never learned.

Ali jerked her head up from where it had fallen. She rubbed her eyes. She didn't even remember when she'd fallen asleep. The creak of a door startled her. She frowned, Leon should have been asleep. Ali turned in her seat to look at the front door. A tall shadow moved with methodical slowness. Ali's stomach dropped to her feet as her thoughts skipped back to the time she was kidnapped. Ali stood carefully as her mind raced.

A trace of white caught her attention. Snowy hair poked out from under a hood.

"Sverre!" Ali whispered, almost jumping the distance across the rooms to reach the figure.

"Shh…" Sverre motioned for silence. "Is Leon asleep?" he asked in a gurgling, fading whisper.

Ali paused and frowned before answering yes. Sverre's voice sounded off. She moved closer though she still couldn't make out many details without the lights on. "Sverre, what's wrong?" Ali asked, fear flooding her as Sverre limped toward his room.

"It's nothing," Sverre said, his voice sounding more tired and faded than before. "Nothing life-threatening or that would decrease my skills… " Sverre gargled again as he coughed for a moment and tilted unsteadily. Ali moved to support some of his weight. Wherever she touched him, her hands were wet with warm liquid that smelled of copper.

Sverre moved, still able to stand mostly on his own, to his room and sank into an armchair in the corner. Ali swung the door quietly shut and locked it behind them. She didn't have to see Sverre to know Leon shouldn't see him right now if he woke up.

Ali steadied her breath and flicked the lights on before slowly turning back around. Sverre's eyes were closed as he struggled to breath. His dark clothes hid most of the blood, but light glinted off the fabric to show it was wet. Ali slowly pulled her eyes down to her own hands. They were red with his blood.

A shift in breathing from the corner brought Ali's attention up again. Sverre shifted and opened his eyes again. He regarded her with half-lidded eyes as she swallowed her nausea and moved toward him. Ali knelt in front of him and tried not to stare. "What can I do?" she asked after she thought she could trust her voice.

Sverre continued to stare for a moment. His already ashen features were a sickly shade of white and blue and his eyes were sunken. He swallowed before speaking, but that didn't stop blood from escaping his mouth when he did.

"You don't owe me anything," he croaked in a whisper. "… don't have to help me."

Ali blinked at his stubbornness but ignored him. She took one of his knives to cut through his already torn shirt and move it away from his chest to get a better look at his injuries. "My aunt was a veterinarian. I spent a lot of time with her and she taught me how to stitch and treat a few wounds," Ali justified as she cut. She left out the part that the sight of blood always made her sick and that she hadn't helped her aunt since before she died.

Pulling back Sverre's shirt, Ali pushed her arm over her mouth and coughed to bite back the bile that threatened to escape. She imagined if someone tried to preform open heart surgery with bolt-cutters, the result would have been prettier.

After taking a moment to steady herself, Ali turned back to the mangled flesh and bones. Her eyes shifted to Sverre's face as she pushed down the idea that Sverre had only made it home in time to die. She couldn't handle that thought. Leon wouldn't be able to either.

Somehow, Sverre wore a loose grin on his face as he watched her.

"What?" she asked after a moment.

His gaze was more unsettling than usual. He gave his head the barest of shakes, but the smile stayed. "Nothing. It's not as bad as it looks."

Ali doubted that.

"It…" Sverre was still trying to talk. "It didn't damage… any of the modifications that clown made to my body." The weak smile was back. "… not human enough this could kill me."

Ali turned back to his injuries to avoid looking at his smile. She didn't understand anything he'd said, but she clung to the idea that the injuries wouldn't kill him.

"Where is that box you used to bandage my head and wrists? Would it have everything we need?" Ali scanned the room as she spoke and spotted the toolbox before she'd finished her second question. She hopped up and grabbed it, heaving it back over to set it down next to the chair.

"Some towels, … warm water," Sverre said, waving a finger toward the attached bathroom before moving to fumble with the latch of the box.

Ali jumped up again and grabbed the towels. She pumped the faucet to get water and found a red tinted bowl under the sink. She filled it when the water was hot and carefully brought it back and place it on the nightstand next to the chair.

Sverre had pulled a pack of EpiPens out of the box and administered one to himself.

"Why are you taking that? Shouldn't you be taking an anesthetic?" Ali frowned and swallowed the lump that had formed in her throat. "That'll make the pain worse, won't it?"

Sverre's brow knitted together and he didn't answer for a moment. "It'll keep me awake," he said finally. "I'll need to be awake to patch this up."

Ali bit hard on her lip before nodding and kneeling in front of him again. She was relieved she wouldn't have to treat the injuries herself, but a knot turned in her stomach, reminding her of how useless she was. He'd probably had to do this alone for years. The thought of Sverre having to treat this kind of injury on his own when he'd first started as a teenager twisted her stomach further.

She swallowed her feelings as Sverre began moving again. He gave instructions for what to do but ended up doing the majority of the work himself. He mentioned the injuries she treated would need to look as though he could have done them himself, in case the clown—whoever that was Ali didn't know—took a closer look at the stitching.

It must have been early morning before Ali had finished playing the role of doctor. She sighed as she bandaged the last finger. She hadn't noticed before that Sverre had been missing most of his fingernails before he'd left. Now they'd all been ripped out and most had little holes where pins had been stabbed through.

Sverre had mentioned Duqa, the clown, as the cause of all the injuries when he'd been stitching earlier. Ali didn't know who this Duqa person was, but as she finished bandaging the last finger, she hated him. She hated the damned clown for all the injuries and scars that adorned Sverre's body.

"Well then, you're officially all patched up," Ali said lightly as she released the hand. The joke fell flat as the lump in her throat was in the way again. "Try to stay that way, 'kay?"

When the words were met with silence, Ali snapped her head up. Sverre's head was slumped against the side of the chair, but his breathing had finally steadied. Ali reached up and gently brushed a few short strands of pale hair off his face. She didn't know how he could possibly be sleeping with all the pain he must have been in. *Practice*, she guessed. The thought wasn't a comfort.

Ali stood and stretched before moving carefully to wash her hands and splash some cold water on her face. She found an empty sack under the sink and began filling it with all the bloody pieces of gauze and other used medical supplies spread out around Sverre's chair.

Next she went to the kitchen to get cleaning supplies and began wiping down the walls and floor leading all the way from the chair to the front porch.

Dawn was just breaking as Ali finally finished and collapsed on her own couch of a bed. She was asleep the second her feet left the floor.

CHAPTER 29

A clattering of dishes woke Ali with a start. She dropped her head back to the pillow after recognizing the familiar sound. A glance out the window showed the dawn was already bright from the morning sun. She stretched and settled back into bed. Leon wouldn't be up yet, so she could sleep a little longer. Something in that thought bothered her as she slipped back to sleep.

Ali jerked awake again within a moment of falling asleep. She jumped out of bed and flew to the kitchen.

Sverre was bustling about, though at a much slower pace than usual, to make breakfast. Still not slow enough, however, for someone with a hole in their chest. Ali's mind screamed the thought loud enough she was shocked Sverre didn't hear it.

He glanced back at her when she entered the room and nodded. "Good morning, Ali. Thank you for your help last night," he said before focusing again on the meal.

"Sverre!" Ali's whispered shout was enough for the man to pause again and look back at her. "What are you doing? You need to be resting," she hissed.

Sverre cocked his head to the side and looked at her as though he couldn't understand what she was saying. His small expression was one of his why-are-you-worried-about-me ones that was infuriating to Ali.

"I'm fine. Would you like some coffee?"

Ali stared at him in amazement. She couldn't believe the words "I'm fine" had just passed his lips. Ali marched across the short distance and grabbed his arm in a place she knew didn't have any injuries. "You're supposed to be resting," she growled again. Sverre raised an eyebrow in surprise.

"Go sit down," Ali ordered, pointing her free hand toward the dining area.

"You don't need to be concerned, really," Sverre said without blinking, still looking surprised at her concern. "I've had worse."

That small part in Ali that said she wasn't useful, twisted again. She ignored that part. "Sit. Down," she ordered again, pulling Sverre carefully to the dining room.

Sverre sat on one of the chairs with only a small, sharp inhale to suggest the movement pained him. He handed over the small tub of oil he'd been preparing to fry eggs in. Ali took the container, careful not to disturb his injured hand any further.

Ali walked back into the kitchen and moved to finish preparing the meal. Every move she made, watchful eyes pierced through her.

After several moments of trying to ignore the gaze, Ali finally turned back to Sverre. He was still sitting and continued staring at her with his head tilted to the side curiously.

Ali crossed her arms and waited… A moment passed without either of them moving or speaking before Sverre broke the silence. "Why are you so concerned about me?"

Ali could have guessed he was going to ask something about that. She just wished she had an answer. "I don't know what you mean. Why shouldn't I be?" Ali deflected, uncrossing her arms and tending to the meal again.

"I mean," Sverre paused a moment. "I bought you as a slave."

Ali flinched. He'd never said or done anything to remind her of that in all the time she'd been there. "Are you saying I should act more like one?" Ali snapped without looking at him.

"No, no, no. Not at all," Sverre said quickly, his voice as close to flustered as she'd heard. A rustle of motion made Ali glance back again. Sverre was standing. He steadied himself with a hand on the table. "It's just…" He continued after a pause, "Most people find me terrifying and would be glad to wish injury or death upon me." His intense soul-searching gaze locked onto hers'. "Why don't you? You have no reason not to."

Ali scoffed. Of course, she had reasons not to wish him pain. She wouldn't wish anyone pain.

"Sit down," Ali repeated in lieu of an answer. "Before you fall on your face. And ribs," she added when he didn't move.

Sverre complied without breaking his stare as he continued waiting for her response.

"I don't know," Ali said with a huff. "Why would I want you to be hurting? Then I'd have to help stitch bloody pieces of you back together... and I don't know if..." Ali broke off from the beginnings of the rant as a tear slid down her cheek.

Sverre blinked. "Are you alright? Would you like a seat?"

Ali gave a sad laugh. "You're the one injured, silly." She wiped another tear away as it threatened to fall.

He motioned for her to have a seat next to him. Ali trudged over to the table and sat. Sverre watched her with such concern in his eyes, Ali had to laugh again. "Why do you get to worry over me, and I can't worry about you?"

Sverre drew back and blinked.

The question caught him off guard, so Ali continued the line of thought. "You spend so much time trying to make sure we're safe and comfortable, and then you think it's odd when someone tries to return the favor."

"Not someone," Sverre corrected. He seemed to have gotten over his shock at the last question. "Just you." He paused before adding, "I mean, Leon, yes—and Dain, of course. I'd expect them to worry. They've known me for years, but it took time for them to learn to trust me. I understand it might be easier for you since Leon is here, but... That doesn't mean you have any need to wish me well. Much less to help me."

Ali thought about it. She had learned to trust that Sverre wouldn't harm her because Leon was around, not because she was disposed to trust a random stranger who bought her. But that didn't seem fair. She'd had to get used to him all on her own. She felt her face morph into a frown—a pout, if she was being honest.

A ghost of a smile touched Sverre's features. The small change shifted his entire look from some kind of devil to angelic. Ali had to pause a moment and blink at him. She'd never seen him smile like that, at least not directly at her.

"What?" Ali tried not to smile back.

"Nothing," Sverre said, though the smile didn't fade. "The eggs are burning."

"Oh!" Ali yelped and jumped up to run back to the pan.

The eggs were indeed burned. A laugh behind her made her smile at the mistake. She turned her pout back toward Sverre. He was gripping the shirt over his chest. Apparently laughing hadn't been a good idea, but he was still smiling.

"Don't laugh," Ali pointed out the obvious.

"I'll try not to." Sverre shifted and released his grip.

Ali started another batch of eggs and poured Sverre some coffee sludge as well as herself. They dropped the heavy topic to discuss smaller matters. Ali brought Sverre up-to-date on Leon's schooling and all the small meaningless events that had happened while he was gone.

Sverre listened attentively and made note of Leon's progress.

The small talk continued until Sverre turned his attention to the kitchen door and cocked his head, listening.

"Leon's up," he said after a moment. He stood carefully to greet the boy.

Ali strained her ears to hear something and finally caught the sound of Leon's door opening and closing. A moment later, Leon screeched and bolted into the kitchen to hug Sverre as tightly as his small frame could manage. Sverre flinched as the boy gripped his torso but returned the hug just as strongly.

"You're back, you're back!" Leon repeated, burying his head in Sverre's side. He stayed that way for a moment before jumping back. "Are you injured? Did I hurt you?"

"I'm fine," Sverre lied again as he smoothed Leon's hair, messy from sleeping.

"Yeah, right," Leon retorted, trying to check Sverre for the injuries he knew would be there. He grabbed Sverre's hand and examined the bandages with a frown.

"Leon," Sverre started, carefully kneeling. "I did receive some injuries, but they're nothing to worry about. I'm back now, and with time off to heal. I'll be fine."

Leon furrowed his brow. "Was it that stupid clown guy again?"

Sverre chuckled a little and glanced at Ali. "Yes, it was that guy."

"That bastard," Leon cursed, clenching his fists in anger.

"Hey," Sverre flicked the boy lightly in the forehead. "Watch your language."

"But—" Leon started, his small face contorting with as much rage as it could hold.

"No 'buts'," Sverre said in his firm parental voice. "You will not go starting your day foul-mouthed on account of that clown. Is that understood?"

Leon stuck out his lower lip. "Yes, sir," he finally conceded.

"Good." Sverre ruffled his hair again as he stood up. "Now, why don't you help Ali with breakfast."

Leon moved slowly at first, but quickly shifted into his exuberant self that had been absent the whole week.

The two of them finished making the meal without any more mishaps or interruptions aside from Ali telling Sverre to 'sit down and shut up' any time he tried offering his help.

The breakfast was served with care and seemed to taste better than anything they'd eaten all week, though that could have been attributed to Ali being left alone in the kitchen. A statement Leon wholeheartedly agreed was a problem.

Ali watched as Sverre coolly joked with Leon, pulling her into a few jokes as well. She sighed at the scene. She didn't know quite when these two had become her boys, but in that moment, she sent up a little prayer of thanks that they were.

CHAPTER 30

"Well, if it isn't the king's pet Shade," General Jeshua Harailt sneered.

Lawr had learned Harailt was the commanding officer in Oroitz just before he learned how much the general hated Bry as king and, by extension, Shad and himself. This hatred seemed to be shared by all the officers in the tavern they had stopped at for a meal.

"Harailt," Shad returned the cold greeting as the other officers circled around.

Lawr hadn't initially thought they'd be in danger since whatever happened here would inevitably get back to Bry, but the aggression seeping from Harailt into his men was enough to concern him. That, and the growing headache he was getting from Shad.

"I should have known the king would send you here. Meddling with military matters he knows nothing about seems to be what *His Majesty* does best after all."

"You'd better mind your tone," Shad snapped back. "Wouldn't want anyone to think you're talkin' treason."

Harailt growled. "No one's talkin' anything of the kind." He glanced around the circle of officers many of whom nodded back. "Not talkin' nothin' at all."

Lawr followed the glance. He didn't like their odds in a fight, but he noticed some of the men in the circle didn't look particularly like they wanted to start one yet either. He cleared his throat and moved from Shad's side to stand slightly in front of him, separating his friend and Harailt.

"Well, glad that's cleared up. I guess we won't be finding a meal here, so we'll just be going."

He pushed Shad around toward the door, moving to break the circle where a younger man stood who didn't look particularly eager to fight.

"Move," he ordered in his best don't-mess-with-me-boy voice.

The circle broke even as Harailt called insults after them. Shad tried to return in kind, but Lawr held his arm at an angle just twisted enough that he reconsidered.

When they were outside Shad shook off his grip. "We could have taken them—or I could have." He glared with more anger than Lawr had seen in his features before. Even when Aarkdal or anyone else was insulting him for his blood, he hadn't looked that angry.

"No, we couldn't have," Lawr stated, even if he didn't think it was true. The headache he still had suggested Shad was more than angry enough to use his powers accidentally. The half-breed could certainly have taken them, but maybe not in a way where they all lived, and certainly not in a way he'd ever forgive himself for. Shad opened his mouth to disagree.

"Not without risking something more valuable," Lawr beat the wraith to speaking.

He tapped the pocket Shad had the AaD tucked away in. It was a good excuse, even if it hadn't been his main concern. Lawr turned and started walking toward their backup option for food, an outdoor court with unappetizing, cheap food that had been set up to serve some of the less well-off officers. He waited for Shad to start walking after him.

"I hate that man," Shad snarled as he followed.

Lawr nodded. He could sense the hatred more than anything in the headache. "I can tell. Why?"

There was a moment of silence as they reached the eating area and ordered a meal. The space in the conversation continued after they'd sat down.

"I don't like most military people," Shad tried, which was an obvious lie. "They're too rule-obsessed."

Lawr raised an eyebrow and remained silent, waiting for Shad to continue.

"It's nothing," Shad tried again. "Just… Harailt really supported Queen Loreda after King Vlasis died. Neither of them wanted to return the throne to Bry. It was almost at the point of war before Loreda yielded." Shad stabbed at his food with such aggression Lawr guessed he was visualizing Harailt's face in it. "Harailt's actions against Bry bordered on treason, actually. That was why Harailt was set out here to guard what was essentially nothing until this fighting started. Bry was trying to give him a second chance by putting him in charge."

Lawr grunted. He didn't have any ideas about what the king had been thinking so he stayed silent and the conversation lagged.

They ate in silence.

"Hey, can I sit here?" A chipper voice with what could have been Australian accent startled Lawr out of his thoughts.

Lawr looked up to see a dark-skinned man standing over him. The man was grinning widely. His pleasant face was almost enough for Lawr to overlook the fact that the stranger was carrying enough weaponry to supply an army. The accessorized rifle he had slung over his back stood out against the too-many other weapons he was sporting. He rested the dominant weapon against the ground and sat without waiting for his question to be answered.

"Of course. You're welcome at our table," Shad chirped back, a firm smile set in place. He introduced himself and Lawr as the man set his own tray of food down before introducing himself as Dain. The two happy-go-luckies skipped off into lighthearted conversation, leaving Lawr to wonder if Shad had noticed the walking armory that sat down at their table. Then again, Dain hadn't batted an eye at the wisps of Shade moving through Shad's skin.

Lawr cleared his throat carefully and tapped his temple when he finally caught Shad's attention.

Are you crazy? Lawr thought as a start to their silent conversation. *The guy's packing a bazooka on his back and you just invite him to lunch.*

Well, actually, it's a high-powered sniper rifle. Shad's correction to Lawr's exaggeration was met with an eye-roll. *Look, I know in some places on Terrae you have strange rules about guns, but not here. Besides, we're in a war-zone. Anyone without some weaponry is more suspicious than not. He's probably just a mercenary or something anyway.*

A mercenary. That doesn't make me feel any better, Lawr thought. Shad just shrugged and turned back to his verbal conversation. Dain was glancing between them and seemed to be waiting for one of them to say something.

"Sorry, what'd ya say?" Shad asked.

"Oh, I just asked what you fellows were doing in this lovely village this time of year?" The stranger asked sarcastically with a grin. "Here for the battle, I suppose."

"Nope. Just bad luck passing through the area. Waiting for a doorway tomorrow," Shad explained but didn't add any more details about their trip or motivation. Lawr mentally crossed his fingers that Dain wouldn't ask further.

Luckily, it seemed to be part of the culture not to ask for more information than was freely given. Dain nodded and continued talking about something else.

Lawr noticed a large burn scar on the man's neck. It looked to be the tip of a scar that might engulf his entire torso. After Lawr noticed one, he couldn't help noticing the dozens of scars etched into the dark man's skin. He looked as though he'd lost a few too many sword fights. And possibly a fight with a brick wall too. His face had a kind of flattened and beaten appearance scarred into it.

"It'll be hard to find a room," Dain was saying as Lawr forced himself to stop staring. "Even for just a night."

"So we've found." Shad sighed. "We already checked everywhere and nothing's available."

Dain hummed a moment. "Well, if it's just for the night, you guys could stay with me. It'll be a bit crowded, but better than sleeping outside. It's started getting colder these last few nights."

"Really?" Shad practically shouted, genuinely ecstatic. "That'd be great, if you don't mind. I hate the cold."

Lawr sighed. "If it isn't inconvenient for you—" Dain shook his head, still beaming. "Then we'd really appreciate it."

"Yeah, don't worry about it. I was able to bargain for a room when I got here. It's not big, but…"

"Better than outside," Shad and Dain said in unison.

"Thanks," Lawr said, suddenly aware that these two were going to talk all night long. "By the way," Lawr began again after a short lull in the conversation. "May I ask what brought you to Oroitz?"

Dain's expression fell immediately. "Oh, just business."

Lawr opened his mouth to ask another question, but a voice in his head warned against it—Shad's voice in particular.

I wouldn't ask too much. Remember? Mercenary. Besides, it's rude, Shad scolded.

Lawr clenched his jaw and remained silent as the two started on another conversation topic. He still wasn't sure what to make of the man's character. Whatever kind of work he did, it seemed completely at odds with his lighthearted and easygoing personality. Lawr frowned.

After they finished their late lunch, Dain offered to show them around Oroitz before returning to the inn where he had a room. Lawr tried briefly to convince the others that he was tired—a true statement—but the energetic two were not to be dissuaded from making him walk around with them.

The trio finally agreed to a short walk around before returning to the inn. Lawr was content with that and spent most of the time in his own head, only half-listening to the conversation going on around him. When the sun sank low and Lawr realized how long their "short" walk was turning out to be, he pulled the two up short and forcefully requested they return to the inn for the night.

They reached the inn and Dain's room in short order. Dain apologized for the mess and started picking it up. Shad didn't bat an eye at the extension of the armory Dain was wearing, spread across every flat surface of the room. Lawr blinked and worked his jaw but remained silent.

After coming up with sleeping arrangements and clearing two human-sized spaces on the floor to sleep, the three were content to tell life stories. Dain and Shad told most of them, as Lawr added comments only enough for them to remember he was there.

Lawr had finally organized his thoughts about Dain and come to a consensus. The sheer force of the man's warm personality and genuinely caring nature made Lawr less wary of him. Now he just had to figure out how that personality was capable of his mercenary job.

CHAPTER 31

Bry pulled himself away from his desk and rubbed his eyes. All day until late in the evening had been spent working without progress. He hoped talking with Klaas and Eleanora might provide more results than the nothing he had to show for the day.

He wandered down the corridors of the castle to the quiet chambers of the Healer. His knock was quickly answered, and Eleanora gave him a hug as soon as he was inside the room.

"Goodness, you have to come visit us more often!" the older woman exclaimed as she released her tight grip. She pulled back and frowned at Bry's bloodshot eyes. "Have you been sleeping?" she asked suspiciously.

Bry forced a wary chuckle and ducked his head away from her watchful gaze. "Not really," he admitted, moving past Eleanora into the kitchen. He sat down next to where Klaas was waiting at the table. "I've been busy."

"Well," Klaas started, pushing the plate of biscuits he'd been eating toward Bry. "Do tell. Else we won't be able to help."

"First things first," Eleanora said, pulling out leftover food and setting a cold salad in front of Bry. "Eat," she ordered as she turned and added the remaining leftovers to a pan on the stove.

"El, I can eat later. I just need some advice…" Bry trailed off in response to the glare leveled at him. He turned to Klaas for help.

Klaas stared back at him for a moment before he seemed to reach a decision. "You look terrible," he stated flatly. "Eat."

Bry grumbled but obliged. He didn't realize how hungry he had been until all the leftovers had disappeared along with half the plate of biscuits.

"Okay," Eleanora said, pouring everyone a cup of tea. "Now you can tell us what the problem is." She sat down and cupped her tea in her hands as she focused again on Bry.

Bry nodded and shared the issues he was having dealing with the Nomads. He mentioned the lack of success his strategies were experiencing for the first time ever.

The older couple listened quietly until he'd finished speaking. Silence settled around them for a few moments.

"Well," Klaas broke the silence first. "I wouldn't trust Harailt. You tried giving him another chance. It sounds like that chance is finished, he failed."

"I don't trust him, of course, but he was the quickest choice to start countering the Nomads. And he is a competent General," Bry explained, the annoyance of days of overwork slipped into his voice despite his best attempts.

"If you don't trust him," Eleanora started in an unusually quiet voice. "How can you trust that he'll succeed against the Nomads?" Bry rubbed his head and sighed but didn't say anything as Eleanora continued, "Replacing Harailt with someone less competent but trustworthy might be a better option."

"And I would, if I could." Bry glanced between them. "But the problem is, I don't have a General I know enough to trust. They're all Vlasis's men."

"Yes." Klaas stroked his beard. "Most of them were Vlasis's friends, promoted because of that fact. Slim pickings, but at least you already know Harailt can't be trusted. Time to learn which of the other Generals can or can't be."

"Klaas has a point, honey," Eleanora said, giving Bry's hand a light squeeze. "I would suggest asking someone who knows the Generals for advice on who to pick."

Bry frowned as he thought for a moment. "I could ask Chesler, I guess. He seems to know everything about the castle and the people in it. He doesn't like me much though."

"Would you trust him to be loyal?" Klaas asked.

"Yes," Bry responded immediately, surprising even himself, then added, "Maybe not to me all the time, but I wouldn't doubt his loyalty to Medius and Sentre."

"Good enough. Then use his knowledge." Klaas nodded to himself.

Bry frowned to himself and nodded. "Great. Now when Shad and Lawr get back with the data we can figure out how to deal with Oracaede."

Klaas hummed and frowned. "You're not going to wait for them to get back to replace Harailt are you?"

"I was planning on it."

"Why? Will any information they bring change your mind about replacing Harailt?"

Bry furrowed his brow as he thought about it. "I guess not. Harailt still has to go."

"Then you might as well do that now. You'll probably want to do that in person, so Istoria should have as much of a heads up as possible."

"Yes, you'll have to deal with Loreda too," Eleanora added. Her lip curled in disgust at her own mention of the woman. "That horrible woman is not someone to trifle with. I'd be concerned with her presence here when you're away."

Bry nodded and pinched the bridge of his nose at the idea. "I know, but I'll have to trust Stori to deal with Loreda and the sphaere in my absence sometime or other. It might as well be now."

"Of course," Eleanora said, taking a moment to try straightening Bry's unkept flames of hair. She continued speaking after he protested by pulling away. "We'll keep an eye on both of them, don't you worry. We can keep Loreda from getting too power hungry while you're away."

"Thanks." Bry managed a grin. "I knew I'd get some solutions to these issues if I came to talk with you guys."

Eleanora nodded vehemently. "Of course, but you know you could come sooner, before you've given up beating your head against a wall. Could save you some time."

"And a wall," Klaas added, taking a sip of tea.

Bry tried to smile as he agreed before his expression darkened again. "Yeah, thanks. Sometimes I just seem to be relying too much on others. A king should be able to solve these problems on his own." Bry shook his head as his frowned darkened. "I'm not doing a very good job as king, you know."

"Posh!" Eleanora exclaimed with a snort.

"The best of kings have advisors," Klaas added. "You can't possibly plan on solving every little problem that arises while you're king. Else you won't be king long."

Bry nodded at the words. They did make sense even if he didn't completely believe them.

I should have done better.

"Alright, well." He stood up. "I guess I should call Shad, tell him the plan. I don't want him rushing to get the data since there isn't a need now."

Klaas and Eleanora nodded and hugs were exchanged as Bry left the sanctuary his surrogate parents provided. He made his way quietly back to his study, avoiding the guards as he went. Once back in his study, Bry dialed Shad's device number and waited as the line beeped trying to find the device to connect. Bry frowned at the longer connection time. Shad must have left Lucianca already.

"Shad," Bry growled to his empty study. "You were supposed to call when you left."

Finally the line connected and started ringing. A moment passed before a groggy voice answered. "What is this?"

Bry frowned at the AaD. The voice didn't sound like either Shad's or Lawr's.

"Shad?" he asked anyway.

"No." The voice drew out a yawn. "This is Dain. You're not Atanas, right?"

"No. I think I have the wrong number," Bry said, checking the number again.

It looks right.

"Wait… This isn't my AaD," the sleepy voice realized, followed by a pause. "Are you looking for Shad, or Lawr, maybe?"

Bry paused before affirming.

"Oh. Well, hold on then," the voice said, followed by the sound of someone falling off something and a yelp.

"Ouch. Oh, Shad's here," the voice mumbled.

A smack sound followed by further exclamations of calamity left Bry frowning at the device in his hands.

"Who kicked me?!" Shad's familiar voice made Bry sigh in relief. He wasn't sure what was happening on the other end of the line, but at least Shad was alive and well-ish.

"Shut up, Shad," another voice Bry recognized. Lawr didn't sound pleased as he continued to grumble, "Humans need sleep to function, unfortunately."

"Oi, Shad," the original voice started. "You've got a call from... someone. I don't know. Here."

Bry listened in silence to a moment of grumbling on the other end before he heard Shad's voice again. "What is it? Who is this? Do you have any idea what time it is? Cause I don't, it's too early. And not a time for—"

"Shad? This is Bry. Where are you?" Bry interrupted the grumbled questions.

"Bry who?" Shad's sleepy voice mumbled. "Oh, Bry!" Realization seemed to have struck. Bry rolled his eyes. "Hi! How are you?"

"Shut up!" two voices shouted in unison in from the background on Shad's side.

"Hang on, Bry," Shad muttered.

Bry sighed and waited as he listened to the rustling of Shad moving around.

"Okay, I'm in the hallway now."

"Hallway? Where are you guys?"

"Uh, Medius. Oroitz." Shad hurried to speak faster. "I was gonna call you, but I got distracted and then it was night, and... sorry."

Bry breathed out heavily. "Shad, what the hell are you doing in Oroitz? I said you didn't have to go there."

"It was the closest point to Lucianca, and I had to get out of that sphaere," Shad explained.

Bry sighed again but remained silent. He couldn't argue with Shad's health in the light sphaere. "Are you guys safe where you are?"

"Yeah. The only thing we need to be safe from here is Harailt. I hate that guy and he hates me. And he still hates you. There's a lot of hate going around here."

"Harailt?" Bry pinched the bridge of his nose. "That's what I was calling about."

"You woke me up to tell me Harailt's an asshole?"

"I'm going to replace Harailt as the leading general with someone else."

"Really? Awesome! Who?"

Bry groaned. "I don't know yet. Still figuring that bit out."

Shad grunted. "You'll have to tell me more when we get back. There's a doorway tomorrow so we should be back within a day or a few at most if the route through the Empty is longer."

"Fine. How did things go on your end?" Bry nodded as he started looking up at where the doorway would be on his AaD.

"Well... We got what we came for. One copy," Shad said vaguely. "That kid I mentioned last time we talked, Biirkon, he's not gonna be an ally."

Bry nodded to himself. "You can tell me more when you get back."

"Yep."

"Alright, talk to ya when you get back." Bry started to hang up but remembered one last thing he wanted to ask. "Wait, Shad. Still there?"

"Yeah," the reply was muffled by a yawn.

"Who answered your AaD? Dan or Bane or something?"

"Oh, Dain. Yeah, we're bunking with him for the night 'cause we couldn't find anywhere else. He's great. A mercenary or something. Fun guy though," Shad explained, his voice shifting as he shuffled about.

Bry had to roll his eyes again. "Shad, you're the only person who could make friends with mercenaries overnight."

"Hey, we were called mercenaries sometimes too, remember?" Shad laughed, "You sound like Lawr. But Dain's real nice. He's not a bad guy at all."

Bry chuckled at that. Shad was right. He did remember people calling them mercenaries more than once. "Yeah, sure."

Shad grumbled something to himself before yawning a goodnight.

Bry ended the call after returning the "goodnight" and shook his head at his friend's ease with making new friends. He started organizing some paperwork for dealing with replacing Harailt at the battlefront. His efforts hardly made a dent against the stack of papers piled on his desk before his head slipped down to rest on his arms for just a moment.

CHAPTER 32

B ry awoke groggily to someone nudging him out of a nightmare. He jerked upright and halfway to standing before he recognized Stori, looking more startled than him and backing away.

"… didn't mean to disturb you, just…"

"It's fine," he interrupted the apology.

He tightened his jaw. This was the second time she'd found him sleeping on his desk. He glanced up, reading her face to see if she was disappointed in him for it. He couldn't tell. Maybe she was good at hiding it. He looked back at the mess of papers he'd been sleeping on and straightened them out a little.

Bry returned he gaze to Stori. "Did you need something?" He grimaced as soon as he said it. It sounded annoyed.

"Oh, uh, nothing. I mean no. I just… didn't mean to disturb," Stori stumbled over her words. It must have sounded like annoyance to her too.

"Hey, it's fine. Sorry for startling you." Bry forced a smile. He waited for Stori to add to the conversation if she wanted to.

Stori remained quiet and watchful for a moment before speaking again. "I was speaking with Eleanora earlier this morning."

Bry glanced out the window with chagrin as he noticed it was already midmorning. He'd slept too long.

"She said you were going to be leaving Sentre for a while."

Bry sighed. He had wanted to tell Stori himself, but Eleanora was always quick to share news. He grimaced at that before looking back up at his wife. "Stori…" he tried to start. Other words didn't come to him. A realization that Stori was standing and waiting while he was sitting comfortably twinged a small guilty part in him.

Bry stood and motioned Stori toward the sofa on the other side of the room. He followed her over and sat down after her. Bry started again, this time giving Stori an overview of what was happening with the Nomads and Harailt.

"Look, Stori," Bry tried again after Stori remained silent for the entire explanation. "I will be leaving for a time. You'll be in charge until I return." Bry noticed Stori bite her lip to keep it from trembling, but he still hadn't finished. "And if I don't return, you're going to be the ruling queen. Trust Eleanora and Klaas, they'll help you. Don't ever trust Loreda though. She shouldn't be allowed anywhere near the throne."

Stori nodded to each point even as her fidgeting had increased, but she frowned at the mention of Loreda. "Why, do you want her away from the throne? If she had a better claim to the throne…"

"She doesn't." Bry frowned.

Why would she think that?

Stori swallowed. "But if she did…" She paused and watched him, waiting for a response.

"If she did—" Bry stressed the *if.* "Then you'd have to challenge her for it." Bry frowned. He hadn't wanted to scare her, but he could also see her preparing for another question. "Stori, if Loreda were to rule, you wouldn't be safe."

Stori stared at him and slowly closed her mouth.

"You, Shad, Klaas and Eleanora, anyone who was close to me. You'd all have to leave. It wouldn't be safe for you in Medius." Bry shook his head. "I'm sorry I don't have any better news to tell you." He focused his gaze back on her with a smile. "Hey, and this is all supposing I die, which I have every intention not to."

Stori offered a pitiful smile in return but continued to stay quiet.

Bry waited too, watching his wife and struggling with a thought. If there was any chance of Stori ruling, she needed to know about Oracaede as soon as possible. "Stori…" Bry tried to start, forcing himself not to be drawn into her attentive eyes. "Stori, Oracaede is still in operation."

Stori drew back and snapped up straight as though she'd been struck. Her big eyes blinked at Bry, as though waiting for him to tell her it was a joke.

"Wha… that can't be! Oracaede's… Ora… It's gone. It's supposed to be gone, Bry."

Bry shook his head.

"We found hints of data that says they are. Do you remember Lawr? The Terranian? I don't know if you met him while he was here."

Stori nodded.

"He found the information. He and Shad were just in Lucianca to find the rest of what they could."

Stori shook her head. "The information could be false. It doesn't—"

"Stori, do you know about Oracaede's Ghost?"

Stori blanched and went stiff. "The assassin?"

"He was here. Came to give Oracaede's congratulations for my coronation." Bry waved his hands at the idea.

"How… did you survive that?" Stori asked, surprising Bry with the concern reflecting in her eyes.

"He didn't try to kill me. I don't know why and it is troubling. Believe me, I know." Bry shook his head. The reason the assassin left him unharmed still eluded him. The only thing he could guess was that Oracaede wanted him alive, and to know they were alive too.

A moment of frowns and silence was shared before Stori broke it. "Are you not going to tell anyone? Your people?"

Bry sighed heavily. "Yes, I'll tell them. But I need proof first. Else they won't believe me. That's what Shad and Lawr are getting. Proof."

Stori nodded and straightened her dress. She startled Bry by clasping his hand with both of hers and holding his gaze with her rare, intense one. "We'll beat them. We can get rid of them completely this time."

Bry tightened his jaw to keep it from falling slack at Stori's intensity. He nodded and smiled. "Yeah, we will."

Stori gave a firm nod in return and released his hand. They sat in comfortable silence for a time before Stori excused herself to work on more of the trade regulations.

Bry escorted her back to her own study room before returning to his.

Somehow talking with Stori had made the day seem less dismal. Now he just had to deal with Harailt.

Bry sent a servant to fetch Chesler. He'd find a replacement general and get the Nomad conflict under control. He returned to his paperwork and writing up a new battle plan as he waited for Chesler to arrive. Time and Vis crawled by as Bry waited with growing impatience.

CHAPTER 33

C hesler had almost finished his report on the peoples' general
attitude toward the king when the same messenger boy that had
come by earlier that morning returned to say the king still needed
to speak with him. Chesler sighed.

*Can't the king bother people who aren't busy with whatever trifles are
bothering him?*

He tried reminding himself that this was Brynte, not Vlasis, but he
swore if Brynte ever called him for advice on feisty bedroom time with the
queen, he would stop trying to pretend the son was any different than the
father.

Chesler dragged himself up the flight of stairs and down the halls to
the king's study. He was admitted after the first knock.

"My apologies, Your Majesty," Chesler offered for his tardiness with a
stiff bow. "Urgent matters required my attention."

That isn't entirely true, Chesler thought. *But more urgent than whatever
is annoying the king today.*

Silence ensued as the king leveled a glare at Chesler. The redhead stood
and moved to lean against the front of his desk with his arms crossed.

Chesler frowned. He didn't know why the new king was always so
adamant that he was nothing like his father when he looked as though he
could have been a copy of the previous king. Chesler tightened his jaw. This
was generally the part where the king, Vlasis or Brynte, it didn't really
matter, would grow annoyed at being kept waiting.

"The matters I need to discuss with you are urgent and important. I don't appreciate your tardiness every time I have to speak with you," the king growled.

"Yes, sir." Chesler tried to keep the disinterest out of his voice. By the darkening of the king's frown, he guessed he hadn't succeeded. "I apologize, sir." Chesler waited a beat before moving along. "What assistance might I provide?"

Brynte remained glaring for a time longer before he stared pacing the same path into the floor that Vlasis always did. "The Nomads, as you know, are not being driven back as efficiently as I'd hoped they would." Brynte started with a glance to Chesler. "I believe some trouble with the leadership on the effort is slowing down the progress."

Chesler could have grinned at that. He assumed the king wasn't talking about himself, but all the reports he'd received said the men at the battlefront thought the king was the problem. From the reports Chesler received, the officers at the front hated Brynte because of his terrible strategies.

"Yes, sir, I think most of the men would agree with that." Chesler couldn't help but jeer.

Brynte squeezed his eyes closed and exhaled heavily before opening them and turning back Chesler. "I don't appreciate those insinuations either," he snapped.

Chesler, quite frankly, was surprised to find the king so self-aware. He would have to start being more tactful about insulting him. "Yes, sir."

Bry scowled. "As I was saying, problems with Harailt's leadership on the front lines are becoming more apparent."

Chesler nodded.

"As such, I'm going to Oroitz to relieve Harailt of his command. I need a suggestion for a General who could better serve Medius."

Chesler made a concerted effort to keep his mouth from falling open. "You're going to replace Harailt?" he asked. He couldn't believe the king was finally going to get rid of that man.

"Do you have any overwhelming reason he should stay?" Brynte asked rhetorically.

Chesler remained silent as the king grumbled to himself.

"I guessed not, since you didn't want Harailt to take over the battle in the first place." Bry continued musing more to himself than for Chesler to hear.

Chesler felt his stomach tighten as he stared at the king for a moment, while he tried to smooth out what must have been shock written on his face. "I didn't—" he considered his word choice. "—agree with that? I never mentioned anything to you about that."

Bry looked at him for a second before bursting out laughing. "Oh, you mentioned it to others then?"

Chesler paled by a few shades and mumbled a bit. "Not about that."

Bry had stopped laughing and glared now. "Your body language at the time said enough."

"Body language?" Chesler stared in puzzlement. "I didn't know you were skilled with..." He paused again, looking for a good word.

Bry scoffed. "Being a person? Yeah, well. Where I grew up, you have to see what people really think about you or you end up dead." He sat down with a huff and leaned over the edges of the mountain of papers, evidently looking for something.

Chesler knew this topic of conversation was closed, but he had one last question. "Are you speaking of your time in exile or the beginnings of your childhood here?"

Bry fixed his eyes on him and seemed to think about it. He brushed a few fingers over the ugly scar across his face. "Both, I guess."

Chesler nodded to himself. That made sense; Vlasis had been hell for him to deal with. He hadn't thought about how Brynte might have had to survive a wrathful father.

"Chesler?" The sound of his name brought Chesler's attention back to the current time.

Brynte was watching him expectantly with an eyebrow raised and pure annoyance etched into his face.

"Yes, sir?" Chesler furrowed his brow as he tried remembering what they'd been discussing.

"A recommendation?" Brynte's irritated expression was more pronounced now.

Chesler remained silent for a moment as he brought his brain back to the matter at hand. And the problem of it. He assumed Brynte was going to replace Harailt because the man was not useful in the position he was in now, but another idea nagged at Chesler. If Bry was planning something devious, he might not want Harailt involved. If he was looking for a disposable General, that would change his suggestion. He considered whether he wanted to risk a friend's life on the off-chance Brynte wasn't the same person as his father.

"Chesler, I'll need an answer." Brynte's tired voice disturbed Chesler's thoughts again. "The Nomads aren't going to drive themselves out."

Chesler remained silent a moment longer.

Why, oh why, does this version of the king seem so trustworthy? he asked himself. Possibly because the new king was obviously a terrible liar and as easy to read as if he had a memo of his intentions pasted to his face.

"General Markus Jair," Chesler said finally. "He is not likely to be listed as one of the active Generals for you to rely on, but he is a solid possibility."

"Why isn't he listed?" Brynte asked before Chesler could continue.

"He had a disagreement with King Vlasis and was put on a hiatus. He has been kept in disuse since," Chesler said slowly, choosing each word carefully.

"Well, a disagreement with Vlasis is always a good start. What was it about?"

Chesler hesitated. He didn't really know. Jair had been his friend since long before the incident and was anything but secretive on any matter except this one. Jair had only said very little about the issue.

"It was about you, I believe," Chesler said cautiously. "The only thing he's said on the matter was that it regarded King Vlasis's heir to the throne."

Brynte hummed a moment before frowning. "So, you know Jair personally?"

Chesler grimaced at having implied having any connection to Jair. *Damn this kid.* Vlasis had never been as sharp. When he spoke to the king in the future he was going to have to be much more on guard to make sure he didn't give any more information away than he wanted. "I know General Jair from times working with him and the previous king. I don't know him well," Chesler lied.

Sharp eyes stared directly through him and the lie. Brynte frowned and shifted his gaze with an annoyed grunt at the explanation but remained otherwise silent for a time before speaking.

"Have him called. I'd like to meet him."

Chesler sighed quietly when Brynte glanced down and started messing with the paperwork in front of him. He hoped it would be enough for the king to want to use Jair for the battles. He knew better, however, than trusting a Godric king.

He nodded and left the room without further ado. He ordered the first servant he found to fetch Jair with instructions to bring him to his office when he returned. The servant paused at the instructions to search the nearby taverns but ran off without a word about it.

Chesler paced back to his office and waited. And waited. Focusing on the papers he'd been organizing before now seemed impossible as the impending prospect of introducing Jair seemed more glaring.

The moments crawled by until a clambering sound in the hallway outside his door was followed by a heavy knock.

Markus's large form stumbled in before Chesler even bid him to enter. "Ar'demus, why you call me 'o dis damned cas'le? Eh?" Jair slurred as he collapsed heavily into one of the office chairs. He wasted no time in reminding Chesler of his hatred for Vlasis. "You know da'd bas'dard's son is here, playing king."

Chesler tried to steady his annoyance at his friend's drunken state.

Markus, the one time I need you sober.

He half-dragged the inebriated man out of his office and down the hallway to the first washroom he found. Chesler drew a bucket of cold and plunged Markus's head into it until he was conscious enough to escape.

"Ar'demus!" Markus flailed and nearly toppled Chesler over as he staggered away. "Da hell are you doing?"

"Feeling any better?" Chesler spat, throwing a towel at Markus's face.

"No!" Jair bellowed as he wiped his face. "You're waysd'en d'wo bod'lles of good spiri'ds ged'n me sober!"

Chesler scoffed. "Not sober enough."

"Da hell was 'ad for?" Markus threw the towel back and stumbled at the effort.

Chesler was glad to note his friend's eyes were a little less clouded. He glanced around the washroom quickly to make sure they were alone.

Satisfied they were, Chesler started slowly, "Listen, the king is going to replace Harailt as the commander at the front lines."

"Abou'd d'ime." Markus snorted with a near perfect show of indifference though his eyes were hungry for more news of the Median military.

"He asked me for a recommendation for a new commander." Chesler stepped up to Markus and straightened his disheveled jacket. "General Jair, when you are a bit more sober, you'll report to the king for the assignment."

Markus blinked and stared for a moment before understanding reached his mind. "Wha'd?! Why da hell d'you recommend me?" He dropped his voice after the first exclamation, looking around the washroom cautiously. His hands worked unconsciously at combing his hair down and smoothing out his jacket.

"Because the king needed a general and you need to get off the liquor," Chesler said with a snap as he moved to the door of the washroom. "We can wait a while in my office until you're a little more sober."

Jair grumbled to himself but followed Chesler obediently to the office. There they waited, going over the battle strategies that were being used against the Nomads. Chesler didn't have access to the plans that had been sent, but he showed Markus some of the things the soldiers had sent him back when they were complaining about the terrible strategies.

The new information didn't elicit any warm feeling in Markus for the new king. Chesler continually reminded him throughout the afternoon and all the way up the stairs until standing in front of the king's study to not piss the man off until he had secured the position.

Markus scoffed again, as he'd done often throughout the day and grumbled something close to "no promises". At the study door, Markus knocked with a heavy fist and waited with impatience for the king to bid them enter.

As they did, Chesler split his attention between watching Brynte for a reaction and watching his friend.

Chesler caught a grimace on Markus's face as they entered and he caught sight of Brynte. Chesler hoped Markus could ignore the distraction long enough not to anger the king. He knew it was a distraction, especially at first. How similar Brynte looked to his father, especially when they both worked with Vlasis when he was that age. The only real difference in their looks, besides the scar, were the eyes. Brynte had Loreda's green ones. Not that it made much of a difference. Loreda was horrid too.

Markus gritted his teeth and the first words out of his mouth were, "You look jus' like your fa'der when he was d'ad age."

Chesler wanted to reach up and smack his friend for his tactlessness. He glanced at Brynte for the king's reaction and hoped he didn't inherit his father's habit of making big decisions based on petty annoyances.

Brynte was grimacing now too as he again absently brushed the scar on his cheek. He stood and moved around to the front of his desk again and leaned against it. "Yes, well, I didn't choose my blood," he said, pulling his attention back to Jair. He stared at Markus for a moment with his head cocked to the side. "General Jair, I presume."

Markus grunted.

Chesler tried not to roll is eyes. "This is General Markus Jair, Your Majesty."

Brynte nodded. "Chesler tells me your skills have been in disuse stemming from a disagreement with Vlasis. Would you mind telling me the nature of this disagreement?" Brynte asked as he shifted his weight against the desk.

Jair half-chuckled, half-scoffed as he stole a glance to Chesler. "Ra'der poli'de for a king, ain'd ya?"

Brynte breathed out a chuckle. "I've only been king a short time. Spent a lot of time with soldiers though and they'll teach respect if not manners. And I was in Lux Aequor a time, too. That'll teach anyone to mind their manners."

"Yeah, da Merii are s'dicklers for proper edique'de." Markus laughed shortly.

Chesler blinked at his friend.

He likes this new king, Chesler thought.

The realization seemed odd. Chesler still hadn't decided if the king was to be trusted, but Markus was always quick to make a decision about people. Chesler frowned at that. Markus was usually right too, which irritated him to no end. It took Chesler ages of careful thought to reach a decision about a person's character.

"Abou'd da dispude wi'd your fa'der," Jair was saying. "I can'd d'ell you any'ding of id."

Chesler stared at his friend. "Markus." Of all the times for Jair to be a stubborn ass about something. He snuck a glance back to Brynte for his reaction.

The king's reaction was limited to a raised eyebrow, and an "Oh?"

Jair clenched his teeth and stood board-straight. "I was sworn 'o secrecy on da ma'dder. Res' assured, id has no relevance 'o any curren'd issues," Jair said stiffly, then they both waited for Brynte's reaction.

The king remained silent, watching Jair. "I see," he muttered, finally looking back to his desk.

Chesler would have guessed he was a little annoyed at the answer, but not angry. It was too early for Chesler to be relieved, but at least the king wasn't angry.

Brynte's attention returned to Jair. "If the matter died with my father, then I will have no issue with it." He paused and waited for Jair to nod affirmation. "Very well. Then when I go to the battlefront, I trust you'll join me to replace Harailt as the commander of this battle against the Nomads."

Jair gave a stiff nod and replied, "Of course."

Chesler tapped his foot, trying to contain his eager excitement.

Brynte nodded as he moved forward to greet Jair with a strong arm grip only a soldier would usually do—and only with an equal.

"Good, good," he muttered to himself a few times. "I'll have any appropriate paperwork completed for this change." He sighed briefly at the mention of paperwork as he turned back to his desk.

Chesler and Jair excused themselves to leave that to him.

"I dink dis calls for celebra'sions," Jair said, standing a bit straighter. Chesler was about to recommend his friend start his trip back to sobriety when Jair started naming restaurants to go to rather than taverns. Chesler smiled.

CHAPTER 34

S had yawned again as he and Lawr made their way slowly through the dark and over dense forest. They would still arrive at the doorway too early, but it was better than staying in town and running into Harailt. Dain had received a surprise call early that morning and immediately packed to leave, though Shad had no idea what for. The dark man could be cryptic when he wanted to and Shad didn't ask. He'd left before the sun was up and Shad and Lawr had to leave the inn too.

The quick breakfast outside hadn't even been warm and now the long walk through the damp forest was making Shad miserable. He yawned again, trying to wake himself. It hadn't worked the first dozen times and it didn't work this time either. Shad still wanted to curl up and sleep more.

Lawr's usual stoic self was ready to not talk. Shad frowned at the back of the older man's head. He'd come to like the older fellow—more than just being able to tolerate his presence like he did with most people. Shad enjoyed the man's quiet company. That, and he was one of so few people who didn't hold Shad's Shade side against him.

Still. Shad frowned, there were times when he'd been in the man's head and sensed some hopelessness. Some fear and panic, though over what, Shad couldn't understand. *He doesn't like being alone.* The realization was strange. *That can't be right. Lawr always wants to be left alone.* Shad frowned again at the thought. It still didn't make sense.

"You keep thinking about me and staring. You're gonna burn holes in my head," Lawr said, glancing back briefly at Shad.

Shad flashed a smile as he jumped out of his mental pondering and stepped quickly to catch back up to the man. "I don't think I could possibly stare that hard, though you could glare holes through granite. How'd you know I was thinkin' 'bout you?" Shad wondered out loud. He hoped Lawr was in enough of a mood for a conversation now that the little bit of talking had woken him up. Maybe he could coax Lawr into answering some of his questions.

Lawr gave a little scoff and looked around at Shad with narrowed eyes. He paused a moment before deciding to speak. "You were focusing hard. I can feel you in my head sometimes, when you do that."

Shad's stomach dropped to his feet. "Oh." He tried to sound his normal state of amused, though he wanted to puke. No one had ever said anything about him getting in their heads. Bry never had, but Bry usually avoided the topic for his sake, unless something was a major problem.

Maybe this isn't a big deal, Shad reasoned to himself. *Maybe it's just Lawr...or something...* That trail of thought didn't make him feel any better. He liked Lawr. He was a good friend. What if he hurt Lawr at some point? Or accidentally manipulated him? The thought terrified him as he glanced back at the man. Given it was Lawr, though, he doubted he would have said anything. Shad swallowed the thought as he focused on his feet again, as well as every thought in his head, trying to make sure none escaped.

A sharp smack to the back of his head snapped Shad's attention back to reality.

Lawr looked at him with an eyebrow raised as he lowered his hand. "Worrying isn't good for your health, you know."

"Neither is being hit over the head!" Shad yelped back. The slap didn't really hurt so much as it surprised him.

Lawr shrugged with a flash of the smirk Shad always thought meant "I know more than you" and kept walking.

Shad scoffed as he tried to think of a way to ask his questions. Nothing subtle was coming to him.

"You're still worrying about it," Lawr stated, glancing back again as he'd already walked a few paces ahead of Shad. "Ask your questions."

Shad laughed. "You sure you're not the mind reader here?" Shad increased his pace to catch up to the man who was somehow always a few steps ahead of him.

"Who said I wasn't?" Lawr smirked again.

Shad thought for a moment then shrugged before ducking his head and returning to the question stream he'd had and tried to pick a good one.

"Has it ever hurt you? When I, whatever you said, focus too hard, or whatever. I didn't know people could feel that." Shad huffed as he looked back up at Lawr. "How often do I get in your head like that?"

Lawr took a moment to think about his answer as he rubbed the graying stubble on his chin. "As I said, only when you focus hard, which, you know, doesn't happen that often." Lawr nodded with contentment at his own answer. "And no. You've never hurt me or anyone I've noticed with this."

"But, doesn't it make you uncomfortable? I mean..." Shad trailed off as he tried to think of a question. It made him uncomfortable just to think about it.

"I can feel it. Think I said that." Lawr paused his walk and cocked his head to the side, staring at Shad. "It isn't that you're manipulating me or anyone without their knowledge."

"Oh?" Shad said, mostly because he couldn't think of anything else he was so relieved. He hadn't been manipulating anyone. Shad would have hugged Lawr if he didn't think the man would dislike it.

They reached the location of the doorway well ahead of time and spent the downtime sitting and talking. Lawr checked the AaD often as he took over the job of opening the doorway. Shad figured he had to do something to thank Lawr for being honest and since a hug wouldn't be appreciated... Then again, now Lawr was focusing extra hard on accurately using the device. Shad shrugged. Somedays, with some people, there was only so much he could do. He'd have to save his questions for later.

Don't wanna annoy the man too much.

The doorway opened without issue and they continued the trek through. This leg of the journey wasn't long. At least, it didn't seem to be nearly enough time in the Empty for Lawr. Shad was excited to get back. He wanted to spar with Bry. Or anybody maybe. He just wanted to fight.

The doorway opened about seven met-reaches from Sentre, and the walking continued.

It had been a good thanks, but not a good thought, Shad considered, letting Lawr handle the AaD. Now he was hardly glancing up from it as he fidgeted with the settings. He only asked what something would do if he thought it might damage the valuable data stored in the little device. All in all, he was rather too entertained by the device to hold much of a conversation.

They arrived in Sentre in relatively good time and made their way through the war-prepping crowds and up through the castle. They looked around in awe at all the preparation taking place.

"I thought he was just going to replace Harailt," Shad growled as they made their way up toward Bry's study. "Is he planning on replacing him with himself?"

Lawr was trailing after him, but Shad could still sense him grinning with some offbeat amusement about the whole thing.

They marched straight to the study and Shad barged in without bothering to knock. "Bry, why are you going off to battle without telling me?" He started speaking again before looking inside, then halted.

Bry, the Castle Manager—Shad forgot his name—and another man Shad didn't recognize all turned to face him at the intrusion.

"Pardon me a moment, gentlemen," Bry said as he walked to Shad and dragged him out of the room to his own bed chambers. Lawr followed without bothering to hide his amusement

"Oh, sorry," Shad called over his shoulder to the other men.

Bry closed the door as they stood in the bedroom and pinched the bridge of his nose. Shad could tell he was trying to decide between scolding Shad for his rudeness and welcoming him back.

"Shad, I'm relieved you're back. Safe and sound by the look of it. But there's a thing called knocking, you know."

"I said sorry," Shad teased as he tucked his concern behind a grin. "Didn't mean to interrupt your top-secret war meeting." He winked and flashed a wider grin as he heard Lawr trying to smother his snickering.

Bry scoffed and rubbed his head. "War meeting? That is Chesler and General Jair." He glanced around his room to make sure they were alone and spoke in a low voice. "General Jair will be replacing Harailt in Oroitz. I'm going to go personally to check the state of things there and determine how the men are faring."

"You're replacing that general." Lawr blinked. "Why?"

Oops, Shad had forgotten to mention that to him.

"Other than because he's an ass?"

"I don't believe he's loyal to Sentre or to myself," Bry said, ignoring Shad.

"I could have told you that," Shad grumbled again. This time he earned a glare from Bry.

"Anyway." Bry moved toward the door of his study. "I was just finalizing some plans and officially putting General Jair in charge—on paper, at least. Want to join?" Bry asked as he paused before opening the door.

"'Course," Shad chirped. Lawr nodded and they both followed Bry back to the other room.

"Gentlemen," Bry said. "This is my friend Shad." He turned to Shad sharply with something close to a sheepish look before he continued speaking. "He'll be coming with me to Oroitz?" Bry's voice lifted at the end, making it a question.

He forgot to ask a moment ago. Shad laughed at that.

"'Course I will be." He nodded to Bry and watched the relief settle onto his face. Bry nodded back in thanks before turning to Lawr. "And this is Lawr from Terrae. He's acting as a technical advisor and is helping with a few issues."

"Sir," Chesler started. The frown lines on his face twisted as he failed to hide his annoyance. "I believe it would be best if only the most necessary members of the court accompanied you to Oroitz."

Shad had to stifle a laugh. "Oh, I'm not a member of the court. I'm…" He glanced at Bry and cocked his head as he tried thinking of a good excuse. "His bodyguard. Of sorts."

Bry raised an eyebrow but said nothing.

"Bodyguard." The word dripped out of Chesler's mouth with more disdain than Shad would have thought possible.

"Yep!" Shad chirped with his best smile in place.

"I had been planning on assigning a personal guard to the king myself."

"And now you don't have to," Shad said, keeping the grin in place.

He didn't like this man. The twist in Bry's face said he didn't like him either. In fact, Bry looked to be getting rather annoyed at this conversation.

Predictable as always.

Chesler's expression finally twisted into something comparable to a smile. "Alright then. If you are to be protecting our king, I'll want to test your skills first."

Shad almost jumped at the chance for a good fight.

Bry, however, had reached his limit with this topic. He stepped in with a snarl. "If we're gonna talk about who gets to protect who, why don't you test my skills first?"

Chesler's grin dropped back to a frown at the proposal. He looked as though it was the worst idea imaginable. "Very well." He managed a growl just loud enough to be heard.

Shad had to cough his laughter into his sleeve as he watched his peeved friend. Lawr tapped his shoulder and leveled a questioning frown at him.

Shad tapped his own temple briefly to let Lawr know he was going to be talking to him.

When we were in exile, Bry and I would take jobs as bodyguards ourselves. And believe me, anyone trying to protect him in battle would just be getting in his way.

Shad listened a moment to the chaos of thoughts and ideas he was always surprised Lawr didn't get lost in before he found a question directed to him.

Doesn't that come with being king?

Shad shrugged and crossed his arms. *Maybe, but Bry's still new to the idea of being king. All this mollycoddling is stifling compared to how we used to work.*

Shad turned back to Bry and Chesler and the new general who had remained quiet for the entire exchange. He was watching Shad with something—not quite suspicion—but close to it. Shad gave him a smile and a small wave without uncrossing his arms. The general frowned back and shifted his gaze.

CHAPTER 35

"I wish Sverre was here," Duqa moaned as he watched the scene in front of him. "He's *so* much more fun than Dain." The darker skinned man didn't even look away from his enlivened conversation with the Avare chief to glare at Duqa.

Duqa pouted. He plopped his head on his hand and sat watching a conversation that was only as interesting as Dain's exaggerated gestures since they were speaking the desert people's language.

Or languages, Duqa thought. Sverre and Dain always said that the Nomads slung multiple languages together. It all sounded like gibberish choked over dust to him. And either way, the gestures were becoming more infrequent and less dramatic. Duqa guessed the conversation was coming to an end.

Duqa's gaze slipped over to the chief's wife, the second in command of the tribe. She was sitting back on her own mat, watching the interaction with shrewd eyes. Duqa thought she could have been pretty at one point; if it wasn't for an oversized nose that had been broken at least a few times. That and the sneer that encompassed her face gave her an ugly look.

Duqa smirked at an idea. He could fix her face. She just needed her nose taken off and readjusted. He could do that. Then she wouldn't be sneering either. Duqa clapped his hands at the happy thought.

The sound drew a glare from Dain for just a moment before he went back to ignoring him. Duqa pouted.

Oh right. Dain had repeatedly told him not to mess with the chief's wife, whatever her name was. Duqa had been all set to ignore him just to see what would happen, but Dain cheated and called Atanas. Even Ata said not to fool around.

"Ugh," Duqa grumbled to himself as he stood and moved outside to search for other entertainment.

Ata had only said he couldn't mess with the chief or his wife. Everyone else was fair game. Duqa exited the tent and looked around for something to play with. He'd hoped to find one of their Wolves on this little expedition. Those boys would probably be a lot of fun.

Not a Wolf in sight.

Duqa turned toward a pair of children playing in the dusty street. He watched the young boy try to convince an older girl to wrestle with him, pushing her around. The boy was getting what he wanted as the girl started shoving him back.

Duqa's attention moved to the boy's hands.

His fingers are too perfect, was the conclusion he came to.

He watched the perfect little hands ball into fists as Duqa absently rubbed his own knotted hands. His fingers had been broken too many times before he'd attached the claws to his hands. The extra hardness under the skin where bones were replaced with metal reminded him that he couldn't even break his own hands anymore. That was annoying.

Damn that boy, Duqa thought in a litany as the child's fingers started bothering him more.

"You need to learn," Duqa hissed as he lunged and grabbed the startled boy by the arm. He twisted as the boy yelped and kicked at him.

"You know you need to learn!" Duqa repeated, kneeling as he wrenched the boy's arm to force him to his knees too. "You only learn to appreciate things once you lose them." He reached and grabbed two of the boy's fingers and snapped them back in a sharp motion.

The boy screamed and Duqa laughed at the pitiful sound. He grabbed two more fingers after his laughter died down and twisted, more slowly this time, and watched the boy's wide eyes as one of the fingers snapped. More screaming. He twisted harder.

A hand grabbed his wrist before the second finger broke.

"Oh, come on," Duqa moaned. He was so close but couldn't quite break the finger with the hand stopping him. He shifted his gaze up the arm to the face of the chief's wife. "Nomad," He started, "You really don't understan—"

His arm was jerked to an odd angle with a snap and the handle of a dagger smashed into his face.

The blow was enough to push him back. His grip on the boy slackened enough for the brat to wiggle away and disappear into the crowded street. Duqa griped at that as the hand released him.

"Aw, come on." Duqa stood and wiped his good hand across his face to find liquid there. *Blood?* He sniffed. The blood was getting on his shirt.

He wiped away more blood as he turned to the warrior woman. Her face was contorted in a vicious snarl. It seemed to be upsetting her that the injuries she'd given him were causing no pain. Duqa couldn't help but laugh at her anger and confusion as he twisted his arm back into place.

"Good effort," he teased, grinning wider as her countenance became more enraged. "Why don't you try again?"

The words were barely out of his mouth before her elbow smashed against his face and another blow he hardly registered moved his leg sideways. Duqa laughed as the force made him stagger back. He glanced down to see she'd kicked his knee to a wrong angle. It did feel a little odd and tingly, but nothing to bat an eye at. Probably something broken he'd have to fix. The biggest problem was his nose bleeding all over his shirt again. This was one of his good shirts.

Looking back up at the woman, the grin on Duqa's face grew. She was staring with a completely stunned look on her ugly face. The last blow would indeed have taken down most opponents. Most normal ones anyway. Duqa smirked. He wasn't even close to normal. He just wished she'd tried to kick his other knee. The metal in that one would have broken her foot.

Duqa started to jeer at her again when a shadow moved between them. Dain stepped up to the woman and started speaking in English.

"Reb, forgive him—though I'd love nothing more than to see you kick his ass." Dain paused and glanced back at Duqa with a smirk. "Unfortunately, Oracaede and Atanas will not look so leniently on you damaging their asset."

The woman, Reb, snarled again, "Thing's not natural."

"Not by a long shot," Dain agreed with his characteristic smile.

They both watched as Duqa made a show of testing his weight on the broken knee. He shrugged and walked a few steps before turning to the dark man.

"Dain, you always ruin my fun. I'll kill you for that one day," Duqa promised. The grin widened at the thought as he cocked his head to the side. One of these days, whenever Atanas said they weren't needed anymore, he was going to have so much fun killing Dain and especially Sverre. The thought warmed his mechanical heart.

Dain laughed off the promise as he turned back to the woman. "Don't mind him, Reb," he said as the woman looked like she was ready to start the fight over again. "As you said, he's not a natural being."

Dain nodded with respect toward Reb and the chief—Duqa hadn't noticed he'd joined them outside—before turning on his heels and walking off passed Duqa. He gave a sharp gesture for Duqa to follow him. Duqa stuck out his lip and considered what might happen if he didn't listen to the man. He looked down at the odd bend of his leg. Probably nothing good to come of disobedience. Dain would just drag him away anyway.

Duqa threw one last smirk to Reb before hobbling after the sniper. It wouldn't have been so difficult to walk if the leg wasn't stuck at such an odd angle. He hopped on one foot and tried straightening his leg out as he followed Dain's weaving path through the market.

Duqa limped at a faster pace to catch up to Dain. The gunman's grin never faltered as he growled, "Why must you antagonize the locals?"

"It was just a bit of fun." Duqa nodded to himself as he watched for Dain's reaction. "Besides, the boy needed his hands fixed."

Dain's expression darkened for a moment before being hidden once again.

He should really work on that soft spot he has for kids, Duqa thought as a grin spread over his face. Dain was even worse than Sverre.

Unfortunately for Duqa's amusement, Dain was quick to change the topic. "They completed the job on time for once. Ahead of schedule even, but they conveniently forgot Atanas wanted the girl when they saw she could be worth a pretty bit of gold. They sold her right after they kidnapped her."

Duqa hummed. This was boring compared to messing with Dain. Or even being able to mess with the girl—the only reason he'd come on this stupid little side job.

"Anyway," Dain continued after a moment of pause.

Duqa realized he'd been waiting for him to comment.

Too late now.

"The chief pointed me to the seller, so we could at least find out who bought her. Maybe that would be enough to track her down, if Atanas wants her that badly."

Duqa heard the stress on the "if". Dain was looking at him again, waiting for him to answer the question.

"Eh, probably not. Ata just wanted some leverage over the hacker. She wasn't that important."

Dain hummed a response as they made their way across the marketplace. Duqa followed as the sniper led them into a large tent filled with tables stacked with gold and other coin, guarded by suspicious, angry traders. Each of the traders had a bodyguard, all armed to the teeth to make sure not a single coin went missing.

Duqa wanted to steal a coin. Just to see what might happen.

"Hey." Dain leveled an impressive glare, something Duqa didn't think the jolly fellow capable of. "Don't even think it."

Duqa made a show of gasping. "How'd you know?"

"You have *stupid idea* written all over your face. And I'm telling you, we need to get out of here alive and you have to report back to Atanas. Do you think he's gonna be happy with the state you're already in?"

A pout formed on Duqa's lips. No, Atanas wasn't going to be thrilled with the state of his leg. He gave a slight nod and Dain backed off.

Dain moved to the center of the tent and glanced around at the traders until he seemed to find what he was looking for. A burly man with tanned skin and beady eyes watched their approach with a growing scowl. The man's hand slipped under the table and rested out of view. Duqa was guessing on the handle of a gun, but he couldn't rule out that the man might be a knife fighter.

Dain quickly started speaking in the Nomad's tongue with the man in his calm, energetic manner. After a moment the tenseness of the trader's shoulders loosened; this was helped by a few coins slipped his direction. After a few moments of talking, and an almost shocked expression Duqa couldn't tell if he'd imagined on Dain's face, they were leaving again. Dain was silent until they were outside and walking.

"Well, that was a dead end. The fellow was nondescript. Dark hair, tanned. The trader thought he might have been from another tribe," Dain said as he weaved through the marketplace, heading toward the stables.

"Case closed." Duqa shrugged.

He would be happy to get back and away from these nasty people. The Avare weren't even on his list of favorite people to torment.

Dain grunted as they reached their animals and untied them. "As much fun as it never is working with you, Duq." Dain gave him a pointed look as he mounted his horse. "Adios, diablo."

"Yeah, yeah. Same to you." Duqa waved flippantly as the gunman rode off. Not that he understood what Dain said at the end.

Dain and all his stupid languages.

Sverre and sometimes even Atanas rubbed it in his face that he couldn't speak anything besides English.

Duqa mounted up and rode off in the opposite direction, homeward at last.

CHAPTER 36

D ain turned at the edge of the marketplace and moved until he
could see the clown leave the mess of tents, well on his merry
way. He turned back into the marketplace and tied up his horse
again. He moved back to the large tent the traders still sat in. The trader,
Kajirn, was even less happy to see him than the first time. Again, a few coins
had to be exchanged before the burly man would listen.

Even more coins were passed as Dain gave the nondescript description
of the buyer that Kajirn should give anyone who asked. He had never been
so thoroughly glad Duqa refused to learn the mess of languages the Nomads
spoke. Otherwise, he might have understood when Kajirn described the
buyer as a devil, clad in black, with white hair and red eyes.

Dain left the tent and returned to the stables as he checked his AaD
for the quickest route to Sverre's house. He mounted up and headed off in
the new direction.

Outside the market, the route was fast, and Dain was through the
Empty before the sun was at its full height in the sky. The few met-reaches
until he reached Sverre's house flew by in an easy gallop. Dain slowed as he
approached the house and dismounted in a smooth motion, keeping his
hands visible until Sverre moved out from the house to approach him.

"Dain, I wasn't expecting a visit from you," Sverre said in his cold tone
as he glanced around, ever cautious.

"No trouble," Dain stated, alleviating Sverre's initial concerns. "Just
needed to talk to ya bout somethin'."

Leon shot out the door before Dain finished speaking. The boy charged into Dain with enough force to drive him back a step at the hug. A laugh escaped Dain along with most of the air in his lungs.

"Man, you're getting strong kid!" Dain laughed as he returned the bear hug. "Seriously, what's he been feeding you?"

"Vegetables!" Leon answered, squirming out of Dain's grip. His bright-eyed face stared up at Dain. "Are you gonna stay awhile?"

"Well, I don't have another job right now." Dain ruffled the boy's hair before he had a chance to move away.

The front door opened, and a young lady stepped onto the porch. She looked for a reassuring sign from Sverre before moving forward toward their little group.

"Though I think Sverre's given my room away." Dain smiled at the woman. "Dara's niece, I presume."

The girl stopped and glanced between Dain and Sverre in confusion.

"Atanas?" Sverre asked with calm caution.

Dain shook his head quickly to disperse that scary thought. He switched his gaze back to the girl. No, if Atanas had any idea Sverre was hiding her... Dain shook his head again and looked back to his friend.

"No, he doesn't know. He just sent Duqa and me to find her in the Aynur's marketplace."

Sverre nodded. "I didn't pay that trader enough, did I?"

"Kajirn? No. I gave him a good bit extra this time to make sure he gets his story straight."

Sverre nodded and motioned the adults toward the house and Leon to take care of Dain's horse. The boy grumbled but just moved quicker to get inside faster.

Dain could feel Sverre's weighted gaze, a silent message that they would continue this discussion later. Sverre was probably going try to pay him back. He was rather particular about owing people. Not that this was fair; Dain already owed the albino more than he could ever pay.

"Will they come back for me?" the girl's soft voice interrupted Dain's thoughts.

"Nope," Dain replied with intentional confidence. "I sent them off searching in another direction in case they try again, but they didn't need to get you that badly. I don't think they're gonna be trying again."

The girl looked relieved, and Sverre did too.

Hmm. Dain almost chuckled at the observation.

"So, Miss…?"

"Ali," the girl said after a moment of hesitation.

Dain had to smile.

She's cute.

"Miss Ali, that's a lovely name." Dain gave the back of her hand a kiss and her eyebrows shot up in surprise. "I'm Dain. It's lovely to meet you—even if you have kicked me out of my room here."

"Oh, I'm sorry." Ali looked flustered as she glanced between Sverre and Dain. "I could sleep on the couch."

"No, Dain can sleep on the couch," Sverre said flatly as Leon came back inside.

"He's staying!" Leon jumped as Sverre grimaced and grumbled something about too many kids in the house already before he waved them all toward the kitchen.

Dain cheered with Leon at his staying over and getting a meal right away. Ali snickered and followed the group into the kitchen. The lunch progressed from the cooking stage, where no one except Sverre did anything helpful, all the way to placing the food on the table, the point which everyone helped. The group gave thanks for their little blessings before Dain and Leon inhaled their food while Ali and Sverre mocked and ate with infuriating slowness. Dain laughed until the meal was over and Leon was excused for more solemn discussions to start.

Sverre remained silent and motioned for Dain to do the same as he waited for Ali to ask whatever had started to bother her during the latter half of the meal.

"So—um—Dain, you…" Ali tried to start. She muttered to herself a moment before finally spitting out her question. "How did you start working for Oracaede?"

Her question surprised Dain. He thought she'd want to know more about what Atanas wanted with her, but she looked concerned for him. Dain glanced at Sverre who gave a brief one shoulder twitch in place of a shrug.

"Well," Dain started, drawing out the word in his sing-song voice as he gathered his thoughts back to the question. "I'd just been discharged from my post in the Australian military when I accidentally crossed worlds to Sylva. Talk about a shock."

"You're from Earth?" Ali sat up a little.

Dain almost laughed at the look on her face. "Yep, born and raised Terranian." He nudged Sverre. "Always wanted to say that." He turned his attention back to Ali. "Yeah, I was Australian Special Operations Force. Two tours."

"I didn't know you could cross between worlds on accident and without an AaD I'm assuming?" Ali glanced at Sverre as if asking a question.

Dain almost had to smile. Sverre never thought he was good with people, but he seemed to have built quite a rapport with the lady. And Ali... Dain could see the trust in her eyes whenever she glanced at Sverre. Most people needed to be around the albino for a long time before they learned to trust him. Dain included himself in that category.

Sverre nodded. "It's not common for the Empty to open a doorway by itself, especially in a world with low Vis, but it can happen. The AaDs were made to alter when that naturally occurs."

Ali hummed and turned back to Dain, waiting for him to continue. Dain pocketed his smile at his joke and obliged. "So, I came to Sylva and was really lucky to meet Ercilia, my wife now." Dain glanced at Sverre to make sure Ali knew he was married already. He received another solemn nod.

Ali tried to smile her little smile, but it was slipping now. Sverre must have explained a few things about this to her, Dain realized. He continued after the short pause.

"Yeah, Erc really saved my life then. We started a family, then Oracaede started to gain more power. My military skills were noted, and they wanted to put them to use. Luckily, Sverre was the one sent to fetch me. Him and his big 'ol heart helped me out. Protected my family." Dain managed to wrap an arm around the albino and give him a half-hug before the solemn one could extricate himself. Dain laughed at it. He wasn't sure even now that Sverre understood how much his kindness and sacrifice for a stranger meant.

He looked up and met Ali's eyes.

She understands—or is starting to.

Ali gave a half-nod and dropped her eyes, almost as if to acknowledge how much Sverre had risked for her as well.

"Don't hug me. You're hurting my ribs," Sverre grumbled, though his face betrayed that he didn't mind.

"Oh yeah, your ribs. Damn man, I forgot." Dain gulped.

He had forgotten Sverre had recently spent too much time with Duqa. He wished for the umpteenth time that his friend was less good at hiding when he was hurt. He didn't even know how bad the damage was.

"Man, if you're hurting, you gotta say something. Let me see how bad it is." Dain started to shift so they could go to Sverre's room. He knew Sverre wouldn't want to show his injuries around Ali, or especially when Leon might return.

"No. I'm fine. It is already patched up." Sverre grumbled and sank further into his seat. "Ali helped."

Dain turned to Ali and must not have kept the shocked look off his face based on the way she pulled back.

But Sverre never likes to look weak. That was how Atanas had raised him. He couldn't imagine he'd have let her help.

"He wasn't in any condition to do that all by himself," Ali defended.

"No, it's good! I'm just… surprised he let you help. He wouldn't, usually," Dain tried to explain.

"He wasn't really in a condition to stop me." Ali frowned as her gaze shifted to Sverre's chest.

Dain blinked. "Sverre?"

"It wasn't that bad."

"You had a hole in your chest!" Ali's eyes were suddenly glistening with tears—angry tears.

Dain stood up so fast he knocked his chair over. "Sverre. Your room. Now." He glared at the younger man, mentally daring him to say something about it. Why did his little buddy have to be so damn stubborn? Dain was almost shaking with rage over it. Why hadn't Sverre called him if he'd been that injured? He should have known to trust him.

"It's not—"

"Get up!" Dain snapped. "We're going to your room. I'll decide if it's 'not that bad'. You'll shut up. Sverre, why the hell can't you ever just ask for help?"

Sverre stared up at him and for an instant, Dain recognized the look of a scared kid waiting to be hit. The look vanished, replaced by indifference, but not fast enough for Dain to miss it. It was a punch to the gut and Dain tried to reel in his anger, even if it was too late. Sverre was always sensitive in recognizing anger. He was even quicker to assume it was directed at him.

Sverre remained silent as he shifted to stand. His gaze moved back to Ali. "I apologize for interrupting the conversation like this."

"You don't have to apologize." Ali's voice was hurt too.

Dain spared a glance at her to see the concern reflecting in her eyes.

Sverre nodded and trudged off to his room. Dain followed close behind until he could close the door after himself. Sverre obediently shrugged off his shirt without having to be told. His unusual passivity had Dain wanting to kick himself for letting his friend see his anger. He'd prefer to kick Atanas, though.

That damned man. He doesn't know how to treat adults. He had no business raising a kid.

Dain removed the bandaging and studied the tidy mess of skin pulled over stapled bone. "She did a good job, at least," Dain grunted as he gently poked at one area and prodded another. "Though I assume you did most of it."

Sverre nodded again. "She did help quite a bit. It surprised me."

"Of course it did. Any act close to kindness always knocks you right off your feet," Dain muttered. His hatred for Atanas resurfaced, but he fought to keep it under control before Sverre noticed.

Sverre remained silent and passive, only squirming a little as Dain, satisfied with the stitching and stapling, began to re-bandage the wound. Dain became aware he was frowning after Sverre's gaze flitted past his face twice without landing in his usual sullen stare.

"I'm not angry at you, Sverre," Dain stated.

He watched red eyes flit over his face again. Judging him for honesty. The albino found enough to say something.

"I was going to let you examine the wound, of course. Just not at lunch when you're just meeting Ali. It would be at an incon—"

"Don't you dare say inconvenient." Dain leveled a finger at Sverre. Red eyes blinked at him. "—inconvenient time."

Dain sighed. "It's not inconvenient to attend to an injury."

"It was already treated."

"You should have called me." Dain leveled his gaze at the younger man.

Sverre blinked then ducked his head. "I figured you would already be here." He chewed his lip as though trying to taste the words before he spoke them. "I had been gone a week in Glacius's time. I thought they would have called you already."

Dain snorted. It was the only response for that kind of thought. "Leon give up on you after only a week? You're kidding me, right."

The albino grumbled at that.

Silence settled as Dain finished bandaging. He put the supplies away and bagged up the bloody, used bandages as Sverre carefully pulled his shirt back on. They moved back to the dining room without another word.

Ali was still there, waiting. Leon had come back in and she had ensnared the boy into helping finish the dishes.

"Sorry for the interruption," Dain said with a bright smile as they entered the room. Ali turned and searched both their faces for reassurance that all was well. She must have found enough in Sverre's for her to relax and smile. Conversations continued with care not to worry Leon as the afternoon progressed.

CHAPTER 37

Chesler moved with grace and care to let his sword be knocked from his hand. Years of practice with Vlasis made the charade of throwing the match easy with Brynte. The old king couldn't take a loss and usually became petty with beheadings after one. Chesler carried through the same motions with the son. He could tell Brynte was good. He just didn't care to see how good at this time. After all, he'd only wanted to test the wraith's skills. And the sooner he could test if the half-breed was capable of protecting the king, the sooner he could move on to other problems.

"Good match, sir," Chesler said, offering his arm to shake.

The king snarled and slapped his hand away. "Don't mock me!" he snapped, attempting to glare holes through Chesler's skull.

Chesler blinked a moment at the sour winner.

Great, he thought trying to keep his eyes from rolling. Now he was going to have to put more effort into letting the king win.

Light clapping at the edge of the sparring ring pulled both of their attentions away from each other. The damned wraith was smiling as brightly as ever. "Fun match, eh?" The cheery voice didn't help Chesler's mood, but it seemed to help Brynte's. "May I request the next one, Your Majesty?"

The verbal salute was offered with such sarcasm, Chesler had to cough back a laugh. He almost missed the mock bow that went with it as the wraith hopped into the ring without waiting for an invitation

"Shad, ready to go a round?" Brynte's anger had dissipated as soon as the wraith spoke.

Shadric pulled a pair of twin Moro blades out of hidden folds of his clothes and shadows.

"Thank you for the match," Brynte nearly spat the words with no patience for Chesler to get out of the ring.

Chesler obliged with a small bow that was ignored. He paced to the fence around the ring and was careful to climb over without catching his cloths. He stood next to Markus and a distance from the king's new friend, Lawrence Dara. He watched carefully as the pair moved to the center of the ring and took up fighting stances. The wraith, at least, looked competent standing still. Chesler hoped he would be at least somewhat useful. Trying to keep another bodyguard near the obstinate king would be an irritation.

A moment of complete silence passed over the ring. It was gone in an instant. Brynte attacked first—and was blocked. One of Shadric's blades descended toward the king's head. It was blocked with a dagger that had materialized in the king's hand.

Brynte pushed the blades back and kicked the wraith in the midsection before moving to attack. Strike after calculated strike were blocked by the wraith until he was pushed into a corner.

The match ended as suddenly as it had started with the king's blade stopping a moment short of taking the shadow's head off. Both combatants straightened and latched hands in a one-armed hug.

"N'other round?" the wraith asked hopefully, apparently less unnerved by his near-death than Chesler was.

He didn't particularly care for the wraith, but this was insane. The thought that Brynte had been going easy on him in their match unnerved Chesler even more.

"You never quit, do you?" Brynte laughed and returned to a fighting stance.

Shadric laughed as he followed suit. "Course not."

He lunged into the first strike.

A flurry of motion held the attention of the onlookers as the match started and Brynte sent both Moro blades flying along with his own dagger. Shadric lunged again at the same time he lost his blades and twisted in a way Chesler was sure a human couldn't until he was behind Brynte. The wraith grabbed Brynte around the neck and held the sword arm away.

A moment of choking and the king dropped the sword. Shadric boxed the king in the ears until the redhead tapped out in submission.

Chesler almost gagged as the king turned to face his friend. One of the wraith's punches had missed his head and caught the king's face. He looked a bloody mess as he snorted blood and held his nose.

For the second time between the two matches, Chesler was worried for the wraith's safety. He knew Vlasis would have any opponent who bloodied him executed before ever leaving the ring. He tried to rationalize that this redhead wouldn't enact that kind of stiff punishment on a friend, but he'd found the Godric line to be unpredictable and their tempers as fiery as their distinctive hair.

Laughter snapped Chesler's attention back to the ring in front of him. The wraith, the stupid wraith, was laughing at Brynte's useless attempts to wipe the blood off his face with his shirt sleeves.

Brynte lunged at the wraith and put him into a headlock the shadow quickly wiggled out of. "Busted my nose, ya asshole!" he yelled, followed by—Chesler couldn't believe it—a laugh. The king was laughing at the messy state he was in. The laugh was followed by several words in the Glasic tongue that Chesler only recognized half of and couldn't imagine anyone saying in civilized society.

He heard a cough next to him and saw Markus staring in surprise at the king's easygoing reaction in as much shock. They both continued staring as the king and the wraith moved slowly toward them after gathering up their weapons. Brynte held his head back and pinched his nose as he walked up to them.

The pair's friend, Lawrence, taking everything in stride, gave a few light claps as they approached and handed Brynte a large colorful cloth handkerchief. "Is it broken?" he asked as Brynte took the cloth and held it to his face.

"Nuh-uh. Least not badly. I'll be fine. I'll go see Eleanora in a minute," the king replied with a shrug.

Shadric hung around the king's side and moved the handkerchief to get a better look at the damage. He moved the king's face this way and that before releasing him. "Oh, it's not broken. It'll just be a little bruised. Maybe you should try getting married again or something. It worked out so well last time." Shadric grinned until the king slapped the back of his head.

"Idiot." Brynte shook his head with half a smile hidden behind blood and cloth.

The wraith just laughed.

The shock of the odd match wore off and Chesler cleared his throat, ready to suggest they go back indoors and the king go to the Court Healer.

"Oh, right." The damned, happy-go-lucky wraith turned to him with his same smile. "You wanted to test my skills. Got so caught up, I forgot."

Chesler growled. He didn't like this wraith half-breed. Never mind his Shade blood, Chesler hated people who smiled all the time. They were too difficult to read and Shadric seemed especially so. Right now, Chesler couldn't tell if the wraith was just happy, or mocking him. He assumed he was mocking him—particularly his faulty assumption that the king would need a bodyguard in the first place.

"I've already seen your skills. They are adequate to provide the king any further protection than what he can provide for himself," Chesler stated, silently hoping none of them would bring up his mistake in thinking the king was going to be useless in battle.

Luckily for Chesler, the fighting pair were too busy critiquing each other and making suggestions for next time to notice. Jair gave Chesler a glance from his position next to the pair that said he'd made the same mistake in thinking.

Lawrence wore a long wondering look that finally landed on Chesler and burned through him with an intensity he rarely felt from other people. The man shifted closer but remained silent for a moment, watching the two younger friends interact.

"They're an interesting pair, aren't they?" he remarked softly enough the two couldn't hear him.

Chesler hummed in agreement as he watched the stranger with a closer gaze. "Interesting is one word."

Lawrence remained silent for a beat. "Their expedition to Oroitz should be interesting too." His sharp gaze shifted suddenly from the pair to

Chesler. "What are you gaining from it?"

Chesler blinked. He hadn't expected this man to be so straightforward in his questions. "I don't understand your meaning," Chesler started to buy time to think of a better response. "It was the king's idea and decision to replace Harailt."

"With your friend? Jair?" His sharp gaze shifted a moment and Chesler noticed his friend stiffen next to him.

"The king asked for my opinion," Chesler stated, focusing on keeping his tone as light and easy as the Terranian kept his.

The man *hmphed.* "So, you're indifferent," Lawrence stated with a tone of unbelief. "Naturally," he mumbled to himself as he shifted away from Chesler and moved back toward the king. He said something softly to them while handing Brynte another handkerchief. They all moved off to return to the castle after a moment.

Chesler moved to follow the trio at Jair's pace, hanging back.

"Wha'd ya d'inking?" Jair asked, as he too watched the group walking ahead.

Chesler shook his head. "I think if we need to work on anything without their knowledge, we'll have to be careful."

"Eh, would we have 'do?" Jair said with a growl. "Da king seems a good guy. Much more easy d'en Vlasis."

Chesler spared a glance at the other man. Jair wasn't one to sneak after all. The idea didn't seem to sit well with his straightforward attitude about everything. Chesler rolled his eyes. He didn't know how Jair survived. Or how he thought the worlds survived without some people sneaking around.

"We'll see," Chesler said quietly.

The group separated once inside with the trio moving off to the Healer's quarters and Chesler and Jair separating, each to prepare anything else they could to make the departure to Oroitz smoother.

CHAPTER 38

D ays passed in uneasy peace, born of avoidance as the final preparations for the king's departure with a new army were made. The reserve soldiers strode about with confidence and jovial jokes. A light trepidation in their step was the only indication of their nervousness at going into battle.

No one else bothered with the confidence. Blacksmiths and weapon makers filled the streets with incessant clanging and yelling. Other suppliers and craftsmen yelled back and bustled about in an anxious fashion as they all hurried to complete whatever momentous requests were made of them.

The bustling stretched its unwelcome reach into the castle as well. The servants and guards all moved as fast as they could, even if their jobs had not been changed by the excitement outside.

Loreda paced the length of her room, wringing her hands at every turn. The longest distance of her room was from a far window to the nook next to her door. She traced the path, walking from the bustle and shouting heard through her closed window — though she assumed this was actually shouting from within the castle — back to the door where the shouting and running was definitely coming from the castle.

Every third turn or so, she reminded herself how silly her impatience and worry were. She straightened her gown and dropped her hands by her side and continued walking, only to be fretfully wringing her hands before she reached another turn. She glanced toward her desk again as she passed it. Everything was set in the same order, and silent, as it had been when she'd last passed by.

As she passed by the window again, Loreda paused to look out at the courtyard below. Frantic arrangements were being completed for the king's departure. The fading light of the late evening hadn't even slowed them down as the torches were lit.

A low pitch from her desk made Loreda jump and sprint to it. She grabbed the AaD to answer. "Jeshua! Are you alright? I've been waiting for your call for ages."

Jeshua Harailt had the nerve to chuckle on the other side. "My apologies, Moon, darling. Didn't mean to worry you so."

"Worry me? I was going to sneak to Oroitz if I didn't hear from you soon," Loreda said with a huff, though the idea sounded silly to her ears now.

Jeshua laughed again in his light tone and offered another sincere apology and a brief explanation of a battle that had carried on. Loreda didn't care as long as he was safe, which he repeatedly assured her he was.

"Jeshua, I must warn you. Brynte is going to Oroitz," Loreda said after a pause. She bit her lip, waiting for a reply.

The deafening silence from the other end of the call scared Loreda as she waited. Finally, the silence was broke.

"Do you know why?" Jeshua asked in a more calculated tone.

"No," Loreda said slowly before adding. "But he's bringing more troops and will be accompanied by General Jair."

"Markus?" Jeshua questioned immediately. "He's on good terms with King Brynte. The lucky bastard." His tone was almost warm as he spoke.

Loreda paused. She knew the rivalry between Jeshua and Jair had never been as sour as they both pretended for Vlasis's benefit. They always seemed to enjoy the competition. Jeshua had almost lost the old king's good favor when he tried to keep Jair in use after the disagreement.

The thought of that disagreement and of Vlasis darkened Loreda's face and made her words harsher than they should have been.

"I doubt he'll stay in favor with him. King Brynte won't trust anybody. He wouldn't dare," she hissed.

A pause followed before Jeshua spoke with a softness in his voice that annoyed Loreda. "Now, Letta, he is your son—"

"He's Vlasis's son," she snapped back before he could finish. "He looks just like him." She paused as her lip curled in remembrance and disgust. "He's that monster's son and he'll never be mine. Don't repeat that idiotic sentiment."

A heavy sigh. "Yes, Moon darling. Never again." A long pause brought the deafening silence back before Jeshua shifted the topic again. "How's our dear Caelyn?" he asked softly.

Loreda squeezed her eyes closed. The topic of children always turned to Caelyn before she was ready for the crushing pain of being away from her.

"When last we spoke," Loreda started, swallowing the lump that had already formed in her throat. "She was thrilled with the horse you got her. The maid said she was sneaking out to try and sleep in the stable." Loreda sputtered a laugh at the thought as tears slipped from her eyes.

Silence was interrupted by a shaky, soft sigh. "When this is over," Jeshua said, emotion beginning to overtake his voice. "She will live in the castle with us and have the best education and the best life. What she deserves. It'll be alright."

More tears fell before Loreda could wipe them away. She just nodded, fearing her voice would fail.

"Moon?" His pet name roused her into the realization that he couldn't hear a nod.

"Yes, yes of course. She will finally have the best," Loreda sputtered in a wet voice. The doubts that had plagued her every waking moment, and often followed her into her dreams, returned and demanded to be voiced. "Can we do this?" she asked, almost too softly to be heard. "Can we, and both return to live here?"

She wished she could take the gnawing doubts back the moment they were voiced. Now her nightmares seemed more real. When only silence ensued, Loreda hurried to explain. She hoped he didn't think she was disregarding all his sacrifices.

"I just mean, of our plan, your job is so much more dangerous." She swallowed again, but the lump in her throat remained, hiding like a coward with her heart. "If you didn't return, I don't know if I—" Loreda broke off as her voice failed, but she pushed through before Jeshua could speak.

"Maybe we should leave. Just take Caelyn and go. We'll be safe. We'll all… be safe."

"No." Jeshua's voice was unmoving. "For what you suffered from Vlasis, you deserve to be Queen. Caelyn… She deserves to live a life out of hiding. If nothing else, if I don't return, promise that Caelyn will live a proper life in the castle. It's her birthright, Loreda. And yours. You both deserve that."

Loreda sniffed. "I want that for her too. So much." She couldn't fit enough emphasis on the words no matter how hard she tried. It was never enough for how much she wanted to give her lovely daughter. "I'm just scared." The words slipped out in a tiny voice without her meaning to.

"You and Caelyn will live in peace," Jeshua stated as though it was already a fact.

Loreda let out a shaky breath. "Promise you'll come back." She hated how much of a child she felt—asking for something no one could promise, but… she needed it. She needed to be reassured.

Jeshua chuckled lightly and without mirth. "I promise I'll try."

Loreda pinched her eyes closed. "I love you. Jeshua, I love you so much. Please come back to me." She was begging again before she could stop herself.

"I love you too," he said with more warmth than Loreda had ever heard from anyone else. "I promise, I will do my best to return. Just wait for me."

Loreda ignored the silence that filled the line again as she tried to control her tears.

"Next week at the usual time?" Jeshua said in a voice that was trying to be light, but couldn't shake the heaviness of emotion.

"Yes, yes." Loreda breathed. "And no later."

"I will try my hardest to be punctual," Jeshua said before wishing her a good night and ending the call.

Loreda set the AaD back down on her desk with a shaky hand. She sank to the floor when her feet wouldn't support her, wrapped her arms around her knees, and cried.

CHAPTER 39

Stori wandered the castle and watched over the preparations for Brynte's leaving. She quietly hoped for every possible delay. Bry's trust in her to rule had overjoyed her until she'd started learning all the different ways she could possibly mess up and break that trust. A weak part of her wished Bry would change his mind and leave Loreda with the job. Loreda would be much better at it. The conversation they'd had about the older woman replayed in her mind, wiping away the silly idea. Loreda would not be a good ruler for Bry or herself.

The thought of the old queen also brought back her questions about if Loreda had some other heir. Stori hadn't talked to Loreda again but felt the burning urgency to find out, no matter how far-fetched. She loathed any conversation she had to have with the woman, but she couldn't shake Loreda's words.

Stori made it back to her chambers, still in thought about her soon-to-be responsibilities. She flipped absently through the endless scrolls and AaDs filled with even more endless judicial laws she still had to work through.

Firm knocking on the door elicited a groan from Stori as it roused her from her dejected thoughts. She waited a moment and glanced around when Leha didn't move to answer it.

Oh, that's right. Leha had gone to volunteer with what preparation she could.

Stori rose and patted her full skirt down before moving at a slow, dignified pace to the door. She hoped whoever was there might leave before she reached it. She opened the door. No such luck.

The young soldier's grin was quickly hidden along with a bouquet of flowers, still visible poking out behind his back. Wide eyes followed with a stuttered, "Your Majesty! I wa-wasn't expecting to find you, ma'am. I apologize." He rushed to speak as his face shifted through several shades of red.

Stori blinked at the stranger who looked just a little familiar.

"I-I'll just be leavin' now." The soldier gave a nervous half-smile as he turned his sharp blue eyes to walk away. The bouquet of flowers moved around front, still not quite out of view.

"Wait," Stori ordered before her brain caught up to her mouth.

The soldier stopped just short of fleeing and twisted his torso around to look back at her. Stori couldn't help but laugh at his face, all flushed and looking as though he could *die of embarrassment*—a phrase Bry had only used when referring to her, but now she could see the look on someone else.

"Yes, Your Majesty?" The man's voice was almost a pleading whine to let him go.

Stori paused another moment as she tried to place why he was familiar.

Leha, was the only thought that came to her. This was the soldier she'd seen Leha flirting with—Chess or something was his name.

"You're looking for Leha?" Stori asked.

Some of the red lessened as the soldier carefully pulled the flowers from behind his back and glanced at them. "Oh, yes, ma'am. I didn't mean to bother you though. I just wanted to say goodbye to Leha." He caught her confused look and hurried to explain, "I'm with one of His Majesty's regiments leaving for Oroitz."

"Oh." Stori hummed softly.

He was leaving. Leha certainly had been busy helping out wherever the soldiers were gathered the last few days.

Any time she could spend with him, Stori guessed.

"What is your name?" Stori asked with a warm smile. She carefully gave him a once over when he wasn't paying attention. He looked strong. Though maybe that was just the uniform. Still, he looked capable of protecting Leha, and the timid nature of his smile spoke of a gentleness to his nature.

"Czesiek Fabian, Your Majesty. Uh, Corporal Fabian." He frowned slightly at his correction. "I just go by Czes, ma'am."

"Oh, Chess, right." Stori nodded. She wasn't sure she was pronouncing it right. It sounded similar to the game Bry and Shad had tried to teach her. "Leha is in the main hall, helping with preparations." Stori nodded down the hallway.

"Oh." Chess made a small sound of surprise. His eyes lit up at the mention of Leha as he looked off in the direction she'd pointed him. "Thank you, ma'am." He gave a low nod and flashed a brilliant smile that made his blue, blue eyes shine even brighter.

He bounced off down the hallway toward the main hall. Stori made a small prayer that he would return, for Leha's sake. Her friend was quite smitten with the man.

Stori closed the door, but she couldn't keep a small smile off her face. She moved to the stair passage between her and Bry's room without even thinking about it. She wanted to see him. That was the only thought she could form about why she was heading upstairs so suddenly.

She gave a light knock and entered without waiting for a reply. She wasn't expecting anyone anyway; he was never in his bedchamber, always in the study. She moved through the dark room to the crack in the door.

Stori stood for a moment in the shadows of the room, watching the much livelier study. Bry and Shad were huddled around the foreigner, Lawr, as he messed around on an AaD. The two were talking back and forth over Lawr's head in what Stori assumed they'd meant to be hushed tones. Neither of them was adept at "hushed tones," however, so it sounded more like they were shouting in a whisper. Every once in a while, Lawr would growl at them to be quiet, but to no avail. They'd insist they were helping and continue talking after the shortest of pauses.

Stori couldn't help the smile that grew on her face. They seemed to be having such a good time, playing serious without actually having to be so.

After a moment of watching, Stori decided she needed to say something before one of them noticed her. She straightened her dress, adjusted her posture, and took a step, pushing the door open and gently clearing her throat at the same time.

The reaction was immediate. Bry and Shad snapped up straight and stepped around in one smooth motion ending with them standing between Stori and Lawr, blocking the view of what he was doing.

They blinked and shouted, "Stori!" in surprise and still in unison.

Stori choked on her laugh at their synced movements. She watched the relief wash over their faces as Lawr peeked around them. The older man gave them both a quick glance then threw Stori a knowing smirk. Stori was glad she wasn't the only one who found the duo amusing.

"I apologize if I interrupted anything important…" Stori said politely. She wasn't even close to sorry. "Is there anything I might assist with?" she asked, serious in her question. If she had some excuse to be around these guys for just a little longer, she might be happy. At the same time, she caught Bry's eye. She wanted to speak with him.

"Well, since you asked—" Shad started, but Bry cut him off.

"No, thank you." Bry moved to her side and glanced back. "We're really just getting in Lawr's way ourselves."

Shad made a sound of disagreement, but Bry ignored him as he caught Stori's hand.

"Could we speak in your room, Stori? It's a bit crowded in here and the walls of my chambers have ears." He cut a sharp, playful look at Shad.

"Now that's not fair," Shad protested.

"Not untrue either," Lawr quipped without looking up from the AaD.

Bry led Stori back through his chamber toward the passage as Shad pretended to be upset at Lawr's betrayal.

"Is something wrong?" Bry asked as soon as they reached her chambers. His face held a concerned frown.

Stori chastised herself for interrupting his fun and chasing away the rare smile. She couldn't recall the last time she'd seen him looking mirthful. Well, that wasn't entirely true. He'd been in good spirits the time he and Shad came to Eleanora with a river of blood flowing from his bruised nose. It had just been harder to see his smile with all the blood in the way.

"No, there's nothing wrong," Stori said quickly, once she'd pulled her attention from the black and blue nose to his eyes. "I just wished to speak with you. I didn't mean to interrupt."

"Oh," Bry paused and gave her a sidelong look, as if waiting for her to add something else. "Alright then," he mumbled.

Fenrir took the time to pad his big self over to Stori and nuzzle her leg. The creature looked up at her with its sloppy, happy look before it moved to nuzzle Bry in greeting also.

Bry smiled at the animal that had grown to stand as tall as mid-thigh since he'd given the creature as a gift to Stori.

"Fen's grown a bit since you last saw him," Stori stated the obvious as Bry straightened up from petting the large creature.

She bit her lip as she watched him. She couldn't find a way to state her worry in a polite way that didn't sound, in her head, as though she doubted him.

"You're worried about me leaving, aren't ya?" Bry shifted his gaze from the creature at his feet to Stori. "Worried I won't come back and you'll have to rule in my stead."

Stori pulled back as she could feel the color flaring up in her face. "No, I'm not worried," she said too hastily after he'd guessed her fears correctly.

Bry raised an eyebrow.

"I mean, I am worried about you, I just…" Stori sputtered as the mischievous smile returned to Bry's face and he rocked on his feet with a look of playful success. "Oh, you make thing's difficult sometimes." Stori shook her head.

Bry shrugged with a casual air but his teasing smile didn't lessen. "It's part of my charm. Gotta use what I can."

"You're very charming," Stori said without thinking. He was. His bright, bright smile had, somewhere amidst her time in Medius, become the highlight of any day. Stori reddened at the thought.

Bry blinked a moment at the compliment but returned to grinning in a moment. "Don't worry." He stepped a little closer and gave her shoulders a squeeze, "You'll do great at this whole ruling thing. It's a piece of cake." His wide grin and raised eyebrow dared her to ask what cake had to do with ruling a sphaere.

She smirked back at him. She could infer he was implying it was easy. Though the near permanent dark circles under his bloodshot eyes and his over-paled skin suggested otherwise. She didn't mention it though. She wouldn't dare. He was smiling. She was happy with that.

Stori shifted close enough to tell the exact color of his eyes were brilliant green with golden flecks. They looked like a forest with sunlight streaming through it.

Bry blinked back at her with surprise written on his bruised and discolored face. He took on the same mischievous look he did when he was going to start joking around—something Stori noticed he only seemed to do when he was either extremely comfortable or the same level of uncomfortable. At this time, she'd guess the latter.

Before he could start talking, Stori reached up and pulled him into a kiss. Bry remained stock still and only after a second did she realize what she'd done. Stori pulled back and clapped a hand over her mouth. She blinked as her face grew hotter. She didn't know why she'd done that.

"Sorry! I..." she sputtered nonsense and glued her attention to her feet, shuffling back a few steps. A sudden arm on her waist stopped her.

"Hey, it's okay." Bry stepped forward to cover the distance again. Cool fingers lifted her chin back to him. "I just wasn't expecting it. How 'bout a do-over?" He leaned over and grazed his lips over hers. Stori closed her eyes and kissed him back, reaching her hand out to run through his messy hair.

After a too short, heavenly eternity, they pulled back but remained entangled. Stori continued tracing her hands through Bry's hair and felt him supporting her with his hands around her waist.

"Well," Bry breathed, leaning his forehead against hers. "I suppose we had to start somewhere before your birthday."

"It's a good start," Stori purred, in the back of her mind noting how relaxed she felt standing next to him. "Just make sure you're back in Sentre by then."

Bry chuckled. "Wouldn't miss it for the worlds."

Stori smiled brightly and nodded as they swayed, almost dancing together.

This is nice, she thought. She wished the moment wouldn't end.

The door burst open, ending the moment as Leha burst in, already speed-talking as she entered. Both she and Stori gave a startled yelp at seeing each other and jumped backward.

Bry grinned sheepishly for a short moment before bursting out laughing. "You know, technically we're married," he reminded her.

"Yeah, but..." Stori cut a sheepish grin toward Leha. She just hadn't talked with her friend about her growing feelings toward Bry in a while. They'd certainly been updated.

"Well, I'll leave you two ladies to talk," Bry said, still smirking as he stepped back toward the passage to his room.

"Yes, yes." Stori shooed him along through the door before turning to Leha.

She wasn't sure where to start and now that Bry was gone, giddy excitement was bubbling up in her chest. Leha rushed to hug her, back to speed-talking as Stori caught sight of a familiar bouquet of flowers. The two girls sank onto a nearby couch, filled with mutual relief and hope.

CHAPTER 40

Ali studied Dain as the dark man prattled on about nothing while re-bandaging Sverre's injuries.

He isn't that handsome in his own right, Ali thought. Rather plain and the scars that painted any exposed skin didn't help the fact. One burn scar in particular that started somewhere below his shirt and ended at his throat, nipping up his cheek, covered such a large swath of discolored skin it was distracting.

No, his physical appearance didn't lend itself to being attractive. It was his nature and personality that did that. It was his smile, and seemingly obsessive nature to make everyone around him smiled. Even Sverre had to twist his lip up in a small grin at some of the things Dain said.

Ali's attention snapped back to what was being said when the name "Atanas" came up and all happy smiles disappeared. The familiar name didn't elicit any good feelings from Ali either.

"Atanas is pushing the Nomads to further their attacks," Dain said absently in a way that sounded far too serious for the smile that still covered his face. "He's been planning a long war for the Nomads to pursue. The Median king's decision to take action has thrown Atanas's plan off."

Sverre hummed at the news but remained otherwise silent as his gaze slid over to Ali.

Ali straightened and pretended she wasn't listening for a half-beat before deciding there was no point. Sverre had already noticed.

"I can step outside, if you want." She swallowed and hoped he wouldn't ask her to.

"No, I'd like you to stay and listen," he said, much to Ali's relief. "This is information that might benefit you to know in the future."

Ali nodded without a word and leaned closer to listen. She hated whenever he mentioned the future. Somehow, the way he spoke always seemed to be saying he wouldn't be there.

Dain nodded to her with his same cheerful smile before continuing. "Atanas was happy, and I use that word loosely, with the trouble they were causing the king. But King Brynte's decision to go directly to the battlefront has shifted some of his people's views of him for the better. Atanas wasn't too pleased with that," Dain said the last part with something between a smirk and a sigh. He seemed pleased that something wasn't going Atanas's way, but the thought was dampened by the trouble it would cause.

"Anyway," Dain started again as he pulled more bandages out to wrap around Sverre's chest. "The Medians are also quite happy with the new, young queen. I don't remember—"

"Istoria Gawain-Godric," Sverre supplied.

"Queen Istoria, yeah. The people like her," Dain picked up without skipping a beat. "Apparently she's been fixing some of the mess Vlasis and Oracaede made of the trade laws. It's already helped a lot of Medians to make a living without having to rely on the black market."

Sverre nodded again but didn't add anything, content to listen and readjust some of the bandaging before Dain smacked his hands away— lightly enough, of course, not to cause his hand injuries further pain.

Ali had to smother a snicker at the duo's dynamics. Without a TV in this world, they'd become the most entertaining thing to watch.

Sverre and Dain both glanced at her at the sound of her muffled laugh. Ali bit back another laugh at the in-sync eyebrow raises.

"Sorry," she sputtered, trying to hide her amusement with a cough. "You were saying?"

"So, back to Atanas," Dain started again with one last questioning glance at Ali. "He's ticked at the king's actions. My meeting with the Aynur's chief didn't go as he wanted. That'll probably irritate him too," Dain said with a smirk and a nod to Ali.

"It's going to be a lose-lose situation for us either way," Sverre stated absently as he snuck a quick readjustment of a bandage layer before Dain could knock his hand away. Dain frowned at him before continuing with a smile and turning to Ali.

"The problem is if they win, Sverre and I are probably going to be the ones sent to rile up the other tribes to fight King Brynte. If they lose…" He shook his head and turned back to Sverre. "We're just gonna be shit out of luck at the start. Your little plan will fall apart here."

Sverre grunted in agreement. A moment passed in uneasy silence before he spoke. "We might want to go to Medius. If things are going poorly, we could lend a hand."

Dain paused his wrapping of fingers and nodded.

"If Atanas gives us an assignment though…" Sverre trailed off.

Dain sighed this time. "We'll do what we can, obviously."

"Sentre will be taking refugees either way. If needed," Sverre said with a quiet glance at Ali.

Dain nodded as he finished bandaging the hand and paused before he moved to the next one. "Getting your family and mine in won't be an issue," Dain said with a nod that Sverre returned. A facial expression passed between them that Ali couldn't quite pin-point and she didn't like. Something about this future talk bothered her.

"Wouldn't…" She paused, waiting for both men's attention to turn to her before continuing to clarify a statement that had bugged her. "Wouldn't someone in Sentre recognize you two?" Ali asked, glancing between the two of them.

"Ali," Sverre started, fixing his sharp gaze on her "If you, Leon, and Dain's family have to go to Sentre, we won't be coming with you."

For a moment, all the air seemed to have left the room.

"What?" Ali breathed.

She returned Sverre's stare, hoping he'd correct his statement or say it was a joke. It wasn't funny. It was so not funny that Ali realized at some point this little group had become family to her. The thought of Sverre leaving pulled at her heartstrings more than she would admit.

"I'm sorry, Ali." Sverre dropped his gaze. "It would only be in case of an emergency."

"An emergency?" Ali repeated. She dropped her gaze to her lap as she twisted her fingers. She glanced at Dain, hoping maybe he'd say something to help, to soften the blow or assure her that would never happen. Maybe she didn't know what she was hoping for now—other than for Sverre to stay and stay safe.

Dain finished bandaging the second hand and released it with the same level of gentle care as always. He didn't look up to Ali though, only at Sverre as another silent conversation passed between them.

"An emergency," Ali repeated. "Then make sure it doesn't happen," she ordered, catching Sverre's eye again. "We won't have to go to Sentre unless you guys aren't safe, so be safe." Ali paused as Sverre continued staring at her, blinking in surprise. "Please," she surprised herself with the pleading tone in her voice.

Ali stood and fled the room, searching for silence—not that painful sad kind that was filling the dining room, but the peaceful kind. Ali moved out the front door before she'd thought anything about it. She leaned against the wooden door frame and closed her eyes as she focused on slowing her breath.

The chill of the desert winter bit into her skin and she wished she'd thought to grab a jacket before leaving the warm house. Ali shook her head. A stupid thought—she had better things to worry about. Like Sverre. Ali knocked her head against the wood of the door. Why did she have to care? She knew she shouldn't, she'd hardly known the man for very long, but...

A tear slipped down her cheek. The thought of him leaving again and coming back bloody and hurt elicited more tears before she could stop them. The worst thought was of him bloody and hurt and not coming back at all. Ali wanted to scream at that thought.

The door suddenly gave way behind her and Ali almost toppled before a strong, ashen arm caught her.

"Are you alright?" Sverre's gentle voice calmed her before she even glanced up at him.

Ali nodded as he pulled the door closed behind him and wrapped a blanket he was holding around her shoulders. Ali sniffed and huddled into the warmth of the blanket and his arms until she noticed he still wasn't wearing any more of a shirt than the bandages around his torso.

"Sverre!" she chided, adjusting the blanket so it wrapped around them both. "You have to take care of yourself too."

Sverre grunted.

The two remained huddled on the porch in silence for a time.

"I don't want you to have to leave."

Sverre let out a heavy sigh Ali could feel from being close to him more than hear aloud. "I don't... want—" He seemed to struggle with the simple word. "—to leave either."

Ali sniffed. Her damned tears were still a looming threat.

"Ali," Sverre's soft voice called her attention. "You know I wouldn't leave you and Leon unless there were no other options. I wouldn't, unless it was safer for you."

Ali sniffed again. "I know." She felt his head nod against hers.

Another moment passed before Sverre's body stiffened and he pulled away a little. "I'm not making you uncomfortable, am I?" he asked in an odd tone, somewhere between doubt and guilt.

Ali tipped her head back to look him in the eyes. He looked unsure at their close proximity and yet reticent to move away.

Ali sputtered a laugh. She shook her head and couldn't help thinking there had been a time when she was scared of this guy. "Not at all."

Sverre nodded again and held her gaze.

The sound of hectic bustling and laughter interrupted the moment as both Ali and Sverre pulled quickly away from each other. Leon rounded the corner of the house full of laughter and covered in mud and a few scrapes.

"Sverre! Ali! You should have seen these birds!" He was ecstatic as he ran to them, already recounting his adventure as Sverre pulled him inside to the tub.

Ali laughed and trailed behind, trying to help and grab the medical box from the dining room for the cuts the boy had.

A shadow blocked her way as she was leaving the room. Dain caught her off guard with a quick hug.

Ali blinked at him as he smiled and leaned down to whisper. "Thank you for caring so much for him. Sverre isn't used to it, but it means a lot."

He flashed her his brilliant, authentic smile as he took the medical box and moved off toward the bathroom.

Ali had to smile to herself. She wiped whatever remained of her tears away as she followed him. The three adults crowded in the small bathroom around Leon to help get him cleaned up.

CHAPTER 41

Lawr's frown darkened as he tried to focus on deciphering the data on the AaD. He usually considered himself a focused person, but even he had his limits. After days of working non-stop to get past the paranoid level of encryption on the data, those limits had been found.

"Shad! I swear to all things *un*holy, if you don't get down from this chair, I'm gonna throw you out the window," Lawr snapped at the wraith.

Shad lost his balance at the sound of his name and toppled from his handstand on the back of the chair with all the grace of a headless chicken.

"Ah man, what gives? That was the longest I'd held a handstand." Shad rubbed his head with more indignation than Lawr would have given him credit for.

"Get. Out."

"Ah, come on," Shad whined. "Bry already kicked me out and I've got nothing to do."

"Then go do nothing somewhere else!" Lawr snapped, turning back to his work.

Shad didn't move but remained silent for only a few blissful moments. "Not to pry."

"Then don't."

Shad continued anyway. "Don't you have a job or something in Terrae that you have to be gettin' back to?"

"Not really." Lawr's tone was stiff. He usually hid his thoughts and, heaven forbid, feelings, on this subject from people in Terrae, but... Shad was different. And he wouldn't know the struggle Lawr had been dealing with because of his age, trying to get his company to fund his projects.

Bastards.

"I'm pretty much retired," he continued. "They won't mind a lengthy absence. It'll just make it easier for them to 'ask' me to resign." He turned a little in his chair to give Shad a pointed look to let the subject drop.

Shad blinked up at him and remained silent. Lawr could see him thinking hard on the topic and he looked to be getting a little angry on Lawr's behalf. Lawr had to grin.

The kid is just too nice.

"It's fine." He nodded that he meant it. "This work is a lot more fun anyway."

Shad grunted. "If you say so." A moment of silence skipped by as he frowned at a thought. "We could go—"

"But we won't," Lawr cut him off.

The indignation in Shad's voice was amusing, but Lawr had to appreciate care and concern where he could find it. Shad grumbled at that and the silence returned for another blissful moment. Shad's shifting and continued grumbling broke the silence a moment later as he got up from the floor and wandered off in search of something else to do.

Lawr watched him leave and hoped his new friend really would drop the subject. He shrugged.

Whatever.

He'd stopped caring about his job on Terrae long before he'd come to Medius.

Lawr sighed in the long-missed silence.

Ali reacted the same way.

He smiled at the memory. She'd been all fire and brimstone when he'd mentioned his frustrations at work.

He scoffed at himself. Lawr had never considered himself the sentimental type, yet here he was, caught in nostalgia. He shook his head and returned his focus to the present. He hoped Ali was at least keeping up with the rent payments.

Hunching over his work, Lawr continued making only slow progress with the data. The silence was so blissful to work in that Lawr didn't notice

227

the afternoon sun until it was reflecting off the window into his face.

He sighed and shifted his position. He worked a few more moments before he remembered Bry was planning on leaving around the afternoon today. A sudden fear gripped his chest that they'd left already and hadn't said goodbye. Lawr shook his head, trying to dislodge that idea. He wasn't successful as he stood and moved to the door. Down the hallways he wandered, looking for signs they were still there. All the equipment that had been prepared and had been blocking part of the hallways had been moved. Lawr reasoned that was fine, it didn't mean they'd left.

He wandered a bit before remembering he should have locked the AaD up before he left the study. *Stupid*, he chided himself as he hurried back to the room. The sound of voices as he reached the study gripped him with new fear for the data. He recognized the voices in a moment though and the fear melted.

Lawr pushed the door open. Bry was puttering around, grabbing last minute things he would need. Like clothes. Shad was laughing about the king forgetting to pack and Lawr was sure the joke was quite funny when Bry had arrived at his room but was growing less entertaining by the second.

Lawr strode back to the study with a calm collectedness he hadn't felt just a few moments prior.

"Oh, there you are." Shad turned his beaming grin toward Lawr as he entered the room. "We were looking for you. And his clothes." Shad jerked his head toward Bry who was still scrambling around and had moved off to his bedchambers to find more clean clothes.

Lawr wasn't sure how the king survived his constant state of mess. Apparently he found a way, just not one Lawr could see or agree with.

Bry reappeared in a moment with a full bag. He turned to Lawr and paused a moment, apparently struggling with what to say. Lawr guessed he was struggling with a proper "kingly" parting. "Lawr," he started.

"Yes, yes," Lawr interrupted to save Bry the trouble. "I'll hold down the fort, watch out for Istoria, don't let Loreda take over, and be in bed by nine." He fixed the redhead with his best smug grin. "Did I miss anything?"

Bry's serious face was lost to reddening and a sheepish grin. "No, I think that about covers it."

"And don't go having any wild parties when we're gone. You know the rules." Shad nodded to himself as he too continued the charade.

"No wild parties, unless you're—" He pointed to Shad. "There. I'll add it to the list." Lawr pretended to write it on his hand.

Bry half-sighed, half-groaned as he clapped a hand over his face. "You guys are weird."

"Wha—?" Shad clutched his heart in mock shock.

Lawr laid a hand on Shad's shoulder. "He's grown up from rebellious teen to responsible adult in such a short time. We should be proud."

Shad nodded as Bry scoffed, "Weird."

Silence settled again for a time as the joking subsided. Lawr reiterated his promise to look out for things while Bry was away and to help Stori however he could.

Shad and Lawr moved off toward the castle entrance as Bry excused himself to say goodbye to Stori. Shad met up with Jair in the courtyard where the officers were waiting. Lawr watched as the wraith teased the older general.

Jair seemed a quick judge of character and had warmed up to Shad as soon as he'd had a conversation with him. He seemed to move by the Shade-blood thing quickly.

Lawr moved away from the courtyard after one last farewell was exchanged with Shad. He walked back inside and up a staircase leading to the balcony overlooking the courtyard. He caught sight of Bry escorting Stori to the same balcony and paused. He considered a moment if it would be appropriate for him to stand on the same balcony as the queen.

The thought was interrupted as Bry hailed him and almost pulled him to the balcony after him. The king said a few words to the officers before he turned and said one last goodbye to both Stori and Lawr before trotting off down the staircase to the courtyard.

Lawr shifted to one edge of the railing where he could see Bry mounting up on his Friesian horse. Lawr spared a glance at Stori to see the young queen watching the same thing.

Her face remained a serene mask of beauty, though Lawr could see the tears welled up in her eyes, threatening to fall at any moment. Her gaze shifted out of the courtyard to the wall that divided the castle from the rest of the town.

Servants, guards, and everyone else in the castle who didn't have to be somewhere stood on the walkway of the wall. They waved at the people they knew among the soldiers amassed on the other side. Stori's gaze searched among the people until she settled on someone.

Lawr followed her line of sight and searched until he recognized a young maidservant he was pretty sure served Stori. The girl was leaning over the wall waving at someone between wiping her eyes with a handkerchief.

A sniff from Stori brought Lawr's attention back to the young queen. She was watching Bry again and had brought out her own handkerchief to dab at her eyes. She needed to do more than just dab with how fast her tears were escaping, but she kept up appearances, at least from a distance.

"He'll come back," Lawr said, startling the young queen out of her head.

She turned to look at him as though she'd forgotten he was there.

"They both will," Lawr continued almost under his breath as his gaze shifted between Bry and Shad.

"I know," Stori said softly. "I know. Bry will. Of course. But..." Her gaze tore from Bry back to the wall. Her maidservant had found flowers which she gently tossed to her man on the other side.

Lawr watched and waited for Stori to speak again.

"Everyone has someone they don't want to lose," she said finally after a light sniffle. "Sons, brothers, lovers." Stori's gaze shifted over the wall. "They won't all come back," she finished in a whisper and wiped her eyes again.

Lawr held her in a sidelong gaze before he sighed and rubbed his face. There was nothing he could say to that.

He returned his focus to the king, who was just preparing his men to move out. Bry glanced up at them and gave one last wave. Stori returned it with a touch more enthusiasm than royalty would be expected to. Lawr gave a short wave without uncrossing his arms.

The line of officers followed the king's lead out of the courtyard and through the city. They were out of sight as soon as they left the courtyard, but Stori and Lawr waited until the line had passed to the lower levels of the city where they were in view again. The procession moved with the soldiers falling in as their units passed beyond the city.

After the front of the line had left the city, Stori wiped away her tears more aggressively than she had before until all were gone. She turned to Lawr and gave a curt nod.

"You must excuse me, Mr. Lawr, I have work I must attend to." She gave a short curtsy and marched—almost stomping—back into the castle.

Lawr smiled after her. At least she bounced back quickly. He sighed and moved off after her. He had work to do as well.

CHAPTER 42

The second full day without Bry in the capital wound down without incident. Stori chided herself. Just because nothing had happened yet didn't mean she could relax. The security of locking herself away in Bry's study wouldn't stop disaster from unfolding around her.

Bry's friend, Lawr, had joined her in taking up uninterrupted residence in the study. He had his own little desk set up in a corner and kept it remarkably clean compared to the rest of the room. He had his own Oracaede related project to work on, though Stori didn't know much about what it was. Lawr wasn't a sharer, she'd found. He was helpful though. Always willing to lend her a hand where he could and make sure she was doing alright. Stori was beginning to suspect Bry told him to do so. Not that she minded, but it made her think of Bry even more.

Stori was consumed with a sense of dread and a knotting in her stomach that she was going to mess something up. She'd started pacing around the room along the same path she'd seen Bry walk. Stori made her fifth pass around the room, still waiting for the floor to fall away under her.

How did Bry handle this? She couldn't help but ponder and compare herself. *How did anyone?* She grimaced as she thought of the warm smile Bry could usually give out to anyone, as though it wasn't hard. She was weak in comparison. She snapped at several servants and Leha in her first few days. She sighed at how graceful Bry and her father had made ruling look and how terrible she was at it.

The hair on the back of her neck rose as Stori became aware of a cold stare piercing through her. She turned to meet Lawr's eyes from where he watched her with indifference as his only expression. Of course, apathy was his default look and she could never tell what he was thinking anyway. She did always appreciate his help, but he was a little scary.

"I can work elsewhere if I'm making you uncomfortable," Lawr said.

Stori flinched. He seemed to be a mind reader, which was unnerving too.

"No, it's not that," she said vaguely.

It was, but other things of more importance were bugging her too.

"Still waiting for the world to come crashing down around you?" he guessed, though he said it as a statement.

Stori gave up trying to hide her thoughts from him. "Yes! I don't know what I'm doing wrong. It seems that... Everything! I'm doing everything wrong." She breathed out heavily as her anger was starting to elicit tears. She sniffed and roughly wiped her face. Why couldn't she be angry like a normal person without crying?

Her thoughts flitted to Loreda. The woman did angry amazingly well.

Stori stomped the thought down as she marched over to the desk and grabbed up her handkerchief to wipe the moisture away. She could still sense Lawr's gaze on her.

"You're not doing it wrong," he stated. Stori tried to explain that yes she was but he stopped her with a raised hand. "It's not wrong, it's hard. And it takes practice."

Stori sniffed and gritted her teeth as she listened. *I'm still doing it wrong.*

"You're thinking of how well Bry does some things, and how well other people do them too," Lawr continued. This time he waited for her to nod before he continued. "You're comparing yourself to people who've had practice. I wasn't here on Bry's first few days as king and neither were you, but Shad has some funny stories about how badly things went. You should ask him."

Stori dropped her gaze.

A groan from Lawr's corner pulled her glance cautiously back to him. Lawr stood and stretched as he glanced at the darkness outside the window.

"It's late. We should go get dinner. It'll be good to step away for a while."

Stori began to protest but was cut short by an order to move that she couldn't disobey. Lawr had a way of acting with paternal authority that she couldn't ignore even when she made the mistake of trying.

They left the study and walked to the dining hall. Stori was going to mention that they should have called a servant to tell the cook they'd be having dinner, as there wouldn't be any food available right now. Lawr however, didn't look as though he'd be listening. He was walking backward with a frown and spinning in every direction, looking at something Stori couldn't see.

"Isn't this wrong?" he asked, coming to a complete stop. He continued to glance around him but didn't take another step. "The guard pattern. It's wrong."

Stori started to tell him he was imagining things when she recognized a few of the day guards were still working. She glanced around, realizing he was right; none of the guards around them should have been working those stations.

"Who would change the schedule?" Lawr started walking aimlessly.

Stori stared at the guards for a moment. She had to remember he wasn't from this sphaere and didn't know about ruling matters. She focused on walking again but paused as she tried to think which direction to go.

"Matters of running the castle are implemented by the Castle Manager, Chesler."

Lawr nodded.

"But those matters are supposed to be agreed upon by the ruling regent, me," she continued.

Lawr hummed. "Then we'd better talk to Chesler and see what the issue is." He turned quickly on his heels to head down a hallway they'd just passed.

"R-right." Stori followed after him.

That had been her thought too, of course. She just didn't know where his office was.

Lawr led the way through the corridors and down a few staircases before leading to a small door, tucked away at the end of a side hallway. Stori didn't bother questioning how the foreigner knew the castle so much better than she did when she'd spent more time in it.

Lawr knocked a heavy fist against the door and poised to open it as soon as he was bid. Lawr had the door half open before a peeved "come in" had finished being spoken.

"Your Majesty, Mr. Dara." Chesler stood, setting aside his dinner with a begrudging sigh as he greeted them each with a nod.

"What's the issue with the guards?" Lawr asked straight away.

"And why was I not informed before you changed the schedule?" Stori added, ignoring the tiny voice in her head saying she just wanted to get a word in rather than stand around looking dumb.

Disgust was evident on Chesler's face as he sat again and shifted a few pieces of paperwork organized into neat little piles on his desk. "I was made aware of possible issues with the scheduling and changed it accordingly." Chesler dragged his gaze over to Stori with something between mockery and disdain. "I didn't want to overwhelm our new queen with such petty matters. I was going to mention it in my next report."

Stori flinched at the comment. She couldn't deny that she might not have noticed the change before the report anyway, if Lawr hadn't pointed it out.

"*Made aware of?*" Lawr raised an eyebrow as he continued. "By who?"

Chesler's gaze focused on Lawr. "The Queen Mother Loreda pointed out a few flaws in the organization and scheduling of the guards."

Stori stiffened at the mention of Loreda. The thought that she needed to work harder to keep the throne safe for Bry bounced around her mind with an internal scream at Loreda.

Doesn't she know ruling is hard enough? Stori brought herself up short of ordering Chesler not to trust anything Loreda said—but only barely.

"Why did you implement Loreda's changes without informing me?" Stori asked in spite of herself.

The annoyance of having to explain himself was clear on his face. "Loreda did make the suggestion," he conceded unhappily. "It was an improvement, so I acted upon it. My apologies for not consulting you first, Your Majesty. It won't happen again." His tone wasn't very convincing.

"Have there been any other changes?" Lawr asked before Stori could reply to the last comment.

Chesler's irritated gaze shifted over to the man, away from Stori. She let out a breath of relief to have his attention off her.

"No," Chesler growled, matching Lawr's glare. The glare lasted until Lawr nodded but didn't turn away. Chesler finally continued, "Loreda also suggested a change to the servants' work-time schedule, but I didn't see it as an improvement and have not implemented it."

"Was the guard schedule change that much of an improvement?" Stori asked before she could stop herself. She could feel the pettiness of her words, but they still forced their way out. "The schedule Brynte set in place was insufficient?"

Chesler's glare swung back to her. Though now it was filled less with disgust and more with amusement, which was even more irritating. "King Brynte hasn't had time to change the scheduling for anyone in the castle. The schedule in question was the one former King Vlasis put in place."

"I see." With that, she nodded a brisk farewell to Chesler that was only gruffly returned before she and Lawr left the room.

They walked down the halls with Lawr deciding the path back.

"Why would she change the schedules?" Stori asked aloud, half to distract herself from her irritation at Chesler and half hoping Lawr might have a brilliant realization.

A pause followed as Lawr thought. They traveled up another staircase and down another hallway before he answered.

"She's testing her power, obviously," Lawr stated.

"Yes, obviously." Stori's tone was snappier than she'd meant as her irritation found voice. She hurried along before Lawr noticed. "But why does she need to prove her power? Unless she truly is planning to make a play for the throne—and soon. If so, how?"

They moved back through familiar passages to the study. Stori returned to pacing.

"I'm going to talk to Loreda," Stori decided after several turns of pacing.

Lawr glanced up at her and held her gaze for a searching moment before nodding. Stori liked that about him; he was never overprotective. He seemed to assess something internally and reach a conclusion without any need to warn her of things she already knew.

Stori nodded and marched out the door, through the hall, and down stairs toward Loreda's room. She practiced what she'd say and more importantly, how she'd sound, all the way. When she reached Loreda's door, Stori tried to mimic the way Lawr knocked on Chesler's door, but it sounded weak in comparison.

Not a good start, she chided herself.

A light, ever lovely "come in" responded from the other side of the door.

Stori opened the door with what she hoped was enough force to make up for the weak knock and entered the room.

Loreda rose from an arm chair she had been lounging in and moved to greet Stori with a warmth that surprised Stori.

"Istoria dear. Are you well?" the older woman gripped her hand and gave it a friendly squeeze.

Stori bit back the instinct to yank her hand away. Instead, she returned the smile, the squeeze, and the greeting with as much warmth as she could muster.

Loreda purred at Stori's greeting and offered her a seat on the couch before starting into polite small talk that Stori didn't bother keeping up with while thinking of how best to ask her question. The warmth in Loreda's tone was stranger than anything else. It distracted her as she thought; it sounded almost... *Sincere?*

After a few moments of one-sided conversation, Loreda ceased and waited for Stori to talk.

This is worse, Stori decided after the silence had stretched on for an uncomfortable length of time.

She finally gave up on finding the perfect wording and decided a straightforward approach would work best.

"Loreda, I wished to ask you about the guard schedule," Stori began, trying to find the words even as she spoke. The older woman's poise was more of a reminder to Stori how childish she must seem in comparison.

"Oh, yes, the change I suggested. A little thing, dear. You shouldn't be bothered with it." Loreda replied as soon as Stori paused. "It was just something I thought of when Vlasis was king and I didn't have time to bother with it when I was ruling," Loreda said, fidgeting just enough that Stori noticed.

"While Brynte is ruling— and in his stead, myself," Stori began, straightening her posture until it felt as stiff as a board. "I will be informed of any changes before you have them implemented." Stori tried to channel her father as she spoke.

His expression would have been cold as stone and relentlessly confident.

Stori wasn't sure how her face compared, but she feared the confidence was lacking—especially if Loreda's chuckle was any indication.

Stori tried not to grimace, but she wasn't sure now if her facial expressions were doing what she wanted. She sunk back into her seat just a little as Loreda apologized for her rudeness though the laugh settled into a smirk on her face.

"Of course, darling. You will be kept abreast of every development and change in the castle," Loreda purred the words though they sounded more like a threat. "Now, is there anything further I might assist you with, or should you be returning to work on those pesky laws?"

Stori's stomach twisted further as the concern returned that she was spending too much time in the study working on the laws and not enough time attending to the castle's business.

Loreda rose from the couch, a sign for Stori to do the same, as she continued polite meaningless talk all the way to the door. Stori followed, mentally kicking herself for not being stronger in the conversation.

Only after Loreda had purred goodnight and closed the door to her chambers, did Stori let her shoulders sag. She trudged away back toward her own room before remembering the piles more of paperwork she still had to attend to and that Lawr would be waiting for her to come back.

Or maybe he won't even care, she thought as she passed her room and took the long way around and up.

Stori sighed. She'd failed at handling the former queen. Stori trudged on as her doubts settled around her shoulders.

CHAPTER 43

Sebastian Atanas stood from his desk for a moment and stretched his arms before walking a tight circle around his office to do the same for his legs. He paused at the couch tucked into the back corner of the office and stared down at its occupant.

Duqa shifted in his sleep and twitched every so often.

Like a dog, Atanas thought.

He sighed. Maybe he had pushed so many experimentations onto one person. But Duqa was special. His defects had made him an excellent test subject.

Atanas picked up the blanket that had fallen to the floor and pulled it over the sleeping man. Duqa shifted again and murmured in his sleep with a twisted smile. Atanas assumed he was having an enjoyable dream. He sighed again as he brushed a hand through the younger man's dark hair. He knew Duqa couldn't even feel the physical contact, but it made Atanas feel better. Somehow.

Atanas straightened and moved back to his desk in a hurry to get away.

Duqa isn't Terrance, he reminded himself with bitter contempt. He wasn't even close to his little brother.

He sat heavily and glanced around his small office space to make sure he was alone before opening one of his drawers and removing the false bottom. He removed the only contents of it and breathed as he stared down at the picture.

He gazed over the photo with a ghost of a smile. Of the two young boys in the photo, Atanas hardly considered that he had been one of them—grinning happily without a care in the world. Especially Terrance. His younger brother always had a smile for everyone and everything.

That must have been it, Atanas thought as he glanced back toward where Duqa slept. They had the same smile; the same stupid grin, even if Terrance hadn't been the same crazy.

At a shifting sound, Atanas instinctively clutched the photo close to his chest. He looked around. The office was still empty; Duqa was still sleeping.

He returned his attention to the photo with a frown. Maybe if Terrance had taken matters more seriously, he'd still be alive. Atanas pushed the picture back into the drawer at the angry thought.

Closing the false bottom again, Atanas shoved the drawer shut. The thought of Terrance still burned in his mind as he tried to focus on his work again.

Another shifting sound made Atanas look up from distracting thoughts. A figure stood by the side door, closing it softly.

"Echo, I told you to knock," Atanas growled as he tried to keep his voice steady.

The silent figure knocked on the back of the closed door twice before moving to Atanas's side and kneeling. The man's unnerving, soulless eyes never left Atanas as he started giving his report.

"The battle in Oroitz has been progressing as you wished. King Brynte will arrive shortly, however, and may shift the outcome," Echo said with an empty, monotone voice that matched his eyes. "The Avare chiefs send their thanks for the support you provided. They extended an invite for you to celebrate with them when the victory is won."

Atanas scoffed, "I would not lower myself to be in the presence of that rabble. You may tell them such when you next meet."

Echo nodded before continuing his report. The information was as Atanas anticipated, as it should be. All the preparations for the aftermath of the fight were also in place, save for a few key personnel.

There's still time for that, Atanas reminded himself.

Atanas almost had Echo dismissed before Duqa woke up, but whatever muse guarded Echo had never been kind.

"Hey-o, Echo," Duqa chirped from the back of the room just as the silent messenger stood to leave. "Have you been avoiding me?" Duqa teased as Echo nodded to Atanas and turned to leave through the side door again.

Atanas scoffed as Duqa followed the man and continued to goad him and ask questions he knew he wouldn't be able to answer. The "training" Duqa had done with Echo to obey the command not to speak unless delivering a message had been some of Duqa's best work.

Maybe Atanas should have Duqa train Sverre again. The damned assassin never learned his lesson properly. Even when he was still Atanas's slave, he'd always been disobedient. Atanas scowled at a thought. He supposed blood did have something to do with a person's character. He scoffed. Or he just hadn't dealt the albino enough pain when he was a child.

The thought made Atanas's scowl darken. He continued growing more annoyed at his former slave until Duqa returned.

"What's up, boss? Ya want me ta kill someone for ya?" Duqa asked with cheerful hope and a psychotic smile as he bounced onto Atanas's desk.

Atanas half-considered the offer, but the albino was still too valuable an asset and a damned good assassin. He sighed. "No, Duqa. No killing today."

Duqa's pout was that of a child denied candy. Atanas almost had to laugh at the antics. Yes, even crazy, Duqa had a lot in common with Terrance.

Duqa blinked at Atanas and looked completely confused by the laugh.

"And Duqa," Atanas smoothed out his features and regained his composure. "Get off my desk."

CHAPTER 44

"So, did it involve Bry? Yes or no?" Shad asked again.

"For da las' 'dime, wrai'd," General Jair said in exasperation at the constant stream of questions he'd been peppered with since leaving Sentre. "Da ma'der's priva'de. I won'd be 'dellen ya anyding."

"Ah, you're no fun." Shad pouted a moment before bouncing right back and turning to Bry for conversation. "Hey, Bry, what if it wasn't about you that Jair was dismissed. You could have and older sister, or brother. Wouldn't that be awesome?" Shad beamed at the idea.

Bry could only sigh. "An older sibling I've never met and who would be the legitimate heir to the throne instead of me. No, Shad, that doesn't sound particularly 'awesome'."

Shad griped about the throne being thrown into the consideration. "I suppose when you add the crown into the mix, it doesn't work, but…" He trailed off as he watched the shadow of his shadows dance along the Empty, away from the torches. "I think it might be fun, having a sibling."

Bry laughed. "Yeah, but I think one brother is all I can really handle." Bry gave Shad a kick from his horse. He missed Shad and kicked the horse's leg. The large animal didn't miss a step at the mild annoyance.

Shad was beaming again as he returned to start another conversation with Jair. He continued jesting with the older general the entire length of the journey through the Empty. Bry was sure his friend had set himself a goal to make great friends with Jair before they reached Oroitz. He was making good progress too, as long as he didn't mention Vlasis or their conflict.

As the front of the army exited the Empty, Bry gave orders for the army and the rest of the officers to head to the battlefront while he went with his retinue toward Oroitz in search of General Harailt.

Riding through the main street of Oroitz, Bry was greeted by several bunches of disorderly officers who were drunk even as the sun had yet to set on the valley. Each group of men they passed didn't seem to have been expecting his or Jair's arrival and hastened to salute their king and the general as they rode past. Their drunken stupor slowed this reaction even more than the surprise of seeing Brynte. One officer was so shocked at seeing the king, he toppled over while trying to salute and stared wide-eyed. Bry couldn't help but glance back at the man picking himself off the ground.

He looks familiar, Bry thought, but couldn't place where he knew him from. He turned to ask Shad, but his friend wasn't paying any attention as he chatted with Jair.

They continued through the town, stopping at each gathering of officers to ask about Harailt's whereabouts. However, the general seemed to have been missing the last two days. He had left standing orders with the men in town and then left for the battle camp even though there hadn't been a battle with the Nomads in several days.

"Why would he leave?" Bry turned to Jair with his question. He had a sense Jair knew Harailt better than any of them.

Jair remained frowning in silence as they approached the house they'd been directed that Harailt stayed in.

They dismounted and Bry was about to ask again when Jair spoke, "D'wo days ago would have been when we lef'd Senr'e."

"You think someone told him Bry was coming and he left? Why?" Shad questioned.

"I don' know," Jair grumbled, chewing his lip. A dark, thoughtful frown remained prominent on his face as they moved toward the house.

The homeowner, a man named Oskar, greeted them warmly, introducing his family and showing off his house before leading them to the room Harailt had been using. Oskar affirmed, amid other endless commentary, that Harailt hadn't returned to his room in the last couple days. He was also more than happy to offer Bry a room to stay in, though he didn't have room enough for Shad and Jair.

Bry only spent a moment looking in Harailt's room. The space was empty of personal affects, even though Oskar insisted the general had commandeered the space for the rest of the month.

The trio gave up on searching out what Harailt had been doing and moved to find sleeping arrangements for the night. Oskar volunteered to lead Shad and Jair to a separate house a short walk across town where there might be space for them to sleep. Bry understood this meant that space would be made for members of the king's entourage, regardless of who was already using that space. He looked toward the house Oskar brought them to with a twinge of guilt.

Oskar's wife Renata led Bry to the only other room they had to spare. She continued apologizing all the way through the little cellar to a small storage room fitted with a single cot and lined with boxes.

Bry glanced around the closet of a room, cramped with boxes and amassed oddball items and had to smile. He couldn't count the number of times he and Shad, and sometimes even Klaas and Eleanora, all had to fit into rooms of this size for the night. The room screamed the warmth of a home more than any of his castle rooms ever did.

Bry voiced that the space look comfortable enough, complete with an attached washroom and a small table, but Renata didn't seem to be listening. She prattled on about the oddity of having the king staying at their house and being in Oroitz at all. The prattling was interrupted with an apology for the state of the rooms in every other sentence.

He finally cut her off mid-apology with assurances that he'd be fine in the space while moving her toward the door.

A sigh escaped Bry as silence finally settled over the now empty room. Her prattle had loosed the nagging reminder that he may have been rash in coming to Oroitz. He grumbled to himself about that, and about Harailt, and all his other problems as he unpacked his bag. Bry dropped old plans he'd brought to review with a partially finished new strategy on the table. The rest of the contents of the bag stayed where they were as he slung it onto his bed to be forgotten.

Bry sat and worked on the strategies, forgoing the family's invitation to join them at dinner. He worked on the plans until his blurry-eyed vision couldn't differentiate between the sprawling diagrams and the nightmares that invaded his sleeping mind.

CHAPTER 45

Nightmares of losing a battle with Harailt enveloped Bry before they morphed into scenes of Stori betraying him and joining Loreda while demanding his execution. He jerked awake, stumbling to his feet. His eyes flashed around the room for any sign of Stori or Loreda. Bry panted, relieved that he was alone and so far from home.

Steadying his breath, Bry moved to the washroom and splashed cold water over his face and head. He took a moment, raking his fingers through his hair to remind himself that he trusted Stori.

Bry moved back to the center of the room and stretched the kink out of his back as he glanced between the table and the unused cot. He wasn't sure there was even enough night left for him to consider sleeping. The faded memory of the nightmare directed him to the table.

He sat and held his head in his hands, staring over the maps before a knock interrupted his thoughts.

"Come in," Bry called over his shoulder as he stood again and straightened the mess of papers to hide his new plans under the old, outdated ones.

"Your Majesty?" Oskar's voice preceded his head through the door as he cracked it open and glanced inside. "Sorry to disturb you so early…" The man's voice waned as his gaze settled on the unused cot before returning to Bry. "You have a visitor, sir."

Bry raised an eyebrow at the early morning intrusion as he gestured for Oskar to let the visitor in. An officer in a wrinkled uniform stepped around the homeowner, giving the man a nod of dismissal as he did. With the door closed again, the officer stood looking at Bry with an expression somewhere between amusement and disbelief.

Bry tried to smile at the early morning interruption. He recognized the officer as the one who'd fallen over when he witnessed Bry riding into town. The man looked even more familiar up close, but Bry still couldn't place him.

"Well, damn Bry! I was gonna say I got a promotion, but I think you've got me beat. This still only counts as one point to ya though."

"*Ammon!*" The mention of points brought back memories. Bry stepped up to greet the tanned man. "Haven't seen you since the Raylex Deal. That facial hair makes you hard to recognize." Bry clapped the man on the back.

"That's First Lieutenant Torvis to you," Ammon turned his shoulder to show off the bright metal work of his rank.

"Well, excuse me." Bry gave him a mock bow. "I've had a bit of a promotion myself."

Ammon nodded, "Yeah, I can see. You've gone from punching bag to king punching bag." He waved to Bry's perpetually bruised face. "Still sparring with Shad, eh?"

Bry chuckled. "Obviously. He's around here too—you should say hi."

"Doubt I could avoid him if I wanted to." Ammon laughed.

"What is it you're doin' here?" Bry asked. "Other than falling over at the greatness of my entrance yesterday."

Ammon's face became somber in an instant. "Well, hating you. Everyone here hates the king. Myself included, until I saw that was you. Had no idea that scrappy mercenary I worked with was the bloody king."

Bry clenched his jaw and nodded. "That bad here?"

"It's not just that it's bad..." Ammon's scoff trailed off as he glanced around the room before settling his gaze on the table. "Do you mind?" he gestured toward the papers.

Bry waved him on and moved to stand next to the mess. He picked up one of the old plans, studied it a moment, then handed it to Ammon.

"I'm still not sure where I went wrong with some of these. Maybe I'm just losing my touch." Bry bit his tongue at hearing the weakness in his voice. He glanced at Ammon, hoping he hadn't noticed. Hawkish brown eyes stared through him for just a moment before turning to the paper.

Ammon remained silent as he scanned the diagrams and details of the plan. He spent several moments that way, head bent over the paper before Bry started shifting with impatience to hear his verdict.

Ammon set the plan back down on the table and turned toward Bry. "Your plans are fine."

Bry finally let out the breath he didn't know he'd been holding. "If they were fine—"

"They are fine." Ammon shoved Bry's shoulder to make the point. "They're exactly the kind of plans I'd expect of you. Problem is, we never received this plan."

Bry stared at Ammon. "Never received it?" he echoed.

"We received a variation of this plan. It was garbage. That's why I was so surprised you were the king. I've seen you make better plans sleep deprived and under siege."

Bry stepped back on unsteady feet as weeks' worth of casualty reports flooded his mind.

"… everyone hates you here," Ammon had continued talking. "And it's for good reason. I hated the king too. Yesterday when I saw it was you I—"

"I'm gonna kill whoever's responsible for this," Bry snarled as the world around him came back into focus.

The silence settled for a moment before Ammon broke it. "I think…" he paused and didn't speak again until Bry's attention had shifted toward him. "It may have been General Harailt."

Bry looked through his old friend, only half-listening. He didn't care who it was, as long as he could kill the person for all the death they'd caused. A quiet voice in his head reminded Bry he needed to know why Ammon thought the General was a traitor, but Bry didn't trust his voice over the rage. He forced himself to wait for Ammon to continue.

Ammon held his gaze for a moment before shifting. "Harailt always had first access to the plans on the AaD as soon as they arrived. He'd take them to review in private before letting anyone else see—said he was making plans for what he'd do to improve them. Since everyone thought your plans were garbage, no one questioned it."

Bry punched the tabletop. "I'm gonna kill him." The general should have been protecting his men, not getting more killed. Bry should have been protecting them too. He ignored the numb ache in his fist as he punched the table again.

I should have seen it. Should have known. The thoughts burned into his mind. He should have been able to put this together sooner.

A hand shaking his shoulder pulled him from his thoughts. "Snap out of it, ya asshole. This ain't no time to be panicking. And stop blaming yourself for everything. Share some damned responsibility, why don'tcha?"

Bry shoved Ammon away. "Stop shaking me, why don'tcha? Gonna make me sick."

Ammon shrugged with a smug grin that showed too many teeth. "Just don't want you to keep being a hog and taking all the blame." His expression sobered. "I'm serious. We all... we shoulda done something. Shoulda seen it."

Bry gave a noncommittal grunt. "I'm the one responsible. That's a king's job."

Ammon snorted. "I don't remember you acting any different before you were king."

Bry rolled his eyes.

"So, what's the plan, boss?"

"I'm still gonna kill him." Bry pulled a hand through his hair, sparing a quick glance at Ammon who nodded. "Have to find him first though. And the men..." Bry trailed off, wondering if he still had an army that would fight for him.

They've never been fighting for me anyways.

Bry frowned at the thought. He'd have to show them he was fighting for them.

Ammon grunted. "Yeah, the men. No one here is on your side, ya know? Murdering someone they trust, assuming you can find him, isn't gonna win ya any favor."

Bry growled and rubbed his head. "We'll arrest him. Then trial and execution."

Ammon nodded agreement.

"So, finding him then. Can you get some men together for a search party? I'll send Shad along to help."

"A search party? He left three days ago. You think he's still around?" Ammon frowned. "And how's Shad gonna help? He gotten over his powers enough to use 'em?"

Bry scoffed. "'Course not, but he might hate Harailt enough to try." Bry moved to grab his boots and coat. "As for Harailt, he put a lot of effort into keeping this charade going. I doubt he'll just walk away."

Ammon hummed at the idea. "I'll gather a posse. Send Shad round to the tavern; we'll meet there." He turned to the door.

"Yeah, yeah. No drinkin' on the job, though. Don't need you fallin' off your horse."

Ammon grumbled a curse and chucked a metal tankard from a shelf next to the door at Bry's head. Bry caught the object with a smirk and Ammon smiled and shrugged before leaving.

Bry's smile faded as he set the mug down and returned his gaze to the maps. He punched the table again.

I should have seen it.

CHAPTER 46

Bry considered his options as he stood outside the door of the house Shad and Jair were staying in. He tried to remain patient as he waited for the owner of the house to awaken in the pre-morning dark to let him in.

After several more knocks, the door finally creaked open and a man peeked out with caution. He blinked at Bry for a moment with a frown before he seemed to recognize him.

"Your Majesty."

"I apologize for disturbing you so early," Bry said, trying to hide the impatience in his voice, and resisting the urge to walk and talk by moving past the man and trying to find Shad's room himself. "I need to speak with two of your guests, Shadric Daemon and General Jair. Right away, if you wouldn't mine." Bry shifted his weight and hoped the man would start showing more signs of life or at least signs that he planned on letting him in.

The homeowner remained stationary as Bry fidgeted and waited. Finally, however, he moved back from the door just enough for Bry to slip inside. Once in the house, Bry still had to wait for the sluggish man to lock the door again and shift past him, leading the way upstairs as he motioned toward two rooms.

Bry murmured a quick "thanks" and moved quietly to knock on Shad's door and let himself in without waiting for a response. Bry stood in the darkness and blinked until his eyes grew accustomed to the dark of the room. He glanced first at the dark lump on the bed, then the two on the floor. Bry assumed the homeowner had disturbed some of his current guests' sleeping arrangements to make room for the king's entourage.

Bry scanned the sleeping forms closer and noted that one of the ones on the floor, farthest from the others, was shifting in form. He moved to Shad and shook him awake.

"Go away," Shad mumbled, throwing a lazy punch in Bry's direction before turning over to better ignore the disturbance.

Bry batted the fist away and jerked the sleeping wraith back to face him. "Shad, wake up," he ordered again.

A groan and grumble from the other side of the room made Bry pause as the sleeping form on the bed rolled and shifted.

Looking back to his friend, Bry saw Shad blinking up at him. "Who're you?" he mumbled again as he tried shoving Bry away.

"Wake up already, ya damn oaf."

The light clicking sound of a gun being cocked made Bry freeze.

"Who's there?"

The no longer sleeping form on the bed had sat up and was pointing what Bry assumed was a pistol at him.

"Identify yourself," the man said again as he shifted to get off the bed.

Bry raised his hands slowly and wiggled his fingers to show he had nothing in them. "I'm King Brynte Godric," he replied, then regretted it. The man wouldn't believe a random stranger in his bedroom at night.

The man scoffed as he shifted closer to the door and lit the Aquarian torch without ever taking his eyes or his aim off Bry.

The dark room flooded with a bright blue glow. Shad groaned louder and pulled his blanket over his head. The other sleeping man in the room also rolled away from the light with a groan.

Bry squinted against the sudden brightness but remained stationary as the man trained the gun on him. The man blinked and stared at Bry for a moment before shifting his gaze to Shad's groaning form as the wraith awoke more and perched himself on his elbows.

"Bry, what are you doing here?" Shad's grumbly voice came with relief to Bry, as did the peripheral movement of Shad sitting up.

The armed man also moved back toward the bed, where he had both of them in view.

"You know him?" the man asked carefully, not lowering the weapon at all.

Shad yelped, finally registering the situation. "Woah! Yeah, man, I know him." Shad used his best, casual, let's-all-calm-down voice. He moved to stand and casually shifted his weight forward, putting himself between the gunman and Bry. "This is Bry—nte. You know, the king."

The man's eyes jumped between Shad and Bry. He hesitated a moment before lowering the gun. "Sorry, Your Majesty. You startled me." The man blinked and fear danced in his eyes for a moment. The fear melted away as soon as Bry caught sight of it, replaced with a look of practiced indifference.

Bry dropped his hands with a noise between a chuckle and a relieved sigh. "You have good reflexes." He offered his arm to clasp in greeting. "I'm the one who should apologize. I shouldn't have barged into your room with such haphazard grace." Bry smiled as the man took his arm with something like relief.

The man looked at Bry with quiet, intense eyes, as if he could read every bit of Bry's character with one look. With that sharp of a gaze, Bry wouldn't have been surprised if he could. It was similar to Lawr's; he wasn't sure if that was a good thing or not.

"May I have your name?" Bry asked, remembering not to refer to the man as "sir" when he was halfway through the sentence.

The man raised an eyebrow and remained silent as he let his gaze slip quickly to Shad than back. "Major Victe Roark, sir."

Bry nodded. "It's good to meet you, Major Roark. I apologize again for disturbing your sleep."

"If you're so sorry—" a deep grumbling voice started from the pile of blankets containing the room's final sleeping occupant. "—then leave. Trying to get some damn sleep."

Bry chuckled and moved back to Shad as the wraith started gathering the few items he'd brought and jumping into his military cargo pants and boots. Bry started to the door as Shad hopped after him, pulling on his last boot. Bry opened the door and Shad hopped into the hallway.

"Get the light, will ya?" Major Roark said as he sat on the bed, carefully lowering the hammer on his gun and tucking it away under the blankets and his pillow.

Bry turned the light off and closed the door. He realized maybe a king shouldn't let his men tell him what to do, but he didn't really care and none of his advisors were there to scowl at him about being un-kingly.

"What's that matter?" Shad asked as he led the way to Jair's room.

Bry shook his head as he refocused on the problem he'd come about. "Harailt."

"Well, he's always a problem," Shad grumbled, knocking on Jair's door. He knocked again after a half-moment of silence.

"Who is id'?" a growling voice called from somewhere inside the room.

"It's Bry and Shad," Bry said just loudly enough he hoped the general heard without waking up the rest of the house's occupants.

"Come in," came the grumbled reply.

Bry opened the door and turned on the torch. Blue light lit up a grumbling Jair sitting on the edge of his bed with a handgun in his lap.

"Bry, wha'd ya doing dis early?" Jair growled as he blinked the sleep out of his eyes.

"We have a problem with Harailt," Bry stated as he moved across the room to grab two chairs huddled around a small table. He checked the room as he moved, just in case Jair had a roommate too. Though he doubted it. The other man on the floor of Shad's room was probably this room's original occupant.

Shad took a seat as soon as Bry sat the chair down and waited expectantly for Bry to talk.

Bry sat heavily in his own chair. "Harailt's been altering the plans I send until they're shit and don't work." Bry rubbed his temple as he shifted his gaze from Shad to Jair.

Jair held Bry's gaze with a cautious yet defiant one. "We'd jus' been assuming you couldn'd plan for shi'd."

"Hey! Bry's an excellent—" Shad stopped when Bry held up his hand for silence.

"I know. An officer—" He turned to Shad. "—Ammon Torvis, from the Raylex Deal—"

Shad's face lit up at the name.

"He came to visit me this morning. He watched us ride into town yesterday and thought there was no way I'd have been the one to send the plans they've been receiving." Bry pulled out the old plan Ammon had confirmed wasn't anything like what they received, unfolded it and spread it out between them, facing Jair.

He watched as the man looked over the plan, reading bits of it and studying the diagram. His natural scowl darkened as he read. Finally, he looked up.

"I saw a plan similar 'o dis. Chesler showed me some of da plans da men had sen'd back 'o complain. Id was much wors' d'ough. Dis one migh'd 'av worked."

Bry nodded and grit his teeth until his jaw hurt. "Yeah, that's what Ammon said. Harailt's the one who gets the plans first and takes it to review in private with no one else seeing it." Bry kicked the bed frame as he clenched and unclenched his fists in a failing attempt to keep calm and not punch something into the ground.

He could feel Shad's eyes watching him carefully. "Don't go beating yourself up about it," the shadow finally said in a calm voice.

"What the hell else am I supposed to do?" Bry snapped, trying to keep his voice low enough not to wake anyone. "There are men dead and dying 'cause I couldn't see that something had to be wrong with the way this campaign was going. My fault!"

"Ids no'd," Jair said flatly.

Bry turned his glare back to the older man.

"Par'd of id is, of course. You're da ruler. You'll always be responsible," Jair said with a nod.

Bry was listening now.

"Bu'd Chesler should have shared da plans he'd been ge'dden back wi'd ya." Jair grimaced. "Harail'd shouldn'd done da'd. Da'd bas'dard is da one who go'd 'dose men injured and killed. He holds da mos'd blame." He unclenched his hands and started folding the map back up along the uneven crease lines with tense fingers, trying not to crumple the paper when they itched to curl into fists again.

Bry sighed and held his head in his hands. "You're right, and Harailt will pay. Shad, Ammon's gonna get some men together to try and find Harailt; you go with. You'll meet them at the tavern in town."

Shad beamed at the mention of Ammon but sobered quickly and

narrowed his eyes at Bry.

"Why're you sending 'da wrai'd for da'd?" Jair frowned as he glanced between them.

Shad groaned and leaned back in his chair. "I'll try, but I can't make any promises."

"Thanks Shad," Bry nodded and turned back to a confused Jair. "Jair, you and I are going to the camp. I'll address the soldiers and we'll talk with the officers camped there. I'm still gonna need an army."

Jair spared a confused glance at Shad before nodding. "I'll ge'd my d'ings."

CHAPTER 47

Istoria sat back in her—Bry's—chair and stared out the window as the sun's bright rays slipped beyond the horizon. The view was gorgeous; she let herself pause and enjoy it. She sighed as she let her mind drift.

Loreda had made good on her threat to overwhelm Stori with all the minute details of the running of the castle. She even started asking Stori's approval for the guards and servants to start and end their shifts. Stori had stomped down the tedious little tasks as fast as she could, ordering the guards and servants to operate as they normally did and asking Chesler to ignore Loreda more often. Stori had tried everything short of talking to the woman again.

Since that worked out so well the last time.

She had taken to avoiding the woman at all costs. She sighed again. Why did Loreda always win whenever they met? She flexed her fingers at the thought. She hated losing to the woman, but avoiding her wasn't winning either.

"Come in," Lawr called, then set a quizzical stare on Stori.

Stori gulped. She hadn't even heard anyone knock.

Eleanora poked her head around the door and scanned the room before stepping inside. Klaas followed with a nod of greeting as he balanced two stacked trays.

"My, my. Bry might get jealous if he knew how much time you spend in his rooms with another man," Eleanora chuckled as she moved toward Bry's desk, winking at Lawr as she passed him.

Stori coughed on a gag and forced a smile.

I don't have time for this… She barely stopped herself from saying the thought aloud.

She watched Klaas set one of the trays down on Lawr's desk with a few words Lawr frowned at.

"I'm teasing, dear," Eleanora finished as she came around the desk and nudged Stori's arm.

Stori forced another equally unconvincing smile. She wasn't in the mood; she still had so much work to finish by the end of the day. Stori turned to Eleanora to say as much, but the frown on the older woman's face made her stop.

Eleanora held Stori's eyes with her inquisitive, judging ones. "Honey, you look as bad as Bry. Your eyes are bloodshot."

Klaas moved to the desk and set the second tray in front of Stori. He pointed to a small bowl of pureed green.

"This is *supposed*—" He rolled his eyes toward his wife and ignored her huff. "—to make up for all the nutrients you haven't been consuming. I won't be leaving until it's empty." He leaned in to half-whisper. "It tastes awful, but don't let that stop you." He stuck a spoon in Stori's hand before pulling back.

Stori looked to Eleanora for help, but the woman wore an ever-deepening frown as her eyes wandered over Stori's appearance.

Stori ducked her head and started on the bowl of greenness. She stopped at the first bite. It tasted like honey.

Klaas winked.

Stori smiled. She watched Lawr try the substance and stare at it perplexed before also turning to Klaas.

"Klaas, why do you tell everyone my medicine tastes bad?" Eleanora's frown softened for a moment as she turned to her husband.

Klaas shrugged. "Most of it does."

Eleanora scoffed before turning her intense focus back to Stori. "Eat up, young lady. We're not leaving until you're finished."

Stori relented. There wouldn't be any quicker way to get back to her work. And now that she'd taken one bite, she was nauseous from how hungry she was. She tried to remain as ladylike as she could while downing the food in as few bites as possible.

Klaas and Eleanora shifted the chairs on the other side of the desk so they could face her and Lawr at the same time.

Stori finished and gnawed her lip over a question she wanted to ask Eleanora. She'd have preferred that the others weren't there, but she had to use any time she could.

"Eleanora," she began quietly. She had to swallow and clear her throat before continuing. She hoped her voice wouldn't sound as scared when she opened her mouth again. "Am I ruling poorly in Bry's absence?" Stori grimaced at the words as soon as she spoke them. How weak and childish they sounded. She glanced at Eleanora, hoping she didn't notice.

"Dear, no one said ruling a world was easy," Eleanora said gently.

Stori ducked her head and blinked the stinging from her eyes.

In other words, yes. I'm doing a horrible job.

Stori remembered all that Loreda had said and forgot to listen to the rest of Eleanora's statement.

"Stori."

Stori snapped her head up. The three were staring at her.

"I was saying," Eleanora said pointedly, wiggling an eyebrow as a dare to Stori to ignore her again. "You're doing just fine." She gave her hand a reassuring squeeze.

Lawr and Klaas nodded with solemn frowns.

Stori tried nodding back as she tucked into herself more. She didn't really believe Eleanora. The older woman was being kind, not honest.

She glanced between the three of them. They must see how poorly equipped she was for this task. Everyone would have noticed by now.

Loreda did.

The thought of the former queen made Stori bristle.

Stop doing that! Stori wanted to scream. Her mind traced back to Bry's warning that no one would be safe if Loreda won. *You're putting everyone in danger.*

"Dear?"

Loreda was someone Stori would have to stop from usurping the throne. She couldn't do that if she was always drooling after the woman for how much better she was.

"Honey, are you listening?"

Stori shook the idea of drooling out of her mind. She had to…

A hand on hers pulled her back to the world around her.

Eleanora stood over her, concern flooding her features. "Are you alright?" she held her hand to Stori's forehead.

Stori blinked before pulling away. "Sorry." She noticed the two men leaning forward in their seats and their frowns had taken on a concerned look. "I'm fine. Sorry."

Lawr stood and moved to lean against the desk. He studied her with a look of… What? Pain? Anger?

Sadness.

He broke his stare. "I can help with more of the mundane tasks. I'll talk with Chesler about how to get Loreda to back off."

"It's fine," Stori lied. "I can and will handle it."

She hated that look, the way it made her feel—like everything was broken.

He held her gaze for a moment. Then the indifference was back in place. He nodded and offered a small smirk.

Stori turned to Eleanora's still worried face.

"It will be fine. I'm not letting Loreda do as she wants."

Eleanora blinked at the change in topic. "Loreda? What is she doing?" Anger appeared in the woman's eyes as she straightened. "Is that woman—?"

"She's not doing anything." Stori clenched her fists, digging her nails into her palms. "I'm not going to let her."

CHAPTER 48

Loreda moved through the halls with importance and a steady gait. She had somewhere to be and an evil king to overthrow. The thought amused her as she felt a faint smile twitch at her lips.

Today is a good day, no matter what.

She was in high spirits. Jeshua was starting his plan. She couldn't help worrying at the thought, but it was too late to go back now. The commitment had already been made and she would see it through.

For Caelyn. And for Jeshua.

Turning a corner as the hallway branched, Loreda moved further from the light and interesting parts of the castle. She didn't know why someone of such importance to the operations of the castle, Sentre, and even Medius itself, to a degree, would content themselves to stay in this back corner of the castle. Loreda shook her head. Some people she didn't understand.

Standing in front of the unimpressive wood door, Loreda swallowed the grimace that had taken up residence on her face and knocked.

A "come in" was sighed from the other side.

Loreda pushed the door open and stepped inside. She glanced around the compulsively organized office until her gaze settled on its sole occupant.

"Queen Loreda," Chesler glared at her with the same disdainful look he used on everyone. "What can I help you with?"

"Chesler, I have something to discuss with you." Loreda took a seat without waiting for an invitation that would never be made. She wasn't going to bother being polite, she'd decided before she even entered. Charm never worked on the tedious man anyway.

A hand was raised as soon as Loreda opened her mouth.

"Let me stop you right there," Chesler said, dropping his hand back to his desk and lacing his fingers together. His bored, ever-irritated eyes never left hers. "The little queen will throw a tantrum if anything is changed without her say so."

Loreda smiled and waved off the concern. "I did have a nice conversation with the queen after she spoke with you. I believe we came to a bit of an understanding—"

"Do you have that in writing?" Chesler interrupted.

Loreda fought the curl her lip wanted to make. She twisted her mouth into a smile and hoped she hid the disgust in time. "I was just saying that we have an understanding. This is nothing the queen will need to have control of. I just had a couple of questions." Loreda gave her best impression of innocent as the dark, cool eyes regarded her with indifference.

"That so?" Chesler said using as little energy as possible.

Loreda hated this man. She again tried to hide the grimace forming on her face. "It's about our new king and queen," Loreda started, as he stared through her with a continued air of boredom. "I just wanted your honest opinion about them. What do the people think of them? I know you keep tabs on the public opinion of our royalty."

Chesler tapped his fingers together at a slow and steady pace as he did nothing but stare through her. Loreda tried to remain just as still, though for some reason she couldn't keep her leg crossing her knee from bobbing up and down.

"My opinion of them hardly matters, but..." Chesler paused as he leaned forward to study her more closely. "Why do you need to know how pleased the people are with them?"

Loreda leaned forward and offered her most seductive smile. Chesler's gaze flickered over her, noting how the new position forced her body into its most flattering pose before locking his eyes again on hers and ignoring the assets she was now displaying.

She hated this man. Hate wasn't even a strong enough word for her loathing. "I just wish to know so that I might better serve Queen Istoria. It must be difficult for her to manage everything. And if the people are opposing her, it would be even harder for the young queen to rule." Loreda smiled and resisted the urge to snap straight upright again.

Chesler leaned back again and started tapping his laced fingers on the desk again. "In my opinion," he started slowly, with a pointed glare to show he was only going to answer the first question. "The king's a bit fresh. He's still growing accustomed to being royalty again and would prefer to be in the action, rather than signing paperwork for it. I assume that's why he was so quick to head off to the battle in Oroitz." He paused and swept a speck of dust off his desk.

Loreda tried not to scoff. She didn't care what Brynte was thinking, as long as he was gone. She must not have hidden her disdain well enough though. Chesler's silent stare was piercing through her again. Loreda swallowed under the intense glare.

"And the queen?" she managed to ask.

"The queen?" Chesler returned the question followed by a moment of silence before he answered. "Queen Istoria is young. She doesn't know how to balance power yet. It will take time, and growing pain, but she'll be an excellent asset to any ruler. The people are starting to realize this too."

Loreda nodded. She had started to realize that as well. She would need to keep the girl around. She almost sighed in relief. She didn't really want to hurt the girl. In any case, she was just a child that didn't have any choice in having to marry a monster like what Brynte would become.

If she was with child, though… Loreda frowned at the thought.

She wouldn't allow any of Vlasis's seed to live. It was too risky. Any child born would have to die. She was settled on that conviction.

"I thank you for your thoughts on the matter," Loreda said mechanically.

Somber thoughts had returned her face to neutral as she stood and turned to leave.

Chesler nodded and stood to walk her to the door. She gave him a polite smile as she left and he slammed the door shut on her heels.

Loreda scowled as she moved away from the door.

That little man will definitely have to go.

Thoughts of how she could have him killed occupied her mind as she marched back to her living chambers. She was so deeply occupied by the idea that she almost ran over someone rounding a corner. She blinked at the familiar face.

Istoria looked back at her in just as much surprise.

"Loreda?" the girl gaped for a half-moment before regaining her composure.

"Istoria, dear. I apologize. I didn't see you." Loreda offered an apologetic smile. She wanted to see how the girl would react to politeness.

Istoria blinked at her for a moment before giving a slight but equally polite curtsy. "Loreda, I wished to speak with you."

Loreda smiled in response to the girl's formality and motioned to a small outcropping in the corridor with comfortable seating. A decision passed over Istoria's face before she marched over and sat with a huff of annoyance at the slow down. The young queen seemed to be focusing hard to keep what Loreda imagined was meant to be a firm look on her face. Loreda's lips parted with a genuine smile as she followed the girl to the seats. The look was less firm than the girl imagined. It was more of a pout and Loreda wanted to laugh. She sat and tucked the genuine smile back away from her face, where it belonged.

"I know you're planning something, Loreda," Istoria started, the pout changing into a more legitimate frown. "I need you to know that I will do all in my power to stop you. The throne isn't yours and I will keep it until Bry returns."

"Well, you are subtle," Loreda noted aloud as a distraction, hoping she kept her face free of the surprise she felt at this declaration of war.

"It is my duty as queen," Istoria stated calmly.

Loreda hummed and tried to keep a twisted grimace from encompassing her face. "What if Brynte were not to return?" She paused and studied the morbid look that settled on the young queen's face.

Odd, Loreda thought. *If Brynte died, Istoria would be free of him. But then she'd have to rule by herself.* Loreda consoled herself that this was the true reason for the girl's concern. After all, it would be impossible for the young girl to earnestly care about what happened to the bastard of a king.

"Why would you suggest that?" Istoria's voice quivered just enough to notice.

"It's a possibility," Loreda assured her. "Men die in war all the time,

Istoria. You must steel yourself to the possibility. Not a single person, no matter how *important*, is safe from the grip of death."

Istoria blinked at her a moment before swallowing and dropping her gaze to her lap. She picked at her fingers and twisted them before catching Loreda's eyes again. "Why do you hate him?" she asked with a pitiful look on her pretty face. "How can you want him dead? He's your son. Why do you hate your own child so?"

Loreda stood too suddenly to be truly graceful. "He's Vlasis's son, not mine," she snapped, then turned and fled before the stupid girl could say another word.

How dare she say such things! Loreda covered her face, unable to school her expression into something acceptable as the words "your son" and "your child" flitted across her mind.

How dare she. Brynte was a monster. *Same as Vlasis.* He was a liar pretending to be different, but Loreda knew the real son of the Godric line. He was the same as his damned father.

Loreda rushed into her room and closed the door quickly behind her, trapping the chaos of stupid, untrue ideas outside with Istoria. The stupid girl didn't know what she was doing—what kind of monster she was helping.

We'll have to move up the timetable, Loreda reasoned as she moved to her desk and snatched the AaD resting there. She was halfway to calling Jeshua before she realized what she was doing. She told herself there was important business for them to discuss, and not that just wanted to hear his voice.

CHAPTER 49

L
ife is good.
It had been for so long that Sverre was waiting for something terrible to happen. But maybe it wouldn't. Atanas was giving him time to heal, just like every other time he had set Duqa on him.

Sverre remained consumed by his thoughts as he half-watched Dain, Ali, and Leon try to make dinner. They had insisted that he 'sit back for once and let someone else do some damn work'. He hadn't argued too much. His ribs were the agony of his existence right now, ever since Dain had made some sort of brace he'd insisted would help them heal faster. The radiating pain was more akin to his ribs being crushed rather than healing, but he didn't mention it.

An over the top reaction from Dain snapped Sverre's attention to the scene in front of him. Ali had dropped a plate. She flushed as Dain teased her over it but bounced back quickly by reminding the man of how much his own clumsiness had already hindered the dinner preparations. Leon handed Ali a broom and dustpan and shook his head in a disconcertingly grown-up manner.

Sverre had to smile. "Are you sure you don't want me to—"

"No!" Three voices shouted in unison.

Sverre blinked. His smile widened just a bit. Life really was good when they were all together. Next time, he'd have to find a way to get Dain's family here as well.

He hoped, even if it was selfish, that he could be alive to see that. Even just once. The somber thought turned his thoughts dark as the smile settled back into an expressionless frown.

The familiar tug of jealousy twisted at his mind as he watched the three of them. Dain in particular. He never understood how the man could so easily convince people to like and trust him. Sverre had worked hard for weeks, months even before Leon would give him the benefit of the doubt about any of his actions. Ali was easier only because Leon was around. But Dain, he could make anyone love him in less than a day. Maybe the dark man was just singularly talented. Sverre wished he could do that.

"Hey, grouch," the chipper voice pulled Sverre's attention to Dain flopping down in a chair beside him. The grinning man was ignoring the glares Ali sent his way as she cleaned up the broken plate.

"Yes?" Sverre questioned.

He stomped down his absurd emotions. He should be damn happy Dain seemed to enjoy his company. The man could be friends with anyone, after all. He certainly had better options.

"Nothin'," Dain beamed at him. "You just looked a bit down. Thought I'd come say hi." A bit of concern slipped past the man's smile and found its way to his face for half a moment.

Sverre clenched his jaw. Now his stupid jealousy was making Dain worry. "I'm fine."

Dain snorted at that. "Yeah. Fine like you have a hole in your chest."

Sverre felt his face twist into a half-grimace that made Dain laugh. "You're not going to stop bringing that up, are you?"

"Nope." Dain winked and grinned.

A small sound, a voice, caught Sverre's attention and immediately broke the happiness of the moment. His AaD chimed, "Atanas calling, Atanas calling" in a litany that burned his ears even though the device was tucked far away in his bedroom.

Sverre stood a little too quickly for his ribs. The movement immediately loosed a slew of retaliatory complaints from the other occupants of the kitchen.

He wanted so badly to listen to them, to let the happy moment continue for just a little longer, to ignore the call. But ignoring Atanas never ended well. He'd learned that lesson all too well as a child.

Instead, he turned to Dain. "The AaD in my room. Atanas is calling." In an instant, all the happiness and light was sucked from the room.

"What?" Leon's voice was so childlike and at the same time almost broken. "But you're not healed. You can't go." He looked around with big eyes at the adults in the room as though one of them could change it.

The smile vanished from Dain's face as he nodded and jogged out of the room down the hallway.

Even Ali, who knew almost nothing about Atanas, had a panicked look to her eyes. Her gaze flitted from Sverre's face to his chest, to Leon beside her, and back to his chest.

Sverre grimaced. He shouldn't have let her help with his injury. The thought returned to him with bitter contempt. He'd dealt with worse on his own. Why couldn't he have been stronger that night? Then she wouldn't be looking at him with such fear.

I should have done better, he chided himself as Dain reappeared with the AaD.

The stupid ringtone pained his ears as he waited for Dain to move to Leon's side and coax the boy into silence. Sverre nodded to Ali to do the same. She knelt on Leon's other side, wiping away tears before hugging Leon.

Sverre answered the call with a curt "sir" in the cold voice he reserved exclusively for work. He listened without expression as Atanas delivered his orders, efficient as always. He could have admired that about the man, if he didn't hate him so much.

"Yes, sir." He caught Dain's eye. "I can find him. We will begin preparations immediately." Sverre hung up as soon as Atanas did.

Sverre tried to ignore the way Ali and Leon flinched at the tone of his voice.

"Dain, you're backup. We leave as soon as possible."

Dain nodded and hugged Leon tighter for a moment before releasing the boy and standing up.

"I'll get our weapons." He moved out the front door toward the attached shed without another word.

Sverre tried to move past the shivering woman and child still enlaced in a hug on the floor. He made the mistake of catching Leon's eye as he

267

moved by. His boy stared up at him with more pain and fear than a child ever should. Sverre would have preferred to be punched in his broken ribs than see the pain in the boy's eyes.

He tried swallowing the lump that had taken up residence in his throat as he moved to his bedroom. Sometimes he hated himself for having taken Leon in. For putting the boy through this every time he when on missions. Leon used to think he was invincible until Sverre had been stupid and forgotten to lock his bedroom door once when he cleaning up Duqa's damage. Now the boy looked at him with those terrified eyes every time he left. He was too young to already understand there would be a day Sverre wouldn't come back.

And now Ali too. One more person who valued his worthless life and would be hurt when he died. Sverre hated how weak he'd been to make these two lovely people care for him—to be so selfish to want them to care about him when he knew he'd die sooner than later.

Sverre took a breath to steady himself as he started taking off his house clothes and pulling on his black work clothes. The clean backup outfit had replaced his bloody and torn one. He was halfway dressed, but the pain from his ribs was preventing him from extending his arms to get the tight shirt on.

He considered jerking the shirt with enough force damage his ribs so he could call Atanas back and tell him he couldn't go. It was a stupid thought. Atanas would still make him go. He'd just be in more pain. A movement by his door made Sverre freeze. He turned his back to the doorway and prayed it wasn't Ali or Leon. They didn't need to see his injuries again. He tried to jerk his shirt on, but his ribs screamed with pain and forced him to stop.

A dark hand rested on his shoulder as another gently guided his arm through the sleeve.

"Sorry," Sverre grumbled as Dain helped him get his other arm into the shirt and pull the material down over his torso.

"There's nothin' to be sorry for, Sverre," Dain said in an unusually somber tone. "Not one damned thing, so don't start."

Sverre shook his head.

Dain moved to grab the sack full of weapons he'd set by the door and emptied it on Sverre's bed. Sverre began gathering his portable arsenal and tucking the weapons into their different pockets and hidden sheaths.

Dain moved back to lean carefully against the wall and the sniper rifle he already had strapped across his back. He crossed his arms with a contemplative look and watched Sverre move. Sverre recognized the look as one that always preceded an idea he wouldn't like.

"Sverre, I'll take the lead on this mission, whatever it is. You'll be backup."

Sverre tucked his pair of Glocks into their holsters. "No. And you know that wouldn't work for Atanas."

Sverre didn't look at his friend. He was more grateful than he could say that Dain even suggested taking the more dangerous job. But Dain had a family too. And he would be much better suited to protecting both their families than Sverre would.

"Atanas doesn't have to know," Dain continued to push. "You're a good shot too. You can just pick an overwatch position a little closer."

"Dain," Sverre turned to his partner as he tucked the last of his weapons, a pair of twin short swords, into their places. "No. You're backup. This isn't up for discussion."

Dain straightened and glared a moment longer. Finally he nodded, but he was still glaring. "Then you'd better make sure you survive. 'Cause I don't want to have to tell them—" He jerked a hand toward the kitchen "—that you aren't coming back."

Sverre nodded. He didn't want that either.

After a moment of silence, they moved back to the kitchen. Ali and Leon were sitting at the table, murmuring in low voices when they walked in.

Leon bounced up and wrapped his small arms around Sverre in a bear hug. Ali stood and stayed back for a moment, twisting her fingers. Her face said she wanted to hug him too but didn't know if she should.

Sverre opened one of his arms a little. It was all the invitation Ali needed to wrap him in a tight hug.

"Please come back," she whispered, low enough that Leon wouldn't hear.

Sverre nodded against her head. He wasn't sure what he could have done to deserve her affection or an ounce of her care, but he still enjoyed it all the same.

Dain circled around and looked as though he was about to join the group hug when Ali and Leon released Sverre and moved a half-step back. Leon bit at his lip as he stared up at Sverre.

"Where are you going?" he asked, just barely holding back his sniffles.

Ali moved to rest a hand on the boy's shoulder and give it a squeeze.

Sverre didn't know if he could fit enough gratitude in his expression for how glad he was that Ali would be able to stay with Leon while he was gone. But he tried anyway as he gave her a small smile before answering Leon's question.

"Medius." He glanced to Dain. "Oroitz."

CHAPTER 50

A permanent frown seemed to have sunken into Bry's features as he stood on the makeshift platform before his army. He hated giving speeches. It was just one more annoyance of many that he wished his job as king didn't have—having to stand up an inspire people. He never knew if what he was saying was reaching his audience or if they were just standing there out of a sense of duty, waiting with impatiences to leave.

A petty part of him griped that they should be able to inspire themselves, like he had to. He stomped down that idea as soon as the thought entered his mind. He had to because it was his job and not theirs. They had their own jobs.

Bry's internal quarrel wasn't helping to settle his already uneasy stomach. He always got nervous and a little nauseous before any kind of speech, but this was ridiculous. The anxiety snake in his stomach seemed to be trying to strangle his intestines before escaping into an un-kingly pile of bile on the ground. Bry swallowed hard. That wasn't going to happen.

"Men, I know the anger you have toward me and if half of what you've heard was true, there would be good reason for it. There isn't." Bry paused and glanced over the crowd. They didn't look any more inclined to kill him, but they didn't look any less inclined either. They primarily looked like they didn't believe him.

"I've talked with your officers and we've discovered there is a traitor in your midst. Someone you've trusted, who has prolonged this war for their own purpose."

"Someone other than you?" a voice shouted.

At that the crowd began shifting with discord. Others shouted insults and questions, but Bry couldn't hear them as a wave of nausea made him pause. He swallowed and pushed the sickening feeling back as he directed his focus back to the crowd. The outrage hadn't died out completely, but it was slackening now that some had said their piece.

"The battle plans I sent to you were altered upon their arrival. They were changed for the worse by General Jeshua Harailt. The officers of your units will confirm this," Bry added the last sentence in haste as the anger of the crowd built toward him.

The crowd was shifting again, everyone ready to disperse and find their officers. They didn't believe a word of what Bry said. They wouldn't until they confirmed it from the people they trusted.

Bry wanted to let them go anyway so he could find a private spot to puke his guts out. He wasn't usually this nervous about giving speeches, but right now the little bit of food he'd been able to stomach when he first got to camp was threatening to make a reappearance.

"Men, hold fast!" Bry bellowed. He wanted to run too, but letting his men slip away wasn't going to cement his role as their leader.

The shifting stopped as his army turned back toward the makeshift stage. They seemed surprised he'd held them there.

"I know your anger. I am angry too. Harailt's crimes are outrageous. But mine are that I did not see this betrayal sooner. I apologize to each and every one of you for the time it took me to discover this treachery."

Silence. The entire crowd fell into a hush. No one moved at the apology from their king.

"Harailt will be tried and executed for his crimes, but this war effort must continue. His crimes cannot stop us from rising to face the threat of the Nomads. If we divide ourselves, we will fail to stop their advance into our villages and homes. In our confusion and suffering, the Nomads have grown stronger. Their forces have grown arrogant, thinking they can defeat us."

Cries of more anger filled the crowd.

"If they are not stopped here, they will continue attacking our towns and villages. Your homes! This must be stopped here, you know better than anyone. For me, I will fight with all I have to protect this sphaere and my

272

people. I ask you to fight with everything you have. Not for the sphaere, but for your homes. Not the nameless masses of people you don't know, but for your families and friends—for those who cannot fight!"

Bry wasn't sure when he had started yelling, but at the end, he was overjoyed he wasn't the only one.

The entire crowd began chanting "fight, fight, fight" back to him in a single voice that was deafening. The sound reverberated through the camp as the crowd continued chanting even as they dispersed. Bry focused every muscle in his face to keep from smiling. Or perhaps from passing out from relief.

He had an army. The relief was overwhelming as he stepped down from the platform. Jair greeted Bry with a smile as they moved through the throng of soldiers. "I didn'd know you could be so inspiring." He looked around at the army. "You did damn good."

Bry laughed. "Thanks. Now I can go back to my tent and puke. Stomach's still rolling."

Jair gave a gruff chuckle as they moved toward the large command tent. The laughs died once they moved inside. The grim faces of all the high-ranking officers in the camp was a quick reminder of the serious situation they faced.

Bry nodded to the few officers he recognized. Including a middle-aged major he remembered from the Raylex Deal. The shock written over the major's face said he remembered Bry too. He kept his distance. They hadn't gotten along at all during the Deal. Bry was pretty sure the major had even tried to get him killed at least twice. Bry ignored the major too, except for a nod of recognition.

Jair started the talk about Harailt's disappearance with more clarity and lack of hostility in conveying the facts than Bry would have been able to manage. Plans for a search party organized before talk turned to the upcoming battle.

Bry moved to the center table and took the battle plan Jair had been carrying and laid it out over the table. The officers gathered in tight to see every aspect and discussions started regarding alterations. Only minor changes were made to the plan to account for recent changes on the battlefield.

Bry's nerves over finally fighting in a pitched battle weren't helping his nausea. The plans he'd made always seemed more real and fragile than they'd ever been for the small battles and ambushes he was used to.

As the evening progressed, the grim expressions on the officers changed, first to relief at a well-made plan, then quickly to anger which grew until the officers were seething. Full understanding of just how much Harailt had been altering the plans was dawning on the officers, along with remembrance of how many men they'd lost.

The weight of the death toll settled onto the shoulders of every man in the tent. For Bry, the weight was almost crushing.

I should have seen it, was the only thought he kept coming back to.

"Hey." Jair nudged Bry and spoke in an unusually soft voice.

Bry's thoughts came crashing back to reality in what wasn't a welcome relief. His nausea hadn't dissipated at all.

Jair frowned at him. "You okay? You don'd look good."

Bry tried to swallow the nausea and smile.

Jair's frown deepened.

Bry guessed he hadn't quite managed the smile. "I'm fine," he mumbled, ignoring everything else as he leaned heavily on the table to keep from falling.

"Your Majesty!" a young soldier ran into the tent and paused just enough to take a breath before continuing. "There is a problem with some of the men."

Bry gave a half-nod as he willed the multiple versions he was seeing of the soldier to stop spinning.

One of the other officers in the room dropped to his knees at that moment and emptied the contents of his stomach. Bry turned slowly enough to not make himself dizzy as he held his breath. Two other officers in the room were ash white and turning green.

"You two," Bry pointed at the two officers. "Take him—" He gestured toward the man who was still heaving on the ground. "—to the med tent, and get yourselves checked out as well."

Bry turned back to the soldier in the entryway of the tent. He had to pause before speaking to make sure he didn't become sick when he opened his mouth. He wished all the officers would leave so he could be sick in private.

The soldier at the entryway looked more and more uncomfortable as the three sick officers left.

"Um, sir," the man started, waiting for Bry's attention to return to him before continuing. "The soldiers from two specific units are getting sick like that. Those officers were from those units."

"Just two units?" Bry ground the question out. He really needed all these people to leave right about now.

"If id jus dwo, 'den id mus' be some'ding added," Jair thought aloud as other officers started to move and mill closer to the exit.

"Something added, like poison," one of the officers said darkly. "If it's just two units, it's not our supply. Someone might have poisoned..." The man trailed off.

Bry couldn't see which officer had spoken as others started talking as well. He leaned heavily against the table. He really needed them to stop moving.

"Those that are sick need to report to the med tent and find out how this happened," Bry snapped.

It was all the men needed to disperse. The officers fled the tent back to their units to check on their own men.

Bry was just glad they were gone. All except Jair, it seemed. The old general was still pacing in front of Bry, grumbling about something or other.

"Jair, please stop moving," Bry choked past the heavy saliva in his mouth. He'd barely spoken before a wave of dizziness made him collapse to his knees. The shock of falling was the last aggregation needed as he purged all over the ground.

A steady hand patted his back as he continued to spit out the vile bits and fluid between heaves. A scrap of cloth appeared in front of Bry after he stopped purging and was left spitting. He took it gratefully to wipe his mouth. The hand on his back disappeared and Bry noticed Jair moving in his corner field of vision.

Bry stumbled and sat back against the table leg, squeezing his eyes closed. He only felt a little less nauseous now. And still just as dizzy. His eyes popped open at a sound somewhere in front of him.

Jair was back. He held a cup of something to Bry's lips. Bry cleaned his mouth as much as he could without moving too much before he was content to lean against the table and do nothing but breathe.

"Mus'a been what you a'de when we go'd 'o camp. You're gonna need 'o see a doc'dor."

"No," Bry mumbled as he tried to sit up, one step closer to standing. "Need to get back to my tent." He wasn't sure how much sense he was making. His voice sounded slow in his own ears.

Jair helped him stand and steadied him as he swayed. "You can'd lead from your d'end. And you need a doc'd—"

"I'll have a soldier fetch a doctor if I need one. In the meantime, I'm not gonna take one away from my men." Bry paused to breathe. "And I won't be leading the men—you will."

Jair's frown settled into a hard line. He nodded and helped Bry out of the tent toward his own as inconspicuously as possible.

They moved carefully through the maze of tents and small groups gathered around campfires. Bry's tent wasn't far from the command tent, but Bry was exhausted by the time he reached it. The nausea was creeping back up and he was only too happy to finally lay down. Bry kept his eyes closed though he could still hear Jair moving about.

"Call a doc'dor if you need one," Jair ordered.

Bry nodded. "Oh—when Shad gets here, don't tell him about me. Just put him to work." Bry cracked an eye to see Jair frowning at the request. Bry tried to smile. "Believe me, if he knows I'm sick you won't be able to get him to do anything. And he won't ever leave. He's too much of a worrier."

Jair grunted. He lifted a bucket for Bry to see before putting it back down next to the bed. A cup of water and length of rag was placed on the small table next to Bry's head.

"I'll send one of da medical aides 'o check on you in a bi'd," Jair said as he stood up.

Bry nodded and waved him off as he shut his eyes again. He held onto the vague hope that he could sleep the nausea off.

CHAPTER 51

D ain's attention seemed focused on watching the clouds overhead,
but Sverre didn't miss the glances his friend kept throwing his
way. He was worried.

"I'll be fine," Sverre assured his partner when he caught another glance
from him.

Dain scoffed. "You wouldn't tell me if you weren't fine."

Sverre grumbled a moment at that. "You'll be watching my back, so
there won't be any problems."

Dain scoffed again with more annoyance this time as he started
grumbling under his breath. Sverre knew as well as him that he'd never find
an overwatch position where he could cover the whole camp. And shooting
anyone in the camp wasn't the plan anyway.

"Just try not to piss him off too much." Dain's voice finally rose above
a grumble. "Know that'd be difficult for you," he continued to grumble.

Sverre grunted back as he readjusted his hood to hide more of his hair.

"Not that it does any good," Dain said as he watched him. "Ya red-
eyed devil. You'll stick out anywhere." Dain smirked.

Sverre nodded, but he was glad Dain wasn't too upset. The worrying
was making the walk even more uncomfortable than his ribs already did.

"Hey! Dain!" A cheery voice called from behind them on the road.
Both men spun around as a cheerful wraith bounded toward them.

Sverre tried hard not to roll his eyes and slap his forehead. "You know
the king's wraith friend," he said as a statement as he glanced to Dain,
waving back.

Dain flinched and shot a look at Sverre, his hand frozen mid wave. "The king's friend?"

Sverre slapped his own forehead. Of course Dain would go around making friends with anyone who passed by.

The wraith reached them and panted a breath before melting into smiles and greetings.

"Wow, you surprised me," Dain started. "I didn't expect you to still be in Oroitz." Dain clapped the young half-breed on the back. "Oh! Shad, this is my friend Sverre." He gestured to Sverre.

"It's a pleasure to meet ya!" Shad beamed as he gripped Sverre's arm in greeting. The same warmth that he greeted Dain with was now directed at Sverre. The wraith didn't even blink at the red eyes or white hair, just smiled all the same. Through with his appearance, Sverre guessed the wraith wasn't going to be one to pass judgment.

Sverre nodded a greeting.

Great.

Not only did he have another overgrown puppy to deal with, but the kid actually seemed pretty nice. He hoped the wraith didn't get caught up or hurt by their actions.

Dain and Shad started off into conversation that Sverre tried hard not to tune out.

"So, what are you doing back here?" Shad asked.

"Just work stuff."

"Fun, fun. Me too."

"Guess there's a lot of work around here…"

Sverre stopped listening. He assumed Dain would tap him if his input was needed. That was their usual protocol.

Sverre watched the wraith out of the corner of his eye. It would be unfortunate if he decided to try and read their minds. Oracaede always trained their operatives to be able to withstand a full blood Shade, but it would raise suspicion for this half-blood.

That, and he was a bit miffed at the wraith. Ali could have been safe in Sentre right now if Shad had been more careful about bringing Lawrence back.

Instead, she was stuck in his house, worrying about him. She was now well within the path of danger, along with Leon.

His frown darkened. He'd lived contentedly with Leon for years, but now that she was there… He couldn't imagine living without her constant presence.

What am I thinking? Sverre tried to shake the idea out of his head. Ali and Leon would be alone when he died. Dain would take care of them, of course, but…

Sverre's thoughts trailed off. It would have been better if they'd never gotten involved with him. He gritted his teeth in anger at his weakness for forcing them to live with him. To get attached to him. He hadn't been fair with that at all.

A tap at his side snapped Sverre's attention back to the reality around him.

Dain was glancing at him with a concerned look between carrying on a conversation with Shad. *"You okay?"* he mouthed the question and waited for Sverre to answer.

Sverre almost had to chuckle. He forgot how perceptive his friend could be. He nodded that he was fine and ignored the frown Dain gave him. He pulled his attention back to the conversation around him with a half-smile to assure his friend he was indeed alright.

The wraith was ranting on about the reason they were there. "… Bry was going to replace Harailt, but the traitor already ran away. The bastard was always a coward."

Sverre frowned at the news. Harailt betraying the king wasn't something he'd heard Atanas mention. The general wasn't working with Oracaede, so why would he do that? The wraith didn't seem to be thinking about why, he just despised the man.

"Why?" Sverre asked anyway, just in case the wraith knew something about it.

He swore Shad jumped at his voice.

He forgot I was here, Sverre thought. People always did.

"Why would one of the generals act against the king?"

"Oh, um…" Shad stuttered as he frowned and thought about it. "No idea. Other than that, Harailt's always been a contemptible ass and was never loyal to Bry."

Sverre inclined his head at the answer. He could tell Shad's questioning gaze was still fixed on him a moment longer before the wraith turned again toward Dain. Dain shrugged and moved the conversation to other topics as they neared the camp.

The trio parted ways once they reached the camp. Sverre and Dain skirted the edge until they were out of Shad's view before doubling back to find a place Dain could set up a perch. Dain offered continual reminders about how much he hated the forest as they trudged through it.

Finally, they found an area that would provide Dain enough cover while also having an overwatch of a majority of the camp. Dain grumbled even more about climbing trees as he started up.

Sverre ignored him as he moved back to the camp. He moved with wary caution through the tents until he passed the medical tent. It was overflowing with occupants. Sverre frowned at that. There shouldn't have been a battle in the past few days.

He moved inside and paused to hold back a gag at the smell. The overwhelming rank in the tent of bile was enough to make him pause as his stomach rolled. He tried holding his breath for a moment, though the smell seemed to penetrate past his skin just from the proximity. He couldn't get away from it.

Sverre swallowed hard and moved into the tent through the rows and rows of cots and makeshift beds on the ground. The men occupying the beds were in various stages of being sick into buckets by their sides. Walking up to one of the aides who looked beyond overworked, Sverre asked about the men three times before the aide even registered that he was being spoken to.

"You didn't hear?" the young man spat, voice already ragged from throwing up. The aide hurried from one bed to another, gathering the filled pails and replacing them with empty, albeit not clean ones. "Someone poisoned the food in a couple of units," the aide explained as he moved, filling any spaces between words with obscene language at each pail he gathered. He grabbed as many full pails as he could and headed to the back of the tent.

Sverre picked up the rest of the pails and followed the man outside through the back. A large hole had been dug and the pails were emptied into it.

The aide looked at Sverre with mild surprise but readily accepted the help in the vile task with a grateful nod. They dumped the buckets of smelly substance into the pit. The smell was almost enough to make Sverre lose his last meal. The aide was sick before they'd finished.

Sverre held onto the man's jacket to prevent him from slipping and falling into the hole. After a moment of retching and spitting the man straightened back up, wiping his mouth with the back of his hand. He mumbled a thanks as he continued spitting the foul taste out of his mouth.

Sverre waited for the man to return to an upright stance before asking another question. "Do you know what the king is doing about all this?" he gestured around them and toward the med tent.

The aide glanced between Sverre and the tent with a nervous and unsure expression. "Look, I'm not supposed to tell anyone…" He paused again to consider if he wanted to tell Sverre this secret. He continued after a glance at the pit of vileness. "The king's sick too. I was sent to check on him a little while ago. He's worse off than a lot of the men, but he wouldn't let a doctor check on him."

Sverre frowned. It might be a problem if the king was too sick to fight. "Why won't he accept a doctor?" he asked as they gathered up the empty pails and moved slowly back to the nauseating tent.

The aide shook his head, "Said it wouldn't do any good. Also, that he didn't want to take one of the doctors away from the men. I mean, we'd really be struggling if we were short a doctor, so I didn't argue."

Sverre nodded in agreement as he glanced around the tent again. He grasped the aide's arm in a warm salute before he turned to depart. He tried breathing the clean air when he was out of the tent, walking twenty reaches from the tent, then forty reaches. Sverre coughed—the smell was following him. It was embedded in his clothes and remained the only thing he could smell as he made his way through the shadows to the tent of the king.

CHAPTER 52

Bry lay as still as he could on his cot and watched the walls and ceiling of the tent sway. He'd told the aide who came to check on him that he didn't want a doctor, but he might be changing his mind. The aide hadn't come when he was getting vertigo from looking over the side of the cot, and now he might see the benefit of having someone there—at least someone who could tell him which of the monsters that formed from the shadows and danced around him were real.

He might have decided to go looking for a doctor, except the time when he could stand without immediately falling over had long since gone. Now he was stuck lying on his cot, watching the world sway, and becoming sick whenever he jerked his lolling head too much.

Of all the monsters that had formed and started moving, Bry didn't question one more with glowing red eyes and odd white hair gliding slowly toward him. This monster did look a bit more stable than the dancing ones, but Bry continued to ignore it, the same as all the others. He was content with ignoring it until it started invading his space. Sitting on the edge of his cot, it held a cool hand to his forehead.

The physical contact helped Bry focus on the monster. None of the others could touch him—his one comfort that they weren't real. Bry concentrated as much as he could without making himself sick. Closer inspection revealed that it was a man, not a monster, though he did have red eyes and white hair, even though he was young. Bry squinted at the man's face and tried to remember why he looked so familiar.

The man, ignoring Bry's intent gaze, never stopped moving. He checked Bry over, took his pulse, and then began rummaging through what seemed to be endless pockets in his cloak. He spoke as he worked too. Most of what the man was saying floated by Bry in an almost tangible, nauseating, stream of words.

"Inorgan... rsnic poison..."

The words floated around Bry as his head lolled trying to catch them all.

"Stay with... —other."

The man held Bry's head steady just as he was getting dizzy. The man pried Bry's clenched mouth open and poured in the contents of a small vial. Something about the man finally clicked into place in Bry's head. Being in his study—an assassin from Oracaede.

Bry jerked back trying to spit out whatever the assassin had given him. The man moved with him, clapping a hand over Bry's mouth and forcing him to swallow.

Bry tried to thrash against the albino but doing so only made him more violently ill. He stopped moving and swallowed. The albino removed his hand but remained close. Bry squeezed his eyes shut and waited for the dizziness to fade out to nothingness.

What is Stori going to do when I'm gone? The question flitted through his mind. *What about Shad?* He wanted his brother there with him more than anything.

Hundreds of scenarios passed before his mind about his wife and brother. Bry's eyes flashed open as he started struggling again. He couldn't leave now, not when he had people to protect.

Bry became aware the man was holding him down as he started talking again. He couldn't hear or make sense of what it was, but he paused his struggling to listen.

The albino leaned in, too close for Bry's comfort, and started talking next to his ear.

"I'm not here to harm you, Brynte. Nor to hinder this war effort."

Bry tried to retort that there was no other reason for Oracaede to send someone here. His retort, however, came out too gurgled and slurred for comprehension. Bry couldn't recognize the words in his own ears.

The albino waited until Bry quieted down before continuing to speak. "I have no orders to cause you any harm or hinderance. I will only have work at the end of this battle. But no matter my orders, I will not hinder you." The albino pulled back a little to hold Bry's gaze.

He looks honest, was the only full thought Bry could hang onto.

The albino nodded at something before speaking again. "Rest now, the medicine will take effect soon and you'll be up before the morning is light."

The albino pulled back and took Bry's pulse once more. He nodded with a satisfied look and stood. He melted back into the shadows and out of the tent without another word.

Bry tried to stay conscious to think about what the albino said, but waves of dizziness and exhaustion rolled over him until he gave in and nodded off to sleep. All time stopped and merged together into blurs of dreams before Bry started becoming aware of his surroundings again.

A bustling noise and someone trying to hold his jaw snapped Bry's sleepy mind back to wakefulness. The memory of the assassin startled him completely awake. He jerked and shoved the person holding him.

A thud and startled yelp made Bry pause. There was no way a cold assassin made that sound. Bry forced his eyes open and blinked his eyes clear before looking over the floor. The same medical aide who'd visited him before was picking himself up off the ground.

"My apologies, Your Majesty," the exhausted young man said with a look that he would have punched Bry if he hadn't been king. "But the medicine will make you better."

The aide dragged himself up to try again, but Bry stopped him with a raised hand. Bry took a quick inventory of how he felt. A bit nauseous and dizzy, but nothing compared to the last time he'd been awake. He could sit up without getting vertigo too.

"I've already had some medicine," Bry grumbled. He almost flinched at the words as they left his mouth. He was trusting Oracaede's Ghost? The thought made him scowl. Why was he—

"Yeah, I figured," the aide interrupted his thoughts. "That ghosty fellow said he gave you the medicine first."

"Ghost?" Bry asked, surprised that the young man would know of Oracaede's Ghost.

He frowned and shook his head. No, the kid didn't know that. He was describing the albino's appearance, of course. The Medians didn't have a word for people like that.

"You accepted help from that... that man?" Bry stuttered.

The aide looked at him with a sideways frown. "Yes." The man sighed and looking as though he was talking to a child as he continued, "The man looked a bit odd, but he gave us a working antidote to the poison and has been helping us distribute it to the men in the med tent. He looked a little demonic at first, but he seems like a good person."

Bry glowered at the aide. Did he really think he didn't like the assassin because he looked odd? The kid must not have met Shad yet. Bry scoffed but remained otherwise silent as he thought. He swung his legs over the edge of the bed, avoiding the pail of nastiness, and paused a moment before trying to stand.

"Sir?" The aide jumped closer to help Bry. "I don't know if you should be up so soon."

Bry ignored him and the vertigo as it came back, bringing a wave of dizziness with it. He swayed and stumbled until firm hands gripped his arm and back to steady him. Bry shook his head and blinked until he could see straight again. He mumbled a thanks to the aide who took a half-step back from holding him up, though he remained close enough to catch Bry if he fell.

"Wait." Bry frowned at something the aide had said earlier. "You said he was helping. Is he still in the med tent?" Bry took a step forward, toward the door.

"No. He left as soon as I was instructed to give you the medicine," the aide said, following Bry's movements with ready arms.

Bry sighed and rubbed his neck.

Of course it won't be that easy.

He thought over what he could remember the assassin saying as he stretched his sore back while continuing to shuffle toward the door. Poking his head out, Bry breathed the clean air of the outside world and watched the camp bustle for a moment.

"Uh, sir?" the aide started from inside the tent. "I might suggest cleaning up a little before you go out."

Bry pulled his head back inside and turned to the aide. The young man looked back at him uncertainly with a hand that fidgeted around his medical kit in one hand and used a rag to hold the pail in his other. He looked anxious to get back to his work.

Bry nodded. "What's your name, and unit?"

The aide grumbled, seemingly at the effort it took to recall such information. "Efijor, sir. Baroen Efijor, Aide in the 2nd unit Medical Command."

Bry noticed he was conveniently forgetting to include his rank, and with a jacket hiding his uniform Bry couldn't tell what it was. Bry nodded as he stepped aside from the entrance and held the tent flap open for the young aide to leave.

"Thank you for your help, Baroen," he said as the kid passed.

"It's my job," Baroen grumbled as he stepped outside and moved off through the mess of tents.

Bry nodded to himself as he searched his desk for a quill pen and some paper, or else an AaD to take note of the aide's name. He wrote it down with his best guess for the spelling. He'd make sure the young man was rewarded for his effort, if he could find him again. He wrote down the major from Oroitz too. He needed to make sure that man had a good post.

Bry shook his head at the mess this whole effort was turning into as he shrugged off his clothes and flinched against the cold until he pulled clean clothes on. Next he spent many moments more than usual cleaning all the bile and rot taste out of his mouth.

By the time he'd gotten his mouth to taste only a little like bile, Bry had worked up an even stronger anger toward whoever poisoned his camp. *Harailt*, he assumed. Not that he knew for certain, but he could assume Harailt would do this. He couldn't count on the general to be at all honorable or value the lives of any of his men now.

Bry fumed over what the general had done as he finished cleaning himself up. He made sure to tuck his grimacing expression away before he stepped out of his tent. He would make Harailt pay, though, no matter what.

CHAPTER 53

"An assassin?" Shad asked with something like a pout. He was upset about not being told of Bry's health issues when he first arrived.

"Yes, the same one as in Sentre before." Bry nodded as he tried ignoring the hurt puppy-dog eyes his friend was sending his way.

Bry'd almost wished he could have talked with Shad alone before telling Jair about this. The older man's expression was deeply unhappy at best. The coincidence of running into the same assassin twice without even attempting to kill Bry seemed to be taxing Jair's suspension of disbelief. Bry still hadn't decided if he should tell Jair about Oracaede yet.

"Are you sure id was da same assassin?" Jair asked, watching Bry with tired eyes.

"Yes, I'm sure. If you saw him you'd recognize him too. He stands out—"

"Oh, shit!" Shad interrupted. His unfocused gaze turned to Bry with a half-apologetic, half-shocked look. "He was albino, with red eyes?"

Bry nodded. Oracaede's Ghost had a distinctive look, everyone knew. Except Jair. He was frowning.

"Albino? Wha'd da'd?"

"Uh, lack of pigmentation," Bry tried to explain. "Pale, white hair, red eyes."

Jair's frown deepened but he remained silent.

Bry turned to Shad, who was looking about as pale as a shadow could look. "Shad? What's wrong?"

"Oh? Yeah, um…" Shad continued stammering for a moment before he managed to actually make sense when he spoke. "The albino, he didn't happen to have a friend with him, did he? Tall black fellow with a big rifle?"

Bry frowned. "No, he didn't bring a friend. Why are you asking?"

"Well," Shad drew out the word beyond what should be possible. "Rem-member my new friend from last time I was in Oroitz? The mercenary Dain?" Shad had begun talking fast, getting all the words out as quickly as possible. "I happen to run into him on my way here. He's back in town for work—"

"Is he albino?" Bry asked, interrupting the speed talking.

"Oh, Dain? No, definitely not. But… he had a friend with him. A really quiet, kinda creepy, albino guy. I think his name was Sverre…" Shad trailed off as Jair balked.

"You know da assassin da'd 'drea'dened Bry, our king?" the old general asked, halfway between disgust and disbelief.

"No, I just met him. I know Dain, a little," Shad defended. He sounded smaller and more defeated with each word. He turned his hurt eyes to Bry and waited.

"Shad, maybe you should consider ending your friendship with this Dain fellow. They probably work for the same people."

"Yeah." Shad hung his head.

Bry nodded and moved on to the next item he needed to discuss before Jair thought too much about the assassin's looks. "Any luck finding Harailt?"

Shad's look of dejection sunk further. "No. I couldn't find anything." He paused his grumbling to glance up and Bry nodded reassurance. He hadn't expected Shad would be able to use his powers well the first time he tried, but he was relieved Shad had at least tried.

A small smile finally found its way to Shad's face before he sobered up again. "The search party isn't doing any better."

Bry scowled and nodded again. "Now, about the poisoning. What do we know?"

"Haraild's responsible."

"We know that for certain?"

Jair nodded. "Da men found a suspicious person wandering around near da affecd'ed uni'ds. He was carrying some pouches of powder."

"Inorganic arsenic," Bry guessed, remembering the jumbled words the assassin had said.

Jair and Shad stared at him for a moment.

"Yeah," Jair finally agreed. "Inorganic arsenic, no'd very common around here, da doc'dors would have 'dake a while longer 'o figure id ou'd."

"How'd you know?" Shad asked, beating Jair to the question.

"Assassin," Bry answered with a shrug.

Two frowns deepened as they stared back at him.

"He diagnosed it, I guess," Bry explained. He wanted this topic changed as much as Shad had before. That damned assassin was creeping him out just to think about. "How does the man you caught relate to Harailt?" Bry tried to shift the topic back again.

"He said so." Jair still frowned, but his focus shifted back to the matter at hand. "Da men helped encourage him 'o 'dalk. Probably should send a doc'dor 'o check him when da o'ders have all been checked."

Bry nodded. The man was likely one of his soldiers, but he didn't have that much sympathy for him given the damage he'd caused. Bry turned his focus to the why.

"Why would Harailt do this though?" he asked the room. "I mean, what does he gain from it?"

The trio frowned in silence as each sorted through their own thoughts about it. Bry noticed a small headache that grew as he thought. He glanced at Shad. His friend seemed to be focusing hard on his thoughts. Jair shifted his weight as his frown deepened. He rubbed his head too. Bry shifted his focus back to Shad. He didn't notice that he was causing them pain.

"So," Bry said loudly. Both other occupants of the tent snapped their attention to him. The headache disappeared. "Any good thoughts?"

He was glad Shad didn't notice he'd been affecting them, but Jair turned a confused frown in Shad's direction before turning the unasked question in a frown toward Bry. Bry gave his head a slight shake and willed the man not to mention it. Jair continued frowning, gave a half-nod, and remained silent.

"I was thinking," Shad started, oblivious to the silent conversation.

"The only thing it really did was cause chaos."

"And pu'd da king oud of use for a while," Jair added, his thoughtful frown focused more on Shad than what he was saying.

"Yeah, but they couldn't have known Bry would get sick. My point is, what they wanted to do and what they did was create confusion." Shad frowned as he spoke and turned to Bry. "There was enough time when everything was a disorganized mess that they could have done something."

Bry glowered and leaned against the table. "You're right. Now we have to figure out what the hell he could have done."

The silence settled as they all, once again, returned to their private thoughts.

Something caught Jair's attention as he straightened up and addressed the entryway. "Dis is a priva'de audience, you have 'o leave."

Bry and Shad spun to face the entryway. A shadowy cloaked figure was leaning casually against one of the tent posts. The man had his hood up, but Bry could still see glimpses of white hair. He may not have even needed to see the hair to know who it was.

"Assassin," he said at the same time Shad called the man, "Sverre."

Bry and Jair had swords in hand in an instant. Shad had his daggers out even faster.

The assassin raised his head enough for Bry to see his blood-colored eyes. "I told you I meant you no harm," he stated as though that would help. He straightened from the post and started walking a semi-circle around the edge of the tent, keeping as much distance from the trio as possible. "If I wanted to, I would have killed you when it was most convenient." He spoke in a deep voice, enunciating each word.

Bry scowled. The assassin did have a point, but it didn't make his actions any more understandable. "So why didn't you?"

The assassin tilted his head to the side. "It wouldn't have benefited me," he said finally.

"You mean it wouldn't have benefited Oracaede." He heard Jair's breath catch and could sense his eyes burning into him.

Well, Bry thought. *They were going to have to tell him Oracaede was still around eventually.*

The albino took in Jair's expression for a moment before turning a calculative gaze back to Bry. His gaze asked a question Bry couldn't read quickly enough before it disappeared. "Maybe that as well," he conceded.

"Sverre? It is Sverre, right?" Shad asked with a half-smile as he stepped forward, just enough to be in front of Bry. Jair also had shifted his position just enough to be a little in front of Bry.

"Yes, that is my name, Shad." The assassin said, his gaze flicking over to Shad for the first time.

Shad's half-smile persisted. "Dain around?"

Bry frowned at the question until he remembered how Shad had described Dain—with a large rifle.

Shit. A sniper, Bry thought.

The albino's expressionless gaze moved back to Bry. "He's around. It is difficult to line up a good shot through a tent, but he is skilled."

"Oh," Shad spared a quick glance at the tent walls. "Tell him I say 'hi' when you see him again."

"So wha'd da hell do you wan'd?" Jair growled, apparently over his shock at hearing about Oracaede.

The assassin spared Jair a glance. "I've only come to deliver a message."

"What's the message?" Bry snapped.

He regretted it as soon as the words left his mouth. Any message from Oracaede would mean blood and a show of force. That was how they operated.

That's probably what the sniper's for, Bry thought, glancing at the tent walls. Bry felt the beginnings of another headache. *Damn this assassin*, he thought. *I'm gonna kill him when I get the chance.*

"Dain is only here for backup," the assassin said calmly, as though he could read Bry's mind. "He will not shoot unless—" His gazed shifted to Bry's sword and dagger for a moment. "—provoked," he finished with a flicker of something that might have been a smile.

Bry glowered at the assassin. *What is he, a mind reader?* Bry paused at the thought; he already had one of those.

His glance flickered to Shad who was already frowning in concentration. That explained the headache Bry was getting. If Shad focused too hard though, he was gonna kill the assassin. They needed answers, not a dead killer.

Bry looked back to the albino. He didn't show any signs he was even aware of Shad's attack. Most people could sense it right away. Shad wasn't good at being sneaky.

"Damn it." Shad's focus dropped and the headache left with it as Shad panted a couple of breaths before staring with a confused frown at the albino.

"You didn't know? Oracaede trains all their operatives against the abilities of Shades," the albino said to Shad. "You can't get into my mind, much less kill me."

Shad panted again. "Wasn't trying to kill you," he grumbled.

The assassin hummed at that.

"What's the message?" Bry repeated. He didn't like the nagging sensation the assassin was toying with them. He didn't seem interested in delivering whatever message he had either. Bry frowned.

He seems more interested in watching us react.

"The message is simply that Oracaede is invested in this war. Whatever the outcome here is, this war will continue."

"Good to know," Bry spat.

It was good to know, but it wasn't worth Oracaede sending two assassins to tell them. Bry held his breath and waited for whatever the rest of the message was. The assassin ended his pacing in front of the entryway before speaking again.

"We will be staying until the end of this battle, but Oracaede will not interfere."

"Will you?" Jair asked suddenly.

The albino gave another ghost of a smile before ducking out of the tent.

Bry ran through the entryway without hesitation, followed by Shad and Jair. He glanced in all directions but the assassin had already melted away into the crowds of milling soldiers carrying about their work.

Damn it, Bry thought for the umpteenth time.

He was gonna kill that damned assassin someday.

After I figure out what he's up to.

CHAPTER 54

C hesler didn't usually go out of his way to make unrequested personal visits. When he did, they weren't to spoiled little queens. And when he did, he expected said queen to be in the king's study. The same place she'd been the past many days. Why did she have to grow an adventurous bone now, when he needed to speak with her?

Chesler sent a guard to find and fetch her. He sighed at the tantrum he assumed she'd throw at the indignity of being summoned. Loreda always had fits when she was first queen. He frowned at the thought. That hadn't changed, actually.

Now he waited. Sitting on the king's sofa in the disaster that was called a study.

How can someone accomplish anything in a place this messy? he wondered as he absently straightened some of the pillows and folded the blankets.

Queen Istoria still hadn't arrived, so he moved on to the bookcases. Half of their contents were stacked on the shelves or on the floor. Chesler grimaced. There was no logic even in the organization of the books that were properly placed on the shelves.

Once the books were as organized as he was going to waste time doing, Chesler glanced around for the next place to organize. His focus paused at a small table in one corner of the room. Every item on the makeshift desk was placed in perfect efficiency. Chesler blinked as he tried to think who the nice, organized space could belong to. He gave up with a shrug. At least he didn't have to organize it.

Chesler's gaze turned to the monstrosity that was the king's desk. Documents and tablets were overflowing from the flat surface and spread to the floor all around it like a moat of information. At least Vlasis had some semblance of organization in his workspace. Brynte was a mess.

Chesler shook his head as he started gathering the mess up and organizing the papers and tablets. He arranged the random piles into sub-piles based on the content and relevancy to Medius. Halfway through the mess, an old message on one of the tablets caught his eye. It was from a Lucian named Aarkdal with *Oracaede* in the title.

Chesler scanned through the message once, then a second time to make sure he hadn't misread. No, he hadn't.

Oracaede is still in operation.

He rested the tablet on the desk and stared into space, processing. How could he have missed this? The thought tumbled around his head followed by another one. Brynte had known this for months now. What was he doing to stop them? Was he doing anything? Chesler grimaced at the thought as he again wondered which side Brynte would choose. For such a straightforward man, Chesler had a hard time predicting how he would react to something like this.

Chesler glanced through the message again, still thinking about Brynte's response. The king hadn't made this information public. Chesler frowned at that. Did that mean the king was working with Oracaede?

No. That's not something this king would do, his gut told him. Then he rolled his eyes. *Making decisions based on your emotions now, huh? Doesn't bode well.*

"Lose something?" a man's voice startled Chesler out of his thoughts as he spun toward the entrance.

Lawrence Dara stood in the doorway, leaning against the frame and studying Chesler with ever calculating eyes.

Chesler hid the tablet behind his back on instinct, then regretted it. Lawrence had already seen what he was reading. The foreigner probably knew more about it than Chesler did anyway. That thought struck him as important. Brynte had brought Lawrence to Sentre within a few days of receiving this message.

Placing the tablet back on the desk as discreetly as possible, Chesler stepped away and waited a moment before noticing Lawrence was still waiting on him to explain his presence in the study.

"I am waiting for Queen Istoria," Chesler stated honestly, brushing his hands together to wipe the dust off. "Do you know when she'll be back?" He tried to make his voice sound natural, but even to his own ears, it didn't.

Lawrence remained stoic, moving from the doorway to the little table in the corner and sitting down. He crossed his arms and continued to consider Chesler. Chesler glowered back. Of course he should have considered that the only organized space in this mess of a room belonged to this man. He was more organized than anyone else the king seemed to know.

"What do you know about Oracaede?" Lawrence finally spoke again.

Chesler grimaced. He hated how this man could be as straightforward as the king, yet still secretive. He pretended to consider the question while really he was just trying to figure out what side this man was on. Safe to say, it was probably Brynte's side, not that it helped.

Still, what did he know about Oracaede? Chesler knew quite a bit. He'd been the one forced to help Vlasis implement terrible idea after terrible idea. But that was not a good question. A good question would be how much was he willing to share with a stranger and a foreigner. The answer was not much.

"I know as much as anyone else," Chesler lied. "What is it you are working on?"

If Lawrence wanted to play a questioning game, Chesler could play too. He hoped the more straightforward approach the man used would work on him since manipulating had never gotten him anywhere with the man.

Lawrence leaned back in his chair and studied Chesler. A moment of increasingly uncomfortable silence grew before Lawrence answered. "Very well, I'll go first. Apparently I found an information leak in my world about Oracaede's recent activity. Brynte brought me to Sentre to work out the info that I found and dig for more." He paused a moment. "Your turn."

Chesler inhaled at the casual way the foreigner stated that Oracaede was still operating. Reading a message about it was one thing but having someone confirm that the monstrosity wasn't gone made the problem so much heavier as it settled on his shoulders. He shook his head. He should have known they wouldn't be defeated so… He hesitated to call the carnage and atrocities of the last war "easy" but compared to what the next war would have to be, it would be.

"I…" Chesler stumbled over words. He still hadn't decided if he should trust this man yet. "What's Brynte doing about this?" he asked instead of answering any question.

Lawrence took a deep breath then sighed. "This is a two-way street, you know."

Chesler frowned as he checked the flooring for a road.

"I mean," Lawrence spoke again. "If I give you information, you need to give me some back. You don't trust me, I don't trust you either. But we're going to have to find a way to communicate, or else we're not going to get anywhere."

Chesler's frown deepened. Somehow, he felt he could trust this man— but he hated making decisions based on feelings.' He despised the idea in fact, but the man did make a point; this standoff wasn't getting him anywhere.

"Fine," Chesler growled. He moved away from the desk and sat down on the sofa. "I worked with Vlasis during his entire rule. Before Oracaede engaged with him, he was a slothful king. After Oracaede became involved… It was brutal. Endless lists of changes, each worse than the last, but he tried to comply with all of them. Otherwise they'd unleash their own specially created hell on Medius. We went from bad to worse to hopeless and then, it seemed, Oracaede was destroyed and we couldn't sink further. Then Vlasis died. The coward had a heart failure and left Medius on the brink of total ruin."

Chesler paused. He hadn't been perturbed by the king's untimely passing, but it had led to different problems. "After Vlasis, Loreda ruled for a short time with no sign of Oracaede. Now with the return of a Godric king, Brynte, Oracaede returns as well. I can tell you, the people will notice that coincidence and it won't help the king win support."

Chesler focused on that for a moment. It wasn't going to be easy to get the people to support Brynte against this returning threat. They would automatically assume he was part of it. He returned his attention to

Lawrence, who was still staring with the same intense focus. "I know almost everything Oracaede did to Medius, so what exactly is it that you want to know?"

"Nothing for now," Lawrence said, taking care to pick each word. "I just wanted to know I could ask in the future."

Chesler snorted. The foreigner didn't need anything other than for him to pass his tests. That was smart. He was irritated beyond words at it, but he could respect the intelligence of it. Now it must be his turn to ask questions at least.

"As for your question about what Brynte is planning," Lawrence started again.

Chesler couldn't help the grimace that slipped onto his face. This man was irritating.

"I don't know what he's planning," Lawrence continued. "But he is going to fight them. We think the Nomads' assault is a retaliation for Brynte rejecting their offer at a union when they sent someone to ask.

"Oracaede sent someone here?" Chesler asked sharply.

Lawrence nodded. "An assassin. The Ghost, or something. Didn't try to kill him though."

"Oracaede's Ghost? *Here?*"

That bothered Chesler. An assassin had been in his castle? Well, technically the king's castle, but his responsibility—and he hadn't even known.

Chesler's glowering was interrupted by Istoria entering the study in a huff. She stopped, surprised to see Chesler, and didn't look happy about the unexpected visit.

"Chesler," she started with a glance to Lawrence. "Is there some development I should know about?" she asked, moving to the desk and sitting down without sparing any energy on proper formalities or good grace.

"No," Chesler tried to hide his annoyance, standing up and moving to the door in as few strides as his short legs would permit.

He'd have to talk with Lawrence more, but not with Istoria around. She was too biased toward Brynte to discuss any of what he wanted to. He also didn't know how much she knew and the fewer people who knew

A Step Through the Empty

about this—until the king acted at least—the better.

"Didn't you say," Lawrence started, then paused and waited until Chesler turned to him. "That you had come here to talk with Stori?"

Chesler growled at the amused look on the foreigner's face. Amused, but guarded. Chesler swallowed his irritation as his mind flitted back to trust and two-way streets.

"Yes, of course. I forgot." Chesler turned toward the little queen, who was sitting at attention behind the desk and piles of paper, staring at him with big soft eyes. "Loreda came to speak with me the other day," he started and watched the way Istoria's face became a scowl at the mention of Loreda's name. He continued, "She wanted to know about the people's good opinion of you and King Brynte."

"Public opinion," Lawrence repeated, pulling Chesler's attention to him. He wasn't the kind of person one considered ignoring, after all. "She wanted to know if the people liked Stori enough that she'd need to keep her around for them to be happy getting rid of Bry," he stated the thought Chesler had reached after a day of thinking about it.

Chesler nodded. He'd wanted to be able to explain that to Istoria himself, but he shouldn't have paused and given Lawrence the chance to catch up so quickly. "That was the impression I got as well," he said. Then, shifting his attention back to Istoria, "I wanted to make you were aware of what may have been her intentions."

Istoria had a lip jutted out, an indication for any who knew her that she was thinking—though to an outsider it might have looked like pouting. Finally, she returned her full attention to Chesler.

"And it took you a few days to decide to make me aware of this?" her tone was soft, but not enough that Chesler could think his loyalty wasn't in question.

He straightened up and glared at her. "My apologies that I didn't reach the same conclusion as Lawrence in as fast a time. I will, however, do the king's bidding and do my utmost to protect his throne until he returns," he stated this with as withering a glare as he could while trying not to let his hands ball into fists.

Istoria returned her own pouting glare. She opened her mouth to say something.

"Stori," Lawrence cut her off before she could speak.

She turned and raised an eyebrow at his interruption.

"Chesler has other matters to tend to. He brought this to our attention in the time he could," Lawrence stated, sparing Chesler half a nod that he took as a dismissal.

Chesler nodded back, gave the queen a stiff nod and marched out of the room.

At least Loreda always had some grace when dealing with these matters, he thought as he finally clenched his hands. His soured mood lasted all the way back to his office.

CHAPTER 55

Stori gave Lawr a sidelong look as Chesler left. She knew the Castle Manager didn't particularly like or trust herself or Bry, but she didn't know Lawr was on good terms with him.

Lawr returned her glance with indifference. "What?" he asked as though nothing in the previous exchange was odd. In the indifference, Stori could see he was waiting for her to ask a question he already knew the answer to.

She grimaced. Stori still had to ask him, even if he was waiting for it. "I didn't know you and Chesler got along so well."

"We don't," Lawr replied immediately. "We just started talking while we waited for you." He paused and watched her.

Stori remained attentive and watched him back. There was more, she just had to wait for him to decide if he wanted to continue. He decided.

"Chesler learned about Oracaede while he was straightening up the office, and then we talked briefly about loyalties."

Stori looked through Lawr like he was crazy. "He found out about Oracaede?" she tried not to shout. "Why'd you let him leave?"

Lawr stared back with an expression of increasing boredom. "As I said, we talked about loyalties. I'm comfortable in where his lie."

Stori continued to gape at him. Was that all there was to it? He trusted Chesler just enough? She blinked at the thought. Lawr didn't particularly seem to trust anyone as far as she could tell.

"Also," Lawr began again as he started shifting the AaD he'd placed on his desk around in what Stori would call excitement for him. "From what I've learned from the information I've been able to access, Oracaede spent a lot of time trying to work around Chesler. He never worked with them."

Stori hummed at that as she watched him. She didn't know he'd been able to access any of the data yet. After watching his almost abashed excitement, she guessed it was a relatively recent breakthrough. "How much of the data were you able to access?" Stori asked. She watched as he stiffened and immediately dropped from excitement to his regular indifference.

"Not all of it. Maybe a quarter. It's been a little easier to unlock. Now that some of it is visible, the rest will fall out."

Stori's brows came together for a moment.

A quarter.

She wondered how long he'd had access to that much data. He just didn't seem to be the type of person to mention anything like this unless it came up in conversation or if she directly asked. She wasn't sure if she should congratulate him on that achievement or not.

He probably wouldn't appreciate it, she finally decided.

Sometimes dealing with Lawr was exhausting. "Even if he wasn't working with Oracaede, that doesn't mean he wouldn't side with Loreda." She waited for his reply, satisfied with her argument.

Lawr blinked at her slowly. A look Stori took to mean the topic was so slow to him that he could barely stay awake through it.

"Chesler wouldn't side with Loreda," he stated as though it was the simplest fact in existence. "He was here when Loreda ruled, before Bry returned, yes?"

Lawr didn't seem to care for an answer, but Stori nodded anyway before he continued.

"If he had decided that she was more fit to rule than Bry, we would know by now. He is loyal to the king, whomever that may be, and it would take a lot more than opportunity to make someone like him try to overthrow the crown. Especially not to replace them with someone of equal or lesser capability to rule, like Loreda."

Stori studied her lap. "Ah. I see. Thank you for the explanation." She gave him a quick smile that he returned with a confused look.

Lawr grunted in response and went back to his work, ignoring her.

Stori sighed again as she tried and failed to complete some of her work as well. She always ended up staring out the window as the sun was starting to set.

A knock on the door was quickly followed by Leha's head appearing around the door. However, she hesitated to enter further. "Miss Stori, is this a good time?" she glanced between Lawr and Stori as she waited.

"Yes, it's fine," Stori said too hastily.

She hated Leha acting standoffish around her, even if it was understandable. Stori was still apologizing for the last time she'd snapped at Leha for no reason other than her own stress.

Leha entered and closed the door behind herself as quietly as possible. "I don't mean to bother you," she started, moving toward Stori in a slow way. "I've just been hearing things around the castle and town that I thought you should know."

Stori tried hard to swallow her grimace before it reached her face. She stretched a weak smile across her face instead.

"Thank you, Leha, but I have to complete this work first. Maybe you could talk to me later tonight." Leha should know Stori didn't have time to talk rumors or idol gossip. She swallowed again to keep from snapping out loud. She was going to be a better ruler than that. She'd already decided.

"No, wait!" Leha almost stomped her foot as she spoke. "This is important." She paused again and waited for Stori's response. Leha's eyes were daring her to say no again.

Stori groaned and glanced to Lawr for support, but he had already returned his attention to his work and taken up ignoring them both. Turning back to her friend, Stori took in her determined glare for half a moment—long enough that she could tell Leha thought this was important. She nodded for her to continue.

Leha released a sigh before straightening again. "It's about King Brynte. There are rumors spreading that he's working with the Nomads. That he made the problem so he can fix it."

Stori snapped her jaws together with an audible crack.

This is going to be a problem. Bry needed the people to support his campaign against the Nomads, no matter how short it was supposed to be.

"The rumors started in the castle?" Lawr's voice startled Stori as she turned her attention to him.

He must have been listening after all. He waited for Leha to nod in agreement that he was correct before turning to Stori and holding her gaze. "Loreda."

Stori scowled. "What would she gain?" she thought aloud, even as the answer became obvious. "Oh."

Lawr nodded.

"That's what I thought, too," Leha started.

"She was already trying to determine if the people liked you and what they thought of Brynte," Lawr pointed out.

Stori squeezed her eyes shut as she tried to drown out the screaming thoughts that flew around her head. What should be done? How was she going to fight rumors? How should she regain support for Bry? What could she do about—

"Stori," Lawr's calm voice cut through her internal panic. She opened her eyes and looked over at the man.

"We need to stop this before it gets out of hand," Stori said breathlessly. "How can we do that?"

She stood and started pacing. She could sense her companions' eyes following her, but she ignored them as she thought.

"I will give a speech to the people," she started—even though the idea knotted her stomach. "A straightforward declaration, however, isn't going to win the people over. We may need to work on a few rumors ourselves." She glanced between her audience of two and received nods of agreement from both.

"We're going to beat her at her own game. I like it." A grin spread across Leha's face.

Lawr's fingers tapped a steady rhythm on his desk. "Any ideas for how?"

Stori shook her head. "Not quite." She smiled as she watched him nodding as a small grin started forming on his face too. "You?"

"I have the beginnings of an idea." Lawr stroked his whiskers for a moment before grabbing at some paper on his desk and beginning to write. "Give me a second and I'll have something we can work with."

CHAPTER 56

Lawr walked down the last hallway to his destination at a slowing pace. This couldn't have been the best way to go about knocking Loreda back. He frowned. Maybe he should have had Stori give her speech first, even if that was what they planned for tomorrow.

He should have come up with a better plan. Or at least a more solid one. Stori expected more from him, he knew.

Lawr stopped mid-step at that thought. She probably expected him to have the ODPAA files opened by now too. She hadn't been very impressed with what he'd been able to access.

Of course she isn't, Lawr chided himself as he started walking again. She expected him to have it finished by now. Bry probably did too. He probably hoped Lawr would already be finished by now so he could send him back to Terrae.

Stupid, stupid, stupid. He used the litany to chase the thought away. *You sound like a child,* he jeered at himself. *Afraid of being sent home.*

He stopped outside the heavy wooden door and swallowed the idea of bashing his head against it.

You still have work to do. Stop whining, he reminded himself as he went back to thinking over the vague strokes of the idea he'd called a plan. This indecision wouldn't work, he decided. Stori was counting on him. Bry and Shad too. Preventing Loreda's takeover was one of his rules, after all. He smiled at the memory, but it didn't warm his heart as he knocked on the door.

A heavy sigh came from the other side followed by the same droning, "Come in."

Lawr entered the office and met Chesler's ever-present scowl. The scowl shifted to a thoughtful frown and remained that way as the man studied Lawr.

"I wanted to continue our conversation, though I'd planned on doing that later," Chesler began as he pushed the stack of papers he was working on to the side. "I wouldn't have guessed you'd—"

Lawr held up his hand to cut him off. "I'm not here about Oracaede, I'm here about Loreda. She's causing problems."

Chesler brought his jaws together as he shifted his focus to what Lawr was saying. He nodded to himself. "I heard a few rumors floating about, regarding Bry and the Nomads. Is that what you're talking about?"

Lawr nodded. "We're planning a bit of a counterattack, if you will. I figured since you're the one who has a handle on the people's opinions of the crown, you might have an idea how we could best correct those rumors and introduce some of our own."

Chesler stared at Lawr with a blank expression. "And the little queen has agreed to this? A little devious for her, isn't it?"

"It was her idea. You shouldn't doubt how far she'll go for this kingdom—and for Bry. She's still learning that herself." Lawr smirked at the man's frown.

"I suppose," he grumbled, pulling out a piece of paper from his desk and beginning to write in the open slots.

Lawr blinked at him for a moment. "You have a form for backbiting an old queen?"

His smirk lessened as Chesler gave him a glare that said that was exactly what this was or at least something close enough. Lawr stayed in the cramped office longer into the evening than he would have preferred, working out the small details with Chesler for this stage of his little plan. Though, by the time he left, fighting rumors with rumors seemed more practical than he had hoped; Chesler had already started putting the ideas into action before Lawr even closed the door on his way out.

He trod back through the halls to check on Stori before giving up on consciousness for the night. He mentally crossed his fingers and hoped she'd made as much progress on her speech for tomorrow as he had with his assignment. The day had already worn him out too much to help with public speaking.

Lawr pushed the door to the study open and poked his head inside before entering. All was silent. He stepped over the threshold and closed the door behind him, careful not to make a sound. The silence remained.

He noticed Stori's maid, Leha, sleeping on the sofa. Lawr scratched his head at the sight. The girl's job was to help Stori, but with the silence of the room, he imagined Stori wasn't in any different position than her maid.

Lawr walked around the desk to find his suspicions correct. The young queen was resting her head on top of a half-written speech. Lawr sighed at the sight.

"You're gonna get a crick in your neck, sleeping like that," he said to himself as he carefully picked her up. "And you need to lose some weight." He struggled to reposition her in his arms without dropping her. "Or just the dress. Bet it weighs as much as you," he grumbled to himself as he staggered once before regaining his balance.

Lawr carefully moved through the doorway to Bry's bedchamber and set Stori down on the bed. He struggled with the blankets until she was under them and he was out of breath. He pulled the blankets back on the other side of the bed and moved to get Leha.

He struggled under the maid's thicker frame and weight until he finally managed to get both girls tucked away in bed before he returned to the study to collapse into Bry's chair.

I'm getting too old for this. He groaned at the thought as he crossed his arms and rested his head on them. *Thought Ali growing up would be the end of it.*

Lawr groaned again and rubbed his eyes. It wasn't true. He'd still had to carry Ali back to her bed when she'd fallen asleep studying. He had to chuckle at the memory of her saying it was good exercise for him. She used that excuse every time.

He blinked at the moisture gathering in his eyes. *Can't believe how much I miss you, kid.*

He closed his eyes for a moment to tread over the carefully protected memories. The moment lengthened until someone shaking his shoulder awakened Lawr. He groaned and shook the hand off.

"What?" he growled, wiping a hand over his eyes to wipe the sleep away.

"Lawr, you shouldn't sleep like that," a soft female voice chastised him.

Lawr frowned. Hadn't he just said that? He removed his hand and sat up straight to glare at... Ali? He shook his head.

No, it was Stori.

"I know that," he snapped, willing the dream of being back in his apartment with his favorite niece to fade faster. He glanced around the well-lit study to see the first morning light peeking through the windows. The reality of the castle took hold and the dream was gone.

Stori reached past him and gathered up the roll of paper she'd been working on the night before. She frowned as she read through it again.

"Well, this is terrible," she said with a sigh.

Lawr sighed and rubbed his head. "Let me see."

He read through the first half of the speech, adding bits and crossing a few things out as he read. He wrote a few sentences beyond where Stori's had gotten before he reached the end of his imagination.

"It's not bad. Not terrible by any means," he said, handing the scroll back to a doubtful-looking queen. "Really, I've written much worse," Lawr reassured her as he stretched out the kink in his neck before shuffling to stand so Stori could sit at the desk.

Stori slumped into the chair and reread the speech as Lawr poked his head into the attached bedroom. Leha was still fast asleep. He pulled the door closed and clicked it shut as quietly as he could.

"Not 'bad'." Stori dropped the paper on the desk. "But is it enough?" She looked at him searchingly for a moment, wide silver eyes piercing his soul.

Lawr had to glance away. The girl had a way of being too intense with no more than a soft gaze. Lawr growled to himself as he patted his messy hair down.

"Enough is what you make it to be. It's your speech. Just write it your way. I'll proofread."

Stori watched him with doubtful eyes. "Alright," she gave up finally, turning back to the paper before her.

"I'm going to get cleaned up. I'll be back," he said as he left the room.

"Alright," he heard her call after him, voice already distracted with the task at hand.

A quick bath and a change of clothes and Lawr was trudging back through the halls before most of the castle was even awake. He stopped by Chesler's office again and was glad to hear he had already put their plan to work. Chesler didn't say much more than that, and Lawr didn't press. The Castle Manager didn't seem to have slept any different from Lawr and was not in a good mood for it.

Arriving back at Bry's study, Lawr was content to collapse in his chair and listen to Stori practice what she'd written of her speech with Leha.

This is going to be a long day, he lamented as he listened to the speech again and started adding pointers.

The whole morning passed in that manner as they prepared for Stori's lunchtime event. Chesler had made the plans for when and how the speech would be delivered. He decided a semi-casual lunch with the nobles of the region would work well enough for the short notice. Stori's talk would be televised using the AaDs so that the common people could see it too.

The plan seemed fine to Lawr, but he could see the stress this sudden lunch was putting on the servants as they dashed around the castle. Accidental or not, they seemed to have forgotten to bring up breakfast. Both he and the queen went down to lunch with growling stomachs but nerves too tightly strung to consider eating.

Lawr grumbled more pointers and encouragement to Stori as she clutched her cut up scraps of paper and speech notes at the table. He watched her as she stood to speak and mentally wished her every good luck he could think of. He wished he could give one of her shaking hands a squeeze, but he thought touching the queen probably wasn't a good move in front of the crowd of nobles. Lawr clenched his fists in his lap instead.

Zoning out of the speech he'd heard a dozen times already, Lawr took up watching the other people at the table.

The table's crowd was composed entirely of strangers he didn't know and assumed Stori probably didn't know either. The twenty or so impressive looking men and women wore hair and makeup perfectly in place and sat with impeccable poise as they listened. Their pampered looks were almost enough to distract from their apathy.

Lawr's gaze shifted from those seated to the back of the large hall where Chesler stood with the other working people, including Leha, and a large piece of equipment Lawr assumed was the Aquarian version of a television camera.

A splotch of red caught Lawr's attention. Loreda stood in a dramatic red dress with her arms crossed on a balcony in the back of the room, overlooking the event. Her scowl was enough to darken even her immense beauty as she watched Stori. She only stayed for a few sentences before she marched out of sight.

Sudden silence brought Lawr's attention back to Stori. She seemed to have finished as she set her notes down and sat again. Lawr watched her a second longer to make sure she didn't hold her breath for too long.

Polite applause sounded around the table and then voices as the nobles fell into general conversation, chattering among themselves. Lawr checked the back of the room where Chesler was getting the camera out and assigning the surrounding people with various tasks.

"Well done." Lawr gave Stori's hand a squeeze under the table.

She nodded back as she watched the nobles interact. "Do you think it helped?" she asked in her gentle voice.

Lawr hummed. "These people? I don't know. I think they already have their opinions. This was for the people listening from outside." He nodded to the large camera being wheeled out of the room through the back door. "For them, I think you did well."

Stori made a face and stared at her food. "You weren't listening."

"No, I wasn't. But you sounded confident, and that's what people will notice. You spoke well."

Stori sighed next to him. "We'll see I suppose."

Lawr picked up his own fork to begin picking at his food. "Yes, I suppose we will."

CHAPTER 57

B ry paced his tent in a show of poorly concealed frustration. All
night they had searched the camp for signs of the assassin. All night
and not a trace. They had found nothing of the sniper either. He
could still be scoping them out and they wouldn't know until it was too
late.

That possibility had become too much of a threat for Jair's comfort.
Early in the evening he had insisted Bry remain in his tent with a suite of
guards. Now there was a counter for each of Bry's movements with several
voices offering a variant of, "Your Majesty, that may not be a good idea.
We can't protect you if you do anything. Please don't move, gesture, or
think without asking first—we will say no regardless."

Shad stayed with Bry. Extra protection, or something. He made light
of the issue at first, but also seemed to have grown tired of the entourage.
He sat frowning in a corner of the tent, evidently bored out of existence.
Bry noticed he'd started practicing shifting from his near-human wraith
form into his Shade form. He could hold the shadowy form for several
moments before slipping back. Halfway through every attempt he'd throw
Bry a "when are we gonna break out" look.

Bry kept shaking his head against the idea. Normally he wouldn't try
to make the guards' job any harder than it already was. That said, if one
more of them mentioned "protecting" him again, he might just green light
whatever Shad's escape plan was.

He wasn't sure how they thought they could protect him anyway.

Shad's description of the gunman and his high-powered rifle didn't give much room for "protecting" if the sniper started firing. That he hadn't started shooting at Bry or anyone else was troubling to Bry as much as the rest of everything involving the assassin. Bry glowered at that thought. Nothing that assassin had said or done made sense.

"Your Majesty, please don't."

Bry dropped the tent flap after a quick glance outside.

"In the open, we can't protec—"

"*Don't*. Say it," Bry snapped, leveling a finger at the older guard. He dropped his hand with a heavy sigh and moved back to the center of the room. "Just don't say it," Bry repeated, raking a hand through his flaming hair and jerking at the tangles they found.

The guard backed toward the other guards with a peaceful wave. The sporadic clenching of his fists was the only sign as to his own anxiety over the situation.

Bry paced back to Shad's side of the room. The gray-blue shadow was almost bouncing in his seat as Bry nodded his agreement to the escape.

Shad jumped up and approached the guards where they were all huddled.

There's a hole by the chair.

Bry didn't blink at the voice in his head as he found a carefully made human-sized hole in the tent next to Shad's chair. He waited until he heard Shad talking with the guards, appealing to their hunger after being cooped up for so long, and offering to bring food.

With the bored and hungry men distracted, Bry easily crept through the hole in the tent and out to freedom. He waited around the back of the tent for Shad to appear. When he did, the two made a quick dash through the array of tents and out of sight before the guards ever noticed the king's absence.

"Took you long enough," Shad scoffed, untying one of the black wraps from his arm and handing it to Bry. "I was ready for us to get out of there ages ago."

"Yeah, yeah." Bry tied the wrap around his head in pirate fashion with practiced ease. He tucked the last strands of his flamboyant hair away as he navigated the short distance toward the command tent.

Shad snatched an old tattered cloak from the edge of one tent and handed it to Bry. With his hair and clean clothes covered, Bry blended in with any crowd of soldiers in the camp.

"And why are we going to Jair?" Shad complained as they reached the back of the command tent and checked their surroundings.

Bry glowered at his friend. Spending the whole evening under close observation and with no sleep had seemed to drain Shad's sense of humor to that of an old grouch.

"Lighten up." Bry elbowed Shad in the gut. "We're talking to Jair 'cause he's running the army. How do you suppose we're gonna do anything if he turns the camp upside down trying to find me?"

Shad grumbled something under his breath but remained otherwise quiet for a moment as they listened to what was going on in the tent. Nothing loud and panicked; the guards hadn't yet arrived to tell Jair of Bry's escape.

Shad sighed again as he stepped around the edge of the tent. "I'll get him out here. You thought of any great argument to convince him?" he asked, taking half a moment to notice Bry's silence and the frown on his face before he started moving toward the tent's entrance. "Great. This'll go well."

Bry grumbled at his friend's poor attitude before trying to think of what he should say to Jair. Somehow, *"Hey, General. I'm going to war and you can't stop me,"* didn't seem like the best approach, but it was all Bry could think of.

The sound of Shad's incessant chatter undercut with Jair's grousing interrupted Bry's stream of thought.

"For da las' 'dime, Shadric, wha' do you need ou'd here?" Jair's exasperated voice asked as they rounded the back of the tent.

Bry had to cough back a laugh at the beaming grin which spread across Shad's face when the old general finally used his name instead of calling him "wraith".

Stepping out of a dark shadow, Bry moved into Jair's line of vision before Shad could either answer or start dancing in joy.

"Jair, we need to talk."

Jair blinked in surprise for half a moment before cutting a sharp, suspicious glance to Shad. "I should'a known."

Shad shrugged as he moved to Bry's side. "You should'a."

"Jair," Bry started, pulling the man's glowering attention back to himself. "I'm not gonna stay locked up in camp when we have a traitor to find, an assassin to capture, and battle to win." Bry fixed the general with a pointed glare. "You may not know me well yet, but Shad'll tell ya, keeping me locked away'll never work."

Bry caught Shad shaking his head in confirmation out of the corner of his eye.

A growl brought Bry's attention back to the general. Jair glared through him a moment. "You don'd need 'o be here for all 'da'd. Sen'dre needs a king 'doo, ya know."

Bry drew back with a scowl. "I can't leave yet," he said before thinking up a good reason for why.

I haven't had a chance to fight anything. Bry swallowed the thought before he could say it.

He needed a better reason.

"I have to stay at least for the battle. I've never had to fight a pitched battle before, and I'm not going to keep sending men to die in something I've never seen. It'll make my planning better too," Bry spewed the explanation before catching and holding his breath to stop himself.

He watched Jair. The general stared right through him and his half-honest reasoning. Finally, he glanced away, leaving Bry enough time to be relieved for a moment, before Jair addressed Shad. "He's never gonna stop dis, is he?"

Shad fixed his mouth in a straight line that puffed out his upper lip as he shook his head again. "Nope. Don't even bother trying. It'll just make it worse."

Jair sighed again as he grumbled something about "damn kids" loud enough for them both to hear.

Bry waited until Jair returned his attention to him before adding, "If it makes you feel better, I'll keep my hair and clothes hidden. Won't be as recognizable—'specially from a distance." He paused and waited for Jair's begrudging nod. "Good. Now, to any outsiders concerned, I'm still in my tent under guard. As long as those guards don't make a ruckus when they notify you of my absence, no one besides the officers will know."

Shad edged closer to Bry as he spoke. "Speaking of ruckus, there goes one of your entourage into the command tent," he said in a low voice.

An annoyed sound from the general brought both their attention back to the older man. Jair continued muttering under his breath as he turned and moved back to the command tent without another word.

Bry and Shad exchanged triumphant looks as they followed. They entered the tent just as Jair was instructing the guards to pretend they were still guarding the king in his tent. Bry gave the old soldier a wink as he passed. The guard somehow managed to remain stone faced while still manifesting an air of much rather preferring to punch a hole in Bry's skull.

"Any developments since I've been away? Any change in the search for Harailt?" Bry asked the room of officers who had gathered round the table in the center of the room. He glanced up from the maps and plans strewn across the table when blank-faced silence was all that met his question.

"Your Majesd'y," Jair started formally addressing Bry. "We haven'd found any 'drace of Haraild," he paused as his frown deepened before he continued. "Da enemy has sd'arded 'o move alone dis valley." He indicated this on the map.

Bry blinked at the formality until the thought struck him that none of the officers recognized him with his hair covered. The sound of muffled snickering behind him told him Shad had just had the same realization. Bry tried not to grimace at the idea. It was annoying.

"Sir?" Jair made sure he had Bry's attention before continuing. "Da Nomads have sd'arded mobilizing dese unids." He pointed to a few carved wooden blocks already in place to represent the enemy's position. "We jus' ordered our d'roops 'o sd'ard moving. Dey'll reach dis valley a 'dime afder dawn breaks, before da enemy reaches id dough."

Bry nodded as he took in the map and the positions of the friendly and unfriendly units. "How many units are you mobilizing?"

"Dwelve for now." Jair gestured to the notations for their army. "We don'd know whad da res' of da Nomad army will do yed."

Bry frowned. "We should have the other twelve units on standby in case the other Nomad units move to attack the camp."

"I was planning on jus' having 'den on sd'anby," Jair stated, giving Bry a sidelong glance. "Leave dese d'wo 'o back us up if we need id."

Bry hummed as he looked over the map again. "Alright. If you think it's best, it might be a good idea."

A unison of relieved sighs made Bry glance up and around the room. Every one of the officers, including Jair, had a relieved look on their face as they nodded in agreement. Bry frowned.

They're still testing me to see if I'll act like him—like Vlasis.

Bry balled his fists and tried to smooth the anger out of his expression before anyone saw. Jair gave him a startled look that said he didn't smooth it out fast enough.

Bry swallowed his anger and dismissed the officers to prepare their units as he rolled the papers up and packed them away. He tried extra hard not to crumple any of the maps in his fists.

"Sorry," Jair started as he too moved to leave. "Id's jus'… differend', working wi'd you now."

"Yeah," Bry growled as he finished packing and brushed passed Jair. "I keep trying to tell people that."

CHAPTER 58

Sverre watched from the tree line as the Sentrian army sat around waiting for orders. All the soldiers remained in their normal dress without weaponry or armor—all except one that Sverre could see. This man was in full dress, ready to move. The man's unit mocked his full armor, an immense weight to carry around so early in the morning and without orders. The young man didn't seem to mind the jabs at first, though after a time, he started shifting and pulling at his armor in embarrassed discomfort.

The sun poured light into the valley when the orders came to prepare for battle. Sverre watched the camp jump to life as soldiers ran in every direction in organized chaos. All the soldiers except the one in full armor stood at attention where the line would form before King Brynte.

The young king seemed impressed with the man's preparation and invited him to join his own ranks instead of wait. Sverre almost laughed. The young soldier was obviously ecstatic at the opportunity; he could barely form a sentence to agree. Sverre watched the dark-haired soldier his unit called Chess as he moved into the king's ranks.

Sverre fingered the AaD at his side.

I should call them. He thought again of Leon and Ali. It would be his last chance before the battle.

He started dialing before he could talk himself out of it, as he'd done the last several times. He clenched his fist, trying to figure out what to say as the device kept ringing.

"H-hello?" Ali's voice was fearful when she answered. The fear crushed Sverre's doubts and replaced them with concern.

"Ali, it's Sverre. Are you safe?"

"Sverre!" The relief in her voice made a part of him twinge with guilt.

He had made her worry. Again. He started to apologize when she continued speaking.

"Oh, I'm so glad it's you. I wasn't sure if I should answer and Leon is outside." The rambling paused for a short moment before starting again. "Are you okay? I didn't know you'd call. Are you safe? Can I help with anything?"

A laugh escaped before Sverre could stop himself. *There she goes.*

"I'm fine—"

"From you, that means nothing."

The irritation in her voice made him smile again. He rethought his answer and tried again. "I have sustained no further injuries."

"How are your ribs?"

"Fi—" He caught himself. "Hurting, but manageable."

Ali grumbled at his use of the word "manageable".

"How are you and Leon?" Sverre asked.

A sigh followed before she spoke. "We are *actually* fine. Leon is keeping up in his school, no thanks to me. We miss you. You'd better not have any kind of emergency. Okay?"

"Okay." Sverre paused. He shouldn't have called. He missed them too. Enough to make himself sick.

"Sverre?"

"Yes." Sverre swallowed and focused to keep his voice steady.

"You'd better come back." Ali's voice slipped as she spoke.

Sverre nodded but couldn't think of a response that could do justice to how much he wanted to be home.

Shifting and sniffling came across the line before he heard Ali talking to someone away from the device.

"Leon!" Ali called. "Come here."

He smiled at the sound of more shuffling and unintelligible sounds of excitement before Leon's voice came through the device.

"Sverre! Are you okay? You called. I'm so happy!"

"I'm glad to talk to you. I wanted to check on you two. I won't be able to call again until after I'm finished." Sverre tried to make his words sound confident, rather than what they were—an excuse to hide the emotions that threatened to choke him out.

"You'll call when you're finished though, right? We'll be waiting." Ali's voice came over the line, full of fear and hope.

"Of course." Sverre tried to be reassuring, but he needed this call to end before he fell apart. "I have to go. I only had a minute."

A whined agreement came from the two voices on the other end before Leon spoke again. "Sverre, I love you."

The sad little voice almost broke him.

"Love you too. Goodbye." He hung up before they could hear his unsteady breathing.

Sverre tucked the AaD away and held a hand across his face. He tried to clear himself of emotion as his hitched breathing shook his ribs.

Several moments passed before Sverre could face the world with his working passivity.

The soft rustle of leaves a distance behind him snapped Sverre's attention to his immediate surroundings. Familiar footfalls and the quiet sound of cursing was enough for him to relax and again observe the scene in front of him. He bit the inside of his lip, ignoring the blood as he tried to keep his face otherwise passive. He couldn't let Dain see how close he was to falling apart.

A few moments passed in the near-peace of the morning before Dain stepped up beside Sverre, grumbling as he pulled a twig out of his short fuzzy hair and tossed it to the ground with bitter annoyance.

"I hate the forest. These damn trees. The mud…" Dain's low mumble continued as he used Sverre's shoulder to balance himself as he pulled several burrs out of his socks and the bottom of his pants. He did the same for the other leg and wiped some pine needles and dust from his pants before he finally straightened up.

The grumbling continued as Dain bemoaned having to stay in the forest.

"Your friend," Sverre started after the stream of grumbles had slowed. "Shadric. He says hello by the way."

Dain's expression darkened as he patted one last bit of dirt from his jacket. "He wasn't upset, was he?" Dain flicked a glance to Sverre. "I mean, after you told them? He wasn't too upset, right? He seems like a good fellow, a nice kid, but he gets attached to people quick."

Sverre snorted at that. Dain wasn't one to talk about getting attached too quickly. "He was upset. Probably still is."

"Why?" Dain fixed a pair of wounded puppy eyes on Sverre. "You explained everything, didn't you?" He frowned and rubbed his head. "No. You don't explain anything, but you got the point across, right?"

Sverre tightened his jaw and remained silent.

"You didn't tell them?" Dain gaped for a moment. When Sverre didn't deny it, he threw his hands up, smacking one of them against a tree branch. "Why the hell not? That was our entire reason for being here so early. Atanas didn't even want us in the area until after the battle, but you said the king needed to know our true alliances. Why didn't you tell him?" Dain stopped ranting and waited, rubbing his hand and looking to Sverre for the answer.

"There was a general there I didn't know. The king and wraith also didn't know him enough to tell him about Oracaede before I forced the subject."

"But..."

"I didn't know him," Sverre repeated, holding Dain's gaze and willing him not to push the topic too much. "That means I won't risk our lives on the chance that he doesn't work for Oracaede or might talk to someone who does."

Dain held his glare for a moment longer before turning his attention to the armies and grumbling under his breath. After a moment, he glanced back to Sverre, "Alright, but now they're gonna think we're here to cause trouble on Oracaede's behalf. That's not gonna help us later."

Sverre sighed and pulled his hood down over his distinctive hair. "I know."

They watched in silence as the army started to shift and march toward one end of the valley. The silence was periodically interrupted by clangs of armor and men shouting as Sverre and Dain followed the movement from the tree line.

"Oh, by the way," Dain started. "I found Harailt. I saw him and a small group of soldiers slip back into camp early this morning, right after the poisoning incident. He was dressed as a soldier."

"How many?" Sverre tried not to groan. Protecting the king would be enough of a chore without the disgruntled general trying to kill him too.

Dain thought. "Less than a squad—too many to handle while injured though."

Another sigh. Sverre was tired of this mess. "They'll probably make a move when the army is in battle with the Nomads. There'll be a lot of soldiers to blend in with, and the Avare will be a distraction. Easier to kill the king than slip away."

Dain grunted in agreement then slipped into a discomforting silence. "You could still be the backup. The king wouldn't recognize me."

"No," Sverre answered without thinking about it. "You stay in the trees. If the king or myself need assistance, shoot something."

"Stubborn ass." Dain said nothing more as they stopped walking and watched the king's unit pass by.

Sverre shouldered the old pack he'd taken from a soldier who was still too sick to fight. He adjusted the standard issue Sentrian rifle he took from the same soldier on his other shoulder and pulled the hood of his cloak a little lower.

Dain rested a hand on Sverre's shoulder and gave it a squeeze. "Keep yourself alive out there. Not just the king."

Sverre blinked at his friend a moment. "I think I can manage both."

Dain looked about ready to hug him and he wasn't sure what he'd do with all the affection. He almost added "don't worry," but why bother? Dain would worry no matter what. He was nice like that—too nice.

Sverre gave Dain a quick nod then turned back to the passing army. He spotted a break in the pattern where another soldier had stepped out of line. He moved carefully from the cover of the trees to the open spot, pretending to be hitching up his pants as he fell in line.

"Fall out of ya'r own unit ahready, eh?" the old soldier next to Sverre scoffed and turned to an older soldier on his other side. "Young pups these days, can't even keep to a line f'ur a short momen'."

A grumble of affirmation in response before the old soldier turned back to Sverre. He studied Sverre for a moment with a displeased look. "Ya got demon eyes. Ya'r not a demon, are ya?"

Sverre turned his head to face him and forced his features into his best impression of a human smile. "Maybe. What's it to ya?"

The older man laughed and slapped Sverre on the back. The slap shook Sverre's ribs. He clenched his jaw in a grimace as an alternative to screaming and unclenched his fists before he could punch the man. He smoothed out his features into the same pleasant, "young pup" look before the soldier turned back from his laugh with the soldier on his other side.

"Maybe ya are." The soldier chuckled about it again before turning to gripe about the youth of the other soldiers, and the king, and hell, maybe the Nomads were just some young idiots, too. Their Wolves were just young dumb kids themselves, weren't they?

Sverre relaxed as the man continued in his steady stream of talking. He noticed that he wasn't the only one affected. All the soldiers in hearing distance were relaxed by the familiarity of the old soldier's jabs. Sverre maintained just enough of a presence to chat with the old man. He didn't get a name, but everyone seemed to know him as Pops. Pops was friendly enough, though he didn't care to learn anyone else's names either. He assigned nicknames which the rest of the unit kept up as their proper names.

"Hey, Demon Eyes," Pops elbowed Sverre in the gut when he didn't respond to his new name fast enough. "What unit were ya wi'dth?"

Sverre made a vague gesture forward. "The king's."

"Oh, da elite." Pops laughed. "Ya sure ye'r ok stay'n back here wi'dth us? D'ey might not let ya back in their unit."

"Think I'll manage," Sverre said with a small smirk. Pops scoffed, and the conversation lulled long enough for Sverre to probe for information. "So, what do you think of the new king?"

Pops scoffed again. "Demon Eyes, that young pup gonna be jus da same as 'is father." He shook his head with something close to anger or maybe severe annoyance clouding his expression. "He gave a good speech, bu'd I wouldn't believe a word of id."

Sverre rolled the answer around in his head as a personal question gnawed at him. "Why do you say that? The father bit?"

"Boy, I know." Pops turned toward Sverre as he walked. "I'll tell ya, I worked with ol' Vlasis's fa'ther, Gareen. Seen the way he'd beat ol' Vlasis. I think Vlasis learned from his father and I'm sure he taught that young Red-hair too." Pops shook his head at the thought and kicked a rock at his feet, knocking it into the leg of the soldier ahead of him. The soldier grunted and muttered a few colorful words.

Pops shook his head. "I'm sure Red-hair will be just like that ol' fool. Just give 'im time."

"Not everyone becomes the same as those who raised them." Sverre's tone was harsher than he'd meant it to be, but not harsh enough to shake away the idea of becoming like Atanas. The thought hadn't occurred to him before, but now, there were a lot of similarities between his and Atanas's working persona. A new thought lodged in his mind; had he ever brought that persona home to Leon? The thought made Sverre sick, but he had to consider it. He'd have to ask Leon and Dain too.

Pops stared at him for a moment before looking away. Sverre grimaced and Pops remained in uncharacteristic silence for several moments too long.

"Sorry, kid," Pops grumbled. He lifted his hand to rub his head but stopped before his hand ran into his helmet. He settled for kneading what he could reach of his brow, disheveling the layer of grime on his face as he did. "Don'd always work dat way."

Sverre grunted. He'd already said too much, now this soldier was gonna start watching what he said. Sverre tried to keep the self-directed annoyance away from his face.

Pops looked hesitant to speak for a moment, "I didn'd mean any'ding by id." He turned a bit toward the soldier on his other side and started talking again about the king. "Red-hair does d'alk a good game though, dodn't he?" He elbowed the other soldier with the same jovial spirit as before.

Sverre returned to focusing on the old soldier's words as the man joked and made the mood light once again. He still had a couple of things he'd want to try getting information about, but he let the mood settle back to easygoing before trying to talk to Pops again. A lag in the conversation around Pops was enough that Sverre finally started talking with him again. He made a few small comments about the situation, enough for Pops to loosen up and talk with him normally again. Sverre's sore ribs took even more of a beating as Pops's normal conversation always seemed to involve a lot of elbows and back slaps.

Sverre finally pushed the conversation to ask about Harailt's betrayal. He carefully made sure not to pick sides with his question but kept his voice low.

"I don't know," Pops started, again raising his hand to rub his forehead in a practiced motion, but dropped it before he hit his helmet. He kicked at the ground instead. "Da talkin' either of 'em do means nothin'. Ya'll learn dat, Demon Eyes. Talk's worth a penny a pound. In battle, you'll see who's worth da pound."

Sverre nodded, hoping his reaction was similar enough to an attentive "young pup," but not so engaged as to spawn any more life lessons he'd already learned the hard way as a child.

The conversation shifted and carried on to less messy topics as the march continued. Sverre kept up enough of the conversation not to draw attention by being too quiet, but not enough that Pops would remember him when they parted ways.

CHAPTER 59

Loreda watched work being carried out on the levels of Sentre below her terrace. The midmorning flurry of work was increasing as everyone bustled about their business and, often, the business of others.

The young queen's speech the day before had caused noticeable fuss among the working class of the city. It had also started talk with the nobles—mostly about which side would win and who would be invited for tea to celebrate. Loreda was sure there were bets being made.

She scoffed at the show of effort Istoria put into her little speech—and her apparent sincerity in it. That part Loreda couldn't understand. Surely the child couldn't fathom what a mess her life would be after the king's heir was born. Loreda tried to warn her, but the child seemed content to live in misery—either that or she just didn't understand. Loreda hoped it was the latter. Then there might be a chance she could help the girl.

Loreda sighed at the thought. She mustn't get ahead of herself. She still had to get Vlasis off the throne.

Vlasis's son? The thought made her blink. It didn't matter, it was the same thing.

There was work to do. All her preparations had to be put to action. Nothing Istoria could say would counter her now. Loreda turned away from the view as a new thought occurred to her. She just had to make Stori see the truth. There was no way Stori would consider staying loyal to Vlasis if she could just see. If Loreda could talk to the girl, get her to understand…

She called a servant and sent an invitation for Stori to come to tea. Loreda would make her understand. She left her room and moved down the halls to a small sitting room she had directed a servant to prepare. She sat in one of the rose-colored armchairs and instructed a servant to bring tea after she'd been waiting a few moments longer than she thought Istoria should have needed to get there.

Finally, Istoria arrived just as the tea did, and sat in fidgeting and awkward silence as the servant poured the tea and set out pastries before leaving.

Loreda watched the young queen fidget and struggle to drink even a few sips of tea as she waited for the more experienced queen to reveal why she'd called her. Loreda tried to swallow her smile. How much Istoria reminded her of Caelyn, tartiness and all.

She pushed the small grin away and replaced it with a carefully crafted public smile.

"Istoria, dear, I hope you are well," she started, and waited for Istoria to get far enough past sputtering on her tea to nod back before continuing. "Now look, Istoria. I think the last few days have been trying and maybe a bit confusing. With your speech and based on our last conversation, I think you may have misinterpreted my actions. I'd like to remain friends, if you'd consider?"

Istoria set her tea down and shifted, adjusting and pulling at her sleeves before answering.

"Thank you. I hope you don't think my actions have been crass these last few days. My duties as acting regent require a show of commitment. I'm sure you understand."

Loreda blinked. She almost thought she'd misheard. Was it her imagination or had Istoria placed unnecessary stress on the words "a show"?

What luck! Maybe the young queen could see the truth after all.

"Oh?" Loreda blinked, forgetting what she'd been planning to ask in the light of this new ray of hope.

Perhaps the girl is acting out of mere obligation to her position.

Istoria nodded and fidgeted before straightening and stilling her hands. "I hoped you would understand that I have to make sure there is no doubt as to my loyalties." Istoria clenched her hands into fists. "Even if I could see the benefit in some of your ideas," she said haltingly. "That you have discussed previously—about Bry… not returning."

"Istoria, dear." Loreda leaned across the table and took the girl's hand. She gave it a reassuring squeeze before anything more could be said. She smiled an honest smile and released the breath she hadn't realized she'd been holding. This dear girl could see the truth, she'd realized that anything related to Vlasis could only be a monster.

"I-I wanted to know how… or what you thought might work… or…?" Istoria trailed off into silence as she stared at Loreda's hand covering her own.

"Don't worry," Loreda cooed with an easy smile. She gave the hand under her own a squeeze before drawing back. "I can understand you had to pretend for the sake of when the King returned. But that isn't an issue. He won't be."

Istoria's gaze jumped to meet Loreda's. "Won't be?" the girl asked.

Her big eyes searched Loreda's for the truth of the statement. Loreda's smile grew and as she watched the news settle into the young queen's mind.

"How would… How can you be so sure?" Istoria asked, again with searching eyes. She looked perturbed and uncertain.

Of course she should look so. Loreda pitied the girl. "It will be taken care of, you may be assured of that. A friend of mine will be handling it personally."

"A friend?" Istoria's gaze sharpened but then softened so quickly Loreda wasn't sure what to make of it. "I thought—" the young queen paused before starting again. "I thought the Nomad's…?" She turned her searching gaze to Loreda for the answer.

Loreda smiled. The big eyes staring back at her reminded her so much of Caelyn, even when discussing such an awful topic. "The Nomads will play their part, but I wouldn't leave something so important up to them. General Jeshua Harailt will see to that work himself. Believe me, he is fully capable of dealing with the king."

She gave Istoria a confident nod. She couldn't help the pride that filled her posture at the thought of Jeshua. He would most definitely take care of the damned king. He had made that promise when Vlasis was alive too. Even if he hadn't directly killed the old king, Jeshua was assuredly a great help in aiding the old coward's demise.

Istoria watching Loreda with a stricken look before she shifted her gaze back to her hands, clenched in her lap. "I understand," she said slowly. "I'm just a bit overwhelmed by all this. I didn't know things would be changing so quickly."

Sitting back, Loreda gathered her teacup and saucer and watched her companion as she carefully sipped her tea and tried to keep her own excitement about the girl's allegiance from spilling out.

Istoria switched between sitting passively staring off into space to fidgeting almost violently only to switch back to staring for a few more moments.

Loreda sat her cup and saucer back on the table.

"Dear," she said softly, interrupting Istoria's stare, waiting for her eyes to focus before continuing. "This will be a big change; I can see you realize that. Do you wish for solitude to think everything over? We'll soon have all the free time you could desire, so don't concern yourself with rushing."

Istoria blinked a moment and appeared to be thinking before turning her attention back to Loreda. "I might benefit from time to consider the things that will change as a result of what you've shared with me. If you don't mind cutting our tea time short."

"Of course." Loreda stood in one graceful motion and moved to stand next to Istoria. She rested her hand on the girl's shoulder and gave a comforting squeeze. "It'll all be over soon, don't worry. You'll be free."

Istoria jerked lightly at the sentiment and looked up at Loreda without blinking. "Yes, I guess I will." She sighed at the notion.

Loreda gave her shoulder another squeeze and tried to keep her smile contained before she stepped away and left the sitting room, heading back to her own chambers.

Back in her own room, Loreda could have danced for joy. If only she could contact Jeshua to let him know the good news.

But he is busy with his own part in this, Loreda reminded herself as she forced herself not to skip to her desk.

"Ah, freedom," Loreda whispered to herself.

She had hardly allowed her mind to wander to the thought until now, but with Istoria on her side, freedom from Vlasis's presence was closer than it ever had been. Finally, the idea of being able to live together with Caelyn and Jeshua was enough to bring tears to her eyes.

Loreda stood next to her desk for several moments, thinking only of the life she would give Caelyn before she finally focused enough to sit down and try to work. She failed at making any progress though as her mind continued slipping back to Jeshua and her daughter.

A sudden bang made Loreda jump as her attention flew to the door. It had slammed open and a line of guards poured in.

"What is this?" Loreda was on her feet, glaring at the closest guardsman until he dropped his gaze. "What is going on here?" she asked again, although this time her voice sounded shrill to her own ears.

"Queen Mother Loreda Iano-Godric," Chesler—*that hateful man*—filed in last, already reading from an AaD. "You have been charged with high treason against King Brynte Godric. You will be held, awaiting His Majesty's return for trial and sentencing." He motioned two of the guards forward to take her.

"*What?*" Loreda shouted as two guards stepped beside her. How had this happened? Her mind tumbled over itself even as Loreda clenched her jaw and focused her glare to scare away the tears threatening to fall. "On what basis—?" She swallowed the disgusting, weak whisper that had escaped her lips. "On what basis?" she snapped this time, jerking her arms away from the guards trying to lead her away.

Chesler raised an eyebrow and continued observing her with a nearly indifferent expression. Not indifferent enough to keep a smile from pulling at his mouth as he answered, "Queen Istoria brought the accusation against—"

"Istoria?" Loreda's jaw hung slack as she blinked at the man and waited, hoping he would correct himself. Istoria wouldn't... She was on her side. They'd only just spoken...

Loreda snapped her jaws together with an audible crack. *That bitch.* A trick? The little queen had tricked her? *Impossible.*

The former queen stood frozen, glaring into space as the notion of freedom crashed down around her. She struggled to suck in a breath of air as she felt the guards by her sides again.

She jerked her away again and leveled a glare at Chesler. "If Istoria has made claims against me, you know that her word isn't enough to have me arrested. Her word against mine is a matter we can settle quickly, Chesler. We can talk with her and—"

"It isn't just her word," Chesler interrupted with a smile—an actual smile.

Loreda wanted to strangle the man. She blinked as her anger faded enough that she could understand the implication.

"Evidence?" Loreda's tone wasn't as smooth as she wanted it to be. She pasted a smile onto her face and took a deep breath before continuing. "The little queen has evidence against me? Really, Chesler?"

"Really." Chesler nodded again to the guardsmen. "A recording of you mentioning your plan over tea."

Loreda stared through Chesler and ground her teeth. When had Istoria become so suspicious? Every time they'd spoken, or just today? A thought gripped Loreda. *Did Istoria have a recording of the time she'd accidentally mentioned Caelyn?*

"I need to speak with Istoria!" Loreda blurted out. She tried to rush passed the guards, but the two at her side already had hold of her arms and they didn't let go this time. She turned her gaze back to Chesler, who was regarding her outburst with a tilted head and a frown. "Chesler, I *need* to speak with Istoria." She couldn't stop the desperation from slipping into her voice.

Chesler raised an eyebrow at the request. "I'll let her know. Maybe she'll visit you in jail."

Loreda opened her mouth to protest the urgency, but the impatience on Chesler's face as he motioned the guards to start moving let her know it would be useless. She let the guards lead her out of her chambers and down the halls. Chesler branched off from the rest of the guards and continued on his own while the rest of the guards followed with Loreda.

Her march of shame wove through the castle halls, past the questioning looks of servants and other guards. All who saw her immediately started whispering to each other, too shocked at the sight to bother hiding their stares. Loreda bit the inside of her cheek and held her head high, refusing to meet their hungry eyes.

The guards lead Loreda down one of the back hallways through the lower castle and veered ever closer to the rocks of the mountain until Loreda could only guess they were in the portion of the castle dug deep into the side of the mountain.

The dungeon was as well-lit as the rest of the castle and almost as clean. Loreda moved in a shocked daze as they passed several full and empty cells until the guards stopped at one and unlocked it. They encouraged her into the empty cage then closed and locked the cell door behind her.

Loreda blinked through her daze and the tears threatening to fall for long enough to notice the little essentials and comforts in each cell including her own. The small cot was lined with blankets and a small desk held an AaD, unlinked to the network. Loreda almost scoffed at that. As though she'd be writing a confession.

She sniffled at the thought and stopped taking note of what was in her cell as she sank onto the floor in a corner and buried her head in her skirts. Sobs wracked her body as she mourned how close her freedom had been. Now all was lost. She cried at the thought of Jeshua returning, triumphant as she knew he would, only to find the kingdom hostile to him. She cried most for her sweet daughter, alone and hidden away in a mansion. The girl would never get the life she deserved now. Loreda even shed a tear for Istoria, the poor misguided girl. She thought this would put her on Brynte's good side, but it wouldn't last. Then she would understand, and she would regret what she had done.

Loreda's sobs rang through the dungeon but were lost in the vastness of the stone underground before they could ever escape for an outsider to hear.

CHAPTER 60

Stori paced the king's study along the familiar path as she waited for Chesler's return. She tried calling Bry again, for about the eleventh time, to warn him of the danger Harailt posed. For the eleventh time, she listened to the same empty beeping sound signaling failure—a sound the AaDs had never made before. She glanced at Lawr as he again tried to call anyone on one of the five AaDs he had in front of him.

He had said that on Terrae, this would be the equivalent of getting a "no service" message because satellites didn't cover the area where the intended recipient of a phone call had gone to. But this wasn't Terrae and the AaDs didn't use satellites. They used the Vis and there wasn't anywhere the Vis didn't reach. For once, Lawr didn't have any idea why the calls couldn't be placed, except a guess that something was blocking it.

As another first, Lawr was showing his anxiety over the situation as he obsessively organized his little space between trying to place calls. He tapped his foot rapidly at sporadic intervals without seeming to realize he was doing it.

Stori tried to bite her tongue and ignore the irritating sound. She'd already snapped at him several times to stop it. He had snapped back that he didn't know what she was talking about.

Footsteps announced a presence a moment before the door swung open and Chesler walked in without waiting for an invitation. A rare smile teased his lips, but Stori couldn't relax until he confirmed that Loreda was indeed locked away.

"She went without much of a fuss," Chesler said. "Well, much less of a fuss than I expected. I think she was pretty surprised you tricked her."

Stori sighed. Finally, Loreda was gone. She met Chesler's gaze with a small smile. "I just had a ludicrous idea. The plan was all Lawr's."

"And the acting all yours," Lawr spoke as he spared a glance from the AaDs in front of him.

Chesler gave a slight scoff as he half-turned to leave. "You've called King Brynte to warn him," he said as a statement.

"No." Stori gulped and glanced to Lawr for help.

Chesler's eyes shifted in a moment from tired and victorious to suspicious. "Why not?" he asked in a guarded tone, glancing between the two of them.

Stori raised her hand to stop the thought process she could tell was going through his head. He thought they weren't going to warn Bry. Stori tried to swallow the irritation that had already built from the lack of communication to Bry and sporadic foot tapping.

"The call won't go through," she said, annoyed. "I've tried many times. Lawr tried others in Oroitz too, but nothing is getting through."

Chesler's expression settled back to his normal, irritated frown. He grabbed one of Lawr's AaDs off the desk and tried dialing, then bristled at the static humming coming from the AaD.

"Guard!" Chesler shouted without moving as he messed around on the tablet. "Istoria, grab a paper," he ordered as one of the guards appeared at the door.

Stori grabbed a roll of paper from Bry's desk along with a full ink pen and brought them back to Chesler.

"How long will it take to send a physical message?" she asked, guessing his intention.

Chesler gave a half-grunt as his frown deepened. He grabbed the paper and pen and began scribbling a message against the tablet. "There won't be a doorway within twenty met-reaches of Sentre for another day and a half. Sending a messenger now to the nearest doorway will take about a day, but that's the best option we have. This AaD problem is going to take a while to fix." He handed the paper to Stori. "Sign this too. Brynte knows he can trust your word, but he's probably still cautious of me."

Stori glanced through the message and tried not to let her inner joy about Bry's professed trust in her show on her face. At the end of a concise summary of events describing what happened, Stori added her own message and signature. She cut the paper and rolled it up, addressing one side of it, applying a seal, and handing it to the guard.

Chesler instructed the guard to find a messenger and a fast horse and get the message to Oroitz. The guard left at a run and a moment later the room dared to breathe.

"Do you know something about the AaD problem?" Lawr asked Chesler with the indifferent expression Stori still couldn't read.

Chesler sighed and rubbed his brow as he nodded. "When Vlasis was king, he once had plans to limit the use of Aequorian technology and tax it."

"That was why Bry was exiled," Lawr said with a nod.

"Correct, but Vlasis had much of Oracaede's plan in place for the scheme before the plans were canceled by Brynte's interference. It was never activated, and I thought it hadn't even been finished. But this must be it." Chesler held up the AaD. "I would assume it's Loreda's doing for just this reason, so you couldn't warn Brynte. But she's shut down the entire AaD network in Sentre, if not Medius as a whole. The people have probably noticed, and their reaction isn't going to be good."

"Stori," Lawr said, turning toward her. "I think you'd better prepare another speech to address this and Loreda's betrayal." He turned back to Chesler. "Now, where's this software? I can work on shutting it down."

Chesler raised an eyebrow. "You know how to fix this?" His voice held an odd combination of doubt and hope.

Lawr snorted. "I've worked with software in every capacity for the last two plus decades. If I don't know how to fix it, I can learn."

Chesler blinked. "Decades…" His tone raised in a drawn-out question.

"Never mind. A long time."

Chesler didn't protest further. "You would work best from the central computer of the castle, not an AaD."

Lawr nodded and followed Chesler out of the room after a quick wave to Stori.

Stori blinked after them for a moment.

Why won't this nightmare end already? she thought as she turned back to the desk and sat down at it in a slump. *And why couldn't Loreda have messed something up that didn't require a speech?*

She glanced at the AaD sitting on her desk. Just in case, she tried calling Bry again. The same soulless buzz filled her ears. She set the AaD back down and covered her face for a moment.

Stori sniffed and carefully pulled out a fresh roll of paper to begin writing out everything she could think of that would help explain the situation.

CHAPTER 61

Bry stared across the now bloody valley of grass that had served as the battlefield. He took a breath of blood-tainted air that started to stink of death. He walked around the battlefield in search of Shad, wherever he'd gone off to.

Climbing the one hill in the open space, Bry scanned the valley on either side. The situation on the other side of the hill seemed similar to the one he'd just left; a few Nomads still swinging their weapons around while the rest were either dead or surrendered.

The edge of the forest a distance away seemed to be where most of the excitement was. Bry moved toward the fighting. Even if Shad hadn't migrated toward the fighting, Bry was still itching for more action.

Bry kept one eye on the chaos going on around him with the Sentrian soldiers gathering the surrendering Nomads as others moved around the dead and started bringing the bodies of friends together and preparing a pyre.

A twinge of regret and something darker gnawed at his stomach as he slowed his pace. That darker gnawing turned Bry's focus away from a fight and back to looking for Shad.

A sharp shove caught Bry off guard and sent him tumbling to the ground. He snapped his head around to face his attacker, sword ready. A cloaked soldier had pushed him and taken the edge of a blade that had been aimed at Bry. More blood dripped onto the battle field.

"De-demon Eyes?" The would-be assassin spoke to the cloaked soldier in a tone of shock as he choked on his own blood.

Bry stood and caught sight of the cloaked soldier's blade, sunk into the older soldier's chest before it was ripped out. The would-be assassin crumpled to the ground. Bry opened his mouth to thank his savior, but a motion in the corner of his eye pulled his attention to another soldier stepping toward him. Turning to his new foe, Bry recognized Harailt under the soldier's disguise.

"So, this is where you've been hiding," Bry said with a weary annoyance as he took up a defensive stance.

Harailt smirked as a few soldiers gathering near him turned their swords against Bry.

A sudden pressure against his back pulled Bry's attention behind him. The cloaked soldier was leaning against Bry as he tied a cloth around his bleeding side. Bry saw that a circle of several more soldiers had surrounded them, weapons drawn for a fight.

Bry planted his feet firmly to support his new comrade until the man squared up from treating his injury, ready to fight.

"Time to die, King," Harailt spat, then charged.

Bry twisted his foot into the ground and ignored the instinct to simply dodge the sloppy attack. He could sense his new ally's presence directly behind him, preparing against his own attacks. The familiar feeling of fighting back to back brought a smile to Bry's face as he stepped forward and blocked Harailt's blow.

Bry pulled out his dagger in case of any surprises—like if Harailt turned out to be a good fighter. He countered with a quick kick to the older man's leg. So far, Harailt's skill was better than most of the other generals Vlasis had employed. He just wasn't a match for anyone who fought in a manner unfamiliar to that which he'd trained in.

Blocking another head strike, Bry slashed at Harailt's leg. He sliced through a good portion of thigh before Harailt could move out of range. The general was much slower now. His stiff movements hadn't been enough to counter Bry's creative one when the fight had first started, and now that he was injured his moves became even clumsier.

Harailt seemed surprised at how the fight was going; especially when Bry struck a blow, catching him from one shoulder to the opposite hip. The new wound spilled more blood than a person could afford to lose.

The general collapsed to his knees, the shock written on his face as he gasped for breath. Bry caught him mumbling a few words about his Moon darling and someone named Caelyn as he fell to the ground, adding his own blood to the already soaked battlefield.

Bry paused to breathe a sigh at the end of another traitor before he composed himself enough to turn and look for his new ally. The cloaked soldier was again working on tying a strip of cloth from his cloak around his side wound. He was only half-turned toward Bry, but had evidently been watching the fight for a while.

Lowering his focus, Bry counted more than a dozen new Sentrian forms added to the body count. Bry nodded in a bit of amazement to himself as he stepped around one of the traitors and toward his new ally. Taking a closer look at one of the Sentrian's he stepped around, Bry noticed the soldier had been shot with a large caliber round.

Bry frowned at that. He'd wouldn't have missed someone shooting at that close of range.

A sniper must have made the shot, his brain supplied. Several of the fallen men had been shot from a great enough distance that he hadn't even heard the shots.

That too was odd. Bry's frown darkened. As far as he knew, the Sentrian army didn't employ snipers yet.

Bry turned his focus back to the still-standing soldier. The man seemed impatient to leave as soon as he could finish bandaging his side. He was already half-stepping away even as he bled profusely.

"Thank you," Bry said, taking a couple of large steps to close the gap between them before the soldier could make an escape.

The stranger gave a distracted nod as he finished stifling the flow from the injury he'd taken for Bry.

"How...?" Bry trailed off in the question as he looked over the bodies again.

A sigh came from the soldier, pulling Bry's attention back. He seemed annoyed—or maybe just unprepared to receive any kind of attention.

The man was looking off into the tree line for a moment before he turned to answer. "Skills and a friend."

The familiar, bone-chilling voice made Bry stop and snap his gaze to the cloaked face looking back at him. Bry was too stunned to speak, or keep his jaw from dropping, as he stared at the albino assassin.

Unblinking crimson eyes stared back for another moment before he gave a quick nod and turned on his heels, walking toward the forest.

"Wait!" Bry ran the short distance between them and jerked the man's shoulder around to face him.

The assassin didn't flinch, but his face tightened enough that Bry knew the rough jerk had aggravated his injury. He released his death grip but didn't back away.

"Why the hell did you do that?" Bry struggled to keep his voice under a shout as he noticed more soldiers gathering in the area. Bry tried remembering what Shad had called the man. *Sphere or something?* He wished now he had something to call the man other than "assassin".

"I told you," the albino finally spoke. "Oracaede has no business with this battle, only with the outcome. I, on the other hand, have business keeping you alive." The man reached up and gave Bry's shoulder a quick, awkward pat. "You do not make my job easy." He offered a slight twist of his pale lips—Bry might call it a smile. The albino turned again and started to leave.

Bry blinked in stunned silence as the albino slipped around the soldiers starting to form a circle.

"Hey, wait!" Bry shouted after the man as he tried to follow him through the newly formed crowd—but the crowd pushed back.

"What the hell is this?!" A shout from another point in the crowd distracted Bry from the albino as he noticed the anger that was rolling off the crowd in waves.

Bry glanced around him then down at the faces of the men the albino had killed. Dead Sentrian eyes stared back at him from every direction.

Gulping, Bry finally found words he could spit out. "These men were working with Harailt and attacked me on his command." He pointed to the general's body where it lay.

An irritated, disbelieving grumble moved through the crowd along with a wave of several roughed hand gestures.

"I knew 'em." An older soldier stepped forward and leaned over the body of the first man who had attacked. "Pop's was everybody's friend. He wouldn't be workin' with Harailt." The statement was reiterated by several soldiers as the circle around him constricted.

Bry grimaced at the anger on the faces of his men. A quick glance in the direction the albino had gone revealed not a trace of white hair or red eyes. Bry wondered if his own men decided to attack him, would the albino come back again? If the soldiers kept closing in, he was going to need it.

"Whad's going on here?" a familiar voice boomed through the crowd.

The voice produced a stirring as one side of the circle parted, and Jair stepped through with Shad close on his heels. Jair stopped and stared at the mess of soldiers' bodies on the ground, but Shad continued toward Bry without blinking at the scene. A quick nod was exchanged between them as Shad stood next to Bry, ready to fight if needed.

"Whad—?" Jair started to ask again but stopped when Bry jerked his chin toward Harailt's fallen body. Jair remained silent for a half-moment before nodding back to Bry. "Men, sd'and down. D'ese—" He gestured around to the Sentrian bodies. "—were d'raidors working wi'd Harail'd."

"But," a man in the crowd started. "That's my frie—"

"Friend," Jair finished, his face a mask of stone as he directed some of his attention specifically toward Bry. "I know da'd, and da'd's why when we ge'd back to Sentre, 'dey won'd be named as any'ding more den fallen soldiers. Heroes in dis war."

Bry could feel the general's piercing gaze as he made the statement—almost a dare. Not that Bry could counter it at the moment, not with his men still itching for blood.

He gave Jair a solemn nod in agreement. He hadn't been planning on ruining the lives of the traitor's families anyway. Bry hadn't considered that his men might be worried about their friends' reputations and the backlash it would bring if they were discovered to have taken part in a revolt against the king.

Grumbles moved through the crowd, but the men grudgingly dispersed on Jair's orders. Bry didn't think they were entirely placated by the words of their general, only that they weren't ready to kill him, even if they were ready to kill their king.

Jair remained stationary beside Shad as they waited for the rest to leave.

Bry sighed and rubbed his head. He could assume another long explanation was in order. He still wanted one in regard to the albino, not that he'd have any chance for that now.

The trio formed a huddle as questions and answers and questions were exchanged. The question stream had slowed but not stopped by the time they started moving toward the makeshift camp.

The camp was already being taken down as the men prepared for a long walk back to the Oroitz camp and a good night's rest before the march back to Sentre. Bry and Shad were grimacing at the thought. Marches were never enjoyable, no matter the distance.

CHAPTER 62

I n the day since Loreda's arrest, Stori's pacing wore a new hole into the
rug covering the floor of Bry's study. The servants quickly patched the
fraying as Stori wore holes elsewhere.

The speech she'd given that morning seemed to have placated enough
of the people to not rally against Bry. At least, not yet. She wasn't sure what
they'd do when Bry returned.

If, a small part of her put forward. *If Bry returned.*

Stori strangled that thought with hopes of how life would be when he
returned.

Turning in her path, Stori pulled her thought to the AaD problem and
tried to tie them there. Away from the *if.*

Lawr hadn't left the dungeon area at the base of the castle where the
computer was housed since he'd first gone down there. Stori wasn't certain
if he'd eaten or slept since then either. When she visited him to inquire after
his progress, he was always in his most irritable don't-talk-to-me-I'm-
thinking mood.

In his sense of good taste, he named the program that had caused this
mess the Functionally Complex and Kludging Mess, which he, in equally
good taste, called the FCKing Mess for short. From what he'd grumbled to
Stori, she knew the designer of the FCKing Mess had mostly been using
preexisting programs and code and merely patched them all together into—
well— a mess. Lawr had used many stronger words, but Stori assumed the
point remained the same when she informed Chesler of the issues.

Chesler had started working on who, if anyone, could have helped Loreda activate the FCKing Mess. He'd developed an organized system for finding suspects. All he had discovered thus far were the names of the technicians working with the main computer who had let Loreda mess with the system because she was a queen and they were following her orders. No one else seemed to have any idea of how to activate or deactivate the system, much less how Loreda could have done everything herself.

Chesler's patience wore thin as he again combed through the records of everyone in, near, or around the castle who had either skills or access to the system to help Loreda in any way. The most irritating problem for him was that Loreda wouldn't have known how to activate the FCKing mess, but he still couldn't find a suspect for who could have turned the system on.

Stori spent the last day delivering messages between them and pacing since she couldn't do anything else. She didn't have the skills to try to help Lawr, not that he'd accept help anyway. Chesler had reverted to his usual suspicious nature and refused to hand over any part of his investigation.

Every spare moment was spent worrying about Bry. Every so often, she tried taking a rest from worrying to get some of her other work done. Those breaks were always short, generally useless, and ended with a return to pacing within moments.

When the day was long gone and night had set in, Stori finally stopped and stared around the room, stomping her foot a little as she thought. She was tired of waiting and doing nothing in the meantime.

She didn't care if the only thing she could do was go to the bottom of the castle and hold cabling for Lawr—who would certainly be working through the night—she would gladly do that. She wasn't sure if Lawr was even doing anything with all the cables that filled the main computer room, but she figured doing something was better than nothing.

Stori left the study and marched down the hall, homemade map in hand to locate the main computer room. She wrapped her arms tightly around herself as she walked, hoping to keep all her worry and fear inside as she passed servants and guards.

Maybe she would be better helping Chesler though. Stori stopped her walk when she reached Chesler's floor. She knew he wouldn't appreciate the help and she wouldn't enjoy spending any more time in the man's company than absolutely necessary. Stori gave her own arms a tight squeeze. Now wasn't the time to be concerned with what she'd enjoy. She needed to help Bry. For that she needed to figure out how the FCKing Mess worked and what Loreda had done with who.

Loreda knows. The thought twisted like a snake through Stori's stomach. She would have rather spent all day in rapt conversation with Chesler than talk to Loreda once more.

It doesn't matter what you want. Stori paused and turned her attention with a perturbed frown to the map. She traced the route to the dungeon in her mind. *Have to help Bry,* she told herself as she changed directions, heading toward the castle prison.

Following the map as best she could, Stori only needed to ask for directions twice before she reached the doors to the dungeon. One of the guards on duty complied with her request and led her through the main hall.

At Loreda's cell, the guard nodded and left, promising to return if he was needed. Stori nodded deafly and stared at Loreda through the bars. The old queen's appearance had fallen into a state of unkempt disarray. Stori tried not to stare at the messy braids hanging limply over Loreda's shoulders, or the gorgeous red dress, now smudged with dirt, and the sleeves frayed where the woman had been pulling at them. The most difficult state of disarray to ignore, though, was the red-rimmed eyes glaring back at Stori.

Loreda sat still, posture somehow still immaculate as she looked coolly through Stori. A small grimace on her serene face was the only recognition she gave the young queen.

Stori tried not to squirm under the sharp unfocused gaze. The questions she had thought to ask faded from her mind as soon as she saw Loreda.

I should have prepared for this a bit more.

The uneasy silence was torn by a sharp, ragged laugh from Loreda. "Come to mock me, have you?" her usual purr sounded off, too wet from crying to sound smooth. "No, that isn't really your style, is it? You need something from me, don't you?"

Stori tried not to flinch at the accuracy of Loreda's guess, but her reaction raised another ragged laugh from inside the cell.

"And what is it you're looking for, child?" she continued when her laugher brought only silence. "Realized your mistake yet? In trusting Brynte, that monster?"

Stori clenched her jaw and tried ignoring the comment. She had come here for information, not to listen to Loreda's anger.

"The FCK—" Loreda's eyebrows had a quick meeting with her hairline. "—the system for blocking AaD communication," Stori caught herself. "Did someone help you activate it?"

Loreda made an indignant sound before standing to move further away from the bars. "I activated it myself, of course. You think I'd trust anyone else to do that?" Loreda turned to face Stori with a sneer, clearly insulted at the idea she might need help.

Stori tried to keep the instinctive frown from showing on her face. "But, to activate it—"

"Oh? You're surprised?" Loreda moved a few steps closer to the bars as she started talking, taking the questioning from Stori. "You think it would be too difficult for some useless royalty?" She patted some dust from her dress. "For useless royalty, yes, but I had years of solitude to learn a few tricks."

"Why?" the soft question escaped Stori's lips before she could think of a better one. Loreda cut her a sharp smirk, ready to continue before Stori clarified her question. "Why would you do all this to Bry?"

The smirk turned into an ugly snarl at the mention of Bry. "Because he is his father's son. He'll be the same monster. If you had any sense, you would have helped me." She scoffed again, but this time the anger slipped as her eyes flickered to Stori's midsection and rested there. Loreda let out a sigh before meeting Stori's eyes again. "I suppose it was too late for that."

"Yes, it was." Stori resisted the urge to hide her stomach behind her hands. It was Loreda's mistaken assumption that she was already with child, but she didn't see any need to correct her. Besides, it had been too late since Stori first made the decision to work with Bry.

Another sigh brought Stori's wandering thoughts back to the woman in front of her. Loreda looked as though she'd aged years in the span of moments. When the older woman turned a forlorn gaze to meet hers, Stori almost stumbled at the look of care and hurt.

"Loreda, there's something." There were still questions she was curious about. "I wanted to ask you about… That is, once you mentioned another child."

"Don't speak of that!" Loreda lunged at the bars, snatching at Stori's clothes through the bars as her eyes flashed with wild fear.

Stori lurched back, staggering to regain her balance after she was a safe distance away. She could only stare at Loreda as she tried to make sense of the behavior.

"Please," Loreda's voice was a soft beg as she clutched the bars. The fear in her eyes changed from wild to earnest. "Please, don't let Brynte find out about her. My daughter hasn't done anything wrong."

Stori blinked as she tried to make sense of the words.

Loreda is worried about Bry hurting her daughter.

The notion sounded too ridiculous for Stori to process, but the earnest and utterly terrified look on Loreda's face was beyond serious.

"Bry wouldn't harm your daughter," Stori stated with absolute certainty.

Loreda blinked at Stori as though the opposite was the absolute truth. A choked sound escaped her throat. "You're still young. You don't know Vlasis that way—"

"We're not talking about Vlasis!" Stori lowered her voice as soon as she realized she'd shouted. "We're talking about Brynte—your son. If you'd bothered to get to know him, you'd know he won't harm your daughter out of spite for you."

The snarl on Loreda's face calmed to an almost placid stare. Finally, she sighed against the silence and rubbed a spot on her forehead, leaving a smudge of grime behind.

"You truly believe that, don't you?" the woman asked, giving her an appraising look.

Stori nodded.

"You believe he will be different. Why? Because he's kind to you now? Vlasis wasn't always a monster." Loreda's voice dropped to a near-whisper as her gaze drifted into remembrance. "When he needed me, he was kind too."

"Bry isn't Vlasis," Stori said again.

She'd never heard Vlasis mentioned as anything other than a monster. The idea that he hadn't always been so was… terrifying. A thought slipped into her mind. That Bry would change.

Stori shook her head, hoping to dislodge the thought.

A sad little laugh brought Stori's attention back to the older woman. Loreda's gaze dropped and a pointed finger followed it, directed at Stori's midsection. "Believe me, he will change. That kindness will be gone, as soon as he has his heir. When he doesn't need you anymore, you will know I'm telling the truth."

Stori stayed silent at Loreda's words. They weren't true.

They can't be.

Stori knew that, but it spoke again to her secret fear—the fear that she was only useful because the kingdom didn't have an heir. It was a fear that used to make her toss at night when she first arrived. It had abated of late but still clung to the shadows of her mind, waiting to be proven true.

She clenched her jaw and lifted her head to look at Loreda with as much defiance as she could muster. She had decided to trust Bry, so that was that. She certainly trusted him more than she trusted Loreda.

The older woman looked back at her with a still-pinched expression. "I was trying to save you," Loreda said in a quiet voice. "Don't you understand, child? I was trying to save you." Her eyes were misty and her voice was wet, filled with pain and longing. If Stori listened hard, she could hear the love in it.

"I don't need you to save me." Stori tried to keep her face blank, to neither cry nor grimace.

Of all the people she'd met in the castle, Loreda was the one to make her feel most helpless. She didn't need the old queen to throw her weakness in her face as though she wasn't the one making it worse.

Stori turned on her heels and marched a few steps away before her annoyance faltered, replaced by a new idea. She turned and stepped up to Loreda's cell again.

"If you were to let your daughter live here, she would be well taken care of. She would have everything she deserves as royalty." Stori spoke with as much confidence as she could fit into the words.

Loreda blinked back at Stori. Her mouth opened and closed a few times, face contorting first with anger before returning to thoughtful hope as she worked over the idea.

Stori almost wanted to celebrate that her choice of words finally had an effect on the woman other than to raise her ire.

"You couldn't promise such a thing." Loreda's voice pulled Stori out of her head. The older queen shook her head with what Stori might consider remorse over the idea.

"I could not vouch for what Bry will do with you, but your daughter would be safe. Bry wouldn't harm his sister." Stori held her breath and willed the woman to listen to her.

Loreda gave a tight smile. "Half." She turned sad eyes to meet Stori's. "Caelyn is his half-sister. Jeshua Harailt is her father."

"That wouldn't change anything," Stori said without hesitation. She paused for a moment before asking, "What is she like?"

Loreda gave a sad smile again as she returned to staring into space. "She's fourteen. She likes horses and being out in the woods, and…" Loreda took in a shuttering breath. "She's lived her entire life hidden away in one of my estates. I wanted to give her a life she deserved. Caelyn is royalty." She lifted her gaze toward the ceiling and then to the bars of her jail.

Silence settled between them as Stori waited for Loreda to make some kind of decision on the matter. The older woman knotted her fingers together as she looked around, upward, and outward. Stori tried to follow her line of sight but found nothing. After a moment, her imagination took over and she could see the castle beyond the dungeon walls.

A soft scoff broke the silence as Loreda turned her gaze toward Stori. "None of those promises will matter. Jeshua is going to kill your precious Bry when they meet in battle. Then all will be well."

Stori sighed. She shouldn't have expected Loreda to reach such a major decision so quickly, especially not when she still held out hope for her general. But Stori had what she'd come for. Now she'd just have to hope Bry stayed safe.

"It's an idea to consider," Stori replied, hoping she sounded surer of Bry's success and return than her fear allowed her to feel. "If you want this life for your daughter, she would be taken care of."

Stori turned to leave, hearing only a light scoff from the cell behind her as she made her way to the exit. Once outside the dungeon, she breathed a sigh of relief at being away from the old queen. She chastised herself for being so affected by the woman's words and walked back toward the stairs.

At least she could tell Chesler some good news.

CHAPTER 63

T he one peaceful night of sleep Bry might have enjoyed was
        interrupted by Shad's snoring, grumbling, and general kicking
        that traveled over from the extra cot placed next to him. Bry
quickly became accustomed to the nuisance before he'd been king, but it
had been a while since they'd slept in the same room.

Disassembly of the campsite continued without need for any input
from Bry. The early morning preparations to leave Oroitz continued as Bry
tried again to call anyone on his AaD. Shad had started walking around the
campsite, asking to borrow any AaD he saw, but so far he reported that no
one had any working communication device and hadn't received any calls
on the AaDs in the last several days.

The men hadn't started complaining about the lack of communication
yet as Jair made sure everyone had a useful and distracting task.

Another cold splash of anxiety twisted Bry's stomach as his mind kept
returning to Vlasis's tax law. Something about the scenario immediately
reminded him of it. Once the connection had formed in his mind, he
couldn't shake the dread of thinking about Loreda, and Stori stuck with
her in the capital.

Bry prepared to leave as soon as it would be acceptable, as both Shad
and Jair noted, for the king to leave camp.

"Your Majes'dy?" the voice preceded Jair's entrance into the tent by a
half-moment. "Jus' received a message from Sen'dre."

Bry jumped up at any chance of news at the capital. The sight of Stori's seal on the rolled paper was a relief, even though he had hoped Jair was referring to a working AaD. He read through the short message and breathed in relief that Loreda had been locked up. The news confirmed the AaD problem was what he'd feared—Vlasis's tax mess.

"How is id?" Jair watched Bry with a pinched frown. "Bad?"

Bry gave a half laugh. "Could be worse. Loreda played for the throne; she's in jail now. The AaD problem, though, is just what we thought."

Jair growled at the news and picked up one of the AaDs on Bry's desk. "I didn'd know da old king had so much of id complete."

Bry grunted a response as he finished reading Stori's message. It was a short plea for him to return safely and to not miss her birthday. He couldn't help the smile that crept onto his face. He'd definitely make it back in time for that.

"Bryn'd?"

Bry snapped his attention back to the general with a questioning hum. Jair watched him with a scowl.

Bry tried to wipe the smile from his face and replaced it with all seriousness, but he could still feel the curl in his lip.

"It's nothing," he said quickly before turning away to put the message on his desk and hide his face until he could get it straightened out. He grabbed a blank sheet of paper off a roll and quickly scribbled a message back to Stori.

Jair grunted. "Id'll be good 'o be back in da cidy soon."

Bry glanced back in time to see a rare smile played across Jair's face. The general excused himself to oversee the departure preparations. Bry shook his head and tucked the letter and the rest of his few personal items into his travel bag and called a messenger to ride ahead of the army and deliver the reply as soon as possible.

Bry walked around the camp, watching the tents being dismantled and helping where he could without getting in the way. Eventually he fell into the worst job, helping with the gathering and burning of the bodies. Two burns would be had—one for their soldiers and one for the Nomads, though both would be burned the same.

The only items gathered from the dead Sentrians were their helmets, each inscribed with the owner's name. Wagons full of helmets moved away from the burn to be counted and organized when they returned to Sentre.

The midday sun was high as Bry placed the last Sentrian soldier's body to be burned. Bry could have sworn he'd met the dark-haired man before, though he had that sense about many of the bodies he'd moved. He sent the men who had been helping him ahead as he waited near the edge of the forest for his stomach to stop rolling. The smell of burning flesh, sweat, and urine followed him no matter how far into the forest he went to get away from the smoke.

Bry felt a presence near him before he saw anyone. He relaxed immediately at the familiarity and nearly fell over as the weight of being alone was lifted.

"You thought you could hide your sickness from me again, but not today," Shad said with a half-smile. He rested a hand on Bry's shoulder, stabilizing the dizzying world now that Bry had a grounded connection to his surroundings.

Bry tried to return the smile, but he could tell how flat it had fallen by the concern that flashed over Shad's face.

"That was a joke. You're not going to be sick on me, are you?" The weak smile barely clung to Shad's face as he moved Bry to sit, leaning against a tree.

"I'll be..." The word "fine" stuck in Bry's throat but refused to be vocalized. He wasn't used to lying to Shad. A heavy sigh turned to a sob as he covered his mouth to keep it from escaping. "There are so many people dead. What if there was another way?"

Bry felt Shad reposition himself to sit next to his friend, but he couldn't bring himself to look up. He was supposed to be used to this. Being a bodyguard, they had both been exposed to death—but this was different. Death was a normal part of life, but there should never be that many bodies in one place. There were far too many dead souls entering the Vis in this place.

"Bry?" Shad's quiet voice made Bry's gut twist further in on itself.

It was the first time he wished Shad wasn't there. The pain returned with guilt for Shad seeing him so weak.

"Bry, it's different—a pitched battle. It's not the same as guarding against a bunch of bandits."

Bry forced himself to look over at his friend. Shad's eyes were bright with unshed tears. Shad coughed and sputtered for a moment. "Could we stay here for a while? I don't want to have to talk with the soldiers. Not yet."

A grunt was the only response Bry trusted his voice to make as he buried his head in his hands again and leaned further against Shad and the tree. He heard Shad mumbling to himself and ignored the growing headache he was getting as the silence of the forest settled around them.

An indefinite period passed before Bry could bring himself to look up and take in the world around him. He breathed easier as the panic and guilt subsided before being lost into the rustling of the forest around them.

Bry continued sitting in silence until his headache was nearly gone and Shad shifted next to him.

"Ready?" Bry asked quietly so as to not disturb the silence if Shad needed more time.

A grunted reply came with a half-sighed laugh. "Sure thing."

Bry grunted an acknowledgment as he stood up and offered Shad a hand. They both moved off, back toward the disassembled camp without another word.

When they reached the packed wagons, Bry gave orders for the last bit of organizing and then finally, to move out. Shad smiled and joked with Jair, the soldiers, and everyone else with his usual beaming smile.

The journey back to Sentre was quieter then the trip to Oroitz had been. The men were too tired to joke and talk. Even the horses seemed to know better than to expend their energy.

In the silence of the march, the only constant sound came from the wagons as they rumbled along. Bry could tell which wagons carried what, even from the front of the line. The supply wagons were the quietest, followed be the moaning wagons that carried the injured. The wagons of helmets, however, were never silent. Bry could hear the constant, deafening rattle of the helmets though he couldn't see where they were in the line. The rattling seemed to be the only sound all the way through the forest to the Empty and on the plains before Sentre.

Cheers and applause rose from the city as Bry and the head of the army entered. The cheers faded to silence sooner than Bry would have hoped, leaving only the rumble of wagons and rattling helmets until they reached the castle.

Once at the castle, disorder took over as officers and soldiers mixed with the masses of women and children trying to find family. Bry was lost in the mass of pushing and shoving. He looked around and moved toward the nearest familiar shadow. Shad was struggling to keep a smile on his face as he pushed toward a staircase and up to the balcony above.

Bry reached the balcony only to be stopped by a familiar, tear-stained face. Stori was a puffy, red, tearful mess as she hugged him and hurried both him and Shad inside and away from the crowd. In a corner away from the masses, Eleanora, Klaas, and Lawr all materialized as soon as Bry and Shad arrived. Eleanora was less tearful than Stori, but only by a margin. Even Klaas dabbed away some dust in his eyes. Lawr was his usual stoic self but allowed for hugs from both Shad and Bry.

Stori paused the little gathering with a brief message for one of the guards to tell Loreda of General Harailt's demise. Bry didn't know why Stori thought Loreda would care, but he didn't question it. The joy returned as soon as the guard disappeared.

The warmth of his little family started returning Bry to the unstable state he'd been in the forest. He accepted the hugs and kisses offered but was undeniably grateful when the greeting party was cut short by pinched noses and several requests for both he and Shad to have a bath before any more hugs were given. Once he'd escaped to an empty bathroom, he locked the doors to keep the servants out as soon as they'd drawn a bath.

Bry struggled to take his armor off and yelped in surprise after dropping another piece of it from his shaking hands. He bit his lip until he tasted blood and could steady himself, focusing on the pain. He loosened the last bit of armor and dropped it with a clatter to the floor, bringing with it the rattling sound of the helmets.

Bry jumped into the bath without bothering to remove his clothes. He pushed himself under the water and screamed. Even that wasn't enough to drown out the rattling that echoed in his head.

CHAPTER 64

A single day of rest was all that could be afforded after Bry returned before urgent matters again required his attention. Loreda's sentencing being the most pressing one that needed his input.

The trial for the matter had already been completed by Chesler and others of the court before Bry even returned. He was glad at least that had been taken care of without requiring his input. He only wished Chesler could have done the sentencing too; he'd have been far more impartial.

The late morning court function started as all the court matters Bry had to attend did, with endless talking and reading titles from scrolls and AaDs. Discussions followed and drew the matter out past lunch without a break before Loreda was even brought to the main hall. His gnawing stomach tried turning itself inside out as he was reminded it hadn't been a good idea to skip breakfast now that he was also forced to miss lunch.

Bry tried to remain still where he sat on the throne but couldn't seem to stop shifting as he fought the urge to pace. He wanted to think on what should be done with her. He couldn't find it in himself to hate her, but...

How am I possibly supposed to sentence her?

He ignored Loreda as best he could when she came in, instead focusing on a lengthy roll of documents he was trying not to tear the edges of. The papers Chesler had given him contained endless suggestions of proper punishments for Loreda's crimes. Top on the list was execution. Second on the list was a different form of execution.

Bry scowled to himself as he read the report behind each suggestion, including the people's likely reaction to each form of punishment. Somehow, they were all negative. Chesler seemed to be of the mind that the Median people would despise Bry no matter what he did with Loreda.

Bry dared a glance at the woman. She kept her head down and didn't look back at him.

Chesler began the process by reading Loreda's royal title followed at length by a list of her crimes. The end of the long list was reached, allowing a time for Bry to be able to speak. A moment of silence passed as he figured out what he was going to say. Another quick glance through the list of penance solidified what he'd wanted to do from the start, what Stori had suggested when he'd first brought it up with her that morning.

"For your crimes, Loreda Iano-Godric, I hereby order you into permanent exile from Medius."

Loreda flinched. Bry watched her body language closely as she looked up at him with confusion and shock. Her eyes glistened with tears.

The moment of silence between them remained in stillness until it was sharply interrupted by the guards shifting to Loreda's sides and pulling her away.

"Wait!" Loreda froze the room with her sudden outcry.

Bry shifted in his seat and leaned closer. He motioned for the guards to wait as he watched indecision and doubt flash across Loreda's face before her gaze went to Stori, seated at his right. The indecision only lasted a moment before determination pushed all other emotions from her expression.

"Your Majesty." Loreda's gaze pierced through Bry. "I must beg a favor from you." She paused and took a shaky breath before continuing. "This is beyond presumptive to ask, but I must. I have a daughter."

The entire room froze. Out of the corner of his eye Bry noticed Stori nodding.

"You what?" Bry barely forced his voice out as he pulled his full attention back to Loreda.

"She's a good girl. She knew nothing of this. I ask you to allow her to live in the castle," Loreda hurried her speech, glancing again at Stori.

Bry followed her gaze. Stori met his eyes with her calm ones and gave a gentle nod. Bry hid his confusion poorly, but she didn't look the slightest bit surprised. Instead her expression was encouraging.

Bry turned back to Loreda who waited anxiously for his response. Bry could only keep staring at her as he tried to think of a proper response. A shifting near his side caught his attention as Shad moved and shifted his weight.

"Bry has a sister. Are you kidding?" Shad's voice hissed loudly, filled with all the shock and disbelief Bry wished he could show. "How does he have a sister?"

Loreda glowered at Shad for a moment before looking back to Bry. Bry raised an eyebrow and gave his head a slight jerk toward Shad. He wanted that question answered too.

"Half-sister," Loreda spoke in an uncharacteristic mumble. "Caelyn, my daughter, is Brynte's half-sister. Jeshua Harailt is—was—he was her father." Loreda paused for only a moment before continuing with emphasis. "Please, I beg you, do not hold the sins of her parents against her. Caelyn is fourteen. She has lived her entire life in my country estates. She has never been made part of this strife."

Bry stood and made a half-attempt at pacing before remembering it wasn't kingly. He stopped in front of Stori and held her calm gaze with a quizzical one of his own. Stori's eyes were soft, seeming to look into the depths of Bry, seeing everything he'd like to hide. She caught his hand and gave his fingers a gentle squeeze before her eyes moved toward Loreda and back again. She raised an eyebrow and waited for him to answer.

"Caelyn, huh?" Bry muttered.

Stori's face lit with a brilliant smile.

Bry turned back to Loreda. "She will, of course, be looked after. I will see she has the best life here in court."

Loreda let out a half-sigh, half-sob. She took a moment to straighten out her features before looking at Bry again, making eye contact with him for the first time Bry could remember.

"Thank you, Brynte."

Bry could only nod as he stared after her as she was led away. He continued to stand in place as the hall emptied out, the matter settled.

Chesler said something about coordinating the girl's travel to Sentre as well as the exiling of Loreda before he stalked out. When only Shad and Stori remained in the room, Bry turned his focus to them.

"Stori?" He frowned at her and tried to ignore the way she flinched at his sharp tone.

She turned big eyes to him with a look of fearful uncertainty before she clenched her jaw as the determined look he'd grown to love filled her features and she moved to stand in front of him, taking one of his hands in hers as she did.

"Loreda let slip the existence of another child to me several months ago." Stori paused at Shad's shocked response to the information. Bry leveled a glare at his friend, a warning to stay silent. Stori remained quiet until Bry returned his full focus to her before speaking. "I was unsure if it might have been a trick or why she was so desperate to keep it a secret from you. I'm sorry for also keeping it a secret from you." Stori pulled her hands back to hide her flushed face. "I wanted to solve one of the problems you face without having to worry you."

She muttered another apology without meeting Bry's eyes. He blinked at her as bits of a familiar conversation they'd had months ago filtered through his mind. Bry rubbed his head and chuckled.

Stori's attention snapped back to him at the sound of his laugh. "You're not upset?"

"What? Of course not. Why would I be?" Bry couldn't help the grin sneaking onto his face. "I'm just glad you got to fight your dragons and win."

A thoughtful frown flitted across Stori's face before it bloomed into a smile. "Yes, I am too."

"Am I missing something?" Shad leaned around and between them, studying both with a frown.

Bry pushed Shad back with a groan. "Yes, you are. And we were having a moment. Why'd you interrupt?"

Stori was already laughing as Shad shuffled to her side. "He seems a little touchy, don't ya think?"

"Shad, don't tease." Stori batted his arm with a smile before linking arms with both of them and forcing them into a walk. "I'm famished from all this. Would you two join me for lunch?" Her bright, playful smile turned back to Bry as his stomach growled.

Bry chuckled as they made their way to Klaas and Eleanora's apartment.

CHAPTER 65

The audience hall was alive with music and laughter that could be heard through the long stretches of hallways leading to the room. Stori walked with extra care, pacing her steps to match Bry's even though she wanted to run to the hall and throw the doors open to see what surprise Bry had created for her birthday.

Bry, in complete opposition, seemed to be walking as slowly as possible, to the point that Stori guessed he was now teasing her. His brilliant smile suggested he was as excited about the party and the night after as she was—he just hid it better.

Stori bit her lip as her thoughts drifted to their plans. The distracting thoughts made her miss a stride. She moved quickly to correct her pace again, trying to banish the embarrassing ideas that flooded her mind.

"Well, you're distracted," Bry said with a wink as he leaned closer. "Thinking something bad?"

Stori ducked her head as heat rose from her neck to her cheeks. The idea Bry had read her mind, or worse, had Shad read her mind and relay what he found made her panicked reddening even worse. Every thought and question she'd had about their night came back to her and swirled around her mind.

A choked cough pulled her attention from herself back to Bry. He seemed to be distracted himself between laughing at her and choking on his own laughter.

"Oh, you're worse than I am," Stori said, failing to hide her own laugh as she patted Bry's back.

"That's hard to beat," Bry teased as soon as he had breath to speak as he wiped away the tears the coughing had produced.

"Hey." Stori gave his back a playful slap before locking her arm within his again as they approached the doors to the hall. They paused still a distance away as the guards waited for some hint that they should open the doors.

She took a few deep breaths to fade her blush. Stori glanced at Bry's still smirking face, giving her no indication at whether she looked any less similar to a pomegranate than a moment before. Stori's hand flitted over her hair again as she steadied herself. The ornamental hair piece seemed to still be in place, but since Leha hadn't checked it, it drew on her nerves. She stopped her hand and snapped it back to her side. How selfish could she be? Leha was still searching for Chess among the injured and Stori was worried about her hair.

"Alright?" Bry's gentle voice interrupted her thoughts.

"Nothing to worry about." Stori smiled back as she pushed the thoughts aside.

Bry's gaze remained teasing as a questioning eyebrow stayed raised.

Stori pouted at the smirk. "Are we going in or not?"

She moved to push the doors open herself without waiting for the guards to assist. She had pushed the door only a little when the guards took over and pushed the heavy doors the rest of the way. Stori nearly tripped and fell into the room before Bry grabbed her arm and looped it through his, keeping her standing as they took a step into the room.

"A little impatient, aren't we?" Bry's teasing voice whispered near her ear.

Stori lost her comeback as she gasped at the light display in the large hall. A huge ball covered in hundreds of little mirrors hung from the ceiling in place of the chandelier. It reflected the blue and orange light of the Aquarian torches lining the wall. The entire room was alive with the dancing of people and flickering lights.

"Do you like it?" an anxious tone in Bry's voice distracted Stori from the lights, drawing her gaze back to him.

"Of course I love it," Stori said, feeling her lips lift into a smile as she watched the tension drain from his face. "It is truly gorgeous, thank you."

Bry gave a sharp nod. "Good. I'm glad you like it. I was worried you wouldn't. It was something Lawr suggested from his world. And Shad thought it was a great idea, so… I wasn't sure." Bry nodded to himself and tried to hide his smile. "Those guys are kind of weird, ya know."

Stori choked at that as she tried not to laugh. Bry raised an eyebrow.

"You're not one to talk about weird, you know."

"What?" Bry gasped with a practiced look of disbelief that made Stori laugh again.

"What, what? Telling secrets?" The sing-song voice distracted Stori from Bry as Shad sauntered over to them. He stopped short of reaching them as his beaming expression took on a tone of mock seriousness. "Wait, do I want to know, or should I start running?"

"Start running," Bry said in a perfect deadpan.

Shad took a step closer. "Make me." His mock serious expression only lasted a half-moment as Bry lurched at him. Shad gave yelped and jumped to Stori's side, taking her arm in his. "Good sir, you should not leave your lady unattended." His mock seriousness was back, but only for a moment before he melted into smiles again.

Bry scoffed as he returned to his original position at Stori's other side and took her free arm.

"See? I told you, Bry! The lights are awesome," Shad started immediately. He peered down at Stori. "Do ya like 'em? I think they're awesome!"

Stori nodded. "They're wonderful. The way they seem to—"

"Float," Shad and Bry said in unison.

The devilish grin widened on Shad's face as he bent down to talk in Stori's ear. "I knew he'd like 'em," he said loud enough for Bry to hear.

Bry glowered at his friend over Stori's head as Shad planted a quick kiss on her cheek before bouncing away into the party.

Stori laughed at his antics as she hugged Bry's arm closer. The warmth of the moment pulled at her heart as she thought on her little family here.

Bry held her close as he walked around the room, greeting those he had to before stopping at a corner table, out of the way of the party where Lawr had made himself comfortable, surrounded by food and empty glasses of liquor.

"Lawr, are you enjoying the party?" Stori asked in greeting.

The older man grunted rather than answer as he continued eating. Stori wondered if he'd remembered to eat at all while he was working on the AaD problem. The way he was inhaling food suggested not.

Bry nodded, accepting that answer. He gave Stori a quick, apologetic smile before turning back to Lawr. "How's the AaD problem coming?"

Lawr took a sip of the hard liquor he'd been nursing. "You mean the FCKing Mess."

Bry gave Stori a sideways look. She read it as both a check of the name and to see if she minded the language. Stori nodded that both were fine.

"Yes, that problem," Bry said, returning his focus to Lawr. "How's it coming?"

Lawr grumbled and rubbed his head before answering. "It's almost fixed. Sorta."

"Almost?" Bry asked at the same time Stori asked, "Sort of?"

"Yeah, sorta almost," Lawr growled as he glowered. "I'm working on it. It'll be done when it's done. Sorry I haven't finished it already."

"Hey, it's fine," Bry said raising his free hand in surrender as he kept up an easy smile. "I was just curious."

Lawr grunted in as close to an apology as Stori knew he would get. "It's coming along. Slowly. It isn't gonna be fixed anytime soon, but I'm doing everything I can."

Bry nodded at the answer. "Whatever you need, just let me know." He paused a moment before adding, "If it'd help, I could try getting the people who implemented it to come and help fix it, but I don't know if that would be useful."

"The FCKing Mess is named that for a reason. The people who implemented it are idiots." Lawr took another sip of his drink before he went back to eating.

"Whatever you need," Bry reiterated with a nod and a wry smile before turning with Stori to continue greeting the rest of the political figures in the room. Stori sighed at the chore that had to be completed before they could consider relaxing and enjoying themselves.

They'd made a full circle around the edge of the dance floor and returned to where they'd entered before all the obligatory greeting was done and a new piece of music started.

"Bry?" Stori asked, leaning closer against him to make sure she had his attention. "Would you like to dance?"

Bry blinked at her for a moment before a smile crept onto his face. "I was just about to ask you." He grinned as he moved to hold her hand and lead her to the dance floor.

Other couples on the floor moved aside to give them the center space. Stori wished she could have melted into the crowd with Bry, but that had never been possible as royalty.

Picking up the melody of the music in an instant, Bry pulled her into the flow of it. Stori effortlessly followed his lead as Bry successfully moved them away from the center and into the flow of the crowd.

They spun past Klaas and Eleanora as the older couple swayed slowly to the rhythm. Stori gave them a short wave before they spun on into the faceless sea of dancers.

The flow of the first dance melted into a second and a third before the stress of the problems in the sphaere returned to the forefront of Stori's mind.

Bry's attention returned to her as she almost missed a step. "You alright?"

Stori nodded and pressed her head against his chest for support. "Just thinking of everything we have to do. How are we going to deal with all of this?"

"All of what?" Bry asked, barely moving his chin from where it rested against the side of her head.

"Everything. Oracaede, Caelyn, the AaDs, the rest of the Nomads. They aren't going to take this defeat and leave. They'll be back. You know that." The panicked feeling of drowning returned before she could stop it.

Bry made a noncommittal grunt as they swayed around the dance floor. "We'll just take things one step at a time, I guess."

A frown caught on Stori's face at the thought. "That's not an answer."

"Isn't it?" Bry pulled back so he could face her. The grin had faded from his face as a frown threatened to take over. "It's the only thing we can do. We can't take on all our enemies at once. We're not strong enough for that. One, maybe two problems at a time is about all we can handle, I think."

Stori grumbled at the answer before remembering her manners as the song ended and Bry bowed. She made a low curtsy in time to not appear rude before Bry escorted her off the floor.

They stood back from the dancing and watched other couples move around the floor in an almost uncomfortable silence. A grumble from Bry pulled Stori's attention from her internal thoughts before they took over.

"Look, time'll pass no matter what we do. Life's just moving from one problem to the next without falling on your face." Bry rubbed his head and glanced around the room as he spoke. He seemed to be trying to remember what he was saying as he said it.

Stori sighed at the answer. She would have preferred a more definite plan, but they didn't have that luxury. "I guess one step at a time is as good a plan as we could hope to have right now."

Bry gave a grunt and a nod. "Klaas always says that bit better, but you know what I mean, right?"

Stori couldn't help but laugh. "Yes, I understand." She paused before turning a mischievous grin of her own toward Bry. "Or maybe I'll just ask Lawr. He seems to have a plan for everything."

Bry laughed—*actually* laughed. It was the highlight of Stori's evening.

"Ouch. You do that, I'll just stand over here with my bleeding heart." Bry chuckled as he held a hand over his chest.

Stori could only grin. She took his hand from his chest and gave it a quick kiss before lacing her arm through his.

Once Bry schooled the surprise on his face, they started walking around the room again. Finding their friends and family in the crowd, they gravitated together for the remainder of the party.

CHAPTER 66

The ragged group of men argued and quarreled among themselves as they trudged out of the large tent into the desert heat, leaving a plume of dust at the entrance. Two pairs of hawkish eyes stared after them as any silence was drowned within the bustle of life outside the fabric barrier.

The eyes turned to face each other. "Ea, Lanxes, Kilker, and Tromix tribes. All destroyed in a Median battle in Oroitz," Erasyl growled, jumping between English and Arabic in the two short sentences.

"Those fools should have listened," Reb snarled at no one in particular in the Glasic tongue. "Tribes were doing fine without Devlet Orospu bastards interfering in Avare business."

Erasyl made a grunt of annoyed disagreement. "We need to grow, Reb. If we're not growing, we're shrinking. If we shrink, civilization will push us out. You don't understand," he finished with a smirk as he rubbed and adjusted his privates.

"I understand plenty, bastard," Reb snapped as she shifted in her sitting position. "We didn't need Devlet Orospu's help to grow. They didn't do anything to help our Avare brothers in battle with the Medians. Devlet Orospu's war with the Median king is not ours. Our brothers died for no cause."

"It is cause, woman. When civilization is done turning around with itself, it comes for us. Avare has nowhere left to wander." Erasyl straightened in his seat and stretched before dropping back to a lazy slouch.

"Devlet Orospu will not provide us support with war. We are their warrior strength—only one enemy left when all is done."

Reb grumbled angry curses in one of their many languages. "We do better by ourselves," she retorted, though with less fire in her voice now.

Erasyl gave a grunt of approval as his gaze traveled up and down Reb's seated form. "We do."

Pointedly ignoring the attention, Reb chewed at her thumbnail as she thought. "We need to call our Wolves," she said finally, returning her gaze to her husband.

Erasyl grunted again as he stood and moved to sit next to Reb. "We'll do that," he agreed, nibbling at her neck.

"*Sikme bastard. Git kendini becer.*" Reb gave him a rough shove. "Erasyl, I am working on a problem."

"I work another problem," Erasyl said, shoving her back and giving her neck a harder bite.

Reb grumbled at him but didn't offer further resistance as she relaxed in his grip and went back to chewing her thumb as she thought. "Wolves'll be back from last assignment in a few days. We'll send them to Medius."

To Be Continued…

ABOUT THE AUTHOR

H. E. Salian is the author of the new series *The Vis Remaining* beginning with the book *A Step Through The Empty*. She lives in the greater Seattle area when not traveling or getting lost. In her free time, she enjoys hiking, welding, and feeble attempts at creating art.

Website: **www.hesalian.com**